SHORT RANGE

STEPHEN LEATHER

ISIS

LARGE
PRINT

First published in Great Britain 2019
by
Hodder & Stoughton
an Hachette UK company

First Isis Edition
published 2020
by arrangement with
Hachette UK

A catalogue record for this book is available
from the British Library.

ISBN 978–1–78541–919–5

Published by
Ulverscroft Limited
Anstey, Leicestershire

Set by Words & Graphics Ltd.
Anstey, Leicestershire
Printed and bound in Great Britain by
T J Books Limited, Padstow, Cornwall

This book is printed on acid-free paper

For Scarlett

Dan "Spider" Shepherd stared at the bottle of water longingly but he already felt the urge to go to the bathroom and adding to his liquid intake would only be asking for trouble. The way things were going there wasn't going to be an opportunity to get to a bathroom in the near future and he didn't want to urinate in the back of the Openreach van, not when he was rubbing shoulders with two other surveillance experts. Openreach was a division of BT, responsible for maintaining the cable and phone network across the UK and, from the outside, the van looked like any of the hundreds of others criss-crossing the capital. It was never given a second glance.

To Shepherd's right was Janet Rayner, a pretty thirty-something brunette, her hair hidden under a wool hat with a bobble on top. Rayner had recently joined MI5 after a decade with the Metropolitan Police's surveillance team. She was handling the video feeds that were displayed on the half-dozen monitors in front of her.

To Shepherd's left was Matty Clayton. Clayton had more than twenty years surveillance experience with MI5 and he was handling comms for the operation.

Long hours sitting in vans eating fast food had played havoc with his waistline. "Victor One has eyeball," he said.

Victor One was one of two Toyota Prius cars that were tailing the target, along with two motorcycle couriers. Each Prius had an Asian driver and a passenger sitting in the back, mimicking the profile of the numerous Uber vehicles running passengers to and from the airport.

The Openreach van was on the inside lane of the M4, heading from Heathrow Airport towards London. Their quarry — Tango One — was a forty-six-year-old Pakistani who had flown into the country on an Emirates flight from Dubai. There had been two MI5 officers in Border Force uniforms waiting at Terminal 3 and they had watched Mohammed Khalid as he used the facial recognition ePassport gates to enter the country. The passport he used was Swedish, and the picture in it was his, but Khalid had never been to Sweden and the name in the passport was not his own.

There was a line of photographs of Khalid taped to the side of the van above the monitors. Four were surveillance photographs taken in Islamabad, the fifth was a head-and-shoulder shot presumably from some official paperwork. Khalid was overweight with several chins, and cheeks pockmarked with old acne scars. In all the pictures he was wearing gold-framed spectacles.

A car had been waiting for Khalid, a blue Vauxhall Corsa hatchback, driven by a bearded Asian man. Khalid had climbed in the back and it had driven out of the airport, closely followed by Victor Two.

2

Victor Two had taken the lead for the first mile and then had driven ahead, its place taken by Victor One. The two courier bikes were hanging back until needed.

Khalid was a financier for Islamic State, channelling the terror group's money to jihadist cells around the world. Most of the time he was based in Pakistan's capital, Islamabad, though he made frequent trips to Dubai for meetings with Islamic State officials. On one of his trips a meeting in a five-star hotel had been bugged by the CIA and they had heard Khalid refer to an upcoming visit to the United Kingdom. The CIA had passed the intel on to MI6 who had begun taking a closer interest in Khalid and once they had confirmed that he had booked a flight via Dubai they had put their MI5 counterparts on alert.

An MI6 officer had boarded the flight from Islamabad to Dubai where he had handed over to an Emirates-based officer who had sat behind Khalid in the business class section of the A380 plane on the final leg of the trip. When he had boarded the plane in Islamabad, Khalid had been dressed in a traditional long dishdasha and a skull cap, but while in the Dubai business class lounge he had changed into a dark blue suit. He was travelling light with just an aluminium carry-on case with wheels.

Shepherd studied a digital map that was showing the Vauxhall's progress along the M4. It was vital that they didn't lose sight of the vehicle because they had no way of knowing where Khalid was going or who he planned to meet.

"We've got an ID on the Vauxhall," said Rayner. "The owner is one Manzoor Hassan. I've an address in Slough."

"So they're not heading to his house," said Shepherd, watching the red dot that marked the position of the Vauxhall. "Anything known?"

"A couple of convictions for indecent exposure but he's not on any watch lists," said Rayner.

"Well he is now," said Shepherd.

The Vauxhall continued east, leaving the M4 and driving along the A4 through Chiswick and towards Hammersmith. Victor One and Victor Two took it in turns to stay close.

As they reached Hammersmith, Clayton announced that the target was preparing to turn off the A4, the Great West Road. A few seconds later the red dot on the digital map showed that the vehicle was heading north

"Let's get the bikes in closer," Shepherd said to Clayton.

Clayton relayed instructions to the surveillance team.

The bikes moved in, one three cars behind the Vauxhall, the other a hundred yards or so ahead. Once the bikes were in position, the two Priuses dropped back. The Openreach van with Shepherd and his team brought up the rear. Progress had slowed now that the Vauxhall had left the main road.

"Spider, there's a mosque up that way," said Rayner. "That could be where they're going."

Shepherd rubbed the back of his neck and sighed. He had been hoping that Khalid had been heading to a hotel. Surveillance at a hotel was hard enough; getting a team into a mosque was a whole different ball game.

"That's going to be awkward," said Clayton, as if he'd read Shepherd's mind. Shepherd nodded. The only way they'd be able to follow Khalid into the mosque would be to use Asians, anyone else would stand out.

Shepherd stared at the dot. "Matty, if they do stop at the mosque, get Rusul and Tahoor out of the cars and after Tango One. The passengers can take over the driving. Just make sure that no one sees the switch."

Clayton nodded and started passing on the instructions to the two Prius teams.

Shepherd tapped on his laptop keyboard and pulled up intel on the Acton mosque. He sat back as he read what was on the screen. The Security Service had identified five men who had worshipped at the mosque as having gone to Syria to fight with ISIS. Two had been killed, two were still there and one had returned to the UK but wasn't considered a threat and so wasn't under investigation. There were several imams at the mosque but none had been red-flagged by the Security Service. The worshippers who had gone to Syria appeared to have been radicalised over the internet and not at the mosque.

Clayton twisted around in his seat. "They'll park up and switch once we confirm that he's going to the mosque," he said.

Shepherd nodded.

"The Vauxhall is approaching the mosque and slowing," said Rayner. "I've got visual from Bravo One."

Shepherd looked over at the screen that was showing the video feed from Bravo One, one of the two motorbike couriers. The driver had a small camera mounted on his helmet and he had turned his head to send them a view of the Vauxhall, which had come to a halt outside the main gates to the mosque. The mosque had once been a pub but ten years earlier it had been purchased by a local Muslim group and converted into a place of worship. It was surrounded by wrought iron railings and a brick minaret had been built on one side. The whole building had been painted white except for the top of the minaret which was gold.

Two men wearing ankle-length thawbs and knitted skull caps walked out of the mosque and over to the target car.

"Get Rusul and Tahoor out now," said Shepherd. "And we need photographs of the men meeting Khalid."

"I'm on it," said Clayton.

Victor One was driving away from the mosque so they lost its visual feed.

Shepherd pressed an intercom to talk to the driver of the Openreach van. "Paul, get us up as close to the mosque as you can."

"Will do," said the driver. Paul Drinkwater was a former black cab driver whose encyclopedic knowledge of the city's streets gave him an edge over the most expensive GPS navigation systems. The van accelerated, then made a left turn and a right turn.

"Tango One is exiting the vehicle," said one of the courier bikers over the radio.

"We've got a visual," said Rayner. She fed the output from one of the cameras hidden in the roof of the van to the screen directly in front of Shepherd. Shepherd watched the screen. Khalid got out of the Vauxhall with his carry-on. The two men embraced him in turn as the Vauxhall drove off.

"Let the Vauxhall go," said Shepherd. "We've got the PNC details." They would need all their resources to keep tabs on Khalid when he left the mosque.

Clayton relayed the instructions to the surveillance team.

The two men who had greeted Khalid patted him on the back and gestured at the mosque. They were clearly about to take him inside. One of the men tried to take the carry-on case from Khalid but he shook his head and kept a grip on the handle.

"Are Rusul and Tahoor on foot?" Shepherd asked.

Clayton flashed him a thumbs-up.

Shepherd scanned the screens. On one he saw Tahoor Farooqi walking along the pavement. Farooqi had joined MI5 straight from university. He was a second-generation British Pakistani whose parents were both teachers at a Bradford comprehensive. Farooqi graduated with a First in English Literature and Philosophy from Reading University and was now in his third year at MI5. He was dressed casually in a puffer jacket and jeans, and had pulled on a skull cap as he walked at a measured pace with his hands in his pockets.

Khalid and his two companions stepped inside the mosque as Farooqi reached the gates.

Shepherd heard Farooqi's voice over his headset. "I have eyeball on Tango One," he said.

Shepherd grinned at Clayton. So far so good. He leaned forward to stare at the screen in front of him. The pavements were now filled with worshippers making their way to the mosque — mainly men but there were also several women including a number wearing full burkhas. Shepherd frowned as he saw two motorbikes heading down the road towards the mosque. "Do you see the bikes, Janet?" he asked.

There were two men on each bike and all had full-face helmets with dark visors. They were all wearing bomber jackets, gloves and boots. They were driving slowly down the middle of the road. Both passengers were looking over at the mosque.

"They're up to something," said Rayner.

Shepherd nodded as he stared at the screen showing the feed from the roof of the van. Rusul Jafari came into view, threading his way through the worshippers as he tried to catch up with their target. He was wearing a leather jacket and brown cargo pants dotted with pockets.

"Jaffa, take a look at the two bikes in the middle of the road," said Shepherd.

On the screen, Jafari looked to his right. "The passengers have got their hands inside their jackets," he said. He stopped. "Shit."

The passenger on the front bike was holding something in both hands.

"Have they got guns?" asked Shepherd.

Before Jafari could answer the passenger threw a cylindrical grey object high into the air. Shepherd knew immediately it was some type of home-made pipe bomb. "Bomb!" he shouted. "It's a bomb!"

The pipe bomb went high into the air, over the railings and hit the ground to the left of the entrance.

Shepherd's mind raced. He wasn't armed and neither were any of the surveillance teams. They hadn't even arranged for an ARV on standby; it was supposed to have been a straightforward surveillance job. He opened his mouth to speak but before he could say anything they felt as much as heard the dull thud of the pipe bomb exploding in front of the mosque. A dozen worshippers crumpled to the ground and others began screaming in terror.

The bike roared off down the road.

"Get our bikes after them, Matty!" shouted Shepherd.

Shepherd reached for the door handle. As he pulled open the door he heard more screams and the slap of feet on the tarmac as people ran away from the carnage. He jumped down onto the road and saw that the second bike had moved forward and was closer to the mosque. No one was paying it any attention — those worshippers that weren't running away in terror were staring at the bloody bodies sprawled on the ground like broken dolls. Several women had rushed to help but most people stood transfixed, in shock from the blast.

As the biker was revving the engine, his passenger pulled a cylindrical pipe bomb from inside his jacket. Shepherd ran towards the bike. "Bomb!" he shouted at the top of his voice. "Get out of the way, now!"

A few heads turned towards him but nobody moved.

The pillion passenger threw the pipe bomb towards the mosque.

"Get down!" shouted Shepherd.

The bomb arced through the air. Shepherd knew that the sensible thing to do was to drop to the ground until after the explosion, but he didn't want the bike to get away. He continued to run.

The biker twisted the throttle and the bike lurched forward. Shepherd threw himself, twisting in the air so that he hit the pillion passenger with his shoulder. The bike toppled and the engine roared. Shepherd fell to the ground, narrowly missing the spinning rear wheel. The bike fell onto the two men, trapping them.

The pipe bomb hit the mosque and clattered onto the paving stones.

"Bomb!" screamed Shepherd again, then he rolled onto his front and placed his hands over his ears. The pipe bomb exploded and there were more screams.

Shepherd got to his feet. Another half-dozen or so bloody victims lay on the ground and more were staggering around.

The two men who had been on the bike were pushing it up. Shepherd took a step towards them. The passenger saw him coming and reached inside his jacket. The driver was concentrating on getting the bike back into neutral and had his head bent over the handlebars.

Shepherd drew back his fist but the passenger pulled out a combat knife and slashed at him. The man's visor was down and Shepherd saw his own reflection as he jumped back to avoid the knife. The man lashed out again and this time Shepherd grabbed his wrist and twisted his arm savagely, at the same time bringing his knee up into the man's groin.

The bike engine roared and there was a loud click as the driver got it into gear.

Shepherd kneed the passenger in the groin again and then pulled the knife from his gloved hand. The helmet meant Shepherd couldn't punch the man in the face or throat and the man's jacket would absorb any blows to the chest. He kicked out at the man's left knee and heard a satisfying crack. The man screamed and fell to the ground.

The bike roared off. Shepherd looked around. Bravo Two had gone in pursuit of the first bike. Bravo One was parked across the road. Bravo One was Neil Geraghty, a relative newcomer to the surveillance team. He had actually worked as a motorcycle courier for two years before joining the Security Service and in his spare time he rebuilt classic motorbikes. He was clearly in shock, staring in horror at the carnage outside the mosque.

"Neil!" shouted Shepherd.

Geraghty looked over. There was a camera fixed to the top of his full-face helmet that was transmitting live video back to the van. Shepherd waved for him to come over. Geraghty twisted the throttle and the bike shot across the road. "After him!" shouted Shepherd, climbing onto the pillion and pointing with the knife down the road after the departing bike.

Geraghty twisted the throttle but before the bike could speed forward, a large bearded Asian man kicked him in the hip. Geraghty yelped and his hand slipped off the throttle. A teenager ran over, screaming, and he grabbed Geraghty's helmet and pulled him off the bike.

The bike fell to the side and Shepherd went with it.

More onlookers ran over, all of them screaming and shouting. Hands clawed at Shepherd's face and the knife was pulled from his grasp.

He hit the ground and he was kicked in the side. He rolled over and was kicked again. He struggled to his feet. All he could see were angry faces.

Geraghty was on the ground, next to his bike. Two teenagers were kicking him and he curled up into a foetal ball. Shepherd tried to get to him but two men blocked his way, thumping him in the chest.

"I'm trying to help!" Shepherd shouted but the mob weren't listening. A punch connected with Shepherd's chin but there was no weight behind it and all it did was push his head back. He put up his hands to defend himself but he was hit from behind, a blow to his shoulder. There was an outbreak of slaps from the men in front of him. Shepherd could easily have fought back but he knew that would only make things worse.

He staggered back under the onslaught of slaps and then someone kicked his shin and he fell to the ground.

12

He tried to get up but he was kicked in the side. All around him were shouts and screams and all he could see were legs and feet, a flurry of blows that blended into one onslaught.

He rolled onto his front and pushed himself up. Around him were more than a dozen angry worshippers, most of them bearded and all of them wide-eyed, screaming at him with hatred.

"I'm not the fucking enemy!" he shouted but his words were lost in the clamour. A hand clawed at his face and he knocked it away.

Something hit him in the back and he staggered forward. He turned just as a teenager threw a punch that glanced off his shoulder. The teenager was crazy with rage, his upper lip curled back in a snarl. He went to punch Shepherd again and Shepherd pushed him away, knocking him back into the crowd.

He was surrounded now, he couldn't see the bike and he'd lost sight of Geraghty. "Neil!" shouted Shepherd but his voice was lost in the baying of the crowd.

"Fucking kafir!" shouted an old man, who spat in Shepherd's face. As Shepherd wiped himself with his sleeve, hands grasped him around the back of his neck. He reacted instinctively, twisting around and ducking down, then firing off two quick punches. The man who had been choking him staggered back, gasping for breath. Shepherd drew back his fist but before he could throw a punch his arm was grabbed by an old man with a grey beard. Shepherd tried to shake him off but more hands grabbed his arms and he felt himself being pulled backwards. He struggled to stay upright, knowing that if he fell to the ground again he'd probably never get up.

A hand grabbed his shoulder and Shepherd tried to pull away.

"Spider!"

It was Jafari.

"We've got to get to Neil, they're killing him!" shouted Shepherd.

Jafari nodded and then started shouting in Urdu at the top of his voice. He pulled away the hands that were gripping Shepherd's arms. The mob ignored him and continued to punch and push Shepherd as they screamed abuse at him. Farooqi shouted louder, raising both hands above his head. This time a few of the worshippers stopped trying to attack Shepherd and looked at him quizzically.

Farooqi pushed his way through the crowd, shouting in Urdu. One of the teenagers started shouting at him and pointed at Shepherd, but Farooqi shook his head emphatically and shouted back.

Gradually the anger subsided. There was still a commotion off to their left and Shepherd pushed his way through to where four young men were kicking Geraghty. Shepherd pulled one of them away. The man turned and sneered when he saw Shepherd, then tried to kick him. Shepherd easily avoided the kick and pushed the man hard in the chest, sending him sprawling over Geraghty's bike. Farooqi and Jafari rushed over to help and together they stopped the worshippers from attacking Geraghty. Shepherd knelt

14

down and gently took off his colleague's helmet. His eyes were closed and blood was trickling from between his lips.

"Is he okay?" asked Farooqi.

Geraghty's eyes opened. "I'm okay," he groaned. "What the fuck happened?"

"They thought we were attacking them," said Shepherd.

"To be fair, you are the only non-Asians here," said Farooqi. "And you were on a bike."

Geraghty tried to sit up but then groaned and lay back. "I think I bust something," he moaned.

"Stay where you are," said Shepherd. "The ambulances will be on their way."

He looked at Farooqi who nodded. "Matty's called it in." In the distance they heard sirens. "Speak of the devil," said Farooqi.

"You and Jaffa help with the wounded," said Shepherd. "I'll stay with Neil."

A woman began wailing hysterically, close to the mosque. There were more sirens now, getting closer. Geraghty had closed his eyes and had gone still. Shepherd took his hand and squeezed it. "Hang on in there, Neil," said Shepherd. "Help's coming."

Geraghty squeezed back but his eyes stayed closed.

The first ambulance arrived within five minutes. By the time a second ambulance pulled up outside the mosque, two police cars had turned up. There were more than a dozen worshippers who had been badly

15

injured in the two blasts and another fifty or so walking wounded. Miraculously, no one had been killed.

It wasn't until the third ambulance arrived that a medic came over to attend to Geraghty. Shepherd explained what had happened. Geraghty was still in pain and bleeding from his mouth, and he was having trouble breathing. "I think his lung has collapsed," said the medic. A colleague hurried over with a gurney and together they loaded Geraghty onto it and took him over to the ambulance.

The third police vehicle to arrive was an ARV, an armed response vehicle. The three firearms officers on board pulled out their carbines but with no one to shoot at they just stood close to their vehicle, eyes scanning the crowds.

Police tape had been strung across the road and uniformed officers were taking names and addresses of worshippers. The highest-ranking officer was a young inspector with a uniform that looked a size too large for him, clearly out of his depth and spending most of the time on his radio.

Shepherd went over to Farooqi. "We should move out and leave the cops to it," he said. "Where's Jaffa?"

Farooqi pointed over to the entrance to the mosque where Jafari was consoling a woman in a burkha who was sobbing into her hands. "We're going to have to give statements, right?" asked Farooqi.

"You can't tell the police about our operation, we don't want our surveillance compromised. Have you seen Khalid?"

Farooqi shook his head.

16

Shepherd waved Jafari over. "Did you see Khalid?" he asked.

"No, it went crazy after the bombs went off. What's going on? Were they after Khalid?"

"No idea," said Shepherd. "It might just be bad luck. What about the guy I pulled off the bike?"

"The cops have got him," said Farooqi. He nodded over at an ambulance where a paramedic was attending to the man's injured leg. Two constables stood either side of him. His helmet had been removed. He was in his teens with a skinhead haircut and a tattoo of a swastika across his neck.

"I'm gonna head off with the van. You guys stay here, okay? And keep a look out for Khalid just in case he's still here."

"The cops will be asking everyone for ID," said Farooqi.

"You're just a couple of worshippers who got caught up in the fracas," said Shepherd.

As Farooqi and Jafari walked away, Shepherd jogged over to the Openreach van and climbed into the back.

"We've been told to get out of Dodge," said Clayton.

"I figured that's what they'd want," said Shepherd. The powers that be wouldn't want an MI5 surveillance operation caught up in the investigation of a terrorist attack. He sat down. "Any sign of Khalid?"

"It was chaos out there," said Clayton. "We didn't see him leave but that doesn't mean anything. Plus there's a back entrance. I think we've lost him."

"I've told Jaffa and Tahoor to stick around, just in case. What about the first bike? Did Bravo Two catch them?"

"They lost them about half a mile away," said Clayton. "We got the registration numbers of both bikes but they seem to be fake."

Shepherd pressed the intercom to talk to the driver. "Back to base, Paul," he said.

"Roger that," said Drinkwater, and the van pulled away from the curb.

"What were they?" asked Clayton. "Grenades?"

"Some sort of pipe bomb, I think," said Shepherd. "Luckily no one seems to have been killed but there are a lot of injured."

"How's Neil?"

Shepherd scowled. "He took a hell of a kicking," he said. "The paramedic thinks a lung has collapsed."

"Bastards," said Rayner.

"There was a lot of confusion," said Shepherd. "They just saw he was on a bike and went for him."

Shepherd's mobile rang and he took the call. It was his boss, Giles Pritchard. "Are you pulling out?" asked Pritchard, as usual getting straight to the point. The director wasn't one for small talk.

"We're on our way," said Shepherd.

"This is a bloody disaster, obviously."

"Obviously."

"Do you have any sense that this attack was linked to Khalid's visit?" asked Pritchard.

"I don't think so," said Shepherd. "It seemed to be more of an attack on the congregation than an attempted hit. Khalid went inside the mosque with two men just before the explosions. We've got pictures of the men so we should be able to ID them asap. There was a lot of confusion after the attack and there's a back way out, so I'm guessing he just cut and ran. I've left two of our people there and they'll keep looking, and we'll get all local CCTV footage checked, but other than that I don't see there's anything else we can do."

"I hear you," said Pritchard.

"What do you want us to do with our video footage?"

"In what way?"

"We have the attack on camera," said Shepherd. "We had the mosque under surveillance when the attack took place and one of our bikes was filming, plus we had the van's camera on it."

"Let's have a look at the footage before we make a decision on that," said the director. "I'm loath to let the police know that we had a surveillance operation running because they have a tendency to leak like a sieve and I don't want the papers getting hold of it. Khalid is going to be spooked anyway, if he hears that MI5 were there we'll never see him again. So mum's the word."

"Not a problem," said Shepherd, and Pritchard ended the call.

"Are you okay?" asked Clayton.

"I've been better," said Shepherd.

"You took a bit of a kicking yourself."

Shepherd shrugged. "I've had worse."

Drinkwater dropped Shepherd, Rayner and Clayton close to MI5's Millbank headquarters, overlooking the

Thames, and drove the Openreach van back to the pool garage. After they had passed through Thames House security, Rayner and Clayton headed up to the mobile surveillance office on the third floor while Shepherd took the lift up to the sixth and walked along to the main incident room. Half a dozen officers were sitting at terminals and the walls were dotted with screens. Sarah Hardy was in charge, a tall no-nonsense brunette who spoke five languages and was a scratch golfer. She was wearing a dark suit and white Nikes — she kept a pair of Prada heels in her desk which she put on for meetings but generally she preferred trainers while she was working.

"We've just been watching your performance," she said with an amused smile on her face. "Is it standard SAS practice to charge towards grenades before they've gone off?"

"Strictly speaking they were pipe bombs and I was winging it," said Shepherd. "Can I see it?"

"Of course," said Hardy. She turned and nodded at one of the officers. "Show us the footage from the van please, Tim."

One of the big screens went black and a second or so later was filled with the view from the camera at the top of the van. The first bike had stopped outside the mosque and the pillion passenger threw his bomb at the building. The bike sped away. Shepherd counted off the seconds without thinking and reached three before the bomb exploded. Half a dozen worshippers, all men, fell to the ground. There was no sound to the footage but he could imagine the screams of horror.

Shepherd appeared on the left of the screen. The second bike had stopped and the passenger had pulled out his pipe bomb. Shepherd started to run towards the bike as the bomb spun through the air. Shepherd reached the bike and hit the passenger, knocking the bike over. The bomb exploded as Shepherd hit the ground and more worshippers fell.

Hardy was shaking her head at what she saw as his stupidity, but Shepherd knew that if he hadn't made the run the bike would have disappeared and they wouldn't have the bomb-thrower in custody.

On the screen, Shepherd got to his feet as the passenger pulled out his knife.

"Nice bit of self-defence here," said Hardy and Shepherd grinned as his on-screen self took the knife off the passenger and kicked out at his leg. The passenger went down. The biker pushed his bike up and drove off. Shepherd waved over at Geraghty and as he climbed onto the back of the bike the worshippers swarmed around them. He and Geraghty were kicked and beaten. Hardy nodded at the officer who froze the image. "Neil's going to be okay, but he has a pneumothorax so he'll be out of action for a week or so," she said.

"What about the guy in custody?" asked Shepherd.

"Name's Tony Hooper, comes from a family of nasty racists," said Hardy. "His dad's been in and out of prison half a dozen times for assaulting Asians and vandalising Asian businesses, and Tony has a couple of brothers who are the same. He's been pouring out bile on social media and has had numerous Facebook and

Twitter accounts blocked. But this is the first time he's been involved in major violence."

"Is he talking?"

Hardy shook her head. "He's in Paddington Green as we speak and refusing to say a word. But it's early days."

"And the other three on the bikes?"

"Both bikes were dumped and set on fire. The registration plates are fake. We've applied for a look at Hooper's phone records and internet usage, hopefully that'll lead us to them."

"Has anyone claimed responsibility for the attack?"

"There's a lot of nasty stuff on social media, 'serves them right', 'time to fight back', and all that sort of nonsense. But no organisation has come forward to say that they did it."

"So lone wolves maybe?"

"We'll know better once we've seen his internet footprint," said Hardy. "But the type of device they used suggests they were amateurs. They threw two of them into a crowd and didn't kill anyone."

"It'll be interesting to see what the tech boys have to say," said Shepherd. "I didn't see a burning fuse and they didn't seem to light anything, so that suggests either an electrical or chemical fuse, which means a degree of sophistication."

"Mr Pritchard says we're to hang onto the footage. He was here ten minutes ago to see what we had and he wasn't happy to discover you'd been filmed."

Shepherd grimaced. "Yeah, I thought that might be an issue."

"His first thought was that we didn't want the police knowing there was a surveillance operation going on, but I think now he's more concerned about your actions being made public. He's not happy. He said he wanted to see you as soon as you got back."

"I'll head on up."

Hardy smiled sympathetically. "Rather you than me," she said.

Giles Pritchard kept Shepherd waiting for twenty minutes before seeing him. Shepherd wasn't sure if it was because the director was busy or if he was just trying to put him in his place. Shepherd had worked for Pritchard for nearly a year but knew almost nothing about him other than that he was career MI5, joining straight from university, initially working in data analysis. So far as Shepherd knew, Pritchard had never run agents or worked in the field; he had spent pretty much his whole career in Millbank. Shepherd wasn't one for gossip, but on the few occasions he'd spoken about Pritchard with colleagues no one could remember him being involved in any major successes — but then no one could tie him into any memorable failures either.

He was sitting behind an uncluttered desk with two computer screens and he had a bottle of Evian water and a glass close at hand. He didn't offer Shepherd a drink, just waved him to one of the two wooden chairs facing him. Shepherd was fairly sure that the choice of uncomfortable chairs was deliberate and that Pritchard wanted to discourage visitors from staying too long.

Pritchard was about ten years older than Shepherd and only a few pounds heavier, his hair slicked back and a pair of metal-framed spectacles perched on his hawk-like nose. He was wearing a dark pinstripe suit and a club tie. Pritchard was said to be a member of White's, the exclusive members-only club that still refused to admit women. It was the oldest gentlemen's club in London and counted Prince Charles and Prince William as members.

As always there was no small talk and the director got straight to the point. "I didn't realise you had played such a starring role in the surveillance footage," said Pritchard, peering over the top of his glasses.

"I was trying to stop them," said Shepherd.

"You were on a surveillance operation. The key to that is staying unnoticed."

"Things changed once the mosque was attacked."

"I understand," said Pritchard. "You made a judgement call. I'm just saying that your actions have put the agency in a difficult position. We can hardly show that video to the police, not with your face clearly on display."

"I couldn't stand by and do nothing," Shepherd said. "And while I failed to stop the bombs being thrown, I did manage to apprehend one of the attackers."

Pritchard wrinkled his nose as if he had just noticed a bad smell in the room. "I'm not disputing that," he said, sitting back in his chair. "But your presence there resulted in a riot that culminated in one of our officers being taken to ICU."

24

"His name's Geraghty," said Shepherd. "Neil Geraghty."

Pritchard flashed Shepherd a withering look. "I'm well aware of his name, Daniel, so don't try suggesting that I'm out of touch with the troops. And just so you know, I was on the phone to the doctor treating him just ten minutes ago. I've also phoned his wife to give her my sympathies and given her my mobile number in case she needs anything."

Shepherd held up his hands. "Sorry," he said. "It's been a tense day."

"Apology accepted," said the director. "But don't forget, it was you calling Neil over that drew him to the attention of the mob. If you'd just stayed in the van, none of that would have happened."

Shepherd gritted his teeth and nodded. He knew from experience there was no point in arguing with the director.

Pritchard watched Shepherd for a couple of seconds to see if Shepherd would respond, and when he didn't the director smiled thinly and nodded. "Anyway, water under the bridge. I have a new job for you. One that will make use of your undercover talents." He paused, but again Shepherd didn't say anything. "How much do you know about county lines drug gangs?" Pritchard asked eventually.

"I've not worked on any cases, but I know the drill," said Shepherd. "Drug gangs in big cities send kids to provincial towns to sell drugs. Usually the high-value ones like heroin and crack cocaine."

Pritchard nodded. "They tend to use young kids, generally fifteen and younger, to work as mules. If the kids get caught they don't face major charges because of their age, and their youth makes them easy to manipulate. The gangs use the child mules to move large amounts of Class A drugs from the big cities. A single line can pull in more than two thousand pounds a day and a gang might have dozens of lines. The local cops in the small towns don't have the expertise to cope, in fact it was only a spate of overdoses across the country that brought it to the attention of the authorities."

"But the National Crime Agency is on the case," said Shepherd.

"It has been for a while," said Pritchard. "They now have more than two hundred active investigations, from Glasgow to London. They have estimated that there are more than a thousand lines up and running at any one time but I feel that's lower than the reality of the situation." He sighed and sipped his water. "Recently the Home Office funded a county lines coordination centre, headquartered in Birmingham, bringing together detectives from the major cities around the UK with NCA analysts with representatives from other agencies that deal with youngsters, such as education, health and welfare."

Shepherd nodded as he waited for Pritchard to get to the point.

"Violent crime — especially knife crime — has soared in the provinces as the various gangs start to fight over turf. In the early days they were moving into virgin territory so there was nothing to fight about, but now pretty much every village and small town has at least one line," said Pritchard. "Over the last few years the violence we are accustomed to in the big cities has been exported to the provinces. Anyway, as part of its ongoing fight against the county line gangs, the NCA has been using undercover agents. The problem is that many of the mules that are being recruited are underage. At least, they are under sixteen. And there are strict procedures that need to be followed when underage covert human intelligence subjects are used."

Shepherd's jaw dropped. "They're using children as undercover agents?"

"No, undercover agent is the wrong term completely. They're not pretending to be something they're not. They're not given legends, they're not acting, they're more like double agents."

"You mean they get caught and they're told they'll be let off if they work for the NCA?"

The director shifted uncomfortably in his seat. "Well, basically, yes."

Shepherd held up his hands. "Who would think that was in any way a good idea?" he said.

"Daniel, this isn't something I dreamed up. This is something being done by the centre in Birmingham with the cooperation of the NCA. But on the question of juvenile covert human intelligence subjects, we have used them here at MI5."

Shepherd frowned. "On what basis?"

"Horses for courses," said Pritchard. "There was a case in Bradford, not that long ago. An imam in a mosque there was part of a child grooming ring. Two of the girls being abused were approached by officers here and they agreed to wear wires."

"While they were being abused?"

"It didn't come to that," said Pritchard. "But the evidence they gathered put a dozen men behind bars for a very long time."

"And what was Five's interest?"

"The imam was an ISIS recruiter and fundraiser. We couldn't put a terrorism charge together but his predilection for young girls was his undoing."

"I get the feeling you're going to tell me that the end justifies the means," said Shepherd.

"There is a logic to that statement that is difficult to refute," said Pritchard.

"Children?" Shepherd shook his head. "It's just wrong."

"You've got a son, right?"

Shepherd nodded. "Liam. But he's not a child any more. He's flying choppers in the Army."

"You must be proud."

"I am," said Shepherd, smiling at the compliment but knowing that Pritchard was playing him. Or trying to play him.

"The kids these days are different, Daniel. They're more streetwise, they know stuff that we never did at their age. When I was a kid, the only way to get porn was to steal a top-shelf magazine from the local newsagent. These days, any sexual perversion you want is a few seconds away on your smartphone. And free at that. Were you ever offered drugs at school? Because I wasn't. My drug was nicotine, a few puffs behind the bike shed between lessons. Cider maybe at night down the local graveyard. But drugs just weren't on our radar."

"Sounds like you had quite a childhood," said Shepherd.

Pritchard flashed him a tight smile. "But at least I had a childhood, Daniel. Most of these kids jump from being toddlers to adults. Sex, drugs, violence, it's all in front of them the moment they learn how to touch a screen. So when we use a juvenile in a case, it's not the same as using a child forty years ago, or even ten. The cops arrest a twelve-year-old these days and all the kid will say is 'no comment' and demand to speak to a lawyer. We've got fifteen-year-olds slashing each other with machetes and schoolchildren dealing in Class A drugs." He shrugged. "Anyway, I don't have to justify departmental procedure to you. Everything that's done is approved by the Home Office. The reason I've called you in is that a juvenile being run by the county lines centre has cut across one of our investigations and I need you on board." He picked up his glass and took another sip of water. "A few years back you worked on a case involving right-wing groups, correct?"

Shepherd tried not to show he was confused by the sudden change of subject. "I've come across them on several occasions, both for the Security Service and for SOCA before that," he said.

"Ever come across a chap by the name of Gary Dexter?"

Shepherd didn't have to consider the question —
with his near-faultless eidetic memory he knew
immediately that it wasn't a name he was familiar with.
"No," he said.

"He was a BNP stormtrooper many years ago,
kicking heads and breaking arms, then he moved to
England First but fell out with them about two years
ago. He left England First and set up his own group,
British Crusaders. There are just over a hundred core
members but many more sympathisers. The Crusaders
hold demonstrations and disrupt Muslim events but the
intelligence we have is that they are planning to become
more proactive. We have had information from Europol
that Dexter and several of his people have been talking
to various right-wing terror groups in Germany and
France with a view to acquiring weapons."

"Firearms?"

"RPGs. And grenades."

"So you think there's a connection between Gary
Dexter and what happened today?"

"Actually, I suspect not," said Pritchard. "The
devices used today appear to be home-made and
Dexter has been trying to acquire commercial
weaponry. But we'll know better once Tony Hooper has
been questioned."

"Apparently he's not saying anything."

"We'll see how he fares after a couple of nights in
Paddington Green," said Pritchard. "But as I said, I
don't think there will be a connection with Gary Dexter
and the British Crusaders. Now, here's the thing. Gary
Dexter has a brother, Micky Dexter. Former

30

Paratrooper, like yourself, did ten years including a couple of tours in Afghanistan. Came back to work in a security firm in Reading. He's an upstanding citizen, by all accounts. Now, Micky has a son, Harry. And sixteen-year-old Harry has fallen in with a bad crowd. He lives outside Reading and young Harry has been bringing in drugs for a Brixton gang. The NCA caught him and he has agreed to help them with their investigation in exchange for any charges being dropped. The drugs investigation is coming along nicely, but then we found out what was going on and realised that young Harry might be the key to putting Gary Dexter behind bars. Gary has had numerous death threats made against him and is the subject of an ongoing fatwa so he never goes anywhere without full security and his home in Bromley is a fortress. The chances of getting a listening device into his home are precisely nil, but every Sunday he visits his brother in Reading for a spot of lunch."

"So what's the plan? To send the kid in wearing a wire?"

Pritchard looked at Shepherd over the top of his glasses, his eyes narrowing, and Shepherd wondered if he had pushed it too far. But he didn't like what he was being asked to do and was finding it difficult to keep the contempt out of his voice. "No, of course not," he said. "But we are giving him a phone that will do the eavesdropping for him. On or off, it transmits anything said within ten feet or so and is virtually undetectable."

"Virtually?"

Pritchard sighed. "Daniel, I'm sure you've used the same equipment on many of your undercover operations," he said. "It looks and feels exactly like a regular phone. If you were to take it apart and if you knew what you were looking for, then maybe you might realise that it had been modified, but really that level of expertise is only found in government labs. Any regular person isn't going to see anything, even if they look at it closely."

"And what about the information you want? Is Harry going to be told what questions to ask?"

"Initially, no. I understand your reservations, a teenager can hardly start questioning his elders without sticking out like a sore thumb. No, we won't even be telling him what the phone does. In fact, he won't even know it's our phone. We've prepared a duplicate of the one that he already has. One of the things you'll have to do is swap it. He's not being told that his uncle is of interest."

"And presumably he's not to know that I'm with Five?"

Pritchard nodded. "You'll be another member of his police handling team."

Shepherd sat back and folded his arms, but realised immediately that he was looking defensive. He put his hands on his knees, but that looked too posed, so he put his hands down by his side and stretched out his legs. "What's the legal position on using children as confidential informants?" he asked.

"If they are under sixteen, a parent or an appropriate adult has to be present at all meetings with their

32

handler. Sixteen and over, they can be on their own. There are procedures in place to ensure the safety of the informant, and any operation can't last longer than four months." Pritchard was looking at him with an amused smile on his face. "I know you're not comfortable with the idea of working with teenagers," he said. "None of us are. This isn't a matter of choice. There are just no alternatives."

"You could put me in," said Shepherd. "I've infiltrated rightwing groups before. We've even got a couple of legends that are still good to go."

"You'll never be able to get close to Dexter. At least not close enough for you to get anything on the record. He's careful. Very careful. The NCA has tried twice and both times the agents were discovered and beaten to within an inch of their lives."

Shepherd sighed in exasperation. "Which is why we shouldn't be using a kid. What's Dexter going to do if he finds out that his own nephew is out to betray him?"

"First, he won't find out," said Pritchard. "Second, you'll be watching over him. You'll be his guardian angel. If there's any sign that he's blown, you pull him out."

"And then what? You take a sixteen-year-old from his family and put him in witness protection for the rest of his life? What about his parents? Do they know what's going on?"

"Of course not," said Pritchard. "If Micky finds out what we're doing then obviously he'll tell his brother."

"I'm really not comfortable with this," said Shepherd.

"Do you think any of us are? But like I said, we have no alternative."

"I've given you one," said Shepherd. "I'll join this British Crusade group and get close to the Dexter brothers."

"That could take months, maybe years, and we don't have the time. There was an arson attack on a mosque in Bradford last month and we're certain the British Crusaders were behind it. And we're sure there are going to be more. There's a lot of chatter among the various right-wing groups that are into this sort of thing, and the word is that the next attack will be in London."

Shepherd folded his arms again and sat back in his chair. So much of what he was required to do in the fight against terrorism ended up with having to choose the lesser of two evils, and this was a perfect example. Use a child as an undercover agent, or have innocent worshippers murdered. Obviously, using the Dexter kid was the lesser evil, but that didn't make it any more acceptable.

"Your NCA point of contact will be an old colleague of yours," said Pritchard. "So at least you'll be working with a familiar face."

Shepherd decided to walk to the Tattershall Castle. It was a bright, sunny day but as always a chill wind blew down the Thames. He'd arranged the meeting for two o'clock and the Tattershall Castle was the obvious choice as it was pretty much equidistant from Millbank and the NCA's South Bank headquarters in Tinworth

34

Street. The Tattershall Castle was a paddle steamer built in the 1930s that had been converted into bars and function rooms. In its glory days it had ferried passengers and goods across the Humber estuary before being retired in 1973 and towed to the Thames. Shepherd often used it as a meeting place as anyone arriving or leaving had to walk along a narrow gangplank so it was easy to spot a tail.

Shepherd grinned when he saw Jimmy Sharpe sitting at a corner bench seat with a glass of lager in front of him, half full or half empty, depending on your point of view. "Razor, you old reprobate," said Shepherd. "Long time, no see."

"More than a year," said the Glaswegian, getting to his feet. He was wearing a black reefer jacket and blue Levi's jeans with gleaming black Doc Martens on his feet. He hugged Shepherd and patted him on the back.

"Closer to two," said Shepherd. "You're looking fit and well."

"Aye, retirement agrees with me," said Sharpe, releasing his grip on Shepherd.

"Retired? Are you serious?"

Sharpe shrugged. "My pension wasn't getting any bigger, so it made sense to take early retirement and then work for the NCA on short-term contracts. What are you drinking?"

"I'll get them," said Shepherd. Sharpe sat down as Shepherd went over to the bar and ordered a Jameson with soda and ice and another lager for his friend, along with a couple of packets of crisps.

"So, how are you getting on with the new boss?" asked Sharpe as Shepherd sat down and sipped his drink.

"He's not that new," said Shepherd. "It's been a year."

"You are burning through bosses, though, aren't you? The fragrant Charlotte Button leaves under a cloud, Jeremy Willoughby-Brown gets shot in his own back garden and Patsy Ellis — well, she took early retirement to spend more time with her family, they say."

"That's what they say."

"But there are all sorts of rumours flying about."

"People do like to gossip, don't they?" said Shepherd. He raised his glass in salute. "Good to see you, Razor."

"And you," said Sharpe. They clinked glasses and drank.

"So this case. You're happy about using a kid?"

"No one's happy," said Sharpe. "But he's sixteen going on twenty-six. His dad's a hard nut and young Harry says that he gets more than his fair share of slappings from him. He's been taking drugs since he was thirteen and got involved with the Brixton dealers a year ago. He's not some namby-pamby kid in short trousers, Spider. He knows what he's doing. He's made some bad decisions and helping us is going to minimise the damage."

"But what happens when it's over? How's the father going to react when he finds out what his son has been up to?"

36

"The feeling at the NCA is that it won't come to that. We'll use the lad to gather evidence and if we get an open and shut case then the drug dealers will plead guilty and there'll be no need for Harry to appear in court."

"I was thinking more about the family connection," said Shepherd. "He'll have to keep what he did a secret from his dad and his uncle for the rest of his life."

"He'll never know, so there's no secret to keep. He won't know that his phone is bugged or that we're targeting his uncle. All we're doing is gathering intel on his uncle, Harry will never have to testify."

"And his parents don't have to be told?"

Sharpe shook his head. "If he was under sixteen then we could only talk to him with a parent or an appropriate adult present, but Harry's sixteen so he can fly solo."

Shepherd sipped his drink and opened one of the packs of crisps. "This is messy, Razor."

"Look, I wouldn't worry about young Harry," said Sharpe. "Some of the kids involved in these county lines are bullied or threatened, but Harry has always been a willing party."

"How did he get dragged into it?"

"He was taking the train into London at weekends to buy small amounts of marijuana for himself and his few friends. His supplier linked up with the gang in Brixton."

"Yardies?"

Sharpe wagged a finger at him. "See now, that's a racist assumption. You hear Brixton and drugs and you automatically think West Indians."

"My apologies. So what sort of gang is it?"

Sharpe grinned mischievously. "Yardies, of course." He sipped his lager. "Anyway, the Yardies convinced young Harry to start selling to his schoolmates and he did. He got up to half a kilo a week and then they encouraged him to start dealing in ecstasy and speed and eventually crack and heroin."

"Crack and heroin to schoolkids?"

Sharpe shook his head. "Once they got him up to sizeable amounts they told him to stop dealing himself. Now he's a middleman. Some of the gear ends up in the schools but the Yardies are using him to transport drugs to some heavier guys in the Reading area. It's a clever system. One of the Yardies takes the drugs on the Tube and meets up with Harry at one of the busier stations, usually at the weekend. They give Harry a backpack and Harry heads back to Reading. No one's going to be worrying about a young kid, and even if he did ever get caught, there's not much he can tell the cops. He doesn't know the person who gives him the drugs and he doesn't know where the Yardies are based."

"But the NCA does?"

"We've had our eye on them for two months. They operate out of a flat above a kebab shop, a clever move because the smell from the takeaway covers up the smell of the drugs. We were getting close to wrapping the case up when your mob started to get busy."

"And Harry's dad — he's not involved in the British Crusaders?"

"Not that we know of. You'd know more than me. The NCA doesn't tend to investigate the right-wing groups unless they do something drastic. Public order is the remit of the Met and you lot look after the terrorism side. There's nothing on the PNC about Micky and he had a good record with the Paras."

"And the mother?"

"Housewife. Harry has two siblings, a brother and a sister, both younger."

Shepherd sipped his drink. The more he learned about the operation the less he liked it. Getting a teenager to lie to his parents was morally wrong, no matter what the legal position was. Sure, the teenager had already been lying to them about his involvement with drugs, but that didn't make what they were doing any less reprehensible.

"How bad an egg is this Gary Dexter?" asked Sharpe.

Shepherd put down his glass. "What have you been told?"

"Not much. Just what's on the PNC really. A few breach-of-the-peace fines, vandalism, drunk and disorderly, but that was all when he was younger. Nothing on file for the last ten years. I Googled him and there's a Facebook page and a Twitter feed where he posts a lot of anti-Islam stuff that could in theory get him into trouble, but no one seems to have taken an interest so far. You know what the cops are like with that sort of thing, they let sleeping dogs lie until somebody makes an official complaint or the media gets hold of it."

"Well, between you and me it looks as if he's gearing up for something more dramatic than a few Facebook posts. He's been making contact with various European terror groups trying to get some heavy weaponry."

"I don't know why they bother," said Sharpe.

"You don't know why who bother to do what?"

"You know what I mean. The Muslims are pissing everybody off and pretty much everyone is turning against them. Why attack them? They're doing a bang up job of hurting themselves as it is, why turn them into victims?"

"You've given this some thought, obviously."

Sharpe laughed. "You can see the way it's going, Spider. Every time there's a jihadist attack, successful or not, the general public doesn't react with fear, they react with anger and hatred. Now, I get that that's what the likes of Islamic State want, because they benefit from the backlash. The more Muslims feel threatened and isolated, the more they'll turn to groups like IS. But at the end of the day they'll lose. Once the majority of the population loses sympathy with Muslims, there'll be a backlash. We're already seeing that across Europe and it'll happen here before long. Groups like British Crusaders just have to bide their time and wait for the pendulum to swing back. If they start blowing up mosques, all they'll do is drum up sympathy for Muslims."

"Maybe you should tell them that."

Sharpe laughed again. "Somebody should."

"Well until you manage to persuade the country's far-right groups to park their hostility, we need to make sure Gary Dexter doesn't get his hands on any heavy artillery. So when can I meet Harry?"

Sharpe looked at his watch. "I figured we go do it this afternoon, after school. We've arranged a safe house not far from where he lives so it's easy for him to drop by."

"Fine by me," said Shepherd. He nodded at Sharpe's lager. "Are you okay to drive?"

"Not a problem," he said. "I'm good to go."

Sharpe's car was an almost-new red Jaguar XE. "Bloody hell, Razor, the NCA's treating you well," said Shepherd when he saw the vehicle parked at the side of the road.

Sharpe laughed as he climbed into the driving seat. "This is mine," he said. "Because I'm a consultant I get to use my own vehicle and they pay me a mileage allowance. The way it's going, the mileage allowance alone is going to pay for three weeks in Spain next year."

Shepherd settled into the passenger seat and fastened his seat-belt. "Good to see you doing so well." The Jaguar still had its new car smell.

"They get their money's worth," said Sharpe. "You should think about moving over, plenty of undercover work on offer, and they're short of good surveillance guys."

"I'm not sure I'd want to move back to police work," said Shepherd.

"It's all the same these days," said Sharpe. "Good guys and bad guys."

"I can't argue with that," said Shepherd.

It took Sharpe just over an hour and a half to drive to the safe house in Reading. It was a neat semi-detached with a green door and a blue Vauxhall Vectra parked outside. Sharpe made a hands-free call when they were five minutes away so they were expected, and the front door opened as Sharpe parked behind the Vectra. They were ushered inside by a woman in her late twenties with short blonde hair and a small gold heart on a chain around her neck. She was wearing blue Wrangler jeans and a pink sweater.

"This is Julie Bacon," said Sharpe. "She's been with Harry since day one."

Bacon closed the door. "Detective Constable Bacon," she said, offering her hand. She had a firm grip as they shook.

"Dan," he said. "Good to meet you."

"The spook," she said. "You guys never seem to have family names." She wrinkled her nose. "I have to say up front I'm not happy about this."

"About what specifically?"

She released her grip on his hand and folded her arms. "About MI5 moving in like this. Harry needs very careful handling."

"My understanding is that you and Razor will continue to run him. Our investigation is to be in tandem."

"There's a world of difference between using a sixteen-year-old to get information on a south London

42

drugs gang and using him to get intelligence on a terrorist group," said Bacon. "Plus there's the whole family thing. If this works out the way you hope it does, Harry's uncle will be behind bars for a long time. What's that going to do to his family?"

"They won't know Harry was involved in the case against his uncle," said Shepherd.

Bacon sighed. "Even so."

Shepherd held up his hands in surrender. "Julie, you're preaching to the converted," he said. "I raised the exact same concerns with my boss. But as always we run into the old 'the end justifies the means' argument."

Bacon opened her mouth to say something, but then had second thoughts and forced a smile. "Coffee? Tea? I've just put the kettle on."

"What time's Harry getting here?" asked Sharpe.

"Just after four-thirty," she said.

Shepherd looked at his watch. It was just before four. "Coffee sounds good," he said. "No sugar and a splash of milk, please."

Shepherd and Sharpe followed Bacon through to a well-equipped kitchen with a marble-topped island. They sat down on stools while Bacon made instant coffee.

"How long have you had this place?" asked Shepherd.

"Since we started running Harry," said Sharpe. "Just over three weeks ago. We figured it would be easier to debrief him here."

"How's the investigation going?"

"All good," said Sharpe. "We've identified half a dozen members of the Yardie gang and that in turn led us to nine county lines in addition to Harry's. Harry has given us four of his contacts here. They're small-time dealers but growing fast. Harry's now bringing in a kilo a week and recently they've been asking him to make midweek deliveries, too."

"A kilo a week isn't much in the grand scheme of things, so I guess it's the supplier to the Yardies that NCA is after," said Shepherd.

Sharpe shrugged. "To be honest, the powers that be are all fired up about the county lines end of it. When inner-city black kids knife each other, overdose or fight over turf, there's a tendency to let them get on with it. But when nice middle-class white kids in the suburbs get involved . . ." He shrugged again.

Bacon put down mugs of coffee and pulled up a stool. "The problem is that it's not just drugs that get exported from the inner cities," she said. "The gang culture that goes with drugs comes with it. We've already seen a rise in stabbings here and it won't be long before we get shootings and the rest of it." She sipped her coffee. "It might already be too late. We've already heard that there are two more lines coming into Reading, so even when we shut down Harry's line the drugs will still be brought in."

"You're almost done with your investigation here?" asked Shepherd.

Bacon nodded. "We caught Harry three weeks ago and he agreed to cooperate almost immediately. He's scared to death that his dad will find out and we promised him that if he helped us he wouldn't be charged."

"And you're allowed to agree something like that with him without the parents knowing?"

Bacon nodded. "It has to be signed off at a senior level, but yes."

"Does he have access to legal advice?"

"He hasn't asked for a solicitor," said Sharpe.

"That's not what I was asking," said Shepherd.

"I know what you're thinking, Spider, but he's not being railroaded, I promise."

"Spider?" said Bacon, frowning.

Sharpe gestured with his mug. "He ate a tarantula many years ago, as a bet."

"Seriously?" said Bacon.

"I'm afraid so," said Shepherd. "It was a one-off."

Bacon laughed. "Now I've heard everything," she said.

"What was Harry told, time-wise?" asked Shepherd. "Does he know how long he'll be doing this for?"

"As long as it takes, that's what he was told. He would let us know where he was doing his pickups and drop-offs, and we had our people there to witness and record. We had real-time access to his phone, calls and texts, and we had him wear a wire on a couple of occasions."

"And he was okay with that?"

"He thinks he's James Bond," said Sharpe. "He seems to be enjoying it now."

"That's dangerous," said Shepherd. "Cockiness leads to mistakes."

"I know, I know, I've tried to calm him down but he's full of piss and vinegar."

Shepherd sighed. The more he learned about the operation, the more uncomfortable he felt.

"I really hoped we'd be done by now," said Bacon.

"We would have been, if we hadn't spotted the link between Micky Dexter and his brother," said Sharpe. "Once we had Harry's name we did a PNC check on his parents and they came up clean. Micky Dexter is a manager with a security company that has council contracts so he has been vetted a few times. Someone at MI5 must have picked up that Micky was Gary Dexter's brother and they started to get busy."

"I think it's a mistake using Harry to gather evidence against his uncle," said Bacon. "That wasn't what he agreed to."

"I hear you," said Shepherd.

"Do you?" said Bacon, her eyes hardening. "Because it seems to me that you're here to do exactly that. You're not interested in the drugs investigation at all."

"Julie . . ." said Sharpe.

"It's okay, Jimmy," said Shepherd. "Julie's entitled to feel protective about Harry. I get it, I'm a father myself."

"And would you want the authorities talking to your child behind your back?"

"Of course not, but then I don't have relatives planning terrorist attacks."

"That's the point, though. Relatives. It's Gary Dexter who is the problem, not Harry's father."

"I agree, it's messy," said Shepherd. "And in a perfect world, MI5 would be pursuing other avenues, but Gary Dexter runs a tight ship and there is no other option."

"These possible terrorist attacks," said Bacon. "What are we talking about?"

Shepherd smiled awkwardly. MI5 and the NCA were working together but that didn't mean that he was in a position to tell her too much about an ongoing case.

She smiled at his hesitation. "I know, I know — you can't tell me and if you did you'd have to kill me."

Shepherd laughed. "You know full well I don't have a licence to kill," he said.

"Let me tell you what I think is going on," she said. Sharpe grinned and winked at Shepherd before sipping his coffee. "We all know what terrorism means. Terrorism is acts of terror, usually ending in the death of innocents. The bombs on the Tube were terrorism. Flying planes into buildings is terrorism. Suicide bombers are terrorism. And we all know who the terrorists are these days." She looked at Shepherd expectantly but he refused to be drawn and simply smiled and waited for her to continue. "It's Muslims. We all know that. And not just Muslims, it's Muslims of Pakistani heritage and more often than not they're called Mohammed. That's just a fact. We know that and the powers that be know that, but in today's PC world they're not allowed to say it because that's racial profiling and we can't have that, can we?"

She looked at Sharpe and he raised his mug in salute. She turned back to Shepherd and tilted up her chin. "The bosses have to appear even-handed, which is why a few months ago they were telling the media that they had thwarted four right-wing terrorism plots so far this year. Well done them, right? Pats on the back all round. But they didn't say what those plots were, did they? Well I was involved with one of those cases and I can tell you it was two skinheads who were planning to nail a pig's head to the door of a mosque. It was never terrorism, it was vandalism. But the commissioner wants it labelled as a potential terrorist attack because it shows how even-handed the Met is. It doesn't matter who or what the terrorists are, the Met will pursue them. Which is fine and dandy, but it's a lie, Dan, and we all know it's a lie." She leaned towards him. "So this is what's bothering me. We got Harry to supply us with intel to help us bring down a south London drugs gang and their suppliers. I wasn't happy about using a kid as a confidential informant but we followed the rules and it worked out okay. But what we're doing now is something completely different. We're lying to him and putting him in harm's way for what seems to me to be a public relations exercise."

She sat back and folded her arms and Sharpe looked at Shepherd expectantly, clearly enjoying his discomfort.

"I hear you," Shepherd said, and immediately put his hands up when he saw the look of contempt flash across her face. "I know, I already said that. But it's true. I do hear what you're saying and I understand and even empathise. I had a very similar conversation with my boss before I was sent over here. Using children as confidential informants makes me very uncomfortable.

But I would say that what we're dealing with is considerably more serious than nailing pigs' heads to mosque doors. Gary Dexter's group has contacted right-wing groups on the Continent with a view to acquiring RPGs, obviously with the aim of attacking mosques."

"Property damage, then," said Bacon.

"Well, I'm sure they'll be firing at mosques but there's a good chance that people will get hurt or killed. Look at that attack on the mosque in Acton. A lot of people were hurt and we were lucky there weren't any fatalities. The European groups involved are heavy-duty organisations, Julie. They're not just a few angry skinheads."

She nodded reluctantly. "I suppose you're right," she said.

He couldn't tell if her comment was sarcastic or not. "Look, if you're uncomfortable with this stage of the investigation, you're free to drop out," he said. "Jimmy and I can handle it."

She shook her head fiercely. "No way," she said. "I got him into this and I'll see it through to the end."

Shepherd flashed her a smile. That's exactly what he had expected her to say. "I'll make sure he's not in any danger," he said.

"I'm not sure that's a promise you can make," she said. "But thank you." She smiled and sipped her coffee.

"So the way I understand it, Harry's status has to be reviewed every month," said Shepherd.

"It's a formality," said Sharpe. "It's supposed to ensure the welfare and safety of the lad and to ensure that the deployment is, to quote the rule book, 'necessary and proportionate'. But really it just goes across a chief super's desk and he ticks a box and initials it."

"No psychological review?"

Sharpe shook his head. "There's a health and safety review, but he doesn't have to see a shrink."

Shepherd scowled. "How do you think he's handling it? The pressure?"

"Like I said, the only problem I can see is overconfidence. He's a cocky bugger."

Shepherd drank his coffee as he considered his options — not that he had too many.

"What are you planning to do?" asked Bacon.

Shepherd took an iPhone out of his pocket. "We need to get him to use this phone. It's the same as the one he already has, so it's just a matter of substituting it."

"What's special about it?" asked Bacon.

Shepherd handed it to her. "Basically it records everything in the vicinity, whether or not the phone is switched on or the sim card is in place. Most crims think that if their phone is switched off it's dead but this one records even when it's off and then sends the recording when the phone is back on. It also records all conversations and text messages along with any internet activity, and sends that in bursts. But I don't want Harry to know that. At some point you need to make a switch."

"Won't he notice that his pictures and stuff aren't there?" asked Bacon.

Shepherd shook his head. "It's a clone. Everything on his phone is on this one."

"How is that even possible?" asked Bacon.

"Don't ask me, but our tech boys can do it. Every photograph, every contact, every call log, it's all on there. They're also able to set it for facial recognition and have all his passwords. And everything he does with the phone can be seen and heard by us."

"What about once he's got the phone?" asked Sharpe. "Do we want him to get closer to his uncle?"

"Initially, no," said Shepherd. "Gary Dexter is around at the house every Sunday so we'll see how that goes."

"You think he'll talk in front of Harry?" asked Bacon.

"We'll see," said Shepherd. "Have you asked him about his uncle?"

"It's never come up," said Bacon.

"Good," said Shepherd. "We obviously don't want him to know that the focus of the investigation is shifting. Have you had the house under surveillance on Sundays?"

"We never watch the house," said Sharpe. "In fact we keep well away from it. This is as close as we get. Why?"

"I'm supposed to attach a tracker and listening unit to Gary Dexter's car if I get the chance," said Shepherd. "We can't get to the car at his own house because security is so tight, and usually he has a driver

51

and bodyguards and they never leave the car alone. But when he visits his brother, he drives himself."

"So you have to do the dirty deed?" asked Sharpe.

"Not me personally, but it's not difficult," said Shepherd. "We just need a few minutes alone with the vehicle."

They all jumped as the doorbell rang. "That'll be Harry," said Bacon.

"Can you introduce him to me?" said Shepherd. "Tell him I'm Inspector David Slater, with the Drugs Squad." He nodded at the iPhone. "Can you look after that and make the switch?"

Bacon nodded and slipped the phone into her pocket before heading down the corridor.

"I think she likes you," said Sharpe.

Shepherd grinned. "You have to admire her commitment to the lad," he said.

"Best not to get too close to your CIs," said Sharpe. "That's my experience."

Shepherd nodded. "Yeah, mine too. But this is different. He's a kid."

They heard the front door open and close and then footsteps. Bacon walked back into the kitchen followed by Harry. Shepherd had already seen surveillance photographs of the boy — he was tall and gangly, much as Shepherd's son Liam had been at that age, and like Liam he had acne across his forehead. He was wearing a school blazer and had his tie at half-mast. He had deep-set eyes and thick eyebrows and piercing blue eyes that narrowed as they scrutinised Shepherd.

"This is Inspector Slater," said Bacon. "He's with the London Drugs Squad."

"Why's he here?" Harry asked Bacon.

"I'm here to offer you any support you need," said Shepherd.

"I don't need no support," said Harry. He looked at Bacon again. "You said no one else would know what I was doing. Just you and him," he gestured at Sharpe. "The whole point of this is that it's a secret, right?"

"Inspector Slater has experience in undercover work," said Bacon. "He might be able to help you with any issues you have."

Harry shook his head. "I'm good."

"We're all very pleased with the way things have been going," said Shepherd. "You're doing a great job."

Harry went over to the fridge, opened it and took out a can of Coke. He popped the tab, watching Shepherd as he drank.

"Has Swifty been in touch?" asked Bacon. Tyrone "Swifty" Taylor was one of the enforcers in the Yardie gang that was using Harry. The leader of the posse was a Jamaican bodybuilder called Jason Morris, who went by the nickname Dancer. Morris ran the posse but usually had his enforcers carry out his instructions, issued from his flat in Brixton.

Harry nodded. "Sent me a text this afternoon. Wants me at Waterloo tomorrow morning."

"Can I see?" asked Bacon.

"Sure," said Harry. He fished his iPhone out of his pocket and held it close to his face for the facial

53

recognition to kick in. Once the phone was unlocked, he handed it to Bacon.

"Have you met Swifty?" asked Shepherd. He stood up and walked over to the fridge. He opened it and took out a bottle of Evian water.

Harry turned to watch him. "A couple of times. He was the one who told me I was gonna start moving different gear."

"What about Dancer?"

Harry shook his head. "I've never met him but Swifty talks about him all time. 'Dancer wants this, Dancer says that', all that shit. They're all scared of him."

Harry now had his back to Bacon and she pocketed his phone and took out the one Shepherd had given her.

"Has Swifty ever threatened you?" asked Shepherd.

"I'm okay," said Harry, but the way he averted his eyes let Shepherd know that he was being less than honest.

"I guess he's happy with the way things are going," said Shepherd. "But do you feel threatened?"

Harry laughed. "Of course I feel threatened." He gestured at Sharpe with his can of Coke. "All he's ever done is threaten me."

"I meant by Swifty. Do you feel as if he could hurt you at any point?"

"If he ever finds out that I'm a grass, hell yeah," said Harry.

"He won't find out," said Bacon.

54

"Yeah, well, the longer this goes on, the more chance there is that he'll realise what I'm doing," said Harry. "You said I'd be done in a few days."

"It won't be much longer," said Bacon.

"But you keep saying that," said Harry.

"Harry, you're not doing anything that you wouldn't be doing if you hadn't been caught," said Sharpe. "If we hadn't got you, you'd still be running the line for Swifty, you'd still be bringing in drugs a couple of times a week. Nothing's changed."

"Now I'm a fucking grass, though," said Harry. "That's what's changed."

"All you're doing is passing on information that Swifty is giving you," said Shepherd. "Our surveillance teams do the rest. If Swifty does ever realise that the police are watching him, there's no reason for him to think that you've been helping him."

"Yeah, well you would say that, wouldn't you?"

"Harry, I know we've only just met and you don't know me from Adam, but I can promise you that I will never consciously put you in harm's way," said Shepherd. "From now on I'm going to be your guardian angel and if anyone tries to hurt you, they'll have to go through me first."

Harry jutted his chin. "Are you strapped?"

"Strapped?"

"Strapped. Carrying. Have you got a gun?"

Shepherd shook his head. "No, I'm not armed."

"So what are you going to do if Swifty and his posse turn up with MAC-10s? Flash your badge?"

"We don't have badges," said Shepherd. "We have warrant cards."

Harry tilted his head on one side. "Yeah? Let me have a look then."

Shepherd hesitated for a few seconds, then took a black leather warrant-card holder from his pocket. On it was the silver crest of the Metropolitan Police. He gave it to Harry who opened it and scrutinised the warrant card inside. "How long have you been a cop?" he asked.

"Twenty years or so," said Shepherd, the lie coming easily. He had memorised all the details of Inspector David Slater's legend. It hadn't been difficult, not with his trick memory.

Harry snapped the warrant-card holder shut and gave it back to Shepherd. "So you flash that and what, Swifty and his posse surrender? You need to get with the real world. The likes of Swifty don't give a flying fuck about the cops."

"Swifty won't get anywhere near you, Harry," said Sharpe. "He's under twenty-four-hour surveillance. If it even looks as if he wants to harm you, we'll protect you."

"But it won't come to that," said Bacon, patting Harry reassuringly on the shoulder. "He's not going to find out."

Harry sipped his Coke.

Bacon gave the phone to Harry and he put it in his blazer pocket without looking at it.

"What will happen tomorrow at Waterloo?" asked Shepherd.

"Someone will give me a bag and then I'll bring it to Reading, on the train."

"What route do you use to get to Waterloo?"

"I get the train to Paddington and then the Bakerloo Line."

"And you're okay with the way things have been going?"

Harry frowned. "What do you mean?"

"Do you feel stressed? Are you sleeping okay? It can't be easy for you, having to do what Swifty tells you and to keep meeting with us."

Harry laughed harshly. "Mate, if it was up to me I wouldn't be dealing with your lot, but it's not as if I have a choice, is it?" He looked over at Sharpe but Sharpe just shrugged. Harry looked back at Shepherd. "I'm between a rock and a hard place, aren't I? If I get caught screwing over Swifty and his posse, God knows what they'll do to me. But if I don't do what you guys say, then I'm fucked."

"Language, Harry," said Bacon.

"What, you gonna arrest me for swearing?" sneered Harry. He scowled at Shepherd. "So no, I'm not sleeping great at the moment. And I don't feel so good. But the way it was told to me, I don't have a choice. If I don't help you then my parents will find out what I've been doing and I'll probably go to prison. At least this way I have a chance of getting my life back to normal."

"That's what we all want," said Shepherd.

"When, then?" asked Harry. "When are you going to stop having me jump through hoops?"

"It won't be much longer, let's see how it goes over the weekend."

Harry looked at his watch. "I've got to go," he said.

"Take care," said Shepherd.

"I always do," said Harry. He headed for the front door with his Coke. Bacon hurried after him.

"I'll take you upstairs and show you what we've got so far," said Sharpe. They heard the front door close as Sharpe led Shepherd into the hallway and up the stairs. Sharpe opened a door to a small bedroom and flicked on the light. A single bed had been pushed up against the wall and four large whiteboards had been placed on easels. The boards were dotted with surveillance photographs and head and shoulder shots. The board on the right had four photographs of Jamaicans on it, two with long dreadlocks, one with short curly hair and one with his head shaved. All were in their thirties and the photographs had apparently been taken in custody suites.

Sharpe waved at the pictures. "From the left: Tyrone 'Swifty' Taylor, Jason 'Dancer' Morris, Winston 'Beamer' Lewis and Lyndon 'Mario' James. They've all got criminal records." He tapped a photograph of a kebab shop. "They're based on the first floor, access through the door to the left of the kebab shop door and there's a fire escape at the rear that leads down to a small yard, which leads out into an alley. That's where they keep their day-to-day drug supplies, but they have a lock-up a short drive away. There's hundreds of kilos in the lock-up so they're all going to go down for a long time once we move in."

58

He moved across to the second whiteboard. "These are the guys who are supplying the Yardies. They're all Scousers but spend most of their time on the Costa del Sol these days." There were three photographs on the board, all taken at long range, presumably with telephoto lenses.

"The leader is a guy called Jerry McAllen. Started off selling wraps of heroin in Liverpool when he was a kid, graduated to big-time marijuana trafficking and now he's one of the biggest importers of cocaine and heroin into the UK. Never been caught, his record is as clean as the proverbial whistle. And even with all the evidence we've collected, we still don't have enough to put him away. He's one of the smart ones. Never goes near the money or the drugs, all communication is through text messages on encrypted phones."

Sharpe tapped the picture on the left. A younger man wearing glasses, with both arms covered in elaborate tattoos, standing by a black Porsche. "This is Jerry's younger brother, Tommy. Their mum died when they were youngsters and their dad was an alcoholic so he dumped them in care and ever since Jerry has taken him under his wing. Tommy's as careful as Jerry."

Sharpe stepped back from the board. "The brothers have enough money invested in property and stocks that they could go legit if they wanted. They've got millions tucked away. But Jerry gets a kick out of it. It's like a game and he's good at it. He loves winning."

"Have you tried getting someone undercover?"

Sharpe shook his head. "To be honest, there's no interest. My boss is after Morris and his crew and

59

wants the county lines shutting down. He doesn't want to put any resources into the McAllens."

"But if you just close down Morris, the McAllens will simply sell to someone else."

"They already are. They've got dozens of customers all over the UK. The thing about the McAllens is that they never rip anyone off. Their word really is their bond. People trust them. Don't get me wrong, they're not softies by any means, but if you play fair with them they'll play fair with you. The only cloud on their horizon is the Albanians. They've moved into the UK drugs scene big time and you don't want to fuck with them. I'd say the Albanians have already taken half of the McAllen's turf yet they don't seem to care. But so far as the brothers go, we have a cunning plan."

Sharpe pointed at the third photograph. The man in the picture was in his late forties or early fifties, barrel-chested and with a weightlifter's build. He had sunglasses pushed up on top of his bald head and was sitting on a patio overlooking the sea with a pretty blonde either side of him and a bottle of champagne in an ice bucket. "Martin O'Connor is their main conduit to Morris and their other customers. He's Irish but hasn't been there in years. He lives on the Costa but is in and out of the UK on a regular basis. We managed to record a couple of conversations he's had with Morris, and Europol have video of him checking out a yacht in Puerto Banus that was later intercepted in British waters with a couple of hundred kilos of cocaine on board. Not enough evidence to put him away, but it's all grist to the mill."

60

"So what's the plan?" asked Shepherd. "Get Morris to roll over on O'Connor and then get O'Connor to give you the brothers?"

Sharpe grinned. "No flies on you, Spider."

"Ha ha," said Shepherd. "I see what you did there. But yeah, it makes sense. Set the dominoes up and knock them down."

"The worst that can happen is that we pull in a Yardie drug gang and shut down their county lines. Best scenario is that we take down a major smuggling ring. Drinks all round."

He gestured at the third whiteboard. There were two surveillance photographs on it, taken with a long lens. "Harry delivers the bags to these guys: Gavin Warwick and Stuart Bradley. Warwick wasn't known to the cops before we had Harry on board, but he's in our sights now." He tapped the photograph on the right. A young bearded man was walking out of an off-licence with a carrier bag. "Warwick is an Essex lad who moved to Reading a couple of years back. Bradley came with him and they share a house. Bradley is known and he's a nasty piece of work." He tapped the second photograph. Bradley was bald with glasses, wearing a Nike tracksuit as he rolled out a wheelie bin. "He has form for drug dealing, selling mainly to youngsters, especially young boys. He has a thing for young boys and getting them hooked on drugs is how he pulls them in."

"Bloody hell, Razor, if you know that why's he still on the streets?"

61

"He was arrested in Chelmsford but two of the boys who were supposed to be giving evidence against him backed out. Presumably they were threatened. Like I said, he's a nasty piece of work. The local cops were giving him a hard time so he moved to Reading. He's a clever bastard. His customers go to the house, always to the back door which isn't overlooked. We managed to get a guy around the back late one night and there's a dog flap in the kitchen door. We reckon they do all their business through the flap and that the door is reinforced. We're going to try and get a look inside at some point, send in a gas man or something."

"But the drugs stay inside the house until they're sold?"

Sharpe nodded. "Yeah. So immediately after a delivery there'll be enough drugs in the house to put them away for a long time. Like I said, we were pretty much ready to go when your mob started to get busy about Gary Dexter." He took a step closer to the fourth whiteboard. "This is the Dexter family. Just so you know who's who."

There were six photographs on the board. Most seemed to have been taken from social media. The two men on the board were Micky and Gary Dexter. Micky was the older, in his late forties. He was a big man and Shepherd figured a career in security was a good fit. He had a strong chin and eyes that looked as if they wouldn't stand for any nonsense. In the photograph he was in the gym, wearing a tight Lonsdale T-shirt and baggy shorts that showed off a dagger tattoo on one calf.

62

Gary Dexter was five years younger, thinner and shorter with sharp features and the look of a man who would have trouble fighting his way out of a wet paper bag. The picture had been taken in a pub and he was holding a pint of beer and grinning as if he had already drunk several. He was wearing a white polo shirt with the red cross of St George on the breast pocket. "They look very different," said Shepherd.

"I know what you mean but they're definitely brothers," said Sharpe. "Same mum, same dad, at least according to their birth certificates. I suppose Micky just got luckier in the gene pool."

"Ten years in the Paras probably helped," said Shepherd.

The third picture was a blonde woman in her late thirties. She was holding a glass of red wine and smiling at the camera. She had long eyelashes that looked fake and her dark roots were showing through, but she had a confident smile as if she didn't care what she looked like. Her eyes were sparkling and Shepherd figured that her husband had taken the picture and that she was very much in love with him.

"That's Micky's wife," said Sharpe. "Debbie. They met as teenagers and she stuck with him right through his Army career." He gestured at the three pictures of the children. "Harry you've met, obviously. His brother is two years younger, Chris. And the girl is Briana. She's nine."

"You said that Micky is tough on the kids. Is that right?"

"Harry claims that his dad hits him every now and again, but you've seen what he's like. If I was his dad I'd be giving him what for."

"You don't hit kids, Razor."

"Sometimes you have to."

Shepherd shook his head. "I never laid a finger on Liam."

"Yeah, well Liam's a good lad. Plus his mum died when he was young."

Shepherd tilted his head to the side. "What do you mean?"

"You know what I mean, Spider. You were his only parent, of course he's not going to play up and risk losing you."

"I never had any problems with him. That's all I'm saying."

"To be fair, you were away most of the time he was growing up. He spent most of his early years with his grandparents and your au pair."

Shepherd opened his mouth to reply but then realised that Sharpe was probably right, so he said nothing.

"The reason we've got so many feral kids knifing each other at the moment is because they don't learn respect at home," said Sharpe. "If you don't respect your parents then why would you respect the police? Or anybody for that matter."

"So you teach them respect by hitting them, is that what you're saying?"

"I got the odd clip around the ear when I was growing up."

64

"And it didn't do you any harm? Come on, Razor. You know that's bollocks. You don't earn respect with violence. Violence breeds violence. But I didn't get the impression that Harry is being abused."

"Me neither, truth be told. I think he was just spinning a line, trying to get our sympathy."

"We need to be sure, Razor. I don't want the dad lashing out at Harry if he finds out what he's been doing."

"Hopefully he won't find out," said Sharpe.

"We need to be sure, Razor."

"He doesn't have a history of violence," said Sharpe. "Other than his military career, obviously."

"Okay, but if I think that Harry is in any danger because of what we're asking him to do, we're pulling him out."

Sharpe patted him on the shoulder. "You're over-thinking this," he said. "If there's any danger it'll come from the Yardies. Harry isn't family to them, he's just a kid to be used. They're the ones that will hurt him, but it won't happen. We've got Morris and his gang under surveillance and if at any time it looks like they've sussed Harry, we'll pull him out."

Shepherd sighed and nodded. Sharpe was a professional with decades of experience working undercover. He was the last person Shepherd needed to be second guessing.

"What do you want to do about monitoring the phone?" asked Sharpe.

"The feed will go to Thames House and I can access it whenever I need to. I can also listen to the live feed through my phone. When does Gary get to the Dexter house on Sunday?"

"Between eleven and twelve."

"Okay if I'm here then?"

"Sure. I'll be here all day and so will Julie."

"And what about Harry's run tomorrow?"

"We'll have people at Waterloo and on the train and at Reading station. We've done a few runs with him so we know the routine."

"You don't do it yourself?"

"We don't use anyone that he knows. And we don't tell him that he's being followed. You know what amateurs are like, if they see someone they recognise, they stare."

"Do you ever see anyone from the gang tailing him?"

Sharpe shook his head. "No. There's just the guy who hands over the bag. It's all pretty casual. They do as many as half a dozen drops a day."

"What about the other lines? Are you turning all the kids?"

"Of the other nine, eight are under fifteen and we can't risk using them. The other one we only spotted a week ago and we're still assessing which way to go. He's a sixteen-year-old but his family are known drug dealers so there's a good chance they know what he's doing. But we can move with just what we have from Harry."

"I'll drop by tomorrow. I'd like another chat with him."

Sharpe took Shepherd downstairs. Bacon offered him another coffee but Shepherd passed. He wanted to get back to Thames House to see how the investigation into the mosque attack was going.

Jimmy Sharpe drove Shepherd back to London and dropped him close to Thames House. Shepherd went in through security and up to the incident room, where Sarah Hardy was eating a sandwich at her desk. On one of the big screens was a live video feed of the outside of the mosque which showed uniformed officers removing the police tape.

"The police are almost done," said Hardy.

"They've done an evidence sweep already?" asked Shepherd. "That was quick."

"They were told to pull their fingers out so that the worshippers could be allowed back in. SOCO and EOD said they would need two days at least but they were overruled."

The scenes of crime officers and the explosive ordinance disposal team should have gone through the crime scene with a fine toothcomb to gather any parts of the bombs that hadn't been destroyed in the explosions. Shepherd assumed that the Met top brass was worried about a confrontation with the Muslim community in the area.

"What about Tony Hooper?"

"Still saying nothing. A lawyer turned up a couple of hours ago."

Shepherd raised an eyebrow. "He has a lawyer?"

"Somebody else is paying for it, but yes, he now has legal representation and I don't think we're going to get a word out of him. Though to be honest I don't think we need a confession or cooperation. The Met has applied to look at Hooper's phone records but we've got a jump on them. He made more than a dozen calls this morning in the hours before the attack, and received six. We've got the names and addresses and it looks as if he was talking to his co-conspirators."

"Are you going to give the info to the Met?"

Hardy shook her head. "No, we'll let them do it in their own time. This is still an SO15 investigation and we don't want to tread on their toes. We're just watching over their shoulder."

"How's Neil?"

"He's in ICU but he's okay. They reinflated his lung but he'll be in hospital for a week or so."

"And have Rusul Jafari and Tahoor Farooqi checked in?"

Hardy nodded. "They went right through the mosque and there was no sign of your Tango One. It looks as if he was spirited out of a back entrance. They got back an hour ago." The phone on her desk rang. She put down her sandwich and picked up the receiver, listened, said "yes" and "of course" and then put it down and smiled at Shepherd. "The director wants to see you. At your convenience."

Shepherd grinned. "He didn't really say that, did he?"

Hardy picked up her sandwich. "I was paraphrasing."

Shepherd went upstairs to Pritchard's office. This time the director kept him waiting for just a few minutes before he was ushered in. Pritchard had taken off his jacket and placed it over the back of his chair.

Gold cufflinks glinted under the overhead lights. He pushed his glasses higher up his nose. "Just so you know, Mohammed Khalid has been booked onto an Emirates flight to Dubai this evening, under the name he flew in on. That suggests he doesn't know he's been watched; if he did he'd probably have gone to ground. The plan is to let him return to Pakistan and keep him under surveillance."

"He left the mosque shortly after the attack?"

Pritchard nodded. "It seems that way, though he wasn't seen. Clearly he was there for a meeting, but what we don't know is if that meeting took place or not. We'll be putting the congregation under the microscope and paying particular attention to the imams, obviously."

"We were just unlucky," said Shepherd.

"So far that's how it looks," said the director. "We'll know better once we've got a clearer idea of what Hooper and his friends were up to. But it's not looking as if Khalid was the target. Just in the wrong place at the wrong time. As they say, shit happens." He smiled thinly. "The good news is that so far the surveillance operation has stayed below the radar. The police know about the attack on Neil but his cover as a courier is holding and they seem to have accepted that he was just an innocent bystander caught up in the reaction to the attack. The descriptions of you are variable, and no one got the registration number or even a decent description of the van you were using." His smile widened a fraction. "So far, so good." He sat back in his chair. "How did it go with the Dexter boy?"

"He has the phone and I'll be at the safe house. He's been asked to make a run tomorrow and I'll watch over that."

"How does he seem?"

"He's a kid. And a cocky one at that. I'd recommend keeping this as short as possible. We're getting him to lie to his parents and parents usually know when their kids are lying."

"I thought all teenagers lied to their parents."

"Do you have children?"

Pritchard's eyes hardened a fraction. "I'm not sure how whether or not I'm a parent has a bearing on your investigation," he said.

Shepherd shrugged. "All kids lie, from an early age. 'I didn't do it' and 'it wasn't me' are pretty much their first words. But as a parent you're not fooled. Then they get older and you ask if they've done their homework and they say they have and you know they're lying. You just know. They get better at lying but a parent can always tell."

"To be fair, you're not just a parent. You've got years of undercover experience, you're an authority on lying."

"Sure, I lie for a living. But parents know their kids and I just worry that his mum and dad will catch him out eventually. Plus, like I said, he's cocky. And overconfidence has caught out many an undercover agent. He's starting to think that it's a game and that he's smarter than the other players."

"I'm assuming you can talk some sense into him."

"I'll try, yes. But the best policy would be to bring the operation to a speedy conclusion."

Pritchard nodded. "Let's see how we get on this weekend."

He looked at his watch, which Shepherd took as a sign that he was being dismissed. Shepherd stood up. Pritchard had already turned his attention to his computer screen as Shepherd left the office.

Jerry McAllen dropped down onto the white leather sofa and smiled up at the cute blonde as she popped the cork off his bottle of Cristal. "You handle that bottle well, darling," he laughed. "I bet you could make me pop like that if you wanted."

"I've had a lot of practice," laughed the girl. She was in her twenties with dark green eyes and an Eastern European accent. Probably Polish, Jerry figured. She was wearing a low-cut top that showed off an impressive cleavage and a short skirt that left little to the imagination. She was just his type. "What's your name, darling?"

"Iwana," she said. She picked up his glass and poured professionally.

"As in, 'Iwana drink'?"

She flashed him a smile. "I've never heard that before," she said.

"Really?"

She laughed and handed him his glass. "Only about a million times," she said.

Jerry's brother, Tommy, dropped down on the sofa next to Jerry. He was eight years younger, a few kilos lighter and with his arms covered in tattoos including skulls, knives, snakes and tumbling dice. Tommy was wearing Diesel jeans and a Ted Baker shirt, the sleeves rolled up to show his artwork. Like his brother he had sunglasses shoved up on the top of his head even though the sun had gone down hours earlier.

Iwana poured Tommy a glass. "You're new," he said as he took it from her.

"I'm twenty-three," she said, putting the bottle back into its ice bucket. "Not new really."

Both men laughed. Jerry ran a hand through his thick jet-black hair. He was wearing a white linen shirt and Versace jeans and had a Rolex Daytona on his wrist. "Why don't you sit down and have a drink with us, Iwana?"

"I can't," she said. "But maybe on my day off."

"Darling, we're VIPs," said Jerry. "Management won't mind."

"Jerry, everyone in this section is a VIP," she said.

"You know me?"

She laughed. "Everyone knows Jerry and Tommy McAllen," she said. She winked and went over to another table.

The two men laughed as they watched her hips swing. "She's fit," said Tommy.

"Fuck off, I saw her first," said his brother. He stretched out his legs and burped. They had eaten at a harbour-side restaurant in Puerto Banus, huge lobsters and thick steaks, washed down with Cristal champagne. The nightclub was a short walk from the restaurant but they had stopped off twice on the way for cocktails. The plan was to spend the rest of the night drinking champagne from the vantage point of the VIP area,

72

cordoned off from the rest of the club by a short flight of stairs, a red rope and two heavily-built bouncers in black suits.

Half the club's clientele were Spanish, but pretty much everyone in the VIP section was British. Jerry knew everyone there, at least by sight, and he had exchanged a few nods and handshakes as he had made his way to his regular sofa. Most of the men he'd shaken hands with were in his line of business, but they weren't competitors, more like friendly rivals.

As he sipped his champagne, he saw a guy in his thirties walk up the stairs towards the red rope. The two bouncers moved to block his way. Jerry smiled to himself. There were always chancers trying to blag their way into the VIP section but only regular big spenders were allowed in and the guy wasn't a regular. He was short and stocky, wearing a Ralph Lauren polo shirt with the big horse on the breast, probably a knock-off. There was a Rolex on his left wrist and a thick chain on his right and Jerry would have bet money that both of those were counterfeit too.

Jerry knew the bouncers. Oskar was a German, a former special forces soldier. He'd done five years in the Kommando Spezialkräfte, the German equivalent of the SAS, before being invalided out with a dodgy knee. His colleague was a Frenchman called Pierre, former Foreign Legion, a tough bastard who took no prisoners. Pierre put a hand on the man's shoulder and said something to him — no doubt telling him to fuck the fuck off. The man held out his hand to shake. Playing the big man. Pierre shook the hand and Jerry could imagine the Frenchman gripping the chancer so hard that tears would spring to his eyes. It was Pierre's party trick — he had a grip like a vice.

The two men shook and as Pierre took his hand away, Jerry realised that the man had slipped him something. Jerry chuckled. Bribing the bouncers with a few euros never worked. They were well paid and their jobs depended on them keeping out the riff raff.

The chancer shook hands with Oskar, then they both patted the man on the back and Oskar unclipped the red rope and ushered him inside. Jerry frowned. That was a first. He'd never seen anyone bribe his way into the VIP area before. Maybe the guy had been before and flashed a lot of money. Or maybe it was one hell of a tip.

The man was walking across the VIP area, his eyes flicking from side to side, taking everything in. There was an arrogance to the way he walked, head up and shoulders back, and Jerry began to wonder if he'd misjudged him.

"Do you know him?" asked Tommy, who was also looking at the new arrival.

"No," said Jerry.

The man was walking in their direction, but he was avoiding eye contact. As he got closer, Jerry could see a jagged scar across the man's left cheek as if he'd been glassed at some point in the distant past. As Jerry stared at the scar the man's eyes met his and Jerry felt his cheeks redden. The man smiled as if sensing his discomfort.

"What the fuck's he grinning at?" asked Tommy.

The man walked up in front of Jerry and nodded. "Jerry?"

Jerry looked up at him. "Do I know you?"

"Not yet. No." The man had an accent, but Jerry couldn't place it. It was European, but not French, not German, and definitely not Spanish. "May I sit down?" He gestured at the sofa opposite them, but then sat down before Jerry could reply. "My name is Frenk," he said.

"Frank?"

"Frenk. With an e. But you can call me Frank if you want. Most of my British friends do."

"Tomato, potato," said Tommy.

Frenk squinted in confusion, not getting the reference.

"What the fuck do you want, Frenk?" asked Jerry. "My brother and I just wanted a quiet drink and maybe a blow job later and I don't think I want to share either of those experiences with you."

Tommy laughed and gulped down his champagne.

Frenk smiled at Jerry but his eyes were ice cold. He leaned towards Jerry and jutted out his chin. It was an old scar, Jerry realised. Very old. Probably done when Frenk was a boy. And close up he realised that the shirt, and the watch, were genuine. The bracelet was gold, too. Several thousand pounds worth. "This is a courtesy visit," said Frenk. "I would appreciate your courtesy in return."

"What do you want?" asked Jerry.

"I am here to inform you that some of the present arrangements you have in the United Kingdom are

75

about to change. I wanted to forewarn you, and to let you know that despite what happens, you will continue to trade as before. It's just that instead of your current customers, you will be dealing with me."

Jerry laughed harshly. "What the fuck are you talking about?"

Frenk continued to smile. "Several of the people you deal with are about to retire, shall we say. And I will be taking their place. It will happen quite soon, and quite suddenly, and I wanted to assure you that other than the change in personnel, it will be business as usual."

"You're going to take out the competition, is that what you're saying?" Jerry shook his head in bewilderment. "Who the fuck are you, Frenk? Russian? Are you Russian Mafia or something?"

"Not that it matters, but I am Albanian," said Frenk.

"Where the fuck is Albania?" asked Tommy. "Is that one of those Arab countries, like Afghanistan?"

"We are Europeans," said Frenk. "We are a small country next to Montenegro, Kosovo and Macedonia. We are north of Greece. So no, we are not a fucking Arab country. But as I said, who I am is not the issue."

"Who exactly are you thinking of replacing?" asked Jerry.

"That is for me to know and for you to find out," said Frenk. "I just didn't want you to have a nasty surprise."

Jerry grinned. "Mate, you'll be the one who gets a surprise if you start throwing your weight around."

Frenk smiled. "We shall see," he said. He waved at the dancers down below. "You are a regular here?"

"You could say that. Yeah."

"Is anyone here a problem for you?"

"A problem?"

"Someone who is giving you trouble."

Jerry laughed and pointed at a man standing by a table on the edge of the dance floor. He was talking to two men sitting on stools. They were all drinking bottles of Sol. "See that arsehole there? The one in the Middlesbrough shirt."

"Middlesbrough?" repeated Frenk.

"It's a football team," said Jerry. "A shit one. The guy wearing the shirt is Simon Close and he's always breaking my balls. He's a fucking scumbag. He took a girl off me a few months ago and he never lets me forget it. She came crawling back after a week but I told her to go fuck herself. And I'm pretty sure he's a grass."

Frenk peered down at Close. Close had just turned thirty. He had shaved his head and had a large diamond in his right ear that glinted in the lights. He had massive forearms, the result of hours in the gym lifting weights and frequent steroid injections. "A grass?" he repeated, as if hearing the word for the first time.

"An informer. We've seen him chatting to the local cops and we had problems with a yacht a while back that we think might be down to him talking too much. If we had proof I'd have offed him myself but I'm not a hundred per cent sure."

"It was him," said Tommy. "He's a fucking arsehole."

Frenk smiled tightly. "I will take care of that problem for you," he said.

"You'll what, now?" said Jerry.

"I will show you that I am a serious person," said Frenk. He stood up and held out his hand. "I will leave you now. Thank you for your time."

Jerry shook his hand but didn't get up. Frenk shook hands with Tommy. He also stayed put on the sofa. Frenk didn't seem to be insulted by their refusal to stand. He nodded and walked away.

"What the fuck was that about?" asked Tommy.

Frenk reached the red rope and Oskar unhitched it for him. Both bouncers smiled and nodded at Frenk and he patted Oskar on the shoulder as he left.

"Just another chancer," said Jerry. "The Costa is full of them." He drained his glass and refilled it. Two blonde girls in very short dresses and impossibly high heels walked over. "Hello ladies," said Jerry. "Why don't you join us?"

The two girls giggled and dropped down onto the sofa. Tommy ordered a second bottle of champagne from Iwana. Frenk reached the bottom of the stairs and headed for the exit, turning to look at Close as he went.

They were halfway through their third bottle of Cristal when Tommy saw the two men walking purposefully across the dance floor towards where Simon Close was standing. "Jerry?" he said.

Jerry looked up from the girl he was kissing, and Tommy nodded over in Close's direction. Jerry turned and his eyes narrowed as he saw the two new arrivals. They were both wearing black leather jackets and had baseball caps pulled down over their faces. The girl tried to kiss Jerry again, but he pushed her away and got to his feet, his eyes widening. Strobe lighting kicked in on the dance floor and in a series of stark images Jerry saw the two men reach inside their jackets and pull out guns. Revolvers. The music was so loud that the shots were lost in the driving beat of the techno track, and the strobe lighting meant the flashes lost their power. The men each fired twice and red flowers blossomed on Close's chest. He was still falling backwards as the two men put their guns back inside their jackets and turned and walked away.

Only the people nearest Close had seen what had happened. A few girls screamed but the screams were lost in the thumping beat of the sound system. One of the men Close had been drinking with knelt down and then started shouting for someone to help. His cries were also swallowed up by the pounding music.

Jerry and Tommy turned to watch the two killers walk calmly out of the nightclub, their heads down.

"What the fuck just happened?" asked Tommy.

"That Albanian fucker just showed us that he's serious," said Jerry. He sat down and picked up his champagne glass. "I think our life just got very interesting."

Tommy joined him on the sofa. "Are we in trouble?"

Jerry grinned. "Mate, if we were in trouble it would've been us that got shot. Frenk is just showing us who he is, that's all. It's just business." He raised his champagne glass. Tommy picked up his glass and clinked it against Jerry's.

As the two men drank, the girls dropped back down on the sofa. "Did yous fucking see that?" said the one Jerry had been kissing. She had a harsh Belfast accent.

"Yeah," said Jerry.

"They fucking shot him to bits," said the girl.

The clubbers on the dance floor had moved away from the body. Two security men in black suits hurried over. Oskar had spotted the body and was heading down the stairs, talking into his headset. The sound system cut off and the lights went on. There were gasps and curses as more clubbers saw the body on the floor. Dozens of smartphones appeared as those nearest the body began recording the carnage.

"Yeah," said Jerry. "Shit happens."

Harry Dexter was so busy playing on his iPhone that he didn't see the NCA surveillance officer who was keeping tabs on him. The follower was in his sixties, wearing a tweed jacket over a dark brown waistcoat and carrying a walking stick. The limp was genuine. The man's name was Oliver Tomkinson and he'd been with the NCA's surveillance unit for five years. His arthritic knee meant that he was of little use in a fast pursuit, but he was such an unlikely tail that he was almost never spotted.

Another watcher parked outside Harry's detached house had made the call that the boy was on his way and Tomkinson had been in place at the entrance to the station with his ticket and a receipt so that he could claim the fare back on his expenses. Once he had seen Harry arrive, Tomkinson walked ahead of him to the platform where the next train to London was expected. Following people by walking ahead of them was a skill that had to be taught and Tomkinson had become something of an expert. His black-framed spectacles had small mirrors at the sides that allowed him to see behind himself as he walked and he was able to monitor the boy's progress without once turning his head.

Tomkinson took a seat on the platform. His task was merely to observe Harry and to check that no one spoke to him or passed him anything. The trip to London was a regular one and they knew where he was going, but that didn't mean that Tomkinson was at all blasé and he kept a close eye on the boy.

All the surveillance officers were using their phones to stay in touch with Sharpe and Shepherd, who were monitoring the operation back at the safe house. If the operation had been critical they would have been using Airwave radios, but they knew exactly where Harry was going and what he was doing and using radios always carried a risk of discovery. The train arrived on time and Tomkinson boarded the same carriage as Harry but sat several seats away. He sent a short text to Sharpe. "ON TRAIN". The boy remained engrossed in his phone all the way to London.

Tomkinson again walked ahead of Harry once they reached Paddington Station. As they walked onto the concourse, another member of the surveillance team was waiting. Andrew Mosley was in his forties, wearing an overcoat and carrying a briefcase, just one of thousands of businessmen criss-crossing the capital on public transport. He sent a text message — "HAVE EYEBALL" — as he followed Harry down into the Tube station. Tomkinson limped over to Starbucks to get himself a coffee and a croissant while he waited for the boy to return.

The phone network disappeared as they moved underground, so Mosley kept close as Harry took the escalator down to the southbound Bakerloo Line platform.

Mosley got into the same carriage as Harry. Harry managed to grab a seat but Mosley stayed standing by the door, pretending to check emails on his phone. Not that Harry was paying any attention to the people around him; he was too engrossed in his own phone.

Harry got out at Waterloo and sat down on the end of a row of four metal seats. He was ten minutes early but his instructions were to stay put and wait. Mosley had taken a seat further down the platform and pulled a copy of the *Financial Times* from his briefcase. Two trains came and went and then a black teenager walked down the platform carrying a grey North Face backpack. The teenager was listening to music through bright red Beats headphones and he was bobbing his head backwards and forwards as he headed towards Harry.

The teenager sat down two seats along from Harry and put the backpack down between them before staring at the far wall, still nodding in time to the music. When the train arrived, the teenager stood up and walked towards the edge of the platform. Harry took hold of the backpack, stood up, and headed for the northbound Bakerloo Line platform.

Mosley didn't follow him. Another NCA officer was already there, waiting for Harry. This one was a woman in her twenties wearing a bobble hat and carrying a tennis bag. Her name was Caroline Connolly and she would follow Harry back to Paddington Station where Tomkinson would board the train with him back to Reading.

"Here he comes," said Shepherd. He had an app on his phone that enabled him to track Harry's progress through the GPS on the iPhone the boy was carrying.

Sharpe nodded. He had been receiving text messages from the surveillance team, updating him on Harry's progress. "Jenny will follow him to the end of the road," he said. "But he was clean all the way there and back."

A few minutes later the doorbell rang and Bacon went to let Harry in. He was wearing a grey hoodie and Adidas tracksuit bottoms and carrying the grey backpack.

"Any problems?" asked Sharpe as he took the backpack from Harry.

"Easy peasy," said Harry. He went over to the fridge and took out a can of Coke.

"Do you want something to eat, Harry?" asked Bacon, standing by the sink.

Harry shook his head. "I'm good."

Sharpe unzipped the backpack and emptied the contents out onto the kitchen table. There was a brick-shaped block of cannabis wrapped in polythene, four Ziploc bags containing white tablets with Batman logos stamped on them and one Ziploc bag with several dozen clear chunky crystals with a yellowish tinge.

"Crystal meth?" asked Shepherd, pointing at the crystals.

Sharpe nodded. He used his phone to take several photographs of the drugs haul, then he pulled on a pair of latex gloves and opened the bag of crystals. He used a pair of tweezers to transfer one of the crystals into a test tube which he then transferred to an evidence bag. He sealed the bag and scrawled his signature and the date on the label.

He took a single tablet from each of the other four bags. He put them in tubes and sealed them in bags, then used a scalpel to pry away some of the tape sealing the pack of cannabis.

"You do this every time?" asked Shepherd.

Sharpe nodded. "We keep a record of every run, taking samples and photographs. And we have CCTV footage from the stations. When we do go to court, it'll be open and shut."

He took a small sample of the cannabis resin, then resealed the package. He returned the drugs to the backpack and handed it to Harry. "Good to go," he said.

"Where do you take it to?" Shepherd asked Harry.

"To their house."

"Do you go inside?"

Harry shook his head. "I go around to the back door and knock. They take it off me."

"Do they ever talk to you?"

"Nah. They don't even say 'thank you'. I asked them for a tip once as a joke and they told me to fuck off." He finished his soft drink and put the can on the table.

"I'll show you out," said Shepherd. He took Harry along the corridor. "How are you feeling?" he asked as they reached the front door.

"What do you mean?"

"Are you worried about anything?"

Harry frowned. "Like what?"

"You're dealing with some not very nice people."

"They don't scare me, if that's what you mean."

"No, you don't need to be scared. Just be careful, Harry."

The teenager grinned. "They're stupid, they haven't a clue what's going on," he said. "When you guys arrest them they'll get the shock of their lives. They won't see it coming." His eyes sparkled and his grin widened. "I'd love to see them being arrested."

Shepherd put a hand on the boy's shoulder. "Harry, you mustn't think that way. All you're doing is giving us some help so that you can go back to being a regular kid and put this behind you."

"Yeah, I know, but they think I'm an idiot. I can tell by the way they talk to me. They don't respect me. I know they don't."

"They're drug dealers, their respect means nothing. You mustn't make it personal."

"Yeah but they're using me, aren't they? You saw what's in the bag. Ten grand of drugs, right? And you know what they pay me?" He unzipped a side pocket in the back and showed Shepherd the envelope there. "Five hundred quid."

Shepherd took the envelope from him and opened it. It was filled with fifty pound notes. "They let you keep this?"

"Sure," said Harry. He grabbed the envelope out of Shepherd's hands as if he feared he wouldn't give it back, then stuffed it into his trousers. "Why not?"

"No problem," said Shepherd. "But what about your parents, don't they wonder where your money is coming from?"

"They don't know," he said. "I keep it hidden."

"Where?"

Harry snorted. "There's no way I'm telling you where I keep my cash," he said.

"I'm just saying, you need to be careful. If they find you're hoarding money they're going to wonder where it came from."

"They won't find it, it's well hidden."

"What do you spend it on?"

"PlayStation games mainly," he said. "And cigarettes."

"Your parents let you smoke?"

He snorted again. "Course not. They don't know I smoke."

"I wouldn't be so sure about that," said Shepherd. "Parents usually have a good idea what their kids are getting up to. And I can smell the smoke on you. You had a cigarette on the way, right?"

"Bloody hell, you can't stop being a cop, can you?"

Shepherd couldn't help but smile. "It's my job, Harry."

"Yeah, but your job here is to arrest Dancer and his crew, innit? Not to give me grief for smoking."

"I'm not giving you grief, Harry. I just don't want you to have a problem with your parents. Just keep your head down and this will all be over before you know it."

Harry shrugged. "I'm okay," he said. "It's fun, what I'm doing."

The boy's overconfidence was a worry, but if Shepherd said too much he might spook him. It was a narrow line that Harry was walking. If he truly realised the danger of his situation he'd become nervous and those around him would spot it. But his cockiness was also dangerous. It was a trap many undercover operatives fell into. The more they got away with lying, the more they wanted recognition, to show how clever they were. Shepherd had sometimes felt that way during long-term operations. He'd spend weeks or months getting close to a target and once he'd won their confidence there'd be an urge to drop a hint of what was to come. Shepherd had never understood where the urge came from though a psychologist had once explained that it was because he was subconsciously feeling guilty about lying and somehow wanted to be punished for it. The way to fight the urge was to accept the fact that under certain circumstances lying was acceptable and that if the aim was to put bad guys behind bars then there was no need to feel guilty.

"Try not to think of it as fun, Harry," said Shepherd. "Just try to act exactly the way you did before you started helping the police. Don't do anything differently."

The teenager flashed Shepherd a sarcastic smile. "You think I'm stupid, too," he said.

"No, I don't. I think you're doing an awesome job. I've worked undercover and I know how difficult it is. I do respect you for what you're doing, I'm just trying to help you through it, that's all."

"So you're what, an undercover cop?"

"I used to be. Not so much these days."

"Did you carry a gun?"

"Sometimes. If I had to."

"Can I have a gun? That would be so sick."

Shepherd couldn't help but smile at the teenager's enthusiasm. He shook his head. "Never in a million years," he said. He opened the door and ushered Harry out, then watched as the boy walked away.

He closed the door and went back to the kitchen. Sharpe was making himself a sandwich.

"So you let him keep the money?" asked Shepherd.

"It was discussed at length," said Sharpe. "Our guv thought we should take the money off him and put it into evidence, but we thought best to let him keep it. That way everything continues as normal and young Harry doesn't get pissed off."

"Whether or not Harry is pissed off isn't the issue, is it?" said Shepherd.

"We just want to keep him as happy as possible, and if we took the money off him he might start resenting us," said Bacon.

"What happens when the case is over and done with? Surely he'll have to give the money back?" asked Shepherd.

"Our guv says no," said Sharpe.

"You just need to be careful is all I'm saying," said Shepherd.

"I think this is us being careful," said Sharpe. "If we took the cash off him it would be put in evidence which means if we go to full disclosure the defence might spot it and realise we had an inside man."

"Inside boy," said Shepherd. "He's a few years to go before he's a man. Razor, if this goes to disclosure the defence is going to know about Harry's role anyway. Even if he's not identified they'll still be able to work out who he is. We need to make sure that Morris and his posse all plead guilty."

"They will, Spider, don't worry."

Shepherd sat down. He picked up his mug of coffee and sipped it thoughtfully. "What about the money?" he asked. "Harry delivers the bag, but how does the money get to Morris?"

"Courier," said Sharpe.

"Are you serious?"

"Three or four times a week they do a courier delivery," said Sharpe. "A large jiffy bag that goes to a post office box company in London. We got a warrant to check the bags last week and surprise, surprise, they were full of cash. One of Morris's men does a weekly pickup. That's how all the county lines pass on their cash, so each pickup is tens of thousands of pounds. Whoever does the pickup then takes the money to a currency exchange on Edgware Road. Presumably they get it into the banking system, for a fee. There's a separate team following up the money angle."

"This is one hell of an operation, Razor." Shepherd raised his mug in salute. "Kudos."

"Yeah, I just wish we could move in now. The longer we leave it, the bigger the risk that something goes wrong. At the moment Morris has no idea what's going on, but if he were to find out . . ." He shrugged and left the sentence unfinished.

"Let's see what happens on Sunday," said Shepherd.

Shepherd had parked his black BMW X5 a short walk from the safe house, as it was his own car and not a pool vehicle. He drove back to his rented flat in Lambeth and parked in the building's underground car park. The flat was tiny, a small sitting room with a kitchen area, a bedroom and a shower room. The reason he had chosen it was because it came with a designated parking space and it was a short walk across Lambeth Bridge to Thames House.

He let himself into his flat and made himself a coffee. The flat was pretty much unchanged from the day he'd moved in, a year earlier. There was nothing of a personal nature, no photographs or mementos, other than a couple of books and a copy of *National Geographic* magazine. When Shepherd used a flat or house to go with a legend, one of MI5's dressers would go in and stamp the legend's personality onto the premises with framed photographs, sports equipment, letters and souvenirs and select a decor and furnishings that would fit. Anyone visiting the Lambeth flat would assume that the occupier had no interests, no social life and no personality, which is just how Shepherd wanted it.

He took his coffee over to the small grey sofa and sat down, swinging his feet up onto the square Ikea pine table. He took out his phone to call Katra. It had been two days since he had last spoken to his girlfriend and he was well aware that he was calling to give her bad news.

He tapped out her number. He never used his phone's address books, he made all calls from memory. "Dan, hi, where are you?" she gushed as soon as she answered.

"London," he said. "Hey, I'm sorry about this but I'm not going to be able to get back this weekend."

"Work?"

He laughed. "Of course it's work," he said. "You think I'd stay away by choice?"

"I'm starting to wonder," she said.

"It's just work, and I can't get out of it," he said. "I'm backed up the rest of this week and then there's a job on Sunday that I have to do. I could get back on Saturday but I'd have to leave so early on Sunday that I wouldn't be relaxed. The weekend after is still on, though, and that's when Liam is coming so we'll have a proper family weekend."

"Promise?" said Katra.

Shepherd winced. He hated making promises because events could easily throw any plans he made into disarray, but he could tell that Katra was upset and he wanted to make her feel better. "I'll be there," he said.

"Okay," she said.

"Is there something wrong?" he asked.

"Just family problems," she said. "Mum's getting short of money."

"I'll sort everything out when I'm back," he said. "Didn't you transfer some money last week?"

"Last month," said Katra. "She's having trouble making ends meet."

"We'll talk it through next week," said Shepherd. "I promise. And we need to talk about moving to London. This commuting is getting on my nerves."

"Mine too," she said.

"Now that Liam's in the Army, maybe now's the time to sell the Hereford house."

"I think that's a great idea," she said. "This house is too lonely now."

"We'll discuss it next weekend," he said.

"Thank you, Dan," she said.

She sounded a bit happier than when he'd started the call, but Shepherd wasn't sure how happy she'd be once they started discussing the finances of a move. Their house in Hereford was lovely with plenty of room and a decent garden and a garage. It had been perfect for when he had been with the SAS, and when Liam was still at school. There was no reason to keep it now that he was London-based, albeit with a fair amount of travel. The problem was the cost. The three-bedroom house in Hereford was probably worth less than half the price of the shoebox in Lambeth. He doubted that Katra realised how expensive London property was, and that if they did have to move, even on his MI5 salary they would struggle to find anywhere close to London that matched the house they had in Hereford.

The Range Rover stopped in front of the single-storey industrial unit and the front passenger side window wound down. Frenk Kriezis pointed the remote control at the red metal door and it rattled up. The car drove slowly inside. It was followed a few seconds later by a white windowless Mercedes van.

The industrial unit was on a small estate in Chingford, northeast London, close to Epping Forest. It was late at night and the other units on the estate were all locked up. Kriezis climbed out of the front passenger seat of the Range Rover. He pressed the remote again and the door rattled down.

The driver climbed out too. His name was Marko Dushku and he was one of Kriezis's oldest friends. He had lived in the next house to Kriezis in his village, the eldest son of a barber. He had been slow as a child and Kriezis had helped him with his homework. What Dushku lacked in intelligence he made up for in brute strength. He was a big child and grew to be an even bigger man, standing six feet six inches tall, broad shouldered and with hands like shovels. Despite his bulk, Dushku's weapon of choice was a cut-throat razor that had once belonged to his father. The razor looked tiny in his massive hand but he wielded it with lethal accuracy. He obeyed Kriezis without thinking; his loyalty was absolute.

The driver of the van opened the door and got out and stretched. His name was Jetmir Shkodra and he too was a big man, standing exactly six feet tall. He had also gone to the same village school but had been in the class below Kriezis and Dushku. His name meant "good life" but Shkodra's childhood had been anything but good. His father had abused him and his mother, getting drunk and beating them in turns with his belt. Shkodra's mother was the family earner, doing laundry in her kitchen and ironing late into the night. The beatings had continued until Shkodra was fifteen. The father hadn't realised that the son had grown into a man and midway through slapping his belt against his son's backside Jetmir had snapped, grabbing the belt and strangling him with it. His mother had hugged Shkodra and assured him that he wasn't at fault, and the two of them staged a suicide, hanging the body from the back of a door with the belt around the neck. The local police did the bare minimum and if they had any doubts about the cause of death they didn't raise them. Shkodra's father was pretty much hated by everyone in the village and while a hundred people attended his funeral, it was more to confirm that he was dead than to pay their respects. Shkodra had been with Kriezis from the start, when they built their own protection business based on a documentary they had watched about the Kray twins of London. There had been no subtitles but their English was good enough to understand the basic business premise: that if you were violent enough and scared people enough they would give you money for the violence to stop. Shkodra was a natural, and meting out beatings to shop owners and businessmen became a way of reliving what he had done to his bastard of a father.

Shkodra walked around to the rear of the van and pulled open the double doors. There were four black men lying on the floor of the van, bound and gagged with grey duct tape. Standing over them was another of Kriezis's men, Gëzim Prifti. Gëzim was the Albanian word for happiness, but Gëzim Prifti was a man who never smiled. He was a former soldier and had served with the Albanian Army in Afghanistan as part of the NATO-commanded International Security Assistance Force in Kabul. He had been badly injured when an IED exploded next to his unit's truck; his left leg was a mass of scar tissue and he walked with a pronounced limp. The Army had discarded him and Kriezis had met the man in a bar in Tirana, Albania's capital city, nursing a tumbler of brandy and glowering at anyone who went near him. Kriezis realised he had met a kindred spirit and a bottle of brandy later they were singing Abba songs in a karaoke bar. Kriezis had offered Prifti a job though he had been suitably vague about what his duties would be. Prifti wasn't stupid and knew that he wasn't being hired for his vocal skills. He became Kriezis's main enforcer, breaking legs and snapping arms as enthusiastically as he belted out "Dancing Queen", and he killed without hesitation when ordered to.

Prifti and Shkodra rolled the four bound men out of the van and onto the ground. They were all conscious, their eyes wide and fearful. Prifti jumped down, grabbed four coils of rope and handed two of them to Shkodra. There were steel girders running across the vaulted metal roof and one by one they threw the ropes over.

Kriezis lit a cigarette as Dushku went over to help. One by one they tied a length of rope around the legs of the bound men and hauled them so that they were hanging by their feet. They tied the ropes to metal benches that were bolted to the walls.

When they had finished, Kriezis stubbed out his cigarette and took a crowbar from the back of the Range Rover. "Which of you is the boss?" asked Kriezis, swinging the crowbar. "Who should I be talking to here?"

Dushku walked along the line of swinging men, ripping the duct tape from their mouths. They all coughed and spluttered as they swung back and forth.

Kriezis banged the crowbar on the concrete floor. "I asked a fucking question," he shouted.

"It's my crew," gasped the man to his left. His head was shaved and it glistened with sweat.

Kriezis walked over to him. "You're the boss? You don't look like a boss to me."

"What the fuck is this about?" asked the man.

"We need to talk about your long-term business plan," said Kriezis. He prodded the man in the stomach with the end of the crowbar. "You look fat. A fat boss sets a bad example to his men."

"Fuck you!" said the man and he spat at Kriezis's leg.

Spittle flecked across Kriezis's jeans and he scowled. "Why the fuck would you do that?" He looked over his shoulder at the two men standing by the van. "Did you

96

see what he did?" He shook his head. "What the fuck, hey?" He looked back down at the man. "What's your name?"

"They call me Vicious."

Kriezis laughed. "Vicious? Are you serious? They really call you that?" He walked along to the man hanging next to Vicious. "Is that his name? Really? That's what you call him?"

"That's his name," said the man. He had long dreadlocks that brushed the floor as he swung backwards and forwards.

"And what's your name?"

"Two-by."

Kriezis frowned. "Two-by? What sort of name is that?"

"It's short for two-by-four."

Kriezis's frown deepened. "What the fuck is two-by-four?"

"It's a piece of wood that measures two by four."

"So you get a nickname from a piece of wood?"

"I broke a guy's legs with a piece of two-by-four."

Kriezis laughed harshly. "I get it now." He looked over at Prifti and Shkodra. "Maybe after today you'll start calling me Crowbar." The two men laughed and Kriezis wagged the crowbar at them. "Don't even think about it," he said. "I hate nicknames. You should be proud of the name your parents gave you, not hide behind a made-up name."

He turned back to the swinging men. He walked slowly over to the third man and prodded him in the groin. "What about you? What do they call you?"

97

"Biggs."

"Because you're fat?"

"Yeah," said Biggs.

Kriezis nodded and prodded the last man in the group. "And you?" He was thin and tall, his head was almost touching the floor.

"Foota."

"Foota? Why?"

"They say I've got big feet."

Kriezis peered at the man's gleaming white Nikes. "You have, too," he said.

He stood back, slowly swinging the crowbar back and forth. "So, we've got Vicious, Two-by, Biggs and Foota. Eeny, meeny, miny, mo." He stepped forward and smacked the crowbar against the side of Vicious's head. The skull cracked and blood splattered across the concrete floor. Vicious went into spasm as blood trickled down his scalp and dripped onto the floor.

Kriezis swung the crowbar again, this time hitting the other side of the man's skull. Several teeth flew across the floor. Kriezis hit him again and again and continued to hit him even after the skull had been obliterated and the floor was splattered with blood and brain matter. When he eventually stopped he was sweating profusely and his face was flecked with Vicious's blood.

"Not so fucking Vicious now, are you?" he said. He laughed and tapped the bloody crowbar onto the floor. "So, who's the number two in this gang? Because it seems to me that number two is now number one."

He walked over to Two-by and prodded him in the chest with the crowbar. "Is it you? Were you his right-hand man?"

"Fuck no," said Two-by.

Kriezis drew back the crowbar. "You look like second-in-command material," he said.

"No!" screamed Two-by. "No fucking way! Foota's the number two. He and Vicious run things. I'm nothing, man. I'm just a gopher. I run fucking errands. I'm nothing, man."

Kriezis smiled. "Is that a fact?" he said. He walked slowly over to Foota. "Is that right, big feet? You're in charge now?"

"Just fucking do what you have to do," said Foota, closing his eyes tightly.

"You were his number two?"

"Yeah, I was his fucking number two. Now get this shit over with."

Kriezis drew back the crowbar, took aim at the side of Foota's head, then relaxed and placed the end of it on the floor. He gestured at Prifti and Shkodra. "Get him down."

The two heavies hurried over to Foota. One untied the rope and the other lowered him to the ground. He used a knife to cut Foota's ankles free. Foota sat on the floor looking up at Kriezis, breathing hard. "How long did you work for Vicious?" asked Kriezis.

"A year. Maybe two."

"Was he a good boss?"

Foota mumbled incoherently.

"Get on your feet," said Kriezis. "Talk to me like a man."

Foota pushed himself up off the floor. The circulation was returning to his legs but he still struggled to stand.

"You understand what just happened?" Kriezis asked.

"You're taking over," said Foota. "I get it."

"The question is, would you be happy working for me?"

Foota sniffed but didn't answer.

"Because you know what the choice is, don't you? I do to you what I did to Vicious and then I give the choice to Two-by. And I think we both know that Two-by's going to agree to anything. The way he gave you up, he'd say or do anything to save his own life." Kriezis smiled evilly. "What about you, Foota? What would you be prepared to do?"

Foota looked Kriezis in the eye, shrugged again, but didn't say anything.

Kriezis transferred the crowbar to his left hand and then reached inside his jacket. His right hand emerged holding a gun. He gave the crowbar to Foota and then stepped back. "If you want to work for me, you're going to have to prove your loyalty. What's your real name? Not your kid's nickname, the name your parents gave you?"

"Noah."

"All right, Noah. Good. I'm looking for someone to head up what used to be Vicious's organisation.

100

Someone who I can trust. Somebody who I know will never let me down. Are you that man, Noah?"

Foota nodded slowly. "Yes," he said. "I am."

"I thought so," said Kriezis. He nodded at Two-by. "You know what you need to do."

Prifti and Shkodra took out smartphones and began videoing him. Dushku stood by the Range Rover, watching impassively.

Foota continued to nod.

"Aw, man, no fucking way!" shouted Two-by. "You can't fucking do this."

Foota walked slowly towards Two-by, swinging the crowbar. The two men moved apart, still filming. Kriezis grinned but kept his gun trained on Foota.

"You're my mate, Foota! You can't fucking do this!" He began to sob. "Please, man. Please."

Foota lifted the crowbar, hesitated, and then swung it with all his might at Two-by's head. It cracked open and blood and brains splattered across the floor. The blow was so severe that the man was almost certainly dead within seconds but Foota hit him again and again and continued to rain blows down on the man's battered skull until Kriezis told him to stop. Foota either didn't hear him or didn't care and he continued to smash Two-by's head to a pulp. Eventually Dushku stepped forward, grabbed the crowbar and pulled it away from him.

Foota turned to look at Kriezis. There was a fire in his eyes, a bloodlust, and he was breathing heavily. He glared at Kriezis, clenching and unclenching his hands.

"So are we good, Noah?" asked Kriezis.

Foota took a long, slow breath, and then he nodded. "We're good." There were flecks of blood all down his trousers and on his shoes.

Kriezis slid his gun back into its holster. He stepped forward, his hand outstretched. Foota reached out and shook his hand. "Welcome to the firm," said Kriezis. He patted Foota on the back. "And your first job is to clean up this mess. I don't care if they find the bodies or not, just make sure there's no connection to this place."

"What about Biggs?"

Kriezis looked over at Biggs, who was staring up at them, wide-eyed. There was a damp patch on the front of his jeans where he'd wet himself. "That's up to you," he said. "It's a management decision and now you are management."

He walked over to the Range Rover and climbed into the front passenger seat. Dushku got behind the wheel as Kriezis pointed the remote at the door and pressed it. The door rattled up and the Range Rover drove out. A few minutes later the van followed.

"Coffee?" asked Sharpe, putting the mug down in front of Shepherd. "And a bacon sandwich." He put the sandwich down next to the coffee. "I always love it when Miss Bacon cooks bacon. It never gets old."

"Detective Constable Bacon to you, Jimmy," said Bacon. "I'm still on staff, remember. You're the hired help."

Sharpe threw her a mock salute before sitting down at the dining room table with his own coffee and sandwich. Shepherd had a MacBook in front of him that he was using to monitor the output from Harry's phone.

It was Sunday morning and they were getting ready for Gary Dexter to arrive at his brother's house for lunch. Sharpe had stationed an NCA surveillance guy in a car down the road from the house. They didn't need video, they just needed confirmation that Gary Dexter had arrived.

"Ketchup or HP?" asked Shepherd.

"Always ketchup on a bacon buttie," said Sharpe.

"Good call," said Shepherd. He bit into the sandwich.

There was an Airwave encrypted handset on the table, the Met's favoured method of communication. As Sharpe picked up his coffee, the handset buzzed three times. That was the signal that Gary Dexter was arriving. "Here we go," said Sharpe.

Shepherd turned up the volume of the laptop. There was the sound of shooting and the occasional grunt and explosion. Harry was playing a shoot-em-up game on his PlayStation.

"Harry!" shouted a woman. "Get the front door will you!" That would be Harry's mother, Debbie.

"I'm busy!" shouted Harry.

"Chris!" shouted Debbie. "Get the door."

"I'm busy too!" shouted Harry's younger brother. He was close to the phone, presumably either watching the game or playing alongside him.

"Ask Briana, she's not doing anything!" shouted Harry.

"I'm busy!" shouted a girl.

"She's playing with her phone, that's all," shouted Chris.

"It's about school," said Briana. "Mum, Chris is only playing his stupid video game, tell him to do it."

"If one of you doesn't answer the bloody door there'll be hell to play," shouted a man, his voice fainter as if he was in another room.

Sharpe grinned. "That'll be Dad. If the kids carry on the way they are I'll go around and give them a clip around the ear myself."

"Your kids never played up?"

Sharpe shrugged. "To be honest I was never home much when they were growing up. I was working in Hargrove's undercover unit and he had us all over the UK. I was away for weeks at a time. You joined well after me, but you remember what it was like?"

Shepherd nodded. He had joined the undercover unit shortly after leaving the SAS and had hit the ground running. He had barely seen his wife Sue or their young son Liam. The operations he was on were all over the country and usually involved the long-term penetration of criminal gangs. He was undercover in a high-security prison when his wife was killed in a senseless car accident, and even when he was a single parent he still had to spend more time away from his son than he was comfortable with. "Yeah. Wish I'd been with Liam more when he was growing up. But I had only the one kid."

"They're all the same at that age," said Sharpe. "It's all about them."

104

"Fine, I'll get it," said Briana.

A few seconds later, Briana shouted to her parents. "It's Uncle Gary!"

"Tell him your dad's in the garden," said Debbie.

"Dad's in the garden," repeated Briana in a sing-song voice.

"Hi Harry, hi Chris," said a male voice that could only have been Gary Dexter.

"Hi Uncle Gary!" chorused the two boys.

Then there was just the sound of the video game and the occasional insult from one or other of the brothers.

Shepherd waited. He needed everyone in the house before he could give Amar Singh the go-ahead to place the bug on Dexter's Mercedes. Singh was in his mid-thirties and was one of MI5's top technical guys. He was usually immaculately dressed, favouring Armani suits and Bally shoes, but today he was in overalls and sitting in a British Gas van not far from where the NCA surveillance team were sitting.

Sharpe and Shepherd ate their sandwiches and drank their coffee and waited. Their time came about ten minutes after Gary Dexter had arrived. They heard his voice again, and this time he was talking to his brother, arguing about football by the sound of it.

Shepherd called Singh on his mobile. "Whenever you're ready, Amar," he said.

"I'm on it," said Amar. "I'll call you when it's done."

Amar Singh climbed out of the British Gas van and closed the door. He was wearing blue overalls with the British Gas logo on them, and a fleece that also sported the logo. He opened the rear door of the van and took out a blue tool kit and a gas detector. The GPS tracking device he was planning to use was in his pocket. It was about the size of a pack of cigarettes, black metal and magnetic. In a perfect world he would have enough time to wire the device into the vehicle's electrical system but Singh had been with MI5 long enough to have learned the world was rarely perfect.

The target was a five-year-old Mercedes parked in the driveway of a house. From what Dan Shepherd had told him, there were six people inside and they were all in the dining room, which was at the rear, so hopefully there wouldn't be anyone looking out of the window. Singh would have only seconds in which to place the device, and he'd have to make it appear that he had a legitimate reason for being in the driveway.

He walked slowly along the pavement, swinging the tool kit. As he reached the driveway to the Dexter house he had a quick look around to check that there were no pedestrians nearby, then checked the windows overlooking the road. He was good to go. As he turned into the driveway he put his hand into his pocket and took out the tracker. There was no on-off switch — it became active automatically once it was placed next to metal. He reached the offside rear of the Mercedes, and as he got to the rear wheel he bent down and slipped the tracker under the arch. He placed it at the high point and heard the dull thunk as the magnet kicked in.

He headed for the front door.

"Alpha Sierra is at the front door," he said into his radio.

"Roger that Alpha Sierra," said Shepherd in his earpiece. "All good. No reaction from inside the house. You can leave."

"Alpha Sierra is leaving," said Singh.

If there had been any indication from inside the house that he'd been spotted he would have rung the bell and given them his prepared story about a possible gas leak in the area. As it was, having received the all clear from Shepherd, all he had to do was walk back to his van.

Shepherd put down his phone. "The tracker's in place," he said. "The battery's good for two weeks, maybe a bit longer."

"Nice," said Sharpe.

The sounds coming through Harry's phone were those of a family tucking into a Sunday lunch. The click-click of cutlery on plates and of drinks being poured. Micky and Gary telling Debbie what a great cook she was, the kids teasing each other. Micky telling his daughter to stop texting.

Shepherd was starting to think that the bugged phone idea was a waste of time, but that changed about ten minutes into the meal.

"Do you fancy coming with me to Serbia next week?" asked Gary.

"Serbia? Why?"

"Boys' weekend," said Gary. "They organise shooting weekends and there's a bunch of us going."

"What, like pheasants, you mean?"

Gary laughed. "No, bruv. It's not shotguns. Big boys' toys. Uzis, Kalashnikovs, hand grenades, RPGs, the works. They've got sniping rifles too."

"Are you serious?" asked his brother.

"Yeah, the gun laws over there are super lax," said Gary. "They've got former Army instructors and it's all safety first, but you can fire pretty much anything you want."

"Why the hell would you want to start shooting heavy artillery?" asked Micky.

"For fun," said his brother.

Sharpe looked over at Shepherd and raised an eyebrow. "Fun?" he said.

"Mate, I spent almost ten years firing guns as a job, the last thing I want to do is shoot for fun," said Micky.

"It'll be a blast," said Gary. "There's six of us going. We can easily fit you in."

"He's not going anywhere to fire guns," said Debbie.

"Debs, it's no big deal. Serbia is a couple of hours away. We fly out Friday afternoon and we'll get back on Sunday."

"We're going to my mum's next Saturday," said Debbie. "It's her birthday."

"Well, I can see who's wearing the trousers," said Gary.

"I'd be very careful saying things like that while Debs is holding a knife," laughed Micky.

"Knife? I'll shove my spoon where the sun don't shine if he says that again."

Sharpe looked over at Shepherd and grinned. "Feisty," he said.

"I'm joking, Debs," laughed Gary. "I was just thinking it might be useful if your man came along to keep us on the straight and narrow."

"The guys you're going with, who are they?" asked Micky.

"Just a few mates," said Gary. "You don't know them."

"You've got to be careful around guns, Gary," said Micky. "They're not toys. And did you say grenades?"

"Yeah, apparently you can throw them at chickens if you want."

"That's gross," said Briana.

"Says the girl who's shoving roast lamb into her mouth," said Harry. "Can I come, Uncle Gary?"

"I think you've got to be eighteen," said Gary.

"I'm almost eighteen."

"You've only just turned sixteen," said Debbie. "And you are not going anywhere near guns. Gary . . ."

"Debs, I was suggesting that Micky goes, that's all. Relive his glory days."

"I don't think of them as glory days," said Micky. "And guns aren't playthings."

"We're not shooting people, Micky. Just targets."

"Up to you, mate. If you want to waste your money firing a few guns, you go for it."

"Did you ever fire an RPG?" asked Gary.

"What's an RPG?" asked Debbie.

"Rocket-propelled grenade," said Harry.

"How do you know that?" asked Debbie.

"Call of Duty," said Harry.

"A video game isn't real life, Harry," said Micky. "Though I know you sometimes get the two confused. But to answer Gary's question, no, I never got to fire one. But I've had a few fired in my direction and they're not toys."

"So it's like a rocket?" asked Debbie.

"It's a grenade that's fired like a rocket," said Micky. "You'll have seen them on the news, usually ragheads shooting at our troops."

"Gary, why would you want to do something like that?" asked Debbie.

Gary laughed. "Debs, we're not shooting troops. Targets. We just want to see what it's like. It'll be a laugh."

"Well Micky's not going, end of."

"Message received," said Gary. "Did I tell you how delicious this lamb is, Debs?"

"No, you didn't."

"Well it is. Bloody lovely."

"No swearing at the table, Uncle Gary," said Briana.

"Bloody isn't swearing," said Harry.

"It bloody well is," said Briana and she giggled.

Sharpe sat back in his chair and stretched out his legs. "What do you think?" he asked, looking over at Shepherd.

"About the trip to Serbia?" said Shepherd. "I think I need to go. Sounds to me like they're setting something up, right? Throwing grenades and firing RPGs."

"Big boys' toys," said Sharpe.

"Except like Harry's dad said, RPGs are definitely not toys. If Dexter is planning to use them in the

110

UK . . ." He grimaced. "It could get very nasty." He shrugged. "Harry was wrong about RPG standing for rocket-propelled grenade, by the way."

Sharpe frowned. "Say what?"

"It actually stands for *Ruchnoy Protivotankoviy Granatomyot* which is Russian for hand-held anti-tank grenade launcher."

Sharpe grinned. "Well, you learn something every day," he said. "Though to be fair, it actually does stand for rocket-propelled grenade."

"Yeah, but that's a backronym."

"A what now?"

"A backronym. The initials came first, from the Russian, but then someone came up with the English words to fit it." He grinned. "I'm not making this up."

"I believe you," said Sharpe.

They sat and sipped their coffee as they listened to the family chatting. There was banter and gentle teasing as the Dexters caught up on each other's lives; they were clearly a close-knit family. There was no more mention of RPGs and the trip to Serbia.

Later in the afternoon, Gary took Harry out into the back garden to kick a football around. Harry left his phone in the sitting room. Sharpe was reading a newspaper and Shepherd was checking for the Serbian shooting trip on his phone. A few minutes on Google took him to a website for a company called Gunfire Tours, based in a town called Sid, to the west of the Serbian capital.

There were photographs of a training ground that looked as if it was in a disused quarry with three heavy-set men in camouflage fatigues holding an assortment of weapons including a Kalashnikov and an Uzi. The company ran shooting courses every weekend throughout the year and offered to set up team-building courses and special events for stag parties. The company also organised bodyguarding courses for people wanting a career in personal protection. There was a long list of personal recommendations from people who had been on the courses, and screenshots of Tweets mentioning the company.

Shepherd checked the booking details and there were four places available for the forthcoming weekend's trip. The only credit cards he had were in his own name so there was no way he could book just then, and besides he'd need to clear it with Pritchard first.

As he flicked through the photographs, he heard Debbie talking to her husband and he looked up from the screen. "You don't think Gary is going to do something stupid, do you?" Debbie said.

Shepherd looked over at Sharpe who was leaning towards the laptop.

"He's my little brother, he's always doing something stupid," said Micky.

"You know what I mean," said Debbie. "What's he up to? You heard him. Grenades. RGPs."

"RPGs," said Micky.

"Whatever they're called they sound bloody dangerous," said Debbie. "Do you think he's up to something?"

"Like what?"

They heard his wife sigh in exasperation. "Don't play silly buggers, Micky. You heard about those grenades that got thrown at that mosque in Acton."

"That wasn't Gary, and you know it. They caught the guy. One of the guys. And they didn't use grenades, they threw home-made pipe bombs."

"What's a pipe bomb?"

There was a silence and Shepherd could picture her husband trying to come up with a way of describing a pipe bomb without using the word "grenade".

"It's a piece of pipe with home-made explosives in it."

"So like a grenade, then?"

"Don't go putting words in my mouth, Debs. You asked and I was trying to explain."

"Then explain to me why your brother wants to learn how to fire an RPG and throw grenades."

"Like he said, it's fun. You heard what I said, I wouldn't find it in the least bit fun but he and his pals are civilians. They'll get a kick out of it. Same as Harry loves his video games."

"Except it's not a game, Micky. You know what Gary's like. Him and that Crusaders group. They hate Muslims, you know they do. What if they read about that attack on the mosque in Acton and decided that they want to do something similar?"

"I think you're letting your imagination run away with you."

"No, I know what he's like. He doesn't mouth off like he used to because he knows I won't put up with it, but we both know what he's like."

"Debs, he's an adult. He makes his own choices."

"If anyone should hate the Muslims it's you, right? You were out there. You were the one they were trying to kill."

"Just the ISIS nutters," laughed Micky. "Most of the Iraqis, the real Iraqis, are as nice as pie. I met loads of decent Muslims, regular guys just trying to earn a living and raise their families, and they were in as much danger as I was. Gary doesn't understand that. He believes what he reads in the *Daily Mail* and on Twitter and on those stupid Facebook pages he posts on."

"You should talk to him."

"I have done. You know I have. But Gary's Gary. He blames everything on the Muslims. But I don't think for one moment he's going to do anything stupid. His bark has always been worse than his bite."

His wife said something but her voice was faint as if she had moved away from Harry's phone. Micky replied but his voice was inaudible and then there was just the sound of the television in the background.

"She is feisty, isn't she?" said Sharpe. "Not afraid to give her old man what for."

"Interesting that the brother doesn't think Gary would be violent," said Shepherd.

"Yeah, but if he knows how the sister-in-law feels, he's not going to start mouthing off, is he?" Sharpe sipped his coffee. "He's got a point, about bad apples spoiling it for everyone."

"What do you mean?"

"You only ever hear the bad stuff about Muslims. But we had a dozen Algerian cops over last month for a surveillance training course. Lovely guys, hard as nails but they were knocking back the red wine like there was no tomorrow. They were Muslims but it was no big thing. I'm pretty sure one of them was gay, but nobody cared."

"No one's saying that all Muslims are bad, Jimmy."

"But the likes of Gary Dexter are," said Sharpe. "That's the problem. We need to be taking out the bad apples not shooting up the whole barrel. That's what's so annoying about the likes of him. You and your mob need to be targeting the ISIS-trained jihadists that are here planning their next atrocity, not wasting your time on Walter Mitty types."

"People were seriously injured in the Acton attack, Razor."

"I know that. But the mosque attacks are a reaction to what the jihadists and fundamentalists have been doing in the UK. If we showed zero tolerance to crap like poppy burning and abuse of our servicemen and the Muslim community brought its bad apples into line, then there'd be nothing for nutters like Gary Dexter to react against."

"You should run for office, Razor. Mayor of London, maybe. Or be an MP."

Sharpe laughed and raised his coffee mug. "My running days are over," he said. "And I've never been one for trying to change the world. I see what the rules are and I follow them. And I put away those people who break the rules. That's my life in a nutshell."

"And to be fair, you have put a lot of people away over the years."

"You never said a truer word," grinned Sharpe.

Gary left the house at just after seven o'clock. Shepherd had an app on his phone that allowed him to track the man's vehicle and he showed it to Sharpe as the Mercedes drove down the road.

Harry's phone continued to broadcast but there was nothing of interest, mainly his mother nagging him to clean his room and his sister telling him to get his feet off the coffee table. At eight o'clock Shepherd decided to call it a day and drove back to London.

"This is good shit," said Swifty Taylor, staring at the large joint in his hand. "I mean, it's really maad shit."

"Too good to share, obviously," said Jason "Dancer" Morris, holding out his hand.

Taylor grinned. "Sorry, Daadie," he said, handing the joint over. "Do yu ting."

Morris took a long pull on the joint and then leaned back on the sofa and tried to blow a smoke ring.

Beamer Lewis laughed. "That is one sorry smoke ring," he said. He was leaning over the coffee table using a gold American Express card to divide a small pile of cocaine into lines.

Mario James was drinking rum from a bottle, and he held out his hand for the joint. Morris passed it over.

They all jumped as the door buzzer burst into life. Morris looked at the diamond-studded gold Rolex on his wrist. It was after midnight and they weren't expecting visitors. "Who the fuck is that?" asked Morris.

116

James gave the joint back to Morris and he went over to the monitor by the door, swinging his bottle as he walked. He looked at the screen. There was a big man standing outside the door on the pavement. He had his head down so James could only see the top of his head. The buzzer went off again and on the screen the man had his hand out. "Can't see his face," said James.

"Tell him to fuck off," said Morris.

James picked up the handset. "Fuck off," he said into it.

The figure on the monitor pressed the intercom and it buzzed again.

"If he does that again, go down and shoot the fucker," said Morris.

James replaced the handset.

Lewis rolled up a fifty-pound note and sniffed a line of cocaine up his left nostril, sat back, then did a second line up his other nostril. "This is quality," he said. He handed the rolled-up note to Taylor.

"I'm okay with the pot," said Taylor. He held out his hand to Morris who gave him the joint.

"Suit yourself," said Lewis. He bent down and did another line. When he sat back up he blinked his eyes and focused on the two men who had appeared from the kitchen, one of them holding a pistol. They were big white guys, definitely not cops. "What the fuck?" he said.

Morris looked over at the kitchen door and his jaw dropped. It took his mind a couple of seconds to process what he was seeing. There was a fire escape leading from the kitchen down to the yard that the

117

kebab shop used to store its rubbish bins. The men must have come up the fire escape and somehow unlocked the door from the outside.

The man holding the pistol was limping as he walked out of the kitchen. He looked at Morris. "You Dancer?"

"Who you, man?"

"I'm the man with the gun, that's who I am."

"You gonna shoot me for what?" asked Morris. "Who the fuck are you?"

"You're coming with us," said the bigger of the two men. He was well over six feet tall with massive hands that he kept clenching as he glared at Morris.

"Like fuck we are," said Morris.

"My boss wants to talk to you."

"Well, tell your boss to use the phone," said Morris. "What the fuck does he want, anyway?"

"He'll explain," said the man. He gestured with his gun. "We've got a car downstairs."

Morris slipped his hand under the cushion next to him. He gripped the butt of the Ingram MAC-10 that he kept there as he continued to stare stonily at the man with the limp. "We ain't gonna do road with you," said Morris. He grinned savagely as he pulled out the MAC-10 but the dope he'd smoked had slowed him down and by the time he'd raised the weapon the man with the limp had shot him twice in the chest. The dope dulled most of the pain and Morris actually smiled before the life faded from his eyes.

James threw his bottle at the guy with the gun but his aim was off and it hit him on the shoulder. James stepped towards a cabinet to the side of the door and pulled open a drawer. "Don't!" shouted the man but James wasn't listening. He whirled around, holding the gun gangster-style and managed to fire one wild shot before two rounds hit him in the chest. "We don't have to do this!" shouted the man with the gun. James slumped to the floor.

The big man cursed out loud. He reached his right hand into his jacket and pulled out a gun.

Lewis groped under the coffee table. There was an Ingram MAC-10 taped to the underside but he had trouble reaching it.

"Put your hands where I can see them!" shouted the big man.

Lewis didn't react. He kept trying to pull the gun free but before he could, the big man fired once and Lewis's face imploded, his body slumping onto the coffee table.

Taylor had pulled a handgun from his belt but before he could aim it the big man shot him in the chest. Taylor continued to bring the gun around so the big man shot him twice in the face and to make absolutely sure the man with the limp put another bullet in his chest as he fell to the ground.

"*Bir kurve*," said the big man as he surveyed the carnage. "Frenk is not going to be happy about this."

Shepherd's mobile phone woke him from a dreamless sleep and he rolled over and picked it up. It was three o'clock in the morning and it was Jimmy Sharpe calling. Shepherd's mind raced into gear. It could only be bad news. "What's up, Razor?"

119

"The shit's hit the fan, Spider. The Morris gang has been hit and hit hard. I'll text you the address."

By the time Shepherd had dressed, the text message from Sharpe had arrived. He took the lift down to the underground car park and got into his black BMW SUV. There was little in the way of traffic and less than fifteen minutes later he was pulling up in front of a kebab shop with more than a dozen police and emergency vehicles parked outside. He saw Sharpe's red Jaguar parked down the road and he left his car next to it and walked back to the scene. A young uniformed constable in a high-vis jacket moved towards him but he was intercepted by Sharpe. "He's with me," said Sharpe.

The constable nodded and went back to his post.

"They're all dead," said Sharpe. "Morris, Taylor, Lewis and James."

"What the hell happened, Razor?"

"Come and have a look for yourself." The door leading up to the flat was being guarded by another uniform, this one a woman with bright red lipstick. She flashed them a smile and stepped out of their way. Sharpe took Shepherd up a flight of stairs. "We're still waiting for SOCO," he said, "there've been four stabbings tonight so everyone's busy. The SIO in charge of the Morris investigation is here, Inspector Victoria Cave."

They reached the top of the stairs. The door was open and inside was a woman in a dark suit, standing in the middle of the room looking at a dead body on the sofa.

120

"You'll need these," said Sharpe, handing Shepherd a pair of shoe protectors and blue latex gloves. As Shepherd finished putting them on, the woman in the dark suit came out. She was in her late thirties, brown eyed with straight dark brown hair. Sharpe made the introduction. "Victoria, this is Dan, he's been riding shotgun with Harry Dexter."

The inspector offered her hand to Shepherd and they shook. "How's that been working out?" asked Cave. She had a trace of a Devon accent.

"He's doing well, considering he's just a kid. How does what's happened affect him?"

"It's all up in the air," said Cave. "There's going to be a briefing at Peel House at midday and we'll know more then. You should be there."

Shepherd nodded. "I will be. What's going to happen here?"

"We'll wait to see what SOCO turns up, and we're canvassing the area for witnesses and CCTV." She looked at her watch and sighed. "They were supposed to be here five minutes ago."

"Busy night, apparently," said Shepherd. He looked around. "So a drug deal went wrong, maybe?"

"There's more to it than that, I think. There were drugs here but they kept most of their stash in a lock-up and that hasn't been interfered with."

"You checked already?"

"We've got it monitored with CCTV. We get a red flag as soon as anyone goes near it and it hasn't been disturbed tonight. Morris only kept relatively small amounts here, not enough for him to be worth killing for."

"Addicts tend not to think too clearly at the best of times," said Sharpe.

"Addicts tend not to carry guns," said Shepherd. "And there must have been at least two of them. Probably more. And the shooting doesn't have an amateur feel to it. Was Morris having problems with another gang moving in on their turf?"

"Not that we know about," said Cave. "That's the whole point of the county lines, they move out into areas where there's little or no competition."

Shepherd looked around at the room and tried to picture what had happened to produce the carnage. Morris dead on the sofa, a MAC-10 on the sofa next to him. James slumped by the door. Lewis sprawled over the coffee table, and another MAC-10 below it. Taylor on the floor, an unfired Glock still in his hand. James was the only one of the four who had managed to get a shot off by the look of it.

"Who broke the door in?" asked Shepherd.

"The uniforms. They got a call about gunshots and decided there wasn't time to call in a locksmith. They didn't know everyone was dead by the time they got there."

"And it was locked?" He smiled. "Sorry, stupid question. If it hadn't been locked there'd have been no need to kick it down."

"No, actually it's the right question to ask. It was locked and bolted from the inside."

"So how did the killers leave?"

"There's a fire exit in the kitchen. It leads down to a yard behind the kebab house and there's an alleyway there to the road."

Cave took Shepherd over to the kitchen. It was long and narrow with a wooden door reinforced with metal plates at the far end. "Was that door bolted?" asked Shepherd.

"Just locked," said Cave. "It's a good quality lock, but as you know all locks are pickable."

Shepherd nodded. So the killers came up the fire escape into the flat, catching the occupants by surprise. Two of them, maybe three. But all four of the Yardies had guns to hand, even though only James had pulled the trigger. If it had been a straightforward hit, the killers would have stepped out of the kitchen without giving the men inside the chance to draw their guns. "I don't know if my opinion counts for anything, but I think they came to talk," Shepherd said to Cave. "They rang the buzzer as a distraction, then the others came in through the kitchen. They wanted to talk to Morris, or at the very least get information from them. But the Yardies were high on drugs and booze and probably weren't thinking straight. They pulled out their guns but they weren't quick enough." He shrugged. "I could be wrong."

"No, that's how I read it," said Cave. "Look, this is part of a bigger picture that you should be aware of. You'll know more once you've heard what the Sheriff has to say."

Shepherd waited until they were out on the street before asking who the Sheriff was. Sharpe laughed.

"Superintendent Ken Sherwood, he runs the Major Incident Room at Peel House."

"I still don't get it?"

"Sherwood Forest. Sheriff of Nottingham."

"Yeah, but it wasn't the Sheriff of Sherwood Forest, was it? Going from Ken Sherwood to the Sheriff of Nottingham makes no sense."

Sharpe slapped him on the back. "You know what your problem is, Spider?"

"No, but I'm sure you're going to tell me."

"You overthink everything," he said. "You always have done."

"We all have our crosses to bear," said Shepherd.

Shepherd drove back to his apartment and grabbed a couple of hours sleep before showering, shaving and putting on a half-decent suit and driving to Peel House in Hendon, north London. Jimmy Sharpe was waiting for him on the ground floor. The Scotsman was also suited and booted. Peel House was part of the Hendon Police College complex. The lower floors were used to train new and serving officers but on the top floor — the fifth — was the Met's Major Incident Room where serious crimes were investigated.

Shepherd didn't have any Met ID so Sharpe had to sign him in. Paperwork completed and with a plastic badge clipped to Shepherd's jacket pocket, they rode up to the fifth floor.

There were close to a hundred men and women in the MIR, most of them detectives but there were also several dozen civilian workers, mainly typists and researchers. At any one time the MIR housed five or six major investigation teams, each one headed by a senior investigating officer. It was where the Met handled all its north London murder investigations.

"It's not usually as busy as this but the guv's brought in people from teams across London," said Sharpe. "He wants to see you as soon as you get in. I'm under orders." Sharpe took Shepherd down a corridor to a glass-sided office where a big man with the build of a rugby player run to fat was sitting behind a terminal. He was wearing a light blue suit and a red tie with black dots on it. He was in his forties but his hair was already steel grey and he was looking at his screen through wire-framed spectacles. He got to his feet as Sharpe knocked on the glass door and opened it.

"Guv, this is Dan Shepherd, from Five. Dan, this is Superintendent Sherwood."

The two men shook hands. Sherwood had a firm grip and an intense stare. "I have to say up front that I'm not happy about the Security Service getting involved in one of our criminal cases," said Sherwood coldly. "I've had investigations turn to shit before because MI5 has gotten busy."

"I'm sorry to hear that," said Shepherd. "I'll try not to make any waves."

"The problem is that your people aren't bound by the likes of the Police and Criminal Evidence Act. No one's disputing the great work you do combating terrorism, but my personal feeling is that criminal investigations are best left to the police."

125

"I understand," said Shepherd. He really didn't want to get into an argument with the superintendent but he had been involved in many cases where police investigations had cut across investigations he was involved with and more often than not it was the cops that caused problems.

"I'm okay for you to sit in on the briefing, but I'd be grateful if you didn't draw any attention to yourself. If you have any queries can you ask them afterwards, either with me personally or through Jimmy here."

"Absolutely," said Shepherd. "I'll be as quiet as a mouse."

The superintendent nodded but didn't say anything. Sharpe tilted his chin and gestured at the door. The two men left as the superintendent got back behind his desk.

"As a mouse?" laughed Sharpe as they walked back to the MIR. "Where did that come from?"

"He doesn't like spooks, does he?"

"He's had a few bad experiences," said Sharpe. "We all have. You know what your mob are like. They're totally unaccountable but everything we do is put under the microscope and God help us if we put a foot wrong."

"We're not totally unaccountable," said Shepherd. "We have rules to follow, same as you."

"They're not the same and you know it." He patted Shepherd on the back. "But I'm not defending the super. He should have been nicer to you."

"I'm a big boy, Razor. I'll get over it."

"Let's grab a coffee, we've got a few minutes before the briefing starts." They took the lift down to the canteen, bought coffee and bacon sandwiches, and took them back to the MIR. When the lift opened, Inspector Cave had just stepped out of another lift, dressed exactly as she had been at the flat above the kebab shop, minus the shoe covers and gloves. She looked at the sandwiches in Sharpe's hand and raised an eyebrow. "Don't suppose one of those is going spare?" she asked.

"Knock yourself out," said Sharpe, holding out the plate.

Cave thanked him and took one of the sandwiches. "The kitchen door lock was definitely picked," said the inspector. "Gunshot wounds seem to have been caused by two weapons but we won't know that for sure until they dig the bullets out. And all their phones had gone. Presumably the killers took them."

"No witnesses saw them leave?" asked Shepherd.

"That part of the city, we tend not to get witnesses to anything," said Cave. "How about we grab a drink after this is over?"

"Sounds like a plan," said Shepherd. He and Sharpe found a spare desk and sat down.

They were halfway through their sandwiches when Superintendent Sherwood walked in and went to stand at the top of the office. He looked around the room, nodding at a few familiar faces, then raised a hand. Everyone immediately fell silent. "Right, thank you for coming at such short notice, ladies and gentlemen, but something has happened regarding the investigations you are involved in and we need to move quickly. Over the last six days there have been a number of attacks against established drugs gangs across London. This culminated last night in the deaths of several members of the Jason Morris gang. Other gangs that have been targeted include Christy "Vicious" Miller and his Southall posse, an Asian drugs gang in Tower Hamlets and a Somalian gang in Ealing."

The superintendent gestured at a screen on the wall and a head and shoulders shot of a man with a sullen stare flashed up. There was an old scar in the middle of his left cheek that looked as if it had been the result of being stabbed with a broken bottle.

"We have intel that suggests that one man is behind all four of these attacks," Sherwood continued, "and probably more that we don't know about. Allow me to introduce you to Frenk Kriezis. Sounds like crisis but you spell it K-R-I-E-Z-I-S. Kriezis is an Albanian but he has managed to acquire a Belgian passport. There isn't much known about him, though that is about to change, obviously."

The picture of Kriezis was replaced by a line of half a dozen head and shoulder shots of grim-faced men. "You might recall these guys, an Albanian gang that received a total of one hundred and twenty-seven years in jail on drugs and human trafficking charges after a year-long investigation by the Central Task Force. These guys were one of the first to set up county lines, running their drugs out of the capital and across the south-east of England. One of the ringleaders of the gang was Frenk Kriezis's elder brother. We're not sure

128

where he has been because he's not in our system and Europol haven't been able to come up with anything on him. The arrest of the gang closed down its county lines, but it looks as if Kriezis is fast-tracking his way back into the industry. The intel we have received from the Drugs Squad is that Kriezis killed Christy Miller and Miller's gang is now working for Kriezis. He brought about a similar change of heart with the Somalian Hot Boyz gang in Ealing. The Hot Boyz have been running drugs from Ealing into towns and villages as far north as Milton Keynes and across to Oxford. Three of the Hot Boyz gang leaders were killed last week. Burnt to death. Covered in petrol and set on fire."

Someone off to Shepherd's left laughed, obviously appreciating the irony of the Hot Boyz being burned alive, but the laughter was cut short by a withering look from Sherwood before he continued. "The word on the street is that the new leaders of the gang report to Kriezis. A similar scenario was played out in Tower Hamlets with the Mahmud Brothers. Mohammed and Faisal Mahmud were found last week, castrated and gutted and covered with streaky bacon. The full details of what was done to them haven't been made public, but obviously the gang knows and they have all switched allegiance to Kriezis. So from a standing start, Frenk Kriezis has burst onto the London drugs scene and now controls at least four gangs and several dozen county lines. We don't know what he is doing in terms of bringing drugs into the country but there have been no signs of a price increase or supply shortage so it looks as if it's business as usual."

The screen went blank, then Frenk Kriezis's picture was back up.

"Those of you working on the cases involving Christy Miller, the Hot Boyz, the Mahmud Brothers and Jason Morris's posse will have already realised the position this puts us in. All four gangs are under active investigation and we were almost ready to move in on two of them — Jason Morris and the Hot Boyz. The other two were well under way and we were confident of putting a lot of people away for a very long time, as well as shutting down dozens of active county lines, and the investigations would hopefully have led to the arrests of the people bringing the drugs into the country." He grimaced. "The problem we have is that several of our prime targets are now dead. And without those prime targets, even if our prosecutions of the survivors were to be successful, we'd only be getting the small fish. And the plan was always to get at least some of those we arrested to give evidence against the overseas suppliers, not the least being the McAllen brothers, who have been a thorn in our side for years. All of that is now up in the air, obviously."

There were several loud groans from around the room. Sharpe looked over at Shepherd and raised his eyebrows. Shepherd knew what he was thinking. This was a major setback, throwing into doubt investigations that had taken up thousands of hours of work. They would all effectively have to start again from scratch.

130

"I know this is the last thing we wanted to hear, but we have to deal with the world the way it is, not the way we want it to be," said the superintendent. "We will continue the investigations that we already have, but I will be setting up a new team investigating the current crop of murders, with Frenk Kriezis as the prime suspect. That team will be headed by Detective Chief Inspector Ron McKee."

A middle-aged detective with his shirt sleeves rolled up raised his hand to identify himself

"Obviously Ron will have access to all the HOLMES databases but he needs to be notified of any major breaks immediately," said the superintendent. "I need him to be aware of where we stand in real time and not playing catch up." HOLMES was the computer system used in all major crime investigations — the Home Office Large Major Enquiry System. Every witness statement, every crime report, every interview, pretty much any action the detectives took, would be entered into HOLMES. The idea was that the computer might spot any links that the detectives had missed, but it also meant that the top brass could watch over everything from the comfort of their padded executive chairs.

Shepherd understood the need for someone to be coordinating the disparate investigations, but he knew that adding the extra layer of administration would just increase the bureaucracy and paperwork. It was the same on the battlefield. The more top brass were involved the slower things moved. That was why the SAS were so successful — generally there would be only one officer involved and he would usually let his men get on with it. It was all about trust. The SAS trusted its soldiers but the Met tended to strictly control their people, binding them with rigid regulations and protocols and making them account for everything they did.

The superintendent asked if there were any questions and when there weren't he called the meeting to an end.

Inspector Cave came over to Shepherd and Sharpe. "It's all getting very complicated, isn't it?" she said.

"Or simpler, depending on how you look at it," said Shepherd. "Before you were looking at several different gangs, now they're all being brought under one banner. And this Frenk Kriezis will be one hell of a scalp."

Cave nodded. "No question of that," she said. "But we all know that nature abhors a vacuum. If we put Frenk Kriezis behind bars, someone else will take his place. They always do." She looked at her watch, a cheap Casio. "How about that drink?"

"Music to my ears," said Sharpe. "The Moon Under Water?"

The Moon Under Water was a few minutes' drive from Peel House and they all went in Sharpe's Jaguar. It was a Wetherspoons pub and despite the early hour it was busy with patrons taking advantage of the cheap beer and food.

"I've never understood the name of this place," said Sharpe as they headed to the bar.

132

"It's from an essay written by George Orwell," said Shepherd. "Back in 1946. It was published in the *Evening Standard* and in it he described his perfect pub and made up the name for it."

"And what makes the perfect pub?" asked Cave. "Other than beer and a busty barmaid."

"He came up with ten criteria," said Shepherd. "They included that the architecture had to be Victorian, the barmaids had to know everyone's name, it should sell tobacco, cigarettes, aspirin and stamps and beer should never be served in a glass without a handle."

"How can you remember all that?" asked Cave.

"Spider here has one of those trick memories," said Sharpe, waving a twenty-pound note to attract the attention of a barman. "Everything he sees, hears or reads, he remembers."

Cave's forehead creased into a frown. "Spider?"

"That's what they call him."

"How would you get a nickname like that?" asked Cave. "Are you good at climbing?"

Shepherd flashed Sharpe a look of annoyance. He didn't like talking about his SAS days to relative strangers. In fact he didn't like talking about it to anyone outside the Regiment. It was the second time Sharpe had done it, and if nothing else it was unprofessional.

"I ate one once, for a bet," he said. "Come on, let's grab a seat while Jimmy does the honours."

They went over to a table by the window and sat down. "So I'm a bit confused," said Shepherd. "I had

133

assumed the NCA was investigating the Jason Morris gang and the county lines. But it's a Met investigation, right?"

Cave nodded. "It's always been done out of Peel House. Initially there were a couple of black-on-black stabbings that were looked at by the Trident team, but once the extent of the county lines became evident the Sheriff decided to set up an MIR team with yours truly as SIO."

"So why did you bring in the NCA?"

"Mainly for their undercover expertise," said Cave. "But also because the kids running the drugs were so young. It was Teflon's idea to bring them in."

Shepherd frowned. "Teflon?"

Cave laughed. "That's McKee's nickname. Nothing sticks to him, and it never has. He's got a knack of never being involved in anything controversial. And whenever something goes wrong he always manages to come out of it smelling of roses. I think he spotted that using underage agents might blow up in our faces so by bringing in the NCA he can shift the blame if there's a problem. If it works then he'll take the credit but if it backfires he'll just say it was their fault. Having said that, Jimmy and his team are real pros and if anyone can make it work, it's them."

Sharpe came over to their table with two pints and Shepherd's Jameson and soda. He sat down and took several gulps of his beer.

"So what does all this mean to the Morris investigation?" asked Shepherd.

Sharpe reached into his pocket and pulled out three packets of peanuts and dropped them in the middle of the table. He ripped one open and picked at them.

"First things first, it's no longer the Morris investigation," said Cave. "With Morris and his posse dead, there's nothing to investigate," she said. "The big question will be who takes over, and that'll take time."

"From what the super was saying, this Albanian guy has been moving in, cutting off the head of the snake and taking over the body," said Shepherd. "But something must have gone wrong when he moved in on Morris and they all got killed. How many were in the gang?"

"Hardcore, fifteen that we knew about. Then there's other guys on the periphery. But in terms of being able to take over the running of the gang, I don't see who else could move in. Do you, Jimmy?"

Sharpe shook his head. "No one comes to mind," he said. "Dancer was the leader. Swifty was his number two and they were as thick as thieves. Dancer and Swifty were the only ones to deal with the McAllens, I don't think anyone else knew where they were getting their drugs from. Beamer was their main enforcer and Mario was their jack of all trades and at a push one of them might have been able to take the reins, but other than that?" He shrugged.

"Those lines were producing thousands a week, someone is going to take them over," said Shepherd.

"We'll be watching and waiting," said Cave.

"What do we know about this Frenk Kriezis?"

"Nothing more than the Sheriff said at the briefing. He's a fucking invisible man. Plenty of gossip on the streets but little in the way of hard facts. I was surprised they had a picture of him."

"It was a passport photograph," said Shepherd. "I'm assuming they just had the one."

"They're fucking rough bastards, the Albanians," said Sharpe. "Most of them come from nothing so they've got nothing to lose. And British prisons are a joke to them. I've put away Albanian gangsters and within weeks they're posting on Facebook and Instagram showing off their drugs and PlayStations."

Cave nodded. "Gangsters from all over the world see London as a soft touch these days," he said. "All our crime stats are going through the roof. Homicides up twenty-seven per cent, robbery up thirty-three per cent, rape up eighteen per cent. We've had a fifty per cent rise in acid attacks and a seventy per cent increase in youth homicide. And a mayor who is more interested in his own political career than in solving the law and order problem." She gulped down some of her beer. Cops the world over liked nothing more than to complain about their lives, but in recent years Shepherd had found that British cops complained more than most. He understood their frustrations. Their resources were being cut to the bone while more was being expected of them. It wasn't a problem that MI5 faced — there was always money available to fight terrorism.

Shepherd tried to steer the conversation back to the matter in hand. "Is it worth holding onto Harry?" he asked.

136

Cave narrowed her eyes. "What do you mean?"

"Well you know where the Morris gang keep their drugs. Just keep an eye on the stash and arrest whoever goes to pick them up. You already have the evidence against the dealers in Reading. Okay, you won't be able to get anyone to turn on the McAllen brothers, but that opportunity has probably gone anyway."

Cave shook her head. "We'd rather bust the Reading dealers knowing that there are drugs on the premises," she said.

"I get that, I just worry that if the Albanians do take over we're going to be putting Harry in harm's way."

"He was in harm's way the moment he began delivering drugs for Jason Morris," said Cave. "And let's not forget that Harry was selling drugs to his schoolmates. He's not some innocent who got caught up in all this. He was a drug dealer who started transferring large amounts of drugs across country who helped us because he didn't want to go to prison."

"He's sixteen," said Shepherd. "Prison was never an option."

"A youth offenders institution, then. But bars are bars. This kid isn't helping us out of the goodness of his heart."

"He's in no more danger now than he was yesterday," said Sharpe. "Nothing has really changed."

"Frenk Kriezis kills to get what he wants," said Shepherd. "Think what he'll do to protect what he has?"

"Dancer was no angel," said Sharpe. "He killed people when it suited him."

"I understand your concern," said Cave. "But Jimmy and Julie Bacon have done a bang up job protecting Harry so far and I'm assuming that will continue."

Sharpe nodded in agreement.

"I'm also worried that the longer this goes on, the more chance his parents will find out what he's doing," said Shepherd.

"We want to tie this up as quickly as possible," said Cave. "But at the moment the ball isn't in our court. And it's even less my call now that Teflon is running the show."

Shepherd nodded and sipped his drink. He could only push it so far and at the end of the day it was never going to be his decision to make.

Cave picked up a menu. "Are we eating?"

Shepherd woke a few seconds before his alarm was due to go off. He rolled over, killed the alarm and padded to the bathroom to shave and shower. His plan was to head to Thames House and spend the morning going through MI5's database to see what intel was available on Albanian drug gangs. As he climbed out of the shower and grabbed a towel, he noticed he had missed a call. His first thought was that it was Katra, but it was Jimmy Sharpe. He returned the call and went through to the kitchen where he had already made himself a coffee. Sharpe answered. "Spider, we've got a problem. Harry has received a text telling him to go to an address in Kilburn."

"A text from who?"

"The text came on Swifty Taylor's phone. It just has an address and a time."

"He can't go, obviously."

"SIO says he should, but under surveillance."

"Razor, Taylor's dead. This is a trap."

"How can it be a trap? There's nothing to be gained in doing anything to Harry, he's just a mule."

"They could just do what they've always done and tell him where to meet to pick up the bag. This is new, right?"

"It's new. Yes. But the way I read it is that they just want to talk to him. Maybe they're going to explain the new regime to him. And if they do, and if we get that on tape, then we're well on our way to making a case."

"And if that tape is put into evidence, they'll know it was down to Harry. The plan was to get the case open and shut so that Morris and his crew would all plead guilty without a court case."

"We can do the same with whoever is taking over."

"Razor, I'm getting a bad feeling about this. The plan was to pull Harry out as soon as possible and now it's looking open-ended."

"I get what you're saying. And Cave is aware of your worries. But the Met's prime concern is to nail Frenk Kriezis."

"So they'll be happy to break a few eggs if it means making an omelette."

"Fuck me, someone got out of the wrong side of the bed today," laughed Sharpe. "Anyway, what's done is done. Harry will be on the two o'clock train to Paddington."

"You'll be following him?"

"We'll have people on the train and the Underground but I'll be going ahead. I could meet you in Kilburn."

"We need at least one ARV on standby, Razor."

"Exactly what the SIO said. He's arranging it."

"And I'd be happier if we had a couple of plainclothes SFOs in attendance." Specialist firearms officers were trained to a higher level than the Met's regular authorised firearms officers and were used in siege situations and to respond to terrorism threats.

"I'll tell him."

Shepherd sighed. It didn't look as if there was any way that he could prevent Harry from attending the meeting. The most he could do was to protect him to the best of his ability. "What vehicle were you planning to use?"

"The Jag."

"Bloody hell, Razor, a bright red Jag?"

"I won't be parking outside, will I? Give me a break."

"I'll get an office vehicle," said Shepherd. "I'd like to be in close and it'll have state-of-the-art comms and video."

"That'll work."

Shepherd sighed. "That's what you wanted in the first place, isn't it?"

Sharpe chuckled. "Aye, you know me so well."

Jimmy Sharpe found a metered parking space for his Jaguar and walked the short distance to the building where Harry Dexter was due to turn up. The Openreach van was parked opposite the building. As he walked towards it, Sharpe shifted his glance between the building and the pavement ahead of him. There were blinds down at the window and nobody seemed to be looking out. Nor did there seem to be any heavies standing outside the building.

They were in a side street off the main Kilburn High Road. There were few pedestrians and no one was paying Sharpe any attention. He was wearing a black reefer jacket and a wool cap and as he walked he pulled on a fluorescent high-vis jacket. The high-vis jacket was the ultimate camouflage, no one ever paid any attention to a man wearing one.

He reached the rear of the van and the back door opened just as he was about to knock. He climbed in. Shepherd was sitting on a plastic stool in front of a bank of monitors, most of which were blank. There were two other men also sitting on stools. One was middle-aged, wearing overalls and a headset. The other was younger with close-cropped hair, wearing a black nylon bomber jacket that was unzipped to reveal the butt of a pistol in an underarm holster.

Shepherd pulled the door closed and nodded at a spare plastic stool. "This is Craig Bird, he's an SFO," said Shepherd, nodding at the armed cop.

"The gun gives it away," said Sharpe. He shook hands with the firearms officer. "Are you here alone?"

"We've another SFO kitted out as a street-sweeper," said Bird.

"And there's an ARV parked up two minutes away," said Shepherd. "They're too visible to have them any closer." He nodded at the man in the headset. "This is

Matty Clayton. He's handling the video feed. We have four cameras giving views all around the van, but the only one we're interested in is the one of the building." He pointed at one of the monitors. It was showing the front door of the building and the window to its left.

Sharpe's phone beeped to indicate that he had received a text message. He took it out and looked at the screen. "Harry has just arrived at Paddington station," he said. "He'll get the Bakerloo Line up to Kilburn Park so he's ten, maybe fifteen minutes away."

"We'll see him on the GPS map," said Shepherd, pointing at one of the screens which showed a map of their area of London. "While he's on the Underground we don't have a signal but as soon as he's above ground his phone will show up here."

Sharpe put the phone away. "Do we have any idea who's in the house?"

Shepherd shook his head. "Matty's been here since ten and no one has gone in or out."

"So no way of knowing how many are inside?"

Shepherd shook his head.

Sharpe sat back and looked around the van. "This is all very hi-tech, isn't it?"

"We've got video coverage on all four sides and state-of-the-art comms," said Shepherd. "And no one looks twice at an Openreach van. They're always out and about."

"What do you do if you need to pee?" asked Sharpe.

"Do you?" asked Shepherd.

"It's a hypothetical question."

142

Shepherd grinned and held up an empty plastic water bottle.

"I'll try to hold it in," said Sharpe. He stretched out his legs and sighed. "This would do my head in," he said.

"Yeah, it can be a bit claustrophobic," said Shepherd. "If we're actively following a target then you don't notice it so much, but sitting for hours on end . . ." He shrugged. "There are more fun ways of spending the day. Or night."

"Someone's heading to the front door," said Clayton.

Shepherd and Sharpe bent forward to look at the monitor showing the feed from the camera in the roof of the van. It was a man, wearing a dark brown leather jacket with the collar turned up, his hands thrust into the pockets of his jeans. He had his head down so they couldn't get a good look at his face.

"Is that Kriezis?" asked Sharpe.

"Can't tell," said Shepherd.

"This is being recorded?"

"All video feeds are recorded," said Clayton.

The man went up to the front door and knocked. The door opened and he slipped inside. As he went in, they were able to see his face. It wasn't Kriezis.

Sharpe's phone buzzed and he checked it. "Harry's at Kilburn Park Tube station. He'll be here in five minutes."

Shepherd looked over at Clayton. "Make sure Foxtrot One is in position," he said.

"Foxtrot One?" repeated Sharpe.

"The street-sweeping SFO," said Shepherd.

143

As Clayton relayed the instructions to the SFO, Shepherd and Sharpe kept a close eye on the map screen. A red dot appeared and began to move north towards Kilburn High Road.

"How many do you have following him?" asked Shepherd.

"Just the one," said Sharpe. "Asian lady. Shaila. A real sweetheart. Don't worry, she'll give him plenty of room. Anyway, we know where he's going."

Shepherd forced a smile and nodded. He realised he was getting over-anxious. Sharpe was a professional, one of the best undercover agents in the business, and he knew what he was doing. It was pointless trying to second-guess him. "Sorry, Razor," he said.

Sharpe patted him on the leg. "You're worried about him. I get it."

The red dot reached Kilburn High Road and headed north-west.

Sharpe's phone buzzed and he checked it then put it away.

The three men watched the small dot move along the road, then turn into the side street where they were parked.

Harry appeared on the screen. He was wearing his school uniform and had a black backpack over one shoulder. "What did he tell his school?" asked Shepherd.

"Julie rang in to say that he was sick."

Shepherd looked across at him. "Are you serious? What, she pretended to be Harry's mother?"

"I think she chose her words carefully," said Sharpe.

144

"You know what I mean."

"We didn't have a whole lot of wriggle room," said Sharpe. "If the school had phoned his parents we'd be up shit creek in no time."

On the screen, Harry walked up to the front door. Shepherd looked over at Clayton. "Do we have the audio feed from his phone?"

Clayton nodded. "It's through the speakers at the moment but the phone is either in his backpack or his pocket so we're not picking up much of anything."

On the screen, Harry rang the doorbell. Shepherd's heart began to pound. His adrenal glands were kicking into overdrive but there was nothing he could do other than to sit and watch.

The door opened. It wasn't possible to see who had opened it.

"I'm Harry," said Harry. The boy's voice was muffled but Shepherd could hear him clearly. The phone was probably in the boy's pocket.

"Get inside."

Harry disappeared into the house and the door closed behind him. Shepherd bit down on his lower lip.

Clayton had twisted around on his stool and was watching the monitor with them.

"In there," growled the man.

There were a few seconds of rustling.

"Sit down."

Shepherd looked over at Sharpe. "Different voice?"

Sharpe nodded.

"You're Harry Dexter?"

"Yeah."

"You used to work for Morris, right?"

There was no answer and Shepherd assumed that Harry had nodded.

"Yeah, well now you work for me."

"Where's Swifty?" asked Harry.

"Swifty's left the business. I'm running it now."

"Why can't I talk to Swifty?"

"Because he's not fucking here. The stuff you deliver for him, where do you take it to?"

"Reading."

"I know that," snapped the man. "Where in Reading?"

Harry gave him the address.

"So they don't know who the customers are," said Sharpe. "They know about Harry but they don't know who gets the drugs from him."

"Probably got Harry's name and number off one of the phones," said Shepherd.

"We need you to take us to where you normally take the drugs."

"What?" said Harry.

"Are you fucking stupid? You're going to take me to the house where you deliver the drugs."

"Why?"

"Listen you little bastard, you don't ask questions, you do as you're fucking told."

There was a cracking sound, like a twig snapping.

Shepherd looked over at Sharpe. "Did he just hit Harry?"

"I couldn't tell," said Sharpe. "The guy might have just hit a chair or something."

146

"It sounded like a slap, Razor. I'm sending in the cops."

Sharpe held up a hand. "Give it a second."

"Razor . . ."

"Okay, okay," said Harry over the speaker. "I won't ask questions." He sounded apprehensive but not fearful so he probably hadn't been hit after all. Shepherd relaxed a fraction.

"Good lad," said the man.

Sharpe smiled. "He's okay. I don't think he was hit."

"When you deliver the drugs, who do you give them to?" asked the man.

"Just a guy," said Harry. "I knock on the door and the door opens. I give them the bag. I never really see who it is."

"But it's the same house, every time?"

"Sure," said Harry.

"Good boy," said the man. "Now, we need you to take us to the house, that's all."

"On the train, you mean?"

"No, we've got a car outside."

"Shit, they're going to go mobile," said Shepherd. He looked at Clayton. "What are our options, Matty?"

"Few and far between," said Clayton. "This van and the ARV, but the ARV is a non-starter for surveillance."

"There's my car," said Sharpe.

"Yeah, a bright red Jag," said Shepherd. "Best you drive back to Reading ahead of them."

Sharpe nodded. "We know exactly where they're going. It'll take them ninety minutes minimum to get there. That's enough time for me to get something sorted."

"We need to be bloody careful here, Razor. This is going to be a kick bollocks scramble but we can't afford to put a foot wrong."

"We can follow in the van at a safe distance and monitor the audio," said Clayton. "We can track them all the way with the phone's GPS so losing eyeball isn't the end of the world."

Shepherd nodded. "Okay, Jimmy, you get your car and head on back. We'll need full surveillance on the house and a couple of ARVs close by. Can you arrange that with your SIO?"

"No problem. I'll pick up Shaila on the way. She'll come in useful."

"We'll go now," said a man over the speaker. The voice was different from the first man. Deeper, with more of an accent.

Shepherd looked over at the firearms officer. "Craig, the ARV can't come with us because they're not allowed to cross into Thames Valley territory, but are you okay to stick with us? I'd prefer to have armed support on board."

"My guvnor says I'm attached to your unit so long as you need me, so I guess I go where you go," said Bird.

"What about Alan?" Alan Liddle was the second SFO, the one outside pushing the street-sweeping trolley.

"I'm sure he'd be up for it."

Shepherd nodded at Clayton. "Matty, get Alan back here. And can you brief Paul on what we'll be doing?

You're right, we can hang well back because the phone GPS will do the hard work."

Clayton gave him a thumbs-up and began relaying Shepherd's instructions over the radio.

The man was talking again, his voice now more conciliatory. "All you have to do is exactly what you always do. You deliver the drugs and you leave. We'll take it from there."

"Don't you know where I'm taking the drugs?" asked Harry.

"I'll head off," said Sharpe, getting off his stool.

"What we do or don't know doesn't concern you," said the man. "You just need to do as you're told. Do you know what this is?"

"It's a gun," said Harry, quietly.

Shepherd stiffened and looked across at Sharpe. "They've got guns."

"He's not being threatened, Spider."

"It sounds to me like he is."

"That's right it's a gun," said the man. "So I don't want to hear any more questions from you, okay?"

"Okay," said Harry, and even though the sound was muffled Shepherd could hear the uncertainty in the boy's voice.

"Right then," said the man. "You just do as you're told and you'll be fine."

"Okay," said Harry again.

"You just take us to the house. That's all I'm asking you to do. Do you have a problem with that?"

"No," said Harry.

"Are you sure? Because if you do, we need to address that now. I don't want you giving me a problem later."

"It's okay," said Harry. "I'll take you there."

"And you'll do as you're told?"

"Sure," said Harry.

"Good boy," said the man "Right, let's go."

Shepherd nodded at Sharpe. "You should go, Razor," he said, and opened the door for him. Sharpe stepped out and hurried along the road. Shepherd was just about to close the door when Alan Liddle appeared, holding a broom. Shepherd ushered him inside and closed the door.

Liddle put the broom on the floor and sat down, nodding at Bird. "All go, innit?" he said and Bird grinned.

"They're coming out now," said Clayton and everyone looked at the monitor showing the view from the roof camera. A tall man in a knee-length leather coat opened the door and stepped out. He looked around and then made a "come on" motion with his hand. A glum Harry appeared, his backpack on his shoulder. They were followed by a third man and Shepherd recognised him immediately from the picture Superintendent Sherwood had put on display in Peel House.

"That's him," said Shepherd. "That's Frenk Kriezis."

Two more men followed Kriezis out of the house. Big men with wide shoulders and the hard eyes of those who had done a lot of bad things. Shepherd cursed under his breath. Whatever Kriezis had planned, he was going in mob-handed.

Kriezis turned up the collar of his coat against the chill wind as he walked across the road to a black

Range Rover parked behind the Openreach van. One of the heavies pressed the fob to unlock the doors, then climbed into the driver's seat. Kriezis stood by the front passenger door as one of the heavies opened the Range Rover's rear door. The other heavy got in first and waved at Harry to follow him.

Harry looked like he wanted to protest but he saw the warning look flash across Kriezis's face and got in. The remaining heavy sat down next to Harry and slammed the door shut. The boy was sandwiched between the two men with barely enough room to breathe.

The driver put the car in gear and edged around the Openreach van.

"Bloody hell," said Shepherd as they watched the Range Rover drive away on the monitor. "How did we miss that?"

"It was parked there already when we pulled up," said Clayton. "I ran a DVLA check but it wasn't Kriezis." He looked at a notepad. "Marko Dushku. Nothing on the PNC."

"It's an Albanian name," said Shepherd.

"We're in Kilburn, half the people here are from that part of the world," said Clayton.

"Run him through Europol," said Shepherd. "What about their faces? Anything we can use from the cameras?"

Clayton shrugged. "Plenty of Kriezis, he was looking around. The driver, too. The others had their heads down."

The red dot that marked the location of Harry's iPhone was blinking on the map monitor as the Range Rover headed west.

Shepherd pressed the intercom to talk to the driver. "Paul, can you head towards Reading? We're after the black Range Rover that just pulled away but we don't need to get close, we've got them on GPS."

"Will do," said Drinkwater.

A few seconds later the van pulled away from the kerb and drove along the road.

They had been driving for almost thirty minutes when Clayton announced that Europol had a file on Marko Dushku. "Major villain in the Albanian capital, Tirana. Extortion, assault, but nothing after he reached twenty-five years old. A couple of years after that he became a Belgian citizen. I've got a picture."

Shepherd leaned over and looked at Clayton's screen. Dushku was a big man with a heavy jaw and deep-set eyes and his head was shaved. He was definitely the driver.

"Kriezis also has a Belgian passport," said Shepherd. "Presumably they have a guy in the passport office there. How old is he, Dushku?"

"Thirty-three," said Clayton.

"So for the last eight years he's been as good as gold, as he?" His voice was loaded with sarcasm.

"You're thinking he's got police protection in Albania?"

"I'm sure of it," said Shepherd. "Probably from about the time they moved from extortion to drugs.

Most likely they used the cash flow to pay off the cops. Happens the world over."

Jimmy Sharpe phoned Shepherd when the Openreach van was outside London, heading west to Reading. "Cave is on the case," said Sharpe. "She's pulled in two ARVs from Thames Valley and they'll be parked less than a minute away from the house."

"She understands the danger here, right? I doubt that Kriezis is going to be paying them a social call."

"She says it's a risk worth taking," said Sharpe. "And she's spoken to Ron McKee who's getting really excited."

"This isn't about testosterone, Razor. A kid's life is on the line. Cave understands that Kriezis is in a car with three heavies and Harry and a backpack full of drugs, does she?"

"To be fair, we don't know for sure that there are drugs in the bag. It could be a dummy run in which case we'd look bloody silly pulling them over en route."

Shepherd rubbed the back of his neck. That's exactly what he had been thinking. But Sharpe was right. There was no proof that there were drugs in the backpack and if there weren't all they would achieve by stopping the car would be to tip off Kriezis that he was in their sights. But if Kriezis was taking out his competition there was a chance that he meant to harm Warwick and Bradley. And if Harry was a witness then his life would also be on the line. If Harry had been an adult then maybe it would be a risk worth taking but he was a child and that made it a whole different ball game.

"He's in a black Range Rover." Shepherd gave Sharpe the registration number. "The iPhone GPS is working just fine," he said. "I'll let you know when he's outside Reading."

"I'll be close by, Spider," said Sharpe. "With as many of my guys as I can get."

"Are you armed?"

"No," said Sharpe.

"Well they almost certainly are. My advice would be to send in the armed cops as soon as we know that there are drugs in the building."

"I already suggested that to Cave and she passed it on to McKee. But McKee says he wants to prepare a full case against Kriezis and his gang."

"Razor, if we catch them red-handed with drugs and guns they'll go down for decades."

"Don't shoot the messenger, Spider. I'm just telling you what McKee says and he's running the show. Where are you?"

"About ten minutes away from the house. Kriezis's car is about half a mile ahead of us. The two SFOs are with us."

"I'm not sure about the legality of them firing their guns in anger outside the Met's jurisdiction," said Sharpe.

"Let me worry about that," said Shepherd. In fact it had already been playing on his mind. It was one thing to have the two armed officers with him, quite another for them to actually fire their weapons.

He stared at the red dot that was marking the progress of the Range Rover as it made its way along the M4. He wondered how Harry was bearing up. Several times in his career Shepherd had found himself wedged in the back seat of a car with heavies either side, not knowing whether he was in trouble or not. But he had been SAS-trained and usually had back up close by, so while those moments had been tense he had at least known that he had a measure of control over the situation. Harry was just a kid who had been threatened with a gun. Shepherd could only imagine how scared he must be.

Harry kept his head down, staring at the backpack on his lap. He didn't know who the men were or what they intended to do when they got to Reading. The fact that the police were following him didn't make him feel any better. He could tell the men in the Range Rover weren't scared of the police. He doubted they were scared of anything.

He sat in silence. The men talked to each other but he couldn't understand what they were saying. He really wanted to go to the toilet but he was too frightened to say anything. He had a very bad feeling about what was happening. He had never been worried when he was with Swifty. Swifty was a Yardie gangster but he was usually laughing and joking. The men in the Range Rover didn't smile, not once. And Harry was sure they would kill him without a second thought.

They reached Reading and the Range Rover headed towards the house where Harry usually dropped off the drugs. As Dushku slowed the Range Rover, Kriezis

155

twisted around in his seat. "Number eighty-seven you said?"

"That one," said Harry, pointing down the road at a semidetached house with peeling paintwork and an overgrown front garden.

"Park there," Kriezis said to Dushku, who pulled up at the side of the road.

Kriezis climbed out of the Range Rover. Prifti got out of the back and motioned for Harry to follow him. Harry sat where he was. "Do I have to come?" he asked fearfully.

"Yes," said Kriezis. "Now get out of the fucking car before we pull you out by your hair."

Shkodra got out of the other side of the car as Harry joined Kriezis and Dushku on the pavement. Kriezis gripped Harry by the shoulder and the boy looked at him fearfully. "You never use the front door?" Kriezis asked.

"They said I always have to go around the back," said Harry.

"And you deliver the drugs how?"

"What do you mean?"

"Are they in a box? A bag? What?"

"A backpack, like my school bag. A grey one."

"And what happens? Talk me through it."

"I walk around the back to the kitchen door. I've got a special knock. They open the door and I give them the bag."

"What do they give you?"

Harry sniffed. "Nothing."

"Show me," said Kriezis.

Harry began to shake. "Please, I want to go home," he said.

"Do you, Harry?" said Kriezis. "Do you really? Do you want me and my friends to take you home and talk to your mother and father? Maybe knock your father around a bit? Maybe fondle your mother's tits? Maybe take her upstairs and fuck her while your father watches? Is that what you want, Harry?"

Tears trickled down Harry's face. "No," he said. He wiped his eyes with the back of his hands.

"Then do as you're fucking told."

Shepherd looked over at Clayton. The audio quality from the phone in Harry's pocket wasn't great but they had heard enough to follow what was going on. Clayton was as clearly affected by what was happening as Shepherd was. Shepherd called up Sharpe. "Razor, have you got eyeball?"

"Yeah, they're all out of the Range Rover, standing on the pavement."

"Is there any way you can get photos of them, especially the two who were in the rear of the car?"

"Not really, no," said Sharpe. "They haven't paid us any mind but they might well spot a camera. What's going on there?"

"We don't have eyeball," said Shepherd. "We've had to park the van down the road from the house."

Kriezis and his gang weren't stupid and there was a chance they'd notice two Openreach van sightings on one day.

"How does Harry look?"

"Scared shitless," said Sharpe.

"What about the ARVs?"

"They're parked up two streets away, they can be on site within thirty seconds."

"How do you read what's happening, Razor?"

"It doesn't feel like a hit," said Sharpe. "I'm guessing that Kriezis just wants to talk. Hopefully once they get access to the house they'll let Harry go."

"We can't let him go inside with them," said Shepherd. "If they do kill Warwick and Bradley they're not going to leave Harry as a witness."

"If they go inside and start shooting, there won't be time for the armed cops to get there."

"I know," said Shepherd. His mind was racing. He wasn't happy about putting Harry at risk, but Sharpe was right. This didn't feel like a hit. But when the Albanians had arrived at the flat above the kebab shop, they probably hadn't been planning to kill everyone inside either. Situations changed — sometimes for the worse.

Kriezis followed Harry as he walked around the side of the house. His men were behind him. They were all looking around but there was nothing out of the ordinary. They were in the sticks, that's what the British called the towns outside London, and the sticks were generally less threatening than the city. That was what made the county lines so profitable — the market was growing but the risks were negligible.

At the rear of the building was a small garden that hadn't been cared for, the hedge was overgrown and the lawn was dotted with brown patches. The garden wasn't overlooked which Kriezis assumed was why it had been chosen. Customers could come and go without being seen.

Kriezis motioned for his men to move either side of the door. Shkodra and Dushku went to the left and Prifti moved to the right. The door was solid wood with a dog flap at the bottom. There was a security peephole at eye-level. The windows to the right were protected with bars and Kriezis was sure that the door would be reinforced on the inside.

He stood to the side and gestured for Harry to knock on the door. Harry did as he was told. There was no response and he knocked again. This time the door opened a fraction. There was a security chain on. Harry looked up and tried to smile. "Hey," he said. The door closed, there was the click of the security chain being unfastened and then the door opened again.

Prifti put his shoulder to the door and pushed hard. Whoever was holding the door was caught by surprise and staggered back. Prifti quickly stepped inside, pulling a gun from inside his jacket.

Harry gasped in surprise. Kriezis put his hand on the boy's shoulder. "Go now," he said.

Shkodra and Dushku hurried inside after Prifti. There was the sound of punching and the dull thud of a body hitting the floor.

"What's going to happen?" said Harry, his voice a hoarse whisper.

"Don't you worry about it," said Kriezis. "Go home. You'll be sent a text when there is a delivery to be made." Kriezis reached into his pocket and Harry flinched. Kriezis grinned and pulled out a roll of fifty pounds notes. He peeled off four and gave them to the boy. "You did well today."

Harry grabbed the notes as if he feared Kriezis was going to change his mind, then hurried back around the side of the house. Kriezis watched him go, then followed his men inside the house.

"He's coming back," said Shepherd. "Looks like he's on his own." His commentary was unnecessary as everyone in the back of the van was watching the monitor that showed the view of the house. Once Kriezis and his men had gone around the back of the house, Shepherd had told the driver to move the Openreach van to a better vantage point. Now they had a near unobstructed view of the front of the building.

Shepherd called Sharpe on his mobile. "Razor, Harry's on his way. When he's well away from the house pick him up and take him back to the safe house. I need to talk to him."

"Will do," said Sharpe. "What's happening there?"

"We don't know, they went around to the back of the house so we can't see anything. As soon as you pick Harry up, debrief him and call me. We're going to wait here but a fat lot of good it'll do as we can't see anything and we lost all sound when Harry left with his phone."

"McKee says we're not to go in, no matter what."

"Are you serious?"

"His words exactly," said Sharpe. "Even if you hear shots, you're to let it play out. He knows you've got Kriezis and his men on video, he doesn't want a shoot out. If it does turn nasty, we let them go and pick them up afterwards."

"And if Warwick and Bradley are hurt?"

"Collateral damage," said Sharpe. "Again, his words."

"That's cold."

"He's a career cop," said Sharpe. "He wants a high-profile bust. He doesn't just want an assault case and a few kilos of drugs. Okay, I see Harry. I'll see you at the safe house." Sharpe ended the call.

"Craig, can you or Alan hang about outside without looking too conspicuous?" Shepherd asked.

Bird shrugged. "I guess so."

"Be close enough to the house so that if you hear shots you can move in. If we do hear shots the ARVs will be here within a minute."

The two SFOs exchanged a worried look.

"What's wrong?" asked Shepherd.

"No offence, but I'm not sure we can use our weapons in Thames Valley, not without written authorisation," said Bird.

Liddle nodded in agreement. "Craig's right. I think we're okay to be here with you, but I wouldn't be comfortable firing my weapon. And the shit would really hit the fan if there were casualties. This isn't our area."

"Yeah, I get it," said Shepherd.

"We can be outside, that's not a problem," said Liddle. "If we hear shots we can investigate, same as any member of the public could. But I don't see that we could fire our weapons."

"Even if you were under attack?"

"That might be different," said Bird. "But Professional Standards would be all over us and we'd have a hell of a lot of questions to answer."

"Alan, how about you hang around outside until the bad guys are out of the house?" asked Shepherd. "The high-vis jacket will give you some credibility." There was a clipboard hanging on a hook on the side of the van. Shepherd unhooked it and gave it to the SFO. "This should help too," he said.

Alan nodded and Shepherd opened the door for him. Liddle climbed out and walked along the road, pretending to study the clipboard. Shepherd pulled the door shut. All they could do now was wait. Harry was now out of danger, and Kriezis and his team were still inside the house. His two main concerns were to keep Harry out of harm's way and to make sure that the MI5 investigation continued to move forward, but he also had to consider the danger that Gavin Warwick and Stuart Bradley were facing. Kriezis's men had at least one gun, probably more, and they clearly weren't paying a social call. They had already killed Morris and Taylor and two of their men, burned three members of the Ealing Hot Boyz gang and butchered the Mahmud brothers in Tower Hamlets and there were probably other murders that the authorities were still unaware of. But it wasn't Shepherd's problem. Kriezis was an NCA target and nothing to do with MI5.

162

Frenk Kriezis smiled at the two men. "I'm sorry if our entrance was a little dramatic but in my experience men such as yourselves often have guns to hand and I'm not in the mood to get shot today."

The two men were naked and had been tied to wooden chairs with strips of duct tape. They hadn't been gagged but fear alone kept them from crying out.

Shkodra and Prifti pointed their guns at the men while Kriezis had ordered them to take off their clothes. They had resisted at first but Dushku had slashed Warwick across the face with a cut-throat razor and after that both men had done as they were told and allowed themselves to be tied to the chairs. Blood was dripping down Warwick's cheek and onto his shoulder.

Dushku went through the men's trousers and took their wallets over to Kriezis. Kriezis took out the driving licences and tossed the wallets onto the floor. He studied the pictures on the licences, then looked at Warwick. "I'm sorry about the cut, but you needed to know that I am a serious person. You understand that now, right? That I am serious?"

Warwick nodded.

Kriezis looked at Bradley. "And you, Stuart Bradley. You understand now that I am serious?"

Bradley nodded fearfully.

"Good, so we are now, as you say, on the same page. My name is Frenk, and I am here to give you a choice. You can work for me, or you can . . ." He grinned.

"Well, let's just say that's the choice. You can work for me. Up until now you have been working for yourselves, selling drugs that you have been buying from Jason Morris. That is no longer an option."

Bradley frowned, not understanding.

"Morris is dead. So is his number two. And his number three and number four for that matter. The drugs that they used to supply you with will now come from me."

"That's cool," said Warwick, his voice trembling.

Kriezis smiled encouragingly. "So you approve?"

Warwick nodded frantically. "Sure, yes. Whatever."

"We don't care who we get our gear from," said Bradley.

"Well you should care," said Kriezis. "You need to sell a good product. If you sell a good product people are happy to buy and they'll tell their friends. Word of mouth. But if you sell them shit then they'll start trying to buy from elsewhere."

"Sure. Yes. You're right." Bradley smiled and nodded again.

"And you're not just saying that because you know what will happen if you refuse my offer?"

"Frenk, mate, we never fucking liked Dancer anyway," said Bradley. "He was a fucking arsehole. And sometimes he cut his shit before he sold it to us. We were always getting complaints, right Gav?"

Warwick nodded. "Yeah. And when we said anything to him he said we didn't know what we were talking about. Like we were fucking idiots. We were looking to get supplied from elsewhere but we drew a blank. He

164

was regular, was the thing. We wanted a kilo, we got a kilo the next day."

"Well, you can have all the kilos you want from now on, and you have my word your drugs won't be cut. We'll send it to you exactly as it arrives in this country."

"Good. Great. Sounds like a plan," said Bradley.

"It is a plan," said Kriezis. "And as part of the plan I want you to increase your sales. This town is wide open and with my supplying you there's no reason you can't sell ten times what you've been selling."

"I don't know about that, Frenk," said Bradley. "This isn't London."

"No, but there's a university here. And schools. And a thriving middle class who just love a little cocaine to liven up their dinner parties. You need to be more — what is the word — proactive. That's it. You need to be more proactive."

"We can do that," said Warwick. He looked over at Bradley. "We can do that, right?"

"I guess," said Bradley.

Warwick looked back at Kriezis. "Look, we don't give a fuck who supplies us. We're just trying to make money."

"That's good," said Kriezis. He smiled. "It's clear we now understand each other. The deliveries will continue as usual. What about payments? How did you pay Morris?"

"We sent cash to an address in south London."

"I need you to give me the address."

"Sure, no problem."

"But in future you will send the money back with the boy. When he delivers the drugs, you give him the money. These days the cops can check the mail. Using the boy will be safer."

"Sure. We'll do that."

"And you need to find another boy to do deliveries. Maybe a couple. Just using one is bad business."

"I'm on it," said Warwick.

"So we understand each other?" asked Kriezis.

Both men nodded.

"There is only one problem," said Kriezis. He gestured at Warwick. "You are bleeding. Your friend isn't. You can't think that's fair, can you?"

Warwick looked around in confusion, not understanding what he was getting at.

"You'll have a scar and every time you look at it you'll remember what happened and you'll remember that your friend here was unscathed. Over time you will resent that. And with resentment comes betrayal."

"No, I . . ." Warwick began, but Kriezis silenced him with a wave of his hand. "I understand how people think, my friend. And I understand why they do what they do. I know when someone is lying to me and I know when someone is planning to do me harm. You will resent the fact that you were cut and your friend wasn't. It's understandable. And you will want revenge and you will stop working as a team. You might think of betraying him and that might lead to me having problems with the police. You have to know that problems with the police are the last thing I want." He gestured at Dushku who flicked out the blade of his cut-throat razor.

"Oh for fuck's sake, you can't do this," said Bradley. "Please, no . . ."

Kriezis nodded at Dushku. "*Prerë fytyrën e tij. Bëni gjakderdhje.*"

Dushku smiled thinly and stepped towards the two bound men.

Warwick continued to beg and plead, shaking his head from side to side, making the blood flow even more.

Dushku raised the knife, took a step to the right, grabbed Bradley's hair with his left hand and drew the knife across the man's cheek with the other. Blood spurted over the blade and down Bradley's cheek. "Fuck!" shouted Bradley.

Dushku stepped back, wiped the bloody blade on the back of a sofa, then folded the razor and slipped it back in his pocket.

"What the fuck!" shouted Bradley. "We said we'd do it."

"But now you are equal," said Kriezis quietly. "Neither needs to be resentful. We can all put this behind us and move on."

Warwick turned to look at Bradley. "He's got a point," he said.

"Are you fucking serious?"

"I would have been pissed off if I was the only one who'd been cut. But now . . . yeah, fuck it. What's done is done, right?" He looked up at Kriezis. "Right?"

"I'm happy to move on," said Kriezis. "We can all make money. In fact you'll be making more money than before. We're expanding, and as we grow, you'll grow. And we'll be dealing with any competition." He chuckled. "In fact there won't be any competition once I'm done. It'll be a monopoly. We'll be the only game in town. Now are we good? Can I untie you and be on my way? Or do we have unfinished business?"

Warwick shook his head. "No, we're good." He looked over at Bradley. "We're good, right?"

Blood was oozing out of the cut on Bradley's cheek and dripping down his neck, but he nodded slowly. "Yeah," he said. "We're good."

"Here they come," said Clayton, but Shepherd had already seen the men on the monitor, walking purposefully along the side of the house. They didn't look like men who had just committed murder but then again it wouldn't have been the first time they'd killed and with familiarity came confidence.

Kriezis brought up the rear. As they walked towards their Range Rover, the camera got a good look at their faces. Shepherd looked over at Clayton but before he could say anything Clayton nodded. "I'm on it," he said. "I'm sending stills over as we speak." His fingers played on the keys of his laptop. MI5's facial recognition systems would search for a match in more than a dozen law enforcement databases, including the EU and the United States, and would also check against photographs held by Border Force, the Driver and Vehicle Licensing Agency and the Passport Office.

The four men reached the Range Rover and climbed in. Kriezis was in the front passenger seat again.

"Are we going to follow them?" asked Bird.

"I think not, Kriezis isn't our problem," said Shepherd. He didn't want to call Sharpe because he'd be with Harry, but he needed to get the Met on the case. In Shepherd's experience, the higher the rank, the less cooperative the person, so he phoned Cave. The inspector answered her mobile phone straight away and she listened as Shepherd explained what had happened. To her credit, Cave didn't ask any questions, she just said she'd get right on it. Shepherd gave her a description of the vehicle and its registration number and ended the call.

There was a quiet knock on the rear door and Shepherd opened it. It was Liddle. The SFO climbed in and sat on a stool.

"How close were you?" asked Shepherd.

"I was down the road when they came out," said Liddle. "Definitely didn't hear any shots."

"Okay, we're good to go," said Shepherd. "I'll get the driver to drop me off at the NCA safe house and then Paul can take you all back to London."

He used the intercom to give Drinkwater his instructions and the van moved off.

"We've got an ID on the men with Kriezis and Dushku," said Clayton. "The matches came from Europol and not surprisingly they're both Albanians."

Julie Bacon let Shepherd into the house and followed him down the corridor to the kitchen. Harry was sitting

169

at the kitchen table with a can of Coke in front of him. Sharpe was sitting opposite him with a mug of coffee. Sharpe looked up at him inquisitively but he was professional enough not to say anything in front of the teenager. "All good," said Shepherd, and Sharpe visibly relaxed. Shepherd patted Harry on the shoulder. "Everything okay, Harry?" he asked.

Harry shrugged but didn't say anything.

Shepherd pulled out a chair and sat down.

"Coffee?" asked Sharpe.

"Please," said Shepherd. "Splash of milk." He grinned at Harry. "I need the caffeine."

"There's more caffeine in Coke," said Harry.

Sharpe stood up to make a coffee for Shepherd.

"Yeah, but I'm watching my weight," said Shepherd. "So, how did it go?" He had to make it seem as if they didn't know what they had heard over the teenager's iPhone.

"They wanted me to show them the house where I deliver the drugs to."

"Okay. What can you tell me about them?"

"They were four white guys. Foreign. One of them had a gun."

"A gun? Wow. Were you scared?"

Harry nodded. "A bit."

"Did they threaten you?"

Harry screwed up his face. "Not really. But they were pretty shitty the way they spoke to me."

"Did they say why they wanted to know where the house was?"

170

"They wanted to talk to the guys I deliver the drugs to. I told them I never met them but they weren't interested. So we went to the house and they knocked on the back door. When the door opened they pushed in and I think they were hitting the guy. Then the main guy told me to go."

"The main guy? How do you know he was the main guy?"

"The others were always looking at him to see what he wanted them to do."

"Did they tell you their names?"

Harry shook his head. "No."

"What did he look like? The main guy?"

"About as tall as you. Brown hair." He touched his left cheek. "He had a scar here."

"Did they say anything about Dancer or Swifty?"

"No. Well, they said I was working for them now. Oh, wait, they said Swifty had left the business, I remember now. But when I asked them what they meant they got shitty. What's going to happen?"

Shepherd looked across at Sharpe who was adding milk to a mug of coffee. That was the big question. If it had been up to him, he would have sent the armed cops in as soon as Kriezis had gone into the house. They could have pulled Harry out of the county line investigation and continued to use him to pursue his uncle. But Superintendent Sherwood obviously felt that he had bigger fish to fry so, for the time being at least, Harry had to stay in play.

"We carry on as we have been," said Sharpe.

Harry slumped back in his chair. "This isn't fucking fair," he said.

"Language, Harry," said Bacon, wagging a finger at him.

"You said this wouldn't be for long but it's going on and on. And I don't understand what's happened to Swifty. He told me to go to that house in Kilburn but he wasn't there. Why's he messing me around like this? Why send me the message and then not turn up?" Realisation dawned and his jaw dropped. "They did something to Swifty, didn't they?"

"We don't know," said Shepherd, the lie tripping off his tongue easily. It was bad enough that they had put the lad in danger; if he knew the truth he'd be nervous and that could lead to him making mistakes. And if he made mistakes the MI5 investigation could come to an abrupt halt. He chose his words carefully. "All we know is that this guy has taken over from him. It might just be that Swifty and Dancer have decided to do something else."

"All you have to be concerned about is carrying out their instructions," said Sharpe, putting the mug of coffee down in front of Shepherd. "Nothing has really changed." He sat down at the table.

"How can you say that?" snapped Harry. "Everything's changed. I don't know who these guys are. And they had fucking guns. That guy waved a gun in my face."

"Harry, please don't swear," said Bacon.

Harry ignored her and continued to stare at Shepherd. "I don't believe you," he said.

"What do you mean?"

172

Harry sneered at him. "I don't believe that you don't know what happened to Swifty. You know, you're just not telling me."

"Harry, whatever happened to Swifty isn't the issue," said Bacon, but Harry waved her away without looking at her. His eyes were fixed on Shepherd's face.

"You shouldn't be lying to me," Harry said, his voice a low whisper.

Shepherd stared back at him, then he slowly nodded. The boy was right. "Okay," he said quietly.

"Spider . . ." said Sharpe.

"It's okay," said Shepherd.

"Who's Spider?" asked Harry quickly. He looked at Sharpe and then back at Shepherd. "Who the fuck is Spider?"

"It's my nickname," Shepherd said. "That's all. But I hear what you're saying, Harry. What you're doing for us, you deserve the truth. If we lie to you it means we don't respect you, and you need to know that we do respect you and we are grateful to you for your help." He paused and nodded, hoping to get a nod or a smile back but Harry just stared at him sullenly. "You deserve the truth. So here it is. Swifty and Dancer are dead. So are the rest of Dancer's gang. We don't know for certain but there's a good chance that the men you met today killed them."

"To take over their business?"

"Exactly."

"So they could have killed me?"

Shepherd shook his head. "No. They need you and the other kids running drugs out to the provinces. He

173

wants to control the business as is, not rebuild it from the ground up. You were never in danger." Shepherd smiled reassuringly. He had promised to tell the boy the truth but he was still lying. When Shepherd had watched Harry walk into the house in Kilburn, he'd had no idea how it was going to play out. And again when Harry had gone around the back of the house in Reading, Shepherd was equally unsure of what would happen.

"Who is he?"

"He's a gangster who is trying to build a drugs empire quickly and doesn't care who he hurts on the way. That's why we need your help, Harry. You were terrific helping us to put a case against Swifty and Dancer but they're dead so now we need you to help us build a case against these new bad guys."

"You all said I wouldn't have to do this for long," said Harry.

"And you won't. A week or so. We just need you to do a few more runs and let us take samples like we did before."

"A week?"

Shepherd looked at Sharpe who nodded.

"I think so," said Shepherd. "And we'll be watching you every step of the way."

"And then I'm in the clear?" asked Harry.

"Yes, of course," said Shepherd.

"You swear?"

"You won't be facing any charges, Harry," said Bacon. "We've told you that, right from the start."

"And my mum and dad won't know?"

"We won't tell them," said Bacon.

Harry nodded. "Okay," he said. He looked at his watch. "I should be getting back home."

"I'll show you out," said Bacon. Harry finished his Coke and followed her down the hallway.

"Sorry about the Spider thing," said Sharpe.

"Not a problem," said Shepherd.

"Not in front of a kid, no. But a mistake like that in the wrong company . . ." He shrugged.

"You wouldn't have said it in the wrong company," said Shepherd. "You're a cop and, okay, I'm not but I'm as good as, so him knowing my nickname is neither here nor there. Don't sweat it, Razor. In fact him knowing my nickname will hopefully make him trust me more. It works to our advantage."

They heard the front door open and close.

"Maybe," said Sharpe. "Except he thinks your name is David Slater."

"I can't tell him my real name, much as I want to," said Shepherd.

"Secret squirrel."

"It's a rule," said Shepherd. "Officers never use their real names with agents."

Bacon came back into the kitchen. "Is everything okay?" she asked.

"All good," said Shepherd, and he quickly filled her in on what had happened. "I've already expressed my reservations about continuing to use Harry but I've been overruled. We need to make sure that he's safe and that we bring it to a speedy conclusion. Assuming they stick to the format, we can follow whoever delivers

175

the drugs to Harry back to their base. It could be that they'll know about Dancer's lock-up in which case we can tie it up pretty quickly. Also, Kriezis will probably be moving in on the other county lines. The fact that we have surveillance teams already in place means we hit the ground running. A week isn't an unrealistic timeframe."

Bacon sat down. Shepherd could see the concern on her face. "Albanians can be nasty bastards," she said.

"Yes, and they are running true to form," said Shepherd. "They've moved into three other gangs that we know about. And the bodies are piling up."

"We have to pull Harry out," said Bacon. "We can't put him at risk like this."

"We'll be watching over him," said Sharpe. "And if they had been planning to hurt him, they'd have done it already."

Bacon folded her arms. "Jimmy, he's a kid."

"Nothing's changed other than the target," said Sharpe. "Dancer and Swifty weren't pussycats. I don't see that Harry is any more at risk now than he was before."

"Except that we were supposed to be wrapping this up," said Bacon. "The longer it goes on, the more chance there is of something going wrong."

"A week isn't long, Julie," said Sharpe.

"If it goes tits-up, it's long enough," said Bacon. She looked at Shepherd. "What do you think?" she asked.

"You know I've been against this from day one," said Shepherd. "Kids have no place in undercover work. But as I said, I've been overruled. All we can do is keep

176

Harry out of harm's way." He held up his hand as she opened her mouth to reply. "I know, I know, we're putting him in harm's way. But we can keep a close eye on him. And we'll have Kriezis and his gang under surveillance. If we even think they want to hurt Harry we can pull him out."

Bacon didn't look convinced but she nodded. "Okay," she said.

Shepherd's phone buzzed to let him know he'd received a text message. He scowled when he read it.

"What's wrong?" asked Sharpe.

"I've been summoned," said Shepherd. "His master's voice."

Giles Pritchard kept Shepherd waiting for twenty minutes before he was admitted into the inner sanctum. The director waved Shepherd to a seat and as usual got straight to the point. "I'm told you've been using MI5 resources on an MPS investigation," he said, pushing his glasses up his nose with one forefinger.

Shepherd shrugged. "We were running surveillance on Harry Dexter, and he's an MI5 asset."

"He was going to meet his drug dealer, not his uncle, correct?"

Shepherd nodded. "It's complicated. The Met investigation into the county lines is ongoing."

"And not within our brief," said Pritchard.

"I need to make sure that Harry isn't in any danger because if anything happens to him it would jeopardise our operation."

Shepherd didn't like the way Pritchard was second-guessing him but there was no way he could express his annoyance without appearing to be combative. He forced himself to smile and resisted the urge to fold his arms. "He received a text message that he thought was from Jason Morris but we knew that Morris was dead. Something was clearly not right so I organised a team to keep an eye on him. It turned out it was an Albanian gangster who is moving in on the county lines. The Met have put a task force together to target him."

Pritchard nodded. "Frenk Kriezis?"

"That's right. He's started his own crime wave, targeting existing county lines and basically making them offers they can't refuse. Effectively Harry Dexter is now working for Kriezis."

"And you followed Kriezis from London to Reading?"

"Strictly speaking I was following Harry. Our asset."

"Who was in a vehicle with Kriezis and his heavies?"

"Exactly," said Shepherd. He could see where Pritchard was going but there was no way of speeding up the process. He just had to wait for the director to get to the point.

"And you had two Metropolitan Police SFOs with you?"

"They were attached to our operation and were in the surveillance van so it made sense for them to come along."

"Even though you knew you would be crossing into the Thames Valley policing area?"

178

"We weren't expecting them to have to use their weapons," said Shepherd.

Pritchard smiled thinly. "Which begs the question, why did you take them with you?"

"We were moving quickly. It caught us by surprise when Kriezis said he was going to take Harry to Reading. The SFOs were already in the van." Shepherd shrugged.

"You arranged ARV cover in Thames Valley?"

Shepherd nodded. "Through the SIO, Chief Inspector McKee."

"And Chief Inspector McKee also arranged for surveillance in Reading?"

It was phrased as a question but Shepherd knew that his boss already had the answer. That was the key to a successful interrogation — never ask a question that you don't already know the answer to. "It was actually the NCA surveillance expert, Jimmy Sharpe. He put a team together at short notice."

"So at that point NCA had surveillance in place and Thames Valley had arranged armed support?"

"That's right."

"Which again begs the question, why didn't you leave it up to them?"

"I was protecting our asset. As I said."

"Well, you weren't actually protecting him as the SFOs you had with you weren't authorised to fire their weapons. Or were you prepared to charge in and take care of them bare-handed? I gather you do have a tendency to rush in at times."

"We were there for surveillance purposes," said Shepherd. "Thames Valley were responsible for the armed support."

Pritchard sat back in his high-backed chair and steepled his fingers under his chin as he looked at Shepherd over the top of his spectacles for several seconds. "Here's what concerns me, Daniel. Best possible scenario is what happened. Kriezis and his men went into the house, talked to whoever was inside and went back to London. Harry Dexter returned to his home. All's well that ends well." He placed his hands palms down on his desk.

"Exactly," said Shepherd, though he was all too aware that there was more to come.

"But the worst possible scenario, had you considered that? Suppose Kriezis had gone in there with his men and started shooting. Suppose that young Harry had been killed? Where would that have left us? The papers would have had a field day. 'Schoolboy killed in botched MI5 operation'. We would have had a lot of questions to answer, and frankly I wouldn't have had the answers. We would have been involved in any criminal cases or court actions that had arisen as a result, and if your SFOs had gone in it would have been even worse. I shudder to think how that would have ended. We are facing calls from all sides for us to become more accountable and if your operation had gone wrong we would have handed our enemies a loaded gun." He picked up a gold pen and began to toy with it. Displacement behaviour. He fell silent but Shepherd resisted the urge to say something to fill in the gap. He wasn't sorry for what he'd done which meant he was in no mood to apologise. But neither did he want to get into an argument with his boss because it wasn't an argument he could win.

"I understand your background, Daniel. Paratrooper, SAS, undercover cop. And I understand that the SAS encourages its people to think on their feet. But you're not special forces any more. You are a cog in a very large machine and for that machine to function smoothly each of us cogs has to do its job. You were lucky this time. But it must not happen again." He looked over the top of his glasses. "Understood?"

"Absolutely, yes," said Shepherd. "Understood."

Pritchard forced a smile. "Good man," he said. He sat back in his chair and looked at his computer screen, his way of letting Shepherd know that the meeting was at an end.

"There was something I wanted to raise with you," said Shepherd.

Pritchard frowned as he looked back at Shepherd, clearly not happy that he hadn't taken the hint and left.

"Have you had a chance to look at the transcript from Harry's phone this Sunday?"

"I have, yes," said Pritchard.

"In particular where Gary Dexter talks about travelling to Serbia to fire some ordnance. Namely RPGs."

Pritchard nodded. "This coming weekend, he said. It's interesting but it's not against the law. Unless he tries to bring an RPG back with him but I doubt they'll let him on the plane if that's the case." He flashed Shepherd a sarcastic smile to show that he was joking.

"I thought it might be an opportunity to get close to Dexter. The trip is open to the public and they still have slots available."

"This is a surveillance operation, not an undercover op."

"Agreed. But this is too good an opportunity to pass up. Gary Dexter says he's going with five mates. According to the company's website they take up to a dozen people at a time and they are showing vacancies. I just turn up and I'll be put in the group with them. I could use a legend I've used before: John Whitehill, freelance journalist. It's the perfect cover."

"You'll spook him."

"Give me some credit. I'll throw in a few Islamophobic comments and he'll see me as a kindred spirit. I've done it before."

"I'm not disputing your professionalism," said Pritchard. "It's just going undercover overseas is a risk."

"A risk that I'm prepared to take," said Shepherd. "You read the transcript. Other than the trip, Gary didn't give anything away. I don't think his brother is in the least bit interested in the Crusaders and I don't think he knows what Gary is planning."

Pritchard hesitated, then nodded. "Agreed."

"So what I'm saying is that we could spend the next year bugging their Sunday lunches and I doubt we'll get anything we can use against Gary Dexter. But put me next to him shooting heavy artillery and there's a chance he'll open up."

"He's careful."

"Sure, on his own territory, of course he is. But out there in Serbia and me having a rock solid legend is a whole different story. I just think it's worth a try. What's the worst that can happen?"

"The worst is that he'll spot you for what you are and realise that he's being watched."

"From all the anti-surveillance techniques he uses, it's clear that he knows that anyway. But he won't spot me. Trust me."

"It's not about whether or not I trust you. Your record speaks for itself." He had his gold pen in his hand again and he was spinning it around his thumb. "It's whether the reward is worth the risk."

"Limited risk. If it looks like he's reluctant in any way I'll just pull back and play the tourist. But if he's receptive, I'll take it as far as I can."

"He'll have access to all sorts of guns, and Serbia is still the Wild West. You won't have any back up."

"I don't see that I'll need it. It isn't as if I'm engineering a meeting in a seedy nightclub, this is a group of guys on a shooting trip. If it makes you happier I can take back up."

Pritchard's smile was colder this time. "It's not about me being happier," he said. "My happiness is immaterial. I think back up would make you more likely to come a cropper. Anyone not local will stick out."

"They could come on the trip with me."

"Then we'd need two cover stories. If anything we'd be doubling the risk of exposure." The pen slipped off his thumb and spun across the desk. He reached for it, then put it down and steepled his fingers under his chin again. "Okay, you can do it. But softly, softly. If you sense any hostility on his part, you drop it. Immediately."

"I will do," said Shepherd. The director had already turned his attention back to his computer and this time Shepherd took the hint and left.

He took the stairs down to the second floor and walked along to the office where the legends were maintained. There was no sign on the door, just a number. Shepherd went in and was greeted with a warm smile by the lady in the outer office. Susan Murray had been with MI5 since before Shepherd joined. She had a memory that was almost as faultless as his, a prerequisite for a job that called for maintaining identities that had to stand up to intense scrutiny. Murray had been a librarian at the British Library for almost twenty years before she had been recruited by MI5. Her job was to oversee the footies and the shoppers, groups of men and women who spent their days maintaining the legends used by officers working undercover.

In the old days, pre-internet, a driving licence, passport and a credit card were all that an officer needed to venture forth with a new identity. But the internet — and in particular social media — had made life much more complicated. Facebook and Twitter accounts had become the norm, and Google meant that anyone could go looking for a person. And if Google drew a blank, suspicions could be raised.

The job of a footie was to maintain the footprints of all the legends that hadn't yet been retired. Footies maintained Facebook accounts, tweeted, used Oyster cards and railcards, kept flats and houses maintained, and paid utility bills. They made calls on mobile phones in the legend's name and sent and received emails. Shoppers bought things online, used loyalty cards in supermarkets, paid for meals in restaurants with credit cards and bought and used rail and airline tickets. If the legend came with a car they would drive the vehicle, sometimes running up parking tickets and speeding tickets. Many new recruits to the service would spend their first six months working as a footie or a shopper, though there were others for whom it was a long-term career.

"Dan, good to see you," said Murray, taking off her spectacles and allowing them to hang from a slim gold chain. "Off somewhere nice?"

"Serbia," he said.

"So that's a no, then," she said.

"I'd like the John Whitehill legend, if it's ready to go."

She tapped on her computer keyboard and nodded. "Yes, it's up to date. What do you need?"

"The full Monty," said Shepherd. "Passport, credit cards, driving licence and a phone. I'm not sure that I'll need to use the Hampstead flat but I'll need it on standby."

"Vehicle?" she asked.

"Not at the moment," said Shepherd. "I'll let you know if that changes."

Murray tapped on her keyboard again, then stood up. "Give me a couple of minutes," she said, and went through a door into what Shepherd knew was a large storeroom lined with filing cabinets. When she returned she was holding two large envelopes and an iPhone.

"The phone is good to go," she said, handing it to him. "There are messages on it regarding writing assignments and the like. But feel free to pop the sim card into any phone you want. It's an iPhone 6, and it uses your thumbprint and the Whitehill date of birth as the fall-back password."

"I remember," said Shepherd, slipping it into his pocket.

She passed him the two envelopes. "All the ID you need, plus a Mastercard, an Amex card and a First Direct debit card. There's just under two thousand pounds in the account but let me know if you need more. The pin numbers again are the Whitehill date of birth. And just to let you know, if you don't already, accounts are getting very busy about receipts. Pretty much anything over fifty pounds needs a physical receipt these days."

"No problem," said Shepherd. "Though if I end up buying an RPG I doubt I'll be able to get a receipt."

"In that case you'll need special authorisation from Mr Pritchard," said Murray.

Shepherd decided not to tell her that he was only joking. He opened the envelope containing the credit cards and ID and checked them. It wasn't that he

186

didn't trust Murray or her department, but if there was anything amiss it was better to discover it inside Thames House than out in the field when a mistake might well be a matter of life or death.

"Everything okay?" asked Murray as Shepherd flicked through the passport.

"All good, Susan, thanks."

"The other envelope contains articles and blog posts that were placed since you last checked the legend," she said. "You had a wonderful stay in the Maldives earlier this year."

Shepherd laughed. "Lucky me," he said.

She handed him a door key. "The flat is ready so you might as well take the key now. The burglar alarm code is your date of birth, not Whitehill's."

"I remember," said Shepherd.

"Of course you do," she said. Murray handed him a clipboard with a requisition form attached which he signed and dated.

He thanked her and headed out. Shepherd didn't have an office or even a desk of his own at Thames House, but there was a hot-desk room on the second floor with a dozen workstations. There were only two other people in the room, sitting well away from each other. Shepherd sat down at a terminal midway between the two of them and logged in.

The Gunfire Tours website was still showing vacancies for the forthcoming weekend trip. Shepherd opened an account in the name of John Whitehill and entered the Hampstead address and phone number, then he booked a place on the trip using the

Mastercard. His payment was accepted and shortly afterwards he received a confirmatory email. The email explained that the booking was for the trip in Serbia and that he would have to arrange his own flight. He could either make his own way to the hotel or he could be picked up at the airport.

He used the MI5 system to access flight records and searched for Gary Dexter. He had a booking on a Friday evening Air Serbia flight that would arrive in Belgrade at 5p.m. He went to the Air Serbia website and booked himself onto the same flight, paying for it with his Whitehill Amex card. He received a confirmation email within seconds

He sat back and smiled to himself. He was good to go. His phone buzzed and he checked the screen. It was Katra. He answered, cupping his hand over his mouth. "Hi, sorry I haven't called for a while, I've been really busy," he said.

"It's okay," she said. "You're always busy these days."

"I know, I'm sorry. They've had me on several cases at the same time. I've literally not stopped."

"But you're coming back this weekend, right?"

"I'm sorry, something's come up."

She sighed. "Dan, you promised."

"I didn't promise. I know I did say I'd be home but I can't ever promise something like that. That's not how the job works."

"Where are you going?"

"Europe," he said. He wasn't supposed to tell anyone, even family members, where he was when he

188

was on official business. "I'm leaving Friday and I'll be back Sunday evening."

"So that's the weekend gone. Again."

"I know, I'm sorry. But this is important."

"It's always important." She sighed. "I'm sorry, Dan, I don't want to sound like a nag but Liam is coming this weekend, remember? He'll be disappointed."

"He's in the Army now, Katra, he knows the way the world works."

"The job comes first? Yes, he knows. You were always away when he was growing up and now you're both away all the time."

"Why don't you come to London next week?"

"You'll have time?"

"I'll be working, obviously. But all the jobs are either in London or close by, so I'll be able to see you in the evenings."

"Maybe," she said.

Shepherd could tell from her voice that she was still far from happy, but he knew there was nothing he could do to make her feel better.

"We'll have dinner, maybe catch a show," he said.

"Okay," she said. Again there was a hesitation in her voice.

"Is there something wrong?" he asked. There was no answer. "Katra?"

"There's something I need to talk to you about, but it can wait," she said.

"Tell me now."

"It's not something I want to talk about on the phone. It's okay, Dan, it can wait."

"Are you sure?"

"I'm sure."

Again he could hear her uncertainty but before he could say anything she had said goodbye and ended the call. He put his phone away. He sat back in his chair and took the cuttings out of the envelope. He read through them, effortlessly committing them to memory, then used the Whitehill phone to log onto the Whitehill Twitter account. The footies had done a good job of keeping his online presence active, posting at least once a day, usually commenting on something in that day's papers. When he'd finished he ran the cuttings through a shredder.

Shepherd arrived at Heathrow Terminal 4 at about eleven-thirty on Friday morning. He checked in for the Air Serbia flight using his John Whitehill passport. He was wearing a leather jacket and cargo pants and had a black baseball cap with "LONDON" across the front.

He only had carry-on luggage — a small black nylon holdall — and it took him less than twenty minutes to pass through security. As he walked through the departures area he spotted Gary Dexter in the Prince of Wales bar, holding a pint of lager and talking to a group of five other men. They were all casually dressed in jeans, polo shirts and jackets. One of the group was West Indian, and he was laughing loudly at something Dexter had said.

Shepherd walked by the bar, bought himself a coffee and found a seat that gave him a view of Dexter's group. He already knew the identities of the men

190

Dexter was travelling with. Their details had been downloaded from the airline's database through a Europol request. Serbia was not a full member of the European Union but had signed a cooperation agreement with Europol in 2014 and the details had come through within four hours of the request being sent in. Shepherd had called up their passport and driving licence details, and run their names through the Police National Computer.

The West Indian was Charlie Palmer, no criminal record and no driving licence. Other than his name and address, Shepherd knew nothing about him. Two others were also upstanding citizens who had only come into contact with the police through driving offences — four speeding tickets between them. Joe Atkinson was a rubbish collector working for Camden Council, Simon Hewson was a personal trainer with his own fitness company. Shepherd had checked out the company's website — Hewson specialised in boot camps for overweight housewives, usually giving them workouts in local parks.

The remaining two members of Dexter's group were less savoury. Both had served time in prison. Roger Moorhouse had done two years for a serious assault after an argument outside a pub in Beckenham, and Matthew Scott had served five years for an arson attack in Ealing. There had been a racial element to both crimes. The man Moorhouse had attacked had been a British-born Pakistani and the house that Scott had set fire to had been home to a Somalian family. Both men had been to court many times, usually on charges of criminal damage or breach of the peace, and Moorhouse had been cautioned several times over cannabis use. Moorhouse and Scott were both listed as being members of the British Crusaders, and Moorhouse was listed as treasurer on the group's website.

They sank a couple of pints each and at forty minutes before the departure time they headed to the gate. Shepherd followed at a safe distance.

They had to wait again for boarding and Shepherd sat some distance away. They boarded at one o'clock on the dot. Shepherd was sitting at the back of the plane close to the toilets. He dozed through most of the flight.

They landed at Belgrade Airport at exactly 5 p.m. He was one of the last passengers off the plane but immigration was efficient and he was in the arrivals area just half an hour later.

Dexter and his group were standing next to a man in a fleece holding an iPad with the words "GUNFIRE TOURS" on it, along with a middle-aged couple wearing waterproof jackets and carrying backpacks. Shepherd headed over. "Sorry," he said to the man holding the iPad. "John Whitehill. I was at the back of the plane." He looked over at Dexter's group. "Sorry, guys, didn't mean to hold you up."

Dexter waved away his apology. The man checked his iPad and nodded. "Right, we're all here," he said, in a heavy accent. "Follow me to the bus."

Shepherd walked with him as they headed towards the exit. "I didn't catch your name," said Shepherd.

"Branko," said the man. He was a couple of inches taller than Shepherd, wearing a camouflage jacket, baggy cargo pants and heavy boots. His hair was receding and what was left was oiled and brushed back. He had thin lips and grey, slab-like teeth that gave the impression he was wearing a boxer's mouth guard.

"Are you one of the instructors?"

Branko grunted.

"Excellent," he said. "I'm looking forward to it."

"Have you fired a gun before?"

"No," lied Shepherd. "It's going to be a first for me."

"You'll enjoy it," said Branko. "Everyone does."

They left the terminal building. There was a coach waiting, with a "GUNFIRE TOURS" sign in the window. Branko waved for Shepherd to climb on board. He got in and chose a seat halfway down. The middle-aged couple were next and they sat across the aisle from Shepherd. The man leaned over and offered his hand. "Ian McAdam," he said. "This is the wife, Carol."

They shook hands, then Carol reached over and shook. They both looked to be in their fifties. He was grey haired, short with a pugnacious look in his eyes. His wife had brown hair so chestnut that it was almost certainly dyed and had unzipped her waterproof jacket to reveal an impressive amount of cleavage. "Pleased to meet you," she said.

"We're from Cumbria," said the husband.

"Lovely part of the world," said Shepherd.

"When it's not raining," said Carol as she released her grip on his hand.

"You?" asked Ian. "Where are you from?"

"London, these days," said Shepherd.

"Ever done anything like this before?"

"First time," said Shepherd.

"Us too," he said. "Carol here bought it for my birthday present."

"Nice," said Shepherd.

Branko pulled the door shut. "So, this is everyone," he said. "My name is Branko, I'll be taking care of you this weekend. And I'll be one of your instructors." He patted the driver on the shoulder and he twisted around and waved. His was in his sixties with a steel grey crew cut and a Desperate Dan chin. He was wearing a sheepskin jacket that was stained and scuffed from years of use. "This is Gordan," said Branko. "He'll be driving us and is also an instructor. The hotel is about an hour away, maybe an hour and a half, so sit back and enjoy the scenery."

He sat down. Gordan put the coach in gear and drove off.

Shepherd stretched out as best as he could. They drove out of the airport and headed west. They were soon driving through featureless farmland. The road was reasonable but the coach's suspension had seen better days and it wasn't a smooth ride.

At one point they drove through woodland, then more farmland, passing through several small villages, usually a mixture of old stone cottages and new white-painted buildings with orange tiled roofs. Most of the other vehicles on the roads were mud-splattered

194

and rusting, though occasionally they were overtaken by a top-of-the-range Mercedes or BMW.

Shepherd had never been to Sid, but he knew of it. It was the site of the first attack on Serbian soil at the start of the Yugoslav Wars, when Croatian forces had fired artillery rockets into the city, killing four civilians and injuring another dozen. The town was close to the borders with both Bosnia and Croatia though in many places borders seemed arbitrary. Following the war there were virtually no Muslims in the area; the people were predominantly Serbs, Slovaks and Croats.

The drive took just over an hour. Their destination was a hotel in a small village on the outskirts of the town. It looked as if it had once been a farmhouse but the area around it was now peppered with flat-roofed industrial buildings and single-storey houses on small plots.

Gordan parked the coach and Branko opened the door and led them along a gravelled path to the main entrance. The reception area had a low ceiling with thick black beams running across it, and a tiled floor. There was a dark wood-panelled desk behind which stood a middle-aged woman with braided hair in a white blouse buttoned up to the neck. She smiled and welcomed them to the hotel in heavily accented English.

She had arranged envelopes on the desk with their names written on in capital letters. Branko handed them out. Shepherd opened his. Inside was a key with a wooden fob and a typed letter welcoming him, detailing the facilities of the hotel and telling him that if he

195

returned after ten o'clock the front door would be locked and that he would have to ring the doorbell to be admitted.

"We have arranged a buffet dinner for you tonight, in the bar," said Branko. "You can check in and shower, the food is ready whenever you want it." He pointed at a set of double doors to his left.

Shepherd's room was up a flight of stairs and at the end of the corridor. There was a single bed with a crucifix on the wall above it and a cheap dressing table with a mirror that was spotted with age. There was a small window offering him a view over the car park, and a chipboard wardrobe. There were two folded white towels at the foot of his bed, a big one and small one. He opened the wardrobe door and saw a mousetrap tucked away in the corner. He realised there was no en suite bathroom so he sat on the bed and read the letter he'd been given but there was no mention of having to share bathroom facilities.

He took out his mobile phone. He had a signal but only one bar. He phoned Katra but it went straight through to her voicemail. He really wanted to clean his teeth so he picked up his washbag and headed along the corridor. There was a bathroom three doors along. The door was open so he slipped inside and pulled a cord to switch on the light. There was a roll-top bath, a sink with another age-spotted mirror over it, and a walk-in shower with a shower head the size of a dinner plate. He cleaned his teeth, splashed water on his face and then realised there was no towel. He went back to his room and used the small towel on his bed to dry himself. He phoned Katra again but it went through to voicemail. Either her phone was off or she was on another call. He left a short message saying that he missed her and that he would call her back. Then he sent a short text message to a mobile number that connected him to an MI5 computer, just giving his location and confirming that he was okay. Pritchard would be able to access the file if he wanted to, but in all likelihood the message would only be read if something went wrong.

He went downstairs and into the restaurant. There was a bar running the width of the room, a buffet table facing the door, and a dozen or so square wooden tables each with four straight-backed chairs.

Dexter and Moorhouse were standing at the bar with Branko. Branko had taken off his jacket and rolled up his shirtsleeves to reveal a large black scorpion tattooed on his left forearm. Scott, Palmer and Atkinson were huddled together at the far end of the bar.

Shepherd walked up to the bar and ordered a lager shandy from a woman who looked like the daughter or younger sister of the woman at reception. It wasn't his favourite drink but he wanted to keep a clear head. "So you guys were all in the Army, here in Serbia?" Dexter asked Branko.

Branko nodded. "*Republika Srpska*," he said. "The Serbian Army."

Shepherd sipped his shandy and listened. The way Branko said it, he made it sound as if he had served in the Serbian equivalent of the British Army, but it was much more complicated than that. Bosnia and

197

Herzegovina had pulled out of Yugoslavia and at the same time some eighty thousand Bosnian Serb troops left the Yugoslav People's Army. They were joined by four thousand Christian mercenaries. In Britain they were called the Bosnian Serb Army, and were responsible for a host of atrocities across the former Yugoslavia, not the least being the July 1995 Srebrenica massacre when they murdered eight thousand Muslim men and boys.

Among the prime movers in the massacre were a paramilitary unit called the Scorpions, and Shepherd didn't think it was a coincidence that Branko had a scorpion tattoo on his arm. The Scorpions began life in 1991, the brainchild of the head of Serbia's State Security Services, Jovica Stanisic. He gave it to two brothers to run, Slobodan and Aleksandar Medić, and they named the group after their favourite weapon, the Skorpion, a Czech 7.65 mm machine pistol developed for special forces. The Scorpions became stormtroopers, inspiring fear in the non-Serb population. They were so brutal that after the war ended the Medic brothers were sentenced for war crimes. But Shepherd doubted that Branko would be telling them that story any time soon. He took another sip of his drink.

"You must have seen a lot of action," said Moorhouse.

Branko grinned. "Some," he said.

Shepherd was sure that Branko was being modest. The Bosnian War had been a vicious three-sided conflict between Muslims, Serbs and Croats who had been forced to live together in the former Yugoslavia.

198

According to estimates, the war had caused around one hundred thousand deaths and displaced more than two million people. It had been a messy conflict, one that was difficult for outsiders to understand. It quickly became a proxy war with Yugoslavia, Croatia, Muslim countries that supported the Bosnian Muslims, and NATO all throwing in men and weapons as if there was no tomorrow. So, yes, if he had been in the Scorpions, he would have seen a lot of action.

For his part, Shepherd had been in Sarajevo for two months in 1995, part of an eight-man SAS team tracking a deadly sniper who was killing men, women and children from his post high in the hills looking down on the town. The siege of Sarajevo ended in February 1996 after four brutal years during which time almost fourteen thousand people were killed, over a third of them civilians. There was every chance that Branko would have known the sniper.

"And what sort of guns will we be shooting tomorrow?" asked Moorhouse.

Hewson walked in and headed over to Dexter. Moorhouse waved at the barmaid and ordered a pint of lager for him.

"We'll start with some pistol work and some target practice," said Branko. "Then we'll shoot some bigger weapons. Uzis and Kalashnikovs. I have a nice sniping rifle you can all try, a Dragunov. How does that sound?"

Dexter nodded. "That's great. But we talked about some bigger stuff, right? Grenades and RPGs."

Branko pulled a face. "We can arrange that for you if that's what you want. But they're expensive and they'll be extra. The regular weapons and ammunition are included in the price you paid, but there will be an extra charge for grenades and RPGs."

"How much?" asked Dexter.

"Grenades are a hundred euros each. RPG rockets are two hundred and fifty euros."

"But you can definitely get them?" asked Dexter.

Branko waved his bread roll. "Of course. But I will want cash. It will have to be cash."

"And no receipts?" laughed Dexter. "Sure, not a problem. You can put me down for a grenade and a rocket. Charlie?"

"Sure, why the hell not?" said Palmer. You only live once."

Dexter looked at Atkinson and Hewson and they both nodded enthusiastically. "I'm up for it," said Moorhouse.

"Me too," said Scott. "That's why we're here, right?"

"What about you guys?" Dexter asked the McAdams.

They both shook their heads. "It's a bit rich for me," said the husband. His wife nodded in agreement.

Dexter looked over at Shepherd. "What about you, John? Are you a man or a mouse?"

"I'm up for it, yeah," said Shepherd. "But is it legal?"

Branko grinned. "It's a grey area, I think that is what you call it in English," he said. "But we have them in stock and we won't be seen here, so legal or not there's no problem."

"Then sure," said Shepherd. "I'll do it."

"Good man," said Dexter, turning back to Branko. "So that's seven grenades and seven rockets. Is that okay?"

"That's good," said Branko. "I'll need the cash up front."

"Now?"

"Is that okay?"

"I don't see why not," he said. "Give me a couple of minutes."

Dexter left the room and went upstairs to his room. When he reappeared a couple of minutes later he was holding an envelope which he gave to Branko. Branko opened it and ran his thumb along a stack of euros. "Two thousand four hundred and fifty euros," said Dexter. "Plus a couple of hundred for your trouble." Dexter winked at Branko and picked up his pint.

Branko looked over at Shepherd. Shepherd got the message and took out his wallet. He counted out seven fifty-euro notes and handed them over.

"Excellent," said Branko. "It looks as if it will be a fun day."

Liam Shepherd shouldered his backpack and walked out of Hereford station. He was almost six feet tall, his dark hair cut short, and he was wearing wire-framed Ray-Ban Aviator sunglasses. He was casually dressed in a dark blue polo shirt and Levi's jeans, the first time he had been out of Army fatigues in almost a week. He used his mobile phone to call a local minicab firm and a white Prius arrived within five minutes. He recognised the driver, a guy who had occasionally driven Liam from home to school when he was younger. The man asked Liam what he was up to. "I'm flying helicopters, for the Army," he said. "At least I will be when I've got my wings."

"What sort of helicopters?" asked the driver.

"At the moment I'm training on the Juno but I want to fly Apaches eventually."

"The ones that fire those missiles?"

"Yeah, those."

The driver nodded his approval. "Sweet," he said. "So are you being trained in Hereford?"

Liam shook his head. "Nah, I'm at the Defence Helicopter Flying School, RAF Shawbury. In Shropshire. I'm here to visit family."

The driver looked at Liam in his rear-view mirror. "You look bloody young to be a helicopter pilot," he said. "So what rank are you?"

"Second Lieutenant," said Liam.

"Nice. I suppose I should salute you."

They arrived outside the house. Liam climbed out and took his backpack with him. The driver tooted his horn as he drove off. Katra's red Nissan Juke was parked in front of the garage but there was no sign of his father's car. Liam gritted his teeth. It wouldn't be the first time that his father had let him down.

He walked up to the front door and used his key to let himself in. "Katra?" he called, but there was no reply. He went through to the kitchen and put his backpack on a chair, then switched on the kettle. He was bursting for a cup of tea.

He went to the bottom of the stairs. "Katra?" he called, but again there was no reply. He went upstairs. The main bedroom door was open but she wasn't there. The door to his bedroom was closed but he doubted that she would be in there. He was just about to check the spare bedroom when the door to the en suite bathroom opened. She gasped when she saw him. Liam was equally surprised; her eyes were red and her cheeks were wet and she had obviously been crying. "Is it Dad?" he asked, his heart pounding. "Has something happened to Dad?"

She shook her head and dabbed at her eyes. "No. But he's working this weekend. He says he's sorry but something important came up."

"You have to expect that with Dad," he said. "There's no need to get upset."

She forced a smile. "I know," she said.

"So what are you crying about?"

She dabbed her eyes again. "Nothing," she said.

"It's obviously not nothing," he said. "Look, I'll go downstairs and make you a cup of tea and you can tell me what the problem is."

Liam was halfway through his mug of tea when Katra came downstairs. She had redone her make-up but her eyes were still red from crying. She sat down at the kitchen table and he put her tea in front of her. It was in her favourite mug, white with "WORLD'S BEST AU PAIR" on it in pink capital letters. Liam had bought it for her birthday ten years earlier and while the lettering had started to fade she still used it every day. She picked it up and sipped it. She had tied her brown hair back and it emphasised how tired she looked.

"What's wrong?" asked Liam.

"Nothing," she said.

"You were crying."

She shrugged.

"Is it because Dad isn't here?"

She shook her head. "No, I'm used to that. We both are. That's his job. When he works, he often works twenty-four-seven."

"So what is it, then?"

Katra brushed a lock of hair behind her ear. Tears welled up in her eyes again and she looked away. Liam hurried over to the counter top and tore off a piece of kitchen roll for her. She wiped her eyes with it.

"Please, Katra, tell me. Maybe I can help?"

She shook her head. "I don't think anyone can help," she said.

He sat down and looked at her earnestly. "I'm not a kid any more, Katra. Tell me what's happened."

She dabbed at her eyes again. "I have a problem in Slovenia. A big problem."

"What? What happened?"

Katra swallowed and then closed her eyes as if she was gathering her thoughts. "My mother needed money. I said I'd send her some but your dad has been so busy I didn't, then my sister borrowed some money."

"Mia?"

Katra nodded. "She went to a man who helps people, and he did. She took the money from the man but then she had trouble paying him back and now he's making her work in this . . ." She shuddered. "This terrible place."

"What do you mean?"

"She has to work in a brothel to pay back the money she has borrowed."

"What? Where?"

"Not far from where our house is. They won't let her leave but she managed to phone my mum."

Liam sat back. "Katra, you need to talk to the police."

She shook her head. "No, the man she borrowed the money from, he pays the police. It's not like England. Here you can trust the police. In Slovenia . . ." She shrugged. "I don't know what to do, I'm sorry."

"And you haven't told Dad?"

"He's just too busy. I was going to talk to him about it today but now he says he can't come."

"How much money did Mia borrow?"

"Eight thousand euros."

Liam smiled. "Is that all?" He sighed. "I thought you were talking about hundreds of thousands. Katra, I've got that much in my bank right now."

She looked at him tearfully. "Really?"

He laughed. "I'm not a kid any more," he said. "I'm an Army officer. I get paid decent money and I'm training so hard I don't get time to spend it. I can fix this for you."

"Are you sure?"

His smile widened. "Of course. Look, you and I can fly to Slovenia first thing tomorrow, we'll go and see this guy and talk to him and I'll pay what your family owes and we're all good."

"I should talk to Dan first," she said.

"There's no need," said Liam. "We'll fly out tomorrow, back on Sunday, and everything will be sorted. We don't even have to bother Dad."

"Are you sure?"

Liam grinned. "Definitely," he said. "Now wipe your face while I book our flights."

Shepherd set his phone to wake him at seven thirty. He showered and shaved and put on a pair of black jeans and a blue denim shirt. He looked out of the window and decided that it was cold enough to take a pullover in addition to his jacket. He picked up his baseball cap and Ray-Ban sunglasses and went downstairs. The McAdams were already in the restaurant, sitting at a table and tucking into a plate of cheese, salami and fruit, with chunks of what smelled like freshly baked bread.

There was a buffet table against one wall with a coffee maker and two jugs, one regular and one decaf. Shepherd poured himself a mug of regular coffee and added a splash of milk. As he was helping himself to bread and cheese, two men wearing camouflage fatigues walked in. Shepherd recognised one of them from the website, and smiled. "Are you with Gunfire Tours?" he asked.

The two men nodded. The taller of the two stuck out his hand. He was the one that Shepherd had seen on the website. "Luka," he said. He was broad-shouldered and had short curly jet-black hair. He had Oakley sunglasses pushed up onto the top of his head. His shirt sleeves were rolled up and like Branko he had a tattoo of a scorpion on his left forearm. "I'm one of the instructors. This is Neno."

Neno was short and wiry, with dark green eyes and a mischievous smile. He offered his hand to shake. He had a strong grip and he looked Shepherd in the eye as he shook.

"I'm John," said Shepherd. "John Whitehill."

"Are you with the Dexter group?" asked Neno.

"I'm here on my own," said Shepherd.

"Ever shot before?"

"Never," lied Shepherd. "I'm really looking forward to it."

"You'll enjoy it," said Luka, patting Shepherd on the shoulder.

The two instructors picked up plates and began filling them with food. Shepherd sat down at an empty table. After a few minutes Gary Dexter arrived with Charlie Palmer and Joe Atkinson. They were all wearing pullovers and jeans and Nike trainers. They greeted Shepherd and the McAdams, then went over to the buffet. The rest of Dexter's friends arrived shortly afterwards and Dexter pushed two tables together so that they could sit as a group.

Luka and Neno sat at a table and tucked into their breakfast. Shepherd sat alone and ate. He really wanted to be sitting with Dexter and his friends but he didn't want to appear too eager. There would be time enough for bonding, and he was close enough to hear everything that was said. The talk was mainly about football. Dexter and Palmer were Millwall fans, Hewson, Atkinson and Scott supported Chelsea and Moorhouse followed West Ham, so there was plenty of teasing and bantering.

At eight-thirty sharp Branko turned up. Like his colleagues, he was wearing desert camouflage fatigues and Timberland boots. He rounded everyone up and took them outside to where Gordan was already behind the wheel of the coach. They all piled in, Gordan started the engine and they pulled away from the hotel. They drove along the main road for about a mile, then turned onto a smaller road that wound its way through farmland that had been freshly ploughed. The coach slowed and turned onto a narrow muddy track that cut through two low hills. The area was fenced off with chicken wire but many of the posts had rotted and fallen over.

The track curved around to the left and they drove into a large quarry. It was several hundred yards across, a grey wall of granite facing them. There were marks on the quarry wall from where explosives had been used to dislodge the rock. Commercial quarrying seemed to have stopped as there was no heavy equipment around and the quarry faces were covered with moss in places.

Gordan brought the coach to a halt and Branko pulled the door open. As they climbed out they saw a tent off to the left, and behind the tent two blue plastic Portaloos. The sky overhead was clear of clouds and Shepherd put on his Ray-Bans against the bright sun.

208

Two pickup trucks were parked to the left of the tent and two men that Shepherd hadn't seen before were pulling folding tables and chairs from the back of one truck and stacking them on the ground.

About fifty yards from the tents was a line of white-painted wooden targets shaped roughly like armless people with bullseye targets pinned to their chests.

Branko pointed out the toilets to the group, then took them to the tent. There was a large table with a white cloth over it on one side, and on the other was a long metal table on which there was a line of handguns. From where he was standing Shepherd could see they were all Glocks. Next to the guns was a clear plastic bin containing ear protectors and another bin full of safety glasses. Luka and Neno were standing at one end of the table, slotting cartridges into magazines.

Branko went over to a holdall on the floor underneath the metal table and pulled out a nylon holster that he strapped to his hip. Then he picked up a Glock and a magazine. He had the group gather around him and then he slowly described the working parts and how the firearm operated.

When he'd finished he asked if there were any questions. No one had any so Branko divided them into three groups. Shepherd found himself with the McAdams which was a pity but as the other guys were a group it made sense.

Branko took care of Dexter, Palmer and Atkinson, Gordan went with Hewson, Moorhouse and Scott, and Neno looked after Shepherd and the McAdams.

Neno took them over to the table and gave them a gun each and a magazine. Shepherd's was a Glock 17 that looked as if it had been used a lot. The magazine was standard with seventeen 9 x 19 mm rounds in it. Ian McAdam also had a Glock 17 but Neno gave his wife a Glock 19. It was slightly smaller and held fifteen rounds in the clip, but the weight was pretty much the same and the trigger pull was identical, five and a half pounds. Neno described the various parts of the gun again, and pointed out the trigger safety mechanism. Then he told them to help themselves to ear protectors and safety glasses and took them over to the line of targets.

The wall of the quarry was about a hundred feet behind the targets which meant that loose rounds wouldn't be going astray. In between the quarry wall and the targets was a pile of sandbags, about nine feet tall. The sandbags were a good idea as with rock there was always the risk of a dangerous ricochet.

"Right, everyone put on their ear defenders and glasses," said Branko. "Then we are good to go. Those of you wearing sunglasses will need to replace them with the safety glasses."

They all did as they were told. The instructors also put on their ear and eye protection before splitting the group into three. Neno took the McAdams couple and Shepherd over to the far end of the line of targets. "John here is a virgin," said Neno. "What about you two? Have either of you fired a gun before?"

Ian and Carol McAdam shook their heads.

"You can relax," said Neno. "It's great fun. All you have to do is think safety first. When you're not aiming the gun, you keep your finger off the trigger. And you do not point the gun at anything other than the target, not even as a joke. And third, always assume the gun is loaded. The only time you are one hundred per cent sure a gun is not loaded is when you remove the magazine and pull the slide back and look down the barrel with your own eyes. Get it?"

All three nodded and Neno grinned. "Right, let's start with you, Carol. Point your gun down the range and pull back the slide to slot a round into the chamber."

Neno was a good instructor; he was patient and calm and clearly knew what he was doing. He checked that Carol had chambered a round, then stood slightly behind her and talked her through it. Her hands were shaking and she had a fixed grin on her face but Neno continued to talk to her in a soft voice as though he were calming a spooked horse. She pulled the trigger. The gun jerked and the shot went wide. She started to turn to look at her husband but Neno had anticipated the move and his hand was already out to keep the gun aiming towards the sandbags.

He talked her through it again and this time she was calmer, but the shot went high. The third shot hit the target and she squealed with pleasure. Neno smiled at her enthusiasm and explained about the sight picture and how she needed to line the sights up with the target and focus on them.

She fired again but rushed it and this time the round went low, thudding into the stand below the bullseye. Neno explained about breathing, how she needed to take a breath and release half of it before gently squeezing the trigger. She nodded, frowned as she concentrated, and fired. The round hit the absolute centre of the bullseye and she yelped with excitement.

"Well done," said Neno, though he must have known it was a complete fluke.

She fired off the rest of the shots and while none hit the centre again she did have several within the bullseye. Once she had fired off all fifteen rounds, Neno took the gun from her, pulled back the slide to check that there wasn't a round in the chamber and gave it back to her. "Well done," he said. "For a first time, you did well."

Her husband hugged her. "That was such fun," she said.

"I'm going to have to be on my best behaviour from now on," laughed her husband.

There were more shots off to the left. Branko was watching over Dexter as he fired his gun. Dexter fired quickly and by the look of it most of his shots were missing the target. Branko didn't seem to care and when Dexter had finished he took the gun off him and checked it was empty, before waving for Atkinson to fire.

Atkinson pulled back the slide, shrugged his shoulders, then aimed the gun gangster-style, rotated ninety degrees with the butt parallel to the ground.

Shepherd assumed that Branko would correct his technique but the Serb just watched impassively as Atkinson emptied his magazine. To Shepherd's surprise several of his shots were in the bullseye but it was clearly more by luck than judgement.

Moorhouse and Hewson were watching as Gordan corrected Scott's stance and showed him how to support his right hand with his left.

Neno had Ian McAdam chamber a round, then had him shoot at the target. He was marginally better than his wife. When he'd emptied the magazine, Neno took the gun from him and checked it was clear. Then he turned to Shepherd. "Ready?" he said.

"Hell, yeah," said Shepherd. He grinned at the instructor. At this short range he could quite happily have put all the rounds in a fifty-pence piece but Whitehill was a beginner and that was how he had to come across.

He pointed the gun at the ground and attempted to pull back the slide but failed. He flashed Neno an embarrassed smile. "Sorry," he said. He tried again and this time slotted a cartridge home.

He listened as Neno briefed him about the sight picture, but he kept his hand loose as he aimed at the target and jerked the trigger so that the gun jumped in his hand. The round clipped the top of the target. "At least you hit it," said Neno, patting him on the back.

"Thanks," said Shepherd.

"Try again."

Shepherd fired again, this time aiming high. He missed the target completely and the round thudded into the sandbags. "Sorry," he said.

"Relax your shoulders," said Neno. "And tighten your grip. Don't be scared of it. You have to control it, don't let it control you."

"Okay," said Shepherd. He fired again and hit just above the bullseye.

"Better," said Neno. "Now do everything the same but aim just a fraction lower."

Shepherd did as he was told but loosened his grip and the shot went wide. "Shit," he said.

Neno patted him on the shoulder. "It's okay, you're doing fine," he said. "You'll get there."

Shepherd would have loved to have shown the Serb just how proficient he was with a Glock, but that would have blown his cover, so he fired almost randomly, allowing the rounds to pepper the wooden target with only about half in the bullseye. He was mentally counting off the shots but he kept on pulling the trigger after he got to seventeen.

"You're out," said Neno, taking the gun from him. Neno checked to be sure and then gave the gun back to Shepherd.

"You all did really well considering it was your first time," he said. "As soon as they've finished we'll go and take a closer look at your targets and we can take some photographs. Later we'll do some balloon shooting."

"Balloons?"

"Just a bit of fun," said Neno. "You'll love it."

214

They stood and watched as the rest of the group continued to fire at the targets. Roger Moorhouse was the last to finish, watched over by Gordan. Moorhouse was surprisingly good for a beginner. He had a good strong stance and his breathing was controlled. Shepherd wasn't sure if Moorhouse was following Gordan's instructions but he was firing in groups of two, breathing tidally between each group. The last ten shots all went into the inner two rings of the bullseye.

When he'd emptied the magazine, Gordan checked the gun and then raised his hand, the signal that it was okay to approach the targets.

Neno took Shepherd and the McAdams over to the targets and helped them unclip the bullseyes. The husband gave Neno his phone and the Serb took several pictures of the couple proudly showing off the results of their handiwork.

Neno offered to take a picture of Shepherd. It was the last thing he wanted — he could only imagine what his former SAS mates would say if they'd seen how badly he'd shot — but Shepherd faked eagerness, gave his phone to Neno and grinned happily as the man took several shots.

Dexter and his pals were gathered around, comparing results and teasing each other.

Luka, Gordan and Neno took the Glocks back to the tent and returned with a Kalashnikov, an Uzi and a Heckler & Koch MP5, the first carbine that Shepherd had used in the SAS.

"Right, lady and gentlemen," said Branko. "Time for you to experience some more serious fire power." He

215

had them line up some fifty feet from the targets, then had Luka, Gordan and Neno describe the weapons they were holding and demonstrate how they were fired. When they had finished, Branko told the group to form three lines behind the instructors. Shepherd stood with the married couple behind Neno, who had the MP5.

Neno explained how the MP5 worked and set it to fire in bursts of three shots. He had Carol fire it first, aiming at the target on the far right. Off to their left was the *thud-thud-thud* of a Kalashnikov being fired. Shepherd looked over and saw Dexter holding the weapon with Branko standing just behind him.

Carol emptied the magazine and Neno reloaded and gave the gun to her husband. As he fired, Hewson let rip with the Uzi. It had obviously been set to fully automatic and within seconds Hewson had emptied the clip.

Ian emptied the MP5 in bursts of three, and Neno reloaded and gave it to Shepherd. "I just pull the trigger once, right?" asked Shepherd, pretending not to know how the gun worked.

"Each time you pull the trigger it will fire three times," said Neno. "There is very little recoil."

Shepherd aimed and pulled the trigger and felt the familiar triple kick as three bullets thwacked into the target. There were fifteen rounds in the magazine so after five pulls the gun was empty.

"Well done," said Neno, though Shepherd had made sure that his shots were spread all over the target.

216

They waited for Moorhouse to finish firing the Kalashnikov, then Shepherd and the McAdams went over to Branko and the other two groups moved down.

After thirty minutes they had all fired each of the weapons, and once they were checked and cleared they spent another fifteen minutes posing for photographs.

While they took selfies and group shots, Neno and Branko went over to the tent. By the time the group had finished taking their photographs, they had filled several balloons from a large brown metal cylinder behind the table. Brown meant helium, Shepherd knew, then he remembered what Neno had said about balloons. The two men were filling different coloured balloons with the helium and tying strings around the necks. Luka and Neno put the Kalashnikov, Uzi and MP5 on the metal table then took the balloons that had been filled over to the targets. They tied two balloons to each target so that they hovered a couple of feet in the air.

As Luka and Neno headed back to the tent, a van came rattling down the track towards them. It was an old Citroën, with a logo of a leaking tap that suggested it belonged to a plumber. It stopped by the tent and a big bald man wearing a leather jerkin and knee-length leather boots climbed out. Neno and Luka went over as the man opened the rear door of the van. They began pulling out crates and putting them on the ground. One of the boxes had Serbian writing on the side and Shepherd saw M75 among the stencils. Shepherd knew the M75 was a type of anti-personnel grenade, known as a Kashikara, manufactured in Yugoslavia and widely used throughout the Yugoslav Wars.

There were other larger crates that didn't have writing on the side but they looked plenty big enough to hold RPGs. Finally the two men pulled out large serving dishes covered with aluminium foil, and a basket of bread rolls. As the driver got back in the van and drove away, Neno and Luka carried the dishes and basket over to the tables.

"Right guys, we're going to have a competition," said Branko, tying off a blue balloon. He nodded over at the targets where there were already twelve balloons bobbing in the wind. "You'll take it in turns to shoot the balloons. You'll be a bit further away this time but you can take your time. You do six shots each and the one who bursts the most gets a prize." He gave the balloon to Luka, opened his backpack and took out a bottle and held it up. "The one who shoots the most balloons gets this slivovitz," he said. "Plum brandy, one hundred per cent proof. It will put hairs on your chest." He put it on the table.

"I'm not sure I'd want that," said Carol and all the men laughed.

"Branko, this isn't fair," said Scott. "Charlie was in the army. The Royal Anglian Regiment."

Branko squinted at Scott. "Royal Anglian?"

"Infantry," explained Dexter. "Cannon fodder. He did five years. The boy can shoot."

"Rifles," said Palmer, holding his hands up. "I hardly ever touched a handgun."

"A gun's a gun," said Hewson.

218

"And you did get four in the bullseye," said Dexter. He grinned at Branko. "Maybe we could give him a handicap?"

"Yeah, how about a blindfold?" asked Moorhouse.

Branko laughed. "Okay, we'll put Charlie a bit further away," he said.

"Fuck that," said Palmer. "I was never good with a pistol. My hands are too big."

"Here we go, we know what else is big, right?" laughed Dexter.

Palmer laughed and slapped Dexter on the back.

Luka and Neno attached the final balloons to the targets. There were nine targets and eighteen balloons in total, a mixture of red, blue, green and yellow. The targets had been lined up close to the wall of the quarry, about forty feet from where they were shooting. At that sort of distance most handguns were capable of a grouping of less than two inches in a bench firing, but in the hands of amateurs and with the balloons bobbing in the wind that was blowing across the quarry, Shepherd didn't expect to see many of them pop. When he was at the SAS's Hereford base he spent a lot of time on the range there, and one of the instructors had explained to him early on that accuracy on the range was less about the shooter and more about the quality of the gun and the ammunition in the clip. The instructor had said that in his opinion a quarter was down to the shooter, a quarter to the gun and a half to the ammo. Shepherd figured the man was right, but accuracy on the range was totally different to accuracy in combat. When you were shooting at targets who were

219

moving and shooting back, Shepherd knew that it was all down to the man. The type of gun and the ammo didn't really matter when you were ducking and diving and firing on instinct.

"Ladies first," said Branko, slotting a magazine into a Glock. He had Carol face the targets and stood behind her. She frowned as she brought the gun to bear on the balloon on the far right and Branko whispered her some advice. She began to pull the trigger but her grip was scrappy and she didn't seem to be using the sights. All six rounds went wide and thwacked into the quarry wall.

Her husband was next. Branko passed the gun to him. He had clearly been listening to Neno. He had a good firm stance and his left hand was cupped around his right as he gently squeezed the trigger. A balloon tied to the second target exploded and the string holding it flopped down. He laughed. "That's not the one I was aiming for," he said. Everyone laughed but Shepherd was pretty sure the man was joking. The next two shots went wide but his fourth hit the balloon on the far right. The last two shots missed. Branko took the gun from him, clapped him on the back and congratulated him. "Two balloons hit, well done."

Luka and Neno jogged over with a new balloon each and tied them in position.

Branko slotted a fresh magazine into the Glock and handed it to Shepherd. Shepherd could feel his natural competitiveness trying to kick in. He would have loved to have shown them what he could do. He knew that he was perfectly capable of taking out six balloons at double the distance and on the move. But he was John Whitehill and Whitehill was a gun virgin so he figured the best he could do was to match Ian's score. He didn't mind not winning the bottle of slivovitz, he had never been a fan of the fiery brandy, but his professional pride was definitely hurting from pretending to be a lousy shot. He pulled back the slide and slotted a round into the chamber.

"Take it nice and slowly, and remember to use the sights," said Neno, standing at his shoulder.

Shepherd nodded and aimed at the first balloon, then moved the barrel to the right and fired, allowing the gun to jerk in his hand.

"A bit more to the left," said Neno.

This time Shepherd aimed to the left and fired. The round smacked into the sandbags.

"Too far," said Neno patiently.

Shepherd aimed and fired and this time a blue balloon burst. Carol clapped. "Well done, John!" she said.

Shepherd deliberately missed with his next two shots, but popped a yellow balloon with his final round.

"So we have a draw," said Branko, taking the gun from him.

Shepherd stepped back and saw that Luka was looking at him with a slight frown on his face. Shepherd flashed him a thumbsup and Luka smiled back and mirrored the gesture, but his eyes remained hard and Shepherd wondered if the Serb had realised that Shepherd had deliberately missed with four of his shots. He pushed the thought from his mind. One of the problems with being undercover was a tendency to jump at shadows and it was a reaction that had to be controlled.

"Right, who's next?" asked Branko.

Atkinson stepped forward and Branko prepared the Glock for him. Atkinson turned the gun gangster-style and fired six shots in quick succession, all going low and thwacking into the targets.

"Wanker!" shouted Moorhouse.

"The sights are off!" shouted Atkinson.

"You weren't using the bloody sights," said Dexter and they all laughed.

Branko took the gun off him, shaking his head in disgust.

Dexter was next and he managed just two balloons. Hewson managed three to his obvious delight, doing a little victory dance after handing the Glock back to Branko.

Moorhouse only managed to pop one balloon, and Scott hit two.

They left Palmer until last. Branko moved everyone back so that they were another twenty feet away from the targets. Sixty feet in all. Branko gave Palmer the gun. Palmer confidently pulled back the Glock's slide and slotted a round into the chamber.

Palmer's friends fell silent as he took a deep breath, relaxed his shoulders, then stood with his left leg slightly forward and bent, the right hand on the butt of the gun and his left hand cupped around it. "Go on, Charlie!" shouted Dexter, though Shepherd figured it was more an attempt to distract Palmer than to support him.

Palmer sighted on the balloon on the left of the middle target, and squeezed the trigger. The bullet went low and thudded into the head of the target. Palmer took a breath, let half of it out, and squeezed the trigger a second time. The balloon popped and the bits of yellow rubber fell to the ground. He aimed at the other balloon tied to that target and fired again. Another hit.

His friends started whooping and cheering but Palmer was in the zone; he fired three more times and each time a balloon popped. He handed the gun back to Branko and raised his arms in the air. Dexter and Moorhouse hurried over and patted him on the back.

"An almost perfect score!" shouted Branko. "Five out of six. Well done!" Branko checked the gun and put it into his holster. Neno gave Branko the bottle of slivovitz and he presented it to Palmer. His friends took out their phones and began taking selfies.

"Right guys — and girl — it's time for lunch," said Branko. He waved his hand at the metal tables where the aluminium foil had been taken off the serving trays. In the middle one was a whole suckling pig, glistening in barbecue sauce.

Dexter laughed when he saw it. "Not expecting any muzzies, hey, Branko?"

Branko's forehead creased into a frown. "Muzzies?" he repeated.

"Muslims," explained Dexter.

Branko burst out laughing. "Muzzies," he said. "Okay, I get it. No, we don't have any muzzies on these trips."

Gordan mimed shooting a gun. "If we did, we'd use them as targets," he said.

Dexter and his friends laughed.

Shepherd went over to the table. There were dishes of barbecued chicken, sausages, coleslaw, baked potatoes, peppers stuffed with rice and minced meat, and a green bean stew. On the floor next to the table was a blue icebox with a white lid that was full of cans of soft drinks, including Coke, Sprite and Fanta, and bottles of water.

Neno was putting out chairs and tables and Luka was stacking plates, knives and forks. Using the old Army principle that you never turned down food because you never knew where your next meal was coming from, Shepherd went over and filled a plate. The pig was perfectly cooked, the skin crisp and fatty, the meat lean and succulent. He carried his laden plate and a bottle of water over to a table where Charlie Palmer was tucking into a chicken leg with gusto. Shepherd sat down opposite him. "Nice shooting," he said.

"Just lucky," said Palmer. "I've hardly ever fired a handgun. Like I said, I mainly used a rifle."

"So you were in the Army, yeah?" asked Shepherd.

Palmer nodded. "Royal Anglian Regiment. First Battalion, based in Woolwich."

"See any action?"

Palmer shook his head. "I missed all that," he said. "Just training and there were so many cuts that most of that was boring crap. And they counted every round so we hardly did any live fire shooting." He shrugged. "Waste of time if you ask me."

Shepherd knew that Palmer was right. The British Army's staffing and resources had been cut to the bone over the years. The SAS suffered less than most, but there was no doubt that defending the realm was a long way down the government's list of priorities, no matter who was running the country. Despite the cuts, the SAS still spent a small fortune on equipment and training, and an SAS trooper often fired more rounds in a day than a regular soldier would fire in his whole career.

"That's why you left?"

Palmer put down a chewed bone and licked his fingers. "Pretty much."

"What about now?"

"I work security. Close protection when I can get it, static security if there's nothing else."

Shepherd wondered if Palmer worked with Gary Dexter's brother, but there was no way he could raise the subject without causing suspicion, so he just smiled and nodded and tucked into his roast pork.

"What sort of stuff do you write?" asked Palmer.

"Travel features, mainly. Basically I'm a hack, I'll write for anyone who pays me."

"But you're not writing about what we're doing?"

"Not the guys personally. But a travel piece about what's on offer, maybe. I might do a feature on

225

adventure holidays, you know? Skydiving. Paramotoring. Clay pigeon shooting."

"I wouldn't want to see my name in print," Palmer said, picking up another chicken leg.

Atkinson came over with his plate and joined them. "Jammy bastard," he said to Palmer.

"I'm a highly trained professional," said Palmer, then he waved his chicken leg as he laughed. "Mate, I'm as surprised as you are."

Branko walked over to another table, carrying a plate piled high with pork and chicken in one hand, and two bread rolls in his other.

"I could do with a beer, Branko," said Atkinson.

"Alcohol and guns do not mix," said Branko. "But we have cold beer for when we've finished." He nodded at the bottle in front of Palmer. "And we can all drink his prize."

Branko sat down at a table and was joined by Luka and Gordan with piled plates. All three men began tucking in.

Palmer waved his chicken leg at Shepherd. "I was just telling John here, I don't want my name appearing in any article he writes."

"For fuck's sake, no," said Atkinson. "I don't want my bosses knowing I was over here firing guns. Mum's the fucking word."

"Sure, no problem," said Shepherd. "It'll only be a travel piece, not about the people on the trip."

Atkinson waved his knife in Shepherd's face. "You'd better fucking not, that's all I'm saying."

"Trust me," said Shepherd.

226

"It's not about trusting you," said Atkinson. "It's about what we'll do to you if you let us down."

Liam had booked seats on a midday EasyJet flight from Stansted. It was a three-and-a-half-hour drive from Hereford so it was still dark when they left the house. They had checked in online and had no luggage and made the flight in plenty of time. The plane landed at Ljubljana Jože Pučnik Airport five minutes early but it took them almost an hour to get through immigration. They rented a Renault Clio from the Enterprise desk and collected the car outside.

Liam drove and Katra gave him directions. She was wearing a black polo-neck sweater and blue jeans and was holding a sheepskin jacket in her lap. She looked tired and Liam figured that she hadn't slept much the previous night. Truth be told, he hadn't felt much like sleeping and had spent much of the night staring up at the ceiling. He had phoned his father at just before midnight and the call had gone straight through to voicemail. It wasn't unusual for him to switch his personal phone off when he was working. Liam had fallen into a dreamless sleep eventually but he doubted that he had slept more than three or four hours.

Katra's mother lived in a small cottage in a village about five miles from the centre of Ljubljana, a grey stone building with a slate roof and a dozen or so chickens scratching around a coop. There were fields of vegetables all around and in the distance there was a much larger farmhouse. She was a small woman with grey hair done up in a bun and a face that was lined and wrinkled from too many years working outside. Liam figured she wasn't much more than sixty-five but looked older. She beamed when she opened the door and saw Katra there, then rushed forward and hugged her. Katra introduced her to Liam and she gave Liam a hug, too, the top of her head barely reaching his shoulders.

Katra's mother began talking in Slovenian and they headed for the kitchen. Liam followed. Mrs Novak was wearing a simple black-and-white checked dress and flat shoes that slapped on the stone-flagged floor.

There was a huge wood-burning stove against one wall on top of which were three large pans. There was an oak table with two bench seats and Mrs Novak waved for them to sit down.

She made them cups of tea, and then joined them at the table. She spoke to Katra for a few minutes, then Katra asked a few questions and her mother answered. Katra looked more and more worried as the conversation continued. Eventually she sat back and looked at Liam, ashen-faced. "Mia can't leave the house where she works," she said. "She hasn't been in touch since she called my mum. She used a customer's phone."

"And this place she's being held, it's what? A bar? A hotel?"

"It's a house where men go to have sex," said Katra. "They can buy drinks there but it's not about the drinks, it's the girls. It's on the motorway between

Ljubljana and Zagreb, near a town called Novo Mesto. Men in Zagreb like it because they are driving over the border from Croatia. It makes them feel safer."

"And who runs the place?"

"The big boss is a man called Zivco Žagar. Everyone knows him. He's like a godfather. He helps people when they need help. If you have a problem with the police or the council, Mr Žagar can fix it. If you need money, he can help if the bank won't."

"And if you don't pay, he forces you to work for him?"

"Mia didn't know that. She just thought it was a loan." Her eyes filled with tears and she wiped them away with the back of her hand.

"It's okay, don't cry," said Liam hurriedly. "We can fix this."

Katra forced a smile. "I hope so."

"I know so," said Liam. "He's a businessman, so it's all about the money. I'll pay him what Mia owes plus interest and that'll be that."

Katra nodded.

"So your mum has told you where this place is?"

Katra nodded again. "I'll be able to find it."

"Before we go you need to take me to an ATM," said Liam. "I've got two debit cards and a Mastercard. I don't know how much it'll let me withdraw in one day but with what I got at the airport I should be able to get a few thousand euros together."

"But that won't be enough," said Katra. "My sister borrowed eight thousand euros."

"He's a businessman, he'll be able to take a credit card payment," said Liam. He sipped his tea, then looked at his watch. "We should be going."

Katra's mother started speaking again, then reached out to hold her daughter's hands. Katra replied. From the body language alone, Liam could tell that Katra's mum was telling her daughter to be careful, maybe even asking her not to go. Eventually Katra's mother released her grip. Katra stood up and nodded at Liam. "Let's go before I change my mind," she said.

After they had finished lunch, Branko took the group over to a table that had been set up outside the tent. On it was a Dragunov rifle with a bipod stand supporting the barrel and a distinctive skeletonised stock. Neno was slotting cartridges into a ten-round box magazine.

Shepherd knew that the Dragunov was the sniper rifle of choice for the Warsaw Pact countries, and had been enthusiastically copied by the Chinese. The Russians had designed it as a rifle that could be used by marksmen at infantry level rather than by highly trained snipers. The idea was to disperse the marksmen through the regular infantry so that they would be readily available when needed. Such marksmen were generally accurate up to about five hundred yards, which was well below the skill set of a trained sniper, but more than enough for most battlefield situations. Unlike rifles designed for ultra-long range shooting, the Dragunov also had mounts on the barrel to fix a bayonet. It was lighter than most sniper rifles so that it could be carried for long distances and had been built as a semi-automatic so that it could take out multiple targets in rapid-fire mode.

"Right, gentlemen and lady," said Branko. "Let me introduce you to the Dragunov sniping rifle." He pointed down the quarry where Gordan and Luka were placing a large watermelon on top of an old oil barrel. "Firing a sniper rifle is a world of difference to aiming a handgun. It's a much more technical operation, and because we are so much further from the target, things like the wind become more important. But this isn't about training you to be snipers, it's about the experience. So you'll be firing three shots each. The target is the watermelon, but to be honest I'll be impressed if you hit the barrel."

In the distance, Gordan and Luka were walking away from the target. They stood about fifty yards away next to a couple of carrier bags which Shepherd assumed contained more watermelons.

Branko had a pair of black binoculars hanging around his neck. There were several other pairs on the metal table and he nodded at them. "If any of you want a closer look, feel free," he said. Moorhouse, Atkinson and Ian McAdam went over to get a pair each.

"So I think lady first," said Branko, beckoning for Carol to come forward. He positioned one of the folding chairs next to the table so that she could sit down to fire the gun. Her husband gave his binoculars to Shepherd so that he could film her on his phone.

Branko showed her how to use the telescopic sight and explained that breathing was even more important than when she had been using the Glock. The best way was to take a full breath, then slowly exhale until about half the air was out, then hold it. While holding the breath the trigger had to be gently squeezed. "Pull it so slowly that it feels as if you are trying not to pull it," he explained, which was as good as any way of describing the process.

Neno trained his binoculars on the targets while Branko stood at Carol's shoulder. She pulled the trigger but the motion was jerky and Shepherd saw the round spark off the rock face behind the barrel.

"High," said Neno.

Branko adjusted the sights and Carol fired again. This time the bullet smacked into the oil barrel.

Her husband cheered. "Chest shot," he said. "He'd be dead as dead can be. Nice one, honey."

"We want to hit the watermelon, remember," said Branko. He adjusted the sights again but her third shot hit the barrel again.

Branko congratulated her, then waved for her husband to take her place.

It took almost an hour for them all to have a go with the Dragunov. Palmer was the best by far, though he claimed it was more down to luck than judgement. Shepherd could tell the former soldier was being less than honest. He had his breathing and trigger-pull just about perfect and while the first shot was low it was only a few inches below the watermelon. His second shot hit the dead centre of the watermelon and it exploded into a dozen pieces. Everyone cheered and he raised a hand to acknowledge the praise.

Gordan put a fresh watermelon on the barrel and then went back to stand next to Luka. Palmer's final shot nicked the side of the fruit.

Shepherd went after Palmer. He had fired a Dragunov on several occasions and wasn't a big fan, but he was enough of a marksman to have put all three of his shots into an apple, never mind a watermelon. But he wasn't Dan Shepherd, former SAS sniper, he was John Whitehill, journalist, so he smiled and fumbled his shots, missing the barrel and the watermelon with all three.

"Never mind," said Branko when he had finished. He patted Shepherd on the shoulder. "Snipers train for years, it's not easy."

Of the rest of the group, only Matthew Scott managed to hit the watermelon, grazing the top but revealing the red flesh inside. His two other shots went wide, though.

Hewson hit the barrel with all three shots and actually had quite a tight grouping, but, having watched the man's technique, Shepherd was sure it was down to luck rather than judgement.

When they had all fired their three shots, Branko removed the magazine and checked the breech was clear and passed the rifle to Luka who took it over to the tent.

"Right," Branko said to the group. "It's grenade time." He led the group over to the tent where Neno had placed the crate of grenades onto the metal table and opened it. Inside were a dozen dark green plastic containers, each the size and shape of a pineapple.

Branko took one out and turned to face the group. The container was in two halves and he twisted them to pull them apart and took out a dark grey grenade. Branko held it out so they could all see it. "Right, this is a grenade and so long as this pin stays in, it's totally safe." He pointed to a small metal ring that was connected to a pin that kept the handle in place. Branko tapped the handle with his finger. "When you do pull the pin, so long as you keep the handle pressed against the grenade, it stays inert. You can hold it as long as you want, nothing will happen until you release the handle. The handle is also called the spoon, and it's from the Yugoslav word for spoon that we get the grenade's name, Kashikara. Once the spoon is released, a chemical fuse is activated. It will take just under four seconds to detonate the explosive. The explosion sends three thousand tiny steel balls hurtling through the air. They will rip through anything within a range of fifty feet or so. We will be pulling the pins and throwing them straight away. No counting to three or anything like that. You pull the pin, you throw it, as far as you can."

"You throw the pin?" asked Hewson in a loud voice.

Branko opened his mouth to reply but Dexter interrupted. "He's joking, Branko! He's taking the piss."

Branko frowned. "Taking the piss?"

"It means he's joking," said Dexter. "He's not serious."

Branko shook his head. "These are not toys," he said. "If you are within twenty feet of one of these when it goes, you are dead. Another twenty feet away and you might not die but your life won't be worth living. So no jokes."

"Sorry," said Hewson, his cheeks reddening.

"No problem," said Branko. "But I haven't lost anyone yet on these trips and I don't want to start now. We'll be doing it from behind a line of sandbags on the far side of the quarry. And this is important. Once you have thrown the grenade you duck behind the sandbags. You don't try to watch it go off. Understood?"

He was faced with a wall of nodding heads.

"What I suggest is this. We've set up a point about a hundred metres from the sandbags where everyone can watch safely. That will be a safe enough distance, so we'll split into two groups and one group can watch and film as the other group throws. How does that sound?"

"Perfect," said Dexter.

Branko put the grenade back into its plastic container and gave it to Gordan who put it back into the crate.

"Right, let's go," said Branko. Gordan picked up the crate and hoisted it onto his shoulder.

Shepherd fell into step with Moorhouse as they walked across the quarry. "This should be fun," said Shepherd.

"I know, how fucking crazy is it? Throwing grenades, I mean, I can't believe they'll let us do it. Gary said we could but I thought he was bullshitting."

"They mention it on their website," said Shepherd. "But I was only planning on shooting a few guns. So the trip was Gary's idea?"

Moorhouse nodded. "He loves guns and stuff. His brother was in the Army. I think Gary tried to enlist but didn't get in."

"Yeah? Why's that?"

Moorhouse shrugged. "I don't know. He doesn't talk about it."

Ahead of them was a line of sandbags, about five feet high. Beyond was an open space of about a hundred feet, surrounded by the walls of the quarry. About thirty feet from the sandbags were three stacks of wooden crates.

Gordan put the container at the base of the sandbags and took off the lid.

"Right, we need two groups," said Branko.

"Can we do six and three, Branko?" asked Dexter. "The lads would prefer to stay together."

"Mr and Mrs McAdam aren't doing it, and I'm not sure six and one will work," said Branko. "I mean, if that's what you want that's fine, but you'll only see the one grenade go off, if you see what I mean."

"I'll go with John," said Palmer.

"Yeah, why not," said Scott.

"Okay, that'll work," said Branko. "So why don't I take John, Charlie and Matthew with the McAdams to the viewing area and Gordan can supervise you throwing." He patted Gordan on the back, then started walking away. The McAdams followed him.

"Videos," said Atkinson. "I want a video of this." He took his phone out of his pocket, tapped in the pin code and gave it to Palmer. "Make sure you get it, yeah?"

"Good idea," said Moorhouse. He pulled out his iPhone and gave it to Scott.

"Take mine as well," said Hewson, handing his phone to Scott.

"And mine," said Dexter.

"Fuck me, mate, I've only got two hands," said Scott, holding up the phones.

"John, you okay to video me and the guys?" asked Dexter.

"Sure," said Shepherd.

Dexter pulled his iPhone from his jeans and used the facial recognition ID to open it before giving it to Shepherd. "Cheers, mate," he said, then turned his back on Shepherd to watch Gordan taking the grenades from the box.

Shepherd followed Palmer and Scott as they trailed behind Branko. He couldn't believe his luck. He'd been handed his target's phone which meant he had full access to his messages, his contacts list, everything. The downside was that he was about six feet away from two of Dexter's friends who were almost sure to notice if he started snooping through his phone.

He kept Dexter's phone in his left hand. Palmer and Scott were deep in conversation so he flicked through to the phone's gallery and started going through the photographs. Most of them were selfies with his mates, though there were several with a pretty blonde girl. He stiffened when he recognised two of the men in one

237

photograph, taken in front of the Houses of Parliament. Neil Burnside and Lee Barnett, two members of Combat 18, a neo-Nazi group that had been implicated in numerous attacks on immigrants around the world. Shepherd had seen the men mentioned in a recent MI5 report on the group. Combat 18 had been quiet for a few years, though members of the group were still banned from joining the police and the prison service. MI5 had managed to get an undercover agent into the group's London chapter in an attempt to find out what they were up to but so far he hadn't had much luck. What the agent had discovered was that the group was expanding overseas and now had members in Australia, Germany, Belgium and Northern Ireland, and had recently moved into the United States, with chapters in Texas, Florida and Alabama.

Branko reached a line of sandbags about a hundred metres from the target crates. "Right, everyone stand behind this."

"We're out of range of any shrapnel, right?" asked Carol.

"Of course," said Branko.

"So why do we need to stand behind the sandbags?" asked her husband.

"They're a marker more than protection," said Branko. "You're welcome to stand in front of the bags if you want."

"He will not!" said his wife.

They all took up their positions behind the bags and got their phones ready. Branko held up his hand and waved at Gordan. Gordan waved back.

Dexter was the first to throw. Shepherd aimed the phone and zoomed in to get a better view. Gordan was talking to Dexter, obviously running through what he had to do. Dexter was listening and nodding. Gordan took a step back and Dexter pulled out the pin and threw the grenade. It curved through the air and landed to the left of the crates. Dexter and Gordan ducked down behind the sandbag wall. The grenade lay on the ground for several seconds and Shepherd was starting to think that it might be a dud when it exploded and the boxes were rocked by the blast wave and shrapnel.

There were whoops from Dexter and his group as they stood up to survey the damage.

Gordan opened another plastic container and took out the grenade. He gave it to Atkinson, gave him instructions and watched as Atkinson pulled back his arm and threw it. Gordan ducked down behind the sandbag wall but Atkinson stayed upright, his mouth open. Gordan realised that Atkinson hadn't dropped down and he hurriedly grabbed him by the belt and pulled him to the ground, just as the grenade exploded. It had landed among the pile of boxes and one of them was blown high in the air.

"Wow, did you see that?" asked Scott, a rhetorical question as they had all been watching.

"Got it on video," said Palmer.

Shepherd stopped videoing and while Hewson and Moorhouse were throwing their grenades, he stood behind Palmer and Scott and scrolled through the address book in Dexter's phone, then went through the messages. Most of them were from the guys he was with, but there were some to a girl called Tracey, presumably a girlfriend. He memorised her number and the number of Dexter's phone. There were several messages back and forth with Neil Burnside of Combat 18 talking about the services offered by Gunfire Tours and in one of the messages Burnside mentioned Branko. Shepherd effortlessly committed the messages to memory.

When the final grenade went off, Shepherd slid the phone into his jacket pocket.

Branko took Shepherd, Palmer and Scott across the quarry, meeting with Gordan and his group on the way. Palmer gave Atkinson, Hewson and Moorhouse their phones back. Shepherd took out Dexter's phone and gave it to him. "It looked good, mate," he said.

"Do you want me to video you?" asked Dexter.

Giving Dexter his mobile phone was the last thing he wanted to do, so he shook his head. "Battery died," he lied. "I forgot to charge it last night."

"No sweat, I'll record it on mine and send it to you."

Dexter and his group headed to the viewing point with Gordan. Branko took Shepherd, Palmer and Scott to the line of sandbags. "You must have thrown grenades in the Army?" Shepherd asked Palmer.

"Sure," said Palmer. "The NATO L109A1. A grenade is a grenade, pretty much."

Shepherd nodded. The L109A1 was made in the UK following a design that the Swiss came up with. That had always amused Shepherd, the fact that a country famed for its neutrality would invent a weapon that would kill anyone within a range of ten yards and cause horrific injuries to anyone a few metres further away. Shepherd had thrown plenty of them during his Army career, but once in the SAS his grenade of choice had been the stun grenade, aka the flashbang. The flashbang had been specifically made for the SAS as a weapon that would stun and disorientate, rather than kill. Not that the point was to save the life of the target — the idea was to remove the deadly shrapnel that didn't differentiate between the good guys and the bad. The stun grenade casing was designed to stay intact during detonation but produce the maximum amount of light and sound. There were several different designs, with single or multiple detonations and some with added CS gas.

Branko took out one of the plastic containers and twisted it apart to reveal the grenade inside. He handed it to Palmer. "Might as well have the expert show us how it's done."

Palmer grinned. He held the grenade to his mouth and used his teeth to pull out the pin. He spat the pin to the ground. "Fire in the hole!" he shouted and threw the grenade over the sandbags towards the targets.

They all ducked down and three seconds later there was a dull thud that they felt as much as heard. They stood up. Palmer grinned when he saw that one of the crates had been completely blown apart.

"Interesting technique," said Branko. "But I wouldn't recommend using your teeth like that."

He prepared a second grenade and handed it to Shepherd. Shepherd had zero interest in throwing a live grenade, but it was necessary to maintain his cover. "So I just pull it, right?" he asked Branko.

"That's it. Pull it and throw it."

Shepherd feigned unease. "It's a bit scary, isn't it? Holding something in your hand that can cause an explosion like that."

Branko shrugged. "For soldiers, it's a tool, nothing more. Under the right circumstances, it could save your life."

Palmer patted Shepherd on the shoulder. "You'll be fine. If there was any risk, Branko wouldn't be standing here with us, would he?"

"Fair point," said Shepherd. He put his index finger through the ring, frowned, then pulled out the pin, keeping the spoon pressed to the side. He turned towards the boxes and threw it in a curving arc. He ducked down a fraction of a second before the grenade bounced off one of the crates. The grenade exploded and Shepherd heard whoops of excitement from Dexter and his friends.

Branko took out a grenade for Scott. After he'd thrown it, Branko congratulated them all and took them over to the tent. "Time for the RPGs," he said.

Luka and Gordan had placed the two metal boxes containing the RPGs onto the table and opened them. Shepherd went over and looked at them. They were RPG-7s. It was a simple enough weapon, which is why it had proved so popular in war zones around the world. Since it was first manufactured in 1961, more than nine million had been produced and while most modern armies had phased out its use, it was still being produced in China, Bulgaria and Romania. Basically it was a single-shot smoothbore steel tube, four centimetres in diameter. The midsection of the barrel was covered in wood so that the operator didn't get burned and there were two handles that held the weapon steady when it was mounted on the shoulder. The back end was flared to reduce the recoil.

The RPG-7 could be used over and over again and could fire a variety of rockets including fragmentation, armour-piercing and high-explosive versions. The maximum range of most of the rockets was about a kilometre but they weren't really accurate beyond two hundred metres. Shepherd had seen the results of a series of tests carried out by the US Army that showed that while the weapon was pretty much a hundred per cent accurate at fifty metres, that accuracy fell to fifty per cent at two hundred metres and at five hundred metres fewer than one shot in twenty-five would be expected to hit the target. Shepherd had never actually fired one, but he had been on the receiving end several times during operations in the Middle East.

Branko pulled one out of its box and slung it casually onto his right shoulder. "This is how you hold it," he said. He put his right hand on the forward handle and slipped his finger over the trigger. "You point it and you pull the trigger. It's as simple as firing a handgun. There are sights but at short range you really just point it at the target."

He handed it to Palmer who put it onto his shoulder and looked through the sights. Branko grinned. "A natural," he said.

Palmer gave the launcher to Dexter who heaved it onto his shoulder. "I thought it would be heavier," he said.

"The rocket adds some weight to it, but in total it weighs about eight kilograms," said Branko. "Right, I'll run through how it works, though really all you need to know is that you point it and pull the trigger. You don't have to be a genius to use one. Tens of thousands of very stupid people have used these, peasants have killed highly-trained soldiers right across the Middle East and brought helicopters down in the arsehole of Africa, so you guys won't have any trouble at all."

His audience laughed as Dexter gave the launcher back to Branko.

"Once it is loaded, the rocket sticks out of the front end. The launcher we can use again and again. I've brought two so that we have a spare in case we have a problem. Pulling the trigger fires a gunpowder booster that kicks the rocket out of the launcher. You'll hear a roar and there's a cloud of grey smoke out of the back. You don't want to be standing behind one of these things when the trigger is pulled. Or the front, obviously. Once the rocket is about ten metres out, its onboard motor ignites taking it up to almost three hundred metres a second. Two sets of fins are deployed to get it spinning and keep it on the straight and narrow. Basically the rocket goes where you point it, you can't change where it's going once you've pulled the trigger."

"What's the range?" asked Dexter.

"It can travel more than a kilometre, but there's a fuse that makes sure it detonates if it goes beyond nine hundred metres," said Branko. "We'll be firing at targets about two hundred metres away. Any questions?"

"You said there were different types of rockets," said Shepherd. "How does that work?" He knew all about the different types of rocket, what he wanted to know was what types Branko had access to.

"There are fragmentation rockets designed to take out infantry or small vehicles, then there are high-explosive versions and high-explosive anti-tank versions. There's even one rocket with two warheads to get through serious armour."

"Which type can we fire?" asked Shepherd.

"We'll be using fragmentation rockets," said Branko.

"Can't we use the big ones?" asked Dexter. "Like the ones we see on TV?"

"On the news you probably saw them firing a PG-7V, a high-explosive anti-tank version. They explode with a big bang. We don't want to be doing that here because one hit and there'll be nothing left of the target. We'll be firing at old vehicles but PG-7Vs will destroy them. The rockets we'll be using are real enough, they just won't blow the target to smithereens." He grinned. "Trust me, you'll enjoy it. Right, let's head on down to the target area."

"Do we need the ear defenders and safety glasses?" asked Dexter.

"No, it's a different sort of noise, it won't damage your hearing," said Branko. "And there's no cartridges being spat out. But if any of you feel more comfortable with the ear protection and glasses, help yourself. They won't hurt."

Branko headed off to the left. In the distance were three vehicles and as they got closer Shepherd realised they were all rusting hulks. There was a white van, a black pickup truck and an old red Yugo, the Yugoslavian-made car that was based on the Fiat 127. The wheels had been taken off all of them and the axles were resting on bricks. The group followed him. Bringing up the rear were Luka, Gordan and Neno. Gordan and Neno were each carrying boxes of rockets on their shoulders.

Branko stopped about two hundred yards from the vehicles, positioning himself so that the quarry wall was directly behind them. "As you can see, the rock face is about four hundred yards away, so there won't be time for the fuse to kick in. But I'm pretty sure you'll all be able to hit the targets. Are we ready?"

Everyone nodded and Branko grinned. "So who's first?"

"I'll give it a go," said Dexter.

Branko gave him the launcher and Dexter hoisted it onto his shoulder. "Right, Gordan will prepare the rocket and I'll talk you through it."

Gordan opened one of the boxes and took out a long, thin warhead. Shepherd recognised it as an OG-7 round, basically used to take out infantry. The shrapnel could penetrate body armour plates at up to twenty feet and rip through exposed flesh at up to four hundred feet. Shepherd frowned. They were far too close to the targets; the shrapnel from the OG-7 would be as lethal as the grenades they had been throwing earlier. Gordan took out a pale green cylinder and screwed it into the base of the warhead. Shepherd realised it was a practice grenade, with a much lower explosive charge and none of the metal rings on the casing that could be converted to shrapnel by the blast.

"That's the propelling charge," explained Branko. "Also called a booster. Inside the cardboard container is the explosive charge that kicks the rocket out of the launcher."

"How much recoil is there?" asked Dexter.

"Less than you expect," said Branko. "The exhaust gases go straight out of the back. You feel it go but it won't throw you off balance. But as I said, you wouldn't want to be standing behind one when it goes off."

Gordan slotted the warhead into the launcher on Dexter's shoulder. "Load," he said in a loud voice.

"Right, that's all you need to do to load it," said Branko. "There's a safety, obviously, but it's now pretty much ready to go." He flicked up the sights and showed Dexter how to aim. "Got it?" he asked.

"Sure," said Dexter, though Shepherd could hear the uncertainty in his voice.

Branko nodded at Gordan. "Everyone move to the side, please," said Gordan. Once his instructions had been followed he said "Clear to fire," in a loud voice.

"At this point, you say 'Ready' to let us know you're good to go," said Branko.

Dexter nodded. "Ready," he said.

"Okay, and now Gordan will remove the fuse protector, which makes the warhead live."

Gordan pulled a small cloth strip from the nose of the warhead.

"Right, cock the hammer, aim, and then push the safety to the left. Take your time, there's no rush. Then when you are ready, squeeze the trigger while keeping the sights trained on the target."

"Which one should I go for?"

"Your call," said Branko. "Whenever you're ready."

Dexter nodded, then cocked the hammer with his thumb and moved the safety switch over to the left. He took a deep breath, then pulled the trigger. There was a loud whooshing sound and the rocket flew out of the launcher and sped across the quarry leaving a grey-white trail behind it. The missile hit the rear wheel arch of the white van and exploded. Dexter stood staring at the damage, his mouth wide open. Palmer slapped him on the back. "Nice one," he said. Dexter was frozen to the spot, his eyes fixed on the van. The smoke trail was whipped away by the wind.

Branko took the launcher from Dexter and handed it to Gordan. Gordan checked it and handed it to Palmer, then prepared a second rocket.

"Fuck, I didn't get a video of it," said Dexter.

"It's okay, Luka is filming everything," said Branko. He gestured off to the left where Luka was holding his phone up.

Shepherd turned away and pulled the peak of his baseball cap low over his eyes. The last thing he wanted was a video of his face on a website.

Gordan slotted the rocket into the launcher. Branko ran through the procedure again, and Palmer slid the safety switch over, sighted on the Yugo and squeezed the trigger. The rocket streaked across the quarry and slammed into the front of the vehicle before exploding. "Not bad," said Palmer.

"Bloody brilliant," said Scott. "Or were you aiming for the van?"

"Fuck you," said Palmer, grinning.

"Me next," said Atkinson.

As Gordan checked the launcher, Shepherd kept his back to Luka and put on his Ray-Ban sunglasses.

The wind was starting to pick up, blowing from the left. It was Atkinson's turn to fire. "You're going to have to take the wind into account," said Branko.

"It'll blow the rocket off course, right?" asked Atkinson as he put the launcher onto his right shoulder.

"Yes, but not the way you'd expect," said Branko. "The wind will push the fins away which means that the nose of the rocket will turn into the wind. So you have to aim the rocket in the direction that the wind is blowing."

Shepherd nodded. It was counter-intuitive, and the opposite of what happened to a sniper's bullet.

Gordan prepared the rocket, and loaded it into the launcher. He adjusted the sights. "That should do it," he said. "Centre the sights on the target, you should be fine. Load!"

"Clear to fire," said Branko.

Atkinson pulled the trigger but nothing happened. He twisted around to look at Branko. "It's not working," he said.

"The safety is on," said Branko.

Atkinson's friends laughed and teased him and his cheeks reddened.

"Clear to fire!" repeated Branko.

This time Atkinson flicked the safety into the off position and pulled the trigger. His grip was too loose on the handles and as the rocket fired the launcher kicked up. The rocket soared into the air. The booster kicked in and its trajectory took it over the tops of the vehicles.

"Oh shit . . ." said Atkinson.

Branko looked worried, but Shepherd could see that the rocket's trajectory was taking it directly towards the rock face. The rocket smacked into the rock and exploded into a thousand fragments and a flash of orange. Branko sighed, clearly relieved that the rocket hadn't left the quarry. "And that gentlemen is what happens if you don't keep the sights centred on the target," he said.

"Sorry," said Atkinson.

"No problem," said Branko. He said something in Serbian to Neno and Neno grinned and replied. It clearly wasn't complimentary but both men smiled at

Atkinson. He handed back the launcher. "Sorry," he said again.

"The wind didn't help," said Branko.

Branko spent more time briefing Hewson, Moorhouse and Scott and paid more attention to their technique. All managed to hit their targets.

Shepherd was the last to fire. Branko gave him the launcher and Shepherd put it on his shoulder and looked through the sights. "I've saved the best until last," said Branko.

"I wouldn't say that I'll be the best," said Shepherd.

"Not you, the rocket," said Branko. He nodded at Gordan who reached into the box and pulled out a bulbous green rocket, much bigger than the ones they had fired before. Shepherd recognised it immediately. It was a PG7-VM warhead, capable of taking out an armoured vehicle, though a modern tank would probably shrug it off. From the look of it, it was the real thing and not a practice model.

"Bloody hell," said Dexter. "What is it?"

"It's an anti-tank model, the type we were talking about," said Branko. "I thought we could use the one, just so you can see the damage it will do."

Gordan pulled out a propelling charge and screwed it into the warhead, then gently eased it into the launcher. "Load," he said.

The safety was still on but Shepherd kept his finger well away from the trigger. "Aim at the Yugo," said Branko. "It's on its last legs as a target."

Shepherd did as he was told.

"Clear to fire," said Branko.

"Ready," said Shepherd.

Gordan reached over and pulled out the fuse protector.

Shepherd flicked the safety off and squeezed the trigger, keeping a tight grip on both handles. The rocket roared away. In flight it was no different from the fragmentation rounds they had fired, but when it hit the Yugo the car exploded in a ball of flame.

Everyone cheered — even Branko and Gordan.

The blast lifted the car completely off the ground and when it fell back it was all aflame and the doors were hanging off their hinges.

"Would you look at that?" said Dexter, staring at the burning vehicle. He looked over at Moorhouse. "We've got to get some of those, mate."

"Fuck, yeah," said Moorhouse.

Shepherd handed the launcher to Gordan. Dexter could have meant only one thing by that statement. His group was definitely planning a terrorist incident back in the UK.

They arrived back at the hotel just as the sun was setting. As they filed off the coach in the hotel car park, Branko told them that they had an hour to shower and change before dinner would be served.

Shepherd went up to his room and showered to get rid of the smell of cordite. He changed into a clean shirt and jeans and then sat on his bed and called Jimmy Sharpe. Sharpe answered on the third ring. "How's Harry?" asked Shepherd.

"All good," said Sharpe. "They wanted him to do a run yesterday and he was okay to do it, so yeah, we got photographs of the delivery and we followed the courier back to that house in Kilburn. We took samples from the bag and filmed the delivery."

"So we can pull Harry out sooner rather than later?"

"I don't see why not," said Sharpe. "How's it going there?"

"I'm pretty sure Dexter and his mates are here to see about buying kit to use back in the UK," said Shepherd.

"How are you going to play it?"

"Show that I'm one of the lads and see if they try to pull me in," said Shepherd.

"Let me know if you need any backup," said Sharpe. "You know I always get on well with right-wing nutters."

Shepherd chuckled. "I'll bear you in mind." He ended the call and he phoned Katra. It went through to voicemail. "Hiya, it's me," he said. "Haven't spoken to you for a while, I hope everything is okay. I'm still overseas but I'll be back tomorrow. Let me know if you can come to London. The least I can do is buy you a nice dinner. Love you."

As he put his phone in his pocket, he realised that he had forgotten to ask about Liam. He took out his phone but decided against making a second call. There'd be time enough to catch up when he was back in London.

He went downstairs to the bar. A buffet table had been laid out and Shepherd's mouth watered as he

253

went over to check out the spread. There were four large terracotta pots each with a label in front of them explaining what the pot contained. The first was a Serbian goulash. The second was *podvarak*, which was described as a sauerkraut casserole. Then there was *pasulj*, a bean stew containing ham hock, and *sarma*, cabbage leaves stuffed with rice and minced meat. There were also platters of sausages of various shapes and sizes, grilled strips of pork loin and fried ground pork patties. Like most cuisines in that part of the world, there was little in the way of vegetables, but half a dozen varieties of bread.

Ian and Carol McAdam had already helped themselves to food and were sitting at a corner table with laden plates and a bottle of red wine.

Dexter was standing at the bar with Branko, who had changed into a red linen shirt and blue jeans but was still wearing his Army boots. Both men were drinking bottles of Lav Pivo, a popular local beer. Shepherd went over to the bar and ordered a bottle of the same. As he was handing over his money, Palmer and Moorhouse arrived so he bought them beers as well.

"Branko, mate, this has been a great trip," said Dexter. His friends nodded.

"It's been a fucking blast, literally," agreed Palmer.

"You should come back," said Branko.

"We will," said Dexter. "What about you, John? Have fun?"

Shepherd grinned. "Hell, yeah. Those grenades, huh? And that RPG. That was something."

254

"Must be great to use them for real, hey Branko?" said Moorhouse, his cheeks flushed from alcohol. "Against the enemy."

Branko nodded. "It's a whole different experience, that's for sure."

"Did you see much action, when you were with the Serbian Army?" asked Dexter.

"Some," said Branko, as he had when Moorhouse had asked him the previous night.

"Ever fired RPGs for real?"

"Not so much, I was more of a sniper," said Branko.

"What was all the fighting about back in the nineties?" asked Moorhouse. Hewson arrived and bought himself a beer.

"They were kicking out the Muslims," said Dexter. He looked at Branko. "Right?"

Branko rubbed his chin. "It was complicated. A lot of different people were forced to live together as Yugoslavia, but no one was happy. We Serbs wanted our independence, and we had to fight to get it."

Dexter clinked his bottle against Branko's. "Yeah, but you Serbs did the right thing, getting rid of the Muslims," he said. "That's what we should be doing in the UK."

Branko shrugged and gulped down some beer. "You would think they'd get the message, right? But we've had thousands of them walk by here recently. When that German bitch invited all the Syrians to Europe, a lot of them came walking by Sid to get into Croatia."

"Are you serious?" asked Dexter.

Scott walked in and went over to check out the food.

"They marched right across the cornfields, trampling the crops," said Branko. "They didn't care. They were almost all men. Hardly any women or kids. Some from Syria but we had Afghans and Iraqis. Pakistanis, too. Thousands of them. Parasites."

"Why Croatia?" asked Hewson.

"Because Croatia's in the EU," said Dexter. "If they can get into Croatia then it's border-free all the way to the English Channel. Then they stow away on a truck and the next thing they know they get a council house and benefits."

"They don't all want to go to England," said Branko. "The Croats were worried that they'd set up home there so they started building fences. Now they throw them back. They reckon there are eight thousand of them in Serbia right now. We have become a holding pen for them."

"And they are mainly Muslims?" asked Scott.

Branko nodded. "If they weren't, if they were Christians, it wouldn't be so bad." He grimaced as if he had a bad taste in his mouth. "But Muslims. They are animals."

"So why don't you just kick them out, the same as the Croatians do?"

"We have to be careful," said Branko. "The world is watching. If it was up to me ..." He shrugged and forced a smile. "But it isn't."

"You've got the same problem we've got," said Dexter. "The people want rid of them, but the government won't do anything."

"What is it like in England now?" asked Luka.

"Grim," said Moorhouse. "We've got no-go areas where the cops are too scared to go. We've got gangs of them abusing our girls. Hundreds of them."

"Thousands," said Dexter.

"What happens?" asked Branko.

"They're Pakis usually," said Dexter. "They get underage girls by plying them with drinks and drugs then they pass them around."

"And the police allow this?" asked Luka.

"For a long time they turned a blind eye," said Dexter. "They're scared shitless of appearing racist. So are the local councils. But things are starting to change now that the newspapers have got onto it."

"They should castrate the bastards," said Moorhouse.

"And throw them out of the country," said Hewson.

"If that happened here, they'd be killed," said Branko emphatically. "It's bad enough that they are here, but if they started hurting our daughters . . ."

Branko slapped his palm down onto the bar, making Dexter jump. Dexter laughed to cover his embarrassment. "Yeah, well the tide is starting to turn in the UK," he said. "But the grooming gangs are happening everywhere that have allowed the Pakis in. Finland, Sweden, Germany. It's a fucking mess."

"So what's the solution?" asked Branko.

"The final fucking solution," said Hewson. "That's what's fucking needed."

"We're working on it, Branko," said Dexter.

The McAdams looked uncomfortable at the way the conversation was going. They both stood up and refilled their plates at the buffet, then went and sat at a table at the far end of the room.

Dexter looked over at Shepherd. "Where do you stand on the whole muzzie thing, John?" he asked.

It was Shepherd's opportunity to show that he was one of them. He'd have to tread carefully because he didn't want to appear too keen. "I'm not a fan," he said.

Dexter and his friends laughed. "Neither are we," said Moorhouse.

"Who the hell is?" said Palmer.

"Yeah, but with me it's up close and personal," said Shepherd quietly.

"What do you mean?" asked Dexter.

Shepherd shook his head. "Forget it," he said.

"No, come on, John. Spit it out."

Shepherd continued to feign reluctance, turning away and sipping his drink.

"You're among friends, John," said Dexter.

Shepherd faked a shudder. "You were talking about the grooming gangs," he said. "They got my sister, a couple of years ago. There were a dozen of them, in Leeds, they got sent down eventually but for years they groomed and raped hundreds of girls. My sister was one of them. They got her hooked on drugs and then passed her around like a fucking rag doll."

"Shit, mate, that's fucking terrible," said Dexter.

"She killed herself just before the cops arrested them. Took an overdose." Shepherd blinked as if he was close to tears. "I wish I'd had a gun then, I'd have shot

258

the fuckers, every one them." He took another drink. "Bastards."

Dexter patted him on the shoulder. "I'm sorry, mate. Really sorry."

Shepherd shrugged. "I just wish I'd done something, you know? My parents were worried about what was happening. They'd seen her getting into a car with some Pakis and staying out all night. They called the cops but they couldn't have cared less." It was a totally made up story but Shepherd had rehearsed it enough times in his head so that he could tell it with conviction.

"That's what happens," said Dexter. "The cops are scared shitless of being accused of racism so they bend over backwards to give the muzzies a free pass. You've seen how it works. They burn poppies and they get a twenty-pound fine. Throw bacon at a mosque and you get six months in prison. Where's the fairness in that?"

Shepherd snorted. "No one ever said life was fair."

"Your sister was abused by muzzies and the cops did nothing," said Dexter. "If we went around abusing Muslim girls, we'd be in court faster than you can say 'Islamophobia'. That's what's wrong with our country."

"So what's the answer?" asked Shepherd. "Do what those guys did in Acton? Throw grenades at mosques?"

"They were amateurs, mate," said Dexter. "They weren't grenades, they were home-made pipe bombs. They didn't kill anybody, and one of them got caught."

"What was the guy's name, the one they grabbed?" asked Shepherd. He knew, of course, but he wanted to know if Dexter and his friends knew.

"Tony Hooper," said Moorhouse. "He's a bit of a nutter. I've never met him but I've seen his dad talking at various meetings. His dad's a bit of a legend and I think Tony was trying to impress the old man."

"He's a fucking moron," said Scott. "You can't ride up on a bike in a crowded street and throw pipe bombs. Where was the fucking planning in that?"

"Yeah, but he has the right idea," said Dexter. "You know what the problem is, John?"

Shepherd shook his head.

"The muzzies aren't scared. They can see that they're winning so that just makes them stronger. Then you look at the Jews. They are so fucking scared. You ever walk past a synagogue? They have static security and CCTV all over the place. My brother does security for a couple of synagogues and they are scared shitless of being attacked."

"To be fair, they did have the shit kicked out of them by the Nazis," said Palmer. Shepherd couldn't tell if he was joking or not.

"Not just the Nazis," said Dexter. "The whole of Europe turned against them. Poland and France couldn't hand their Jews over quick enough. And they've never forgotten that. Which is why Jews always keep a low profile. They don't eat pork, but you never hear Jews insisting that all the food in schools or hospitals is kosher. Not like the muzzies do. And the Jews don't block off public streets to pray. Or go around burning poppies. And Jews don't dress differently. Not most of them anyway. They might wear that little cap thing on the way to the synagogue but that's about it. But look at the fucking muzzies. They dress like they're in the desert most of the time. And they make their women dress from head to toe in black, covering their faces and shit. It's like they want to stick out. They want to be different."

It was starting to sound like a prepared speech but it was exactly what Shepherd wanted, an insight into the group's thinking.

"The Jews stay below the radar," continued Dexter, showing no signs of calming down. "They're as keen on their religion as the muzzies, but they don't push it down our throats. They blend. They fit in. They fucking adapt. And they inter-marry, all the time. I've got mates who've married Jews and it's no big thing. But when was the last time you heard of a muzzie marrying outside his religion? It never fucking happens. And why? Because they think they are better than us. It says that in the Koran. They are the chosen, everyone else is the shit on their shoes. What we need to do, what we Christians need to do, is put the fear of God into the muzzies. We need to show them that we're the strong ones, that if they fuck with us we'll blow up their churches."

His eyes were wide and burning with a fierce intensity, and his friends were equally wound up. Palmer was clenching and unclenching his fists as if he was about to lash out, and Scott was transferring his weight from side to side as if he was limbering up.

261

"That's what we need to do, John," said Dexter, his voice dropping to a low whisper. "We need to put the fear of God into them so that they start fucking behaving themselves."

Scott nodded enthusiastically. "And the sooner the better," he said.

"Amen to that," said Dexter.

Later in the evening, Dexter, Moorhouse and Branko sat together at a corner table over bottles of beer, their heads so close that they were almost touching. Shepherd was standing at the bar with Simon Hewson. He would have dearly loved to have been at the table, but it was clear that the men didn't want to be disturbed. "Another?" he asked Hewson, who was already a little the worse for wear. Hewson was drinking gin and tonics and whenever Shepherd had bought a round he'd made sure that the man had been given a double.

"Sure," said Hewson, slurring the word.

Shepherd ordered drinks for them both, and pointed at Joe Atkinson, who was standing further down the bar. "Joe? Another?"

"Cheers," said Atkinson, who was also obviously fairly drunk.

Shepherd ordered a pint of lager for him.

The barmaid put down their drinks and Shepherd paid with a twenty-euro note. "So what do you think Gary and Rog are up to?" he asked Hewson. "Fixing up another visit?"

"They're shopping," said Hewson, and he giggled.

262

"Shopping?" repeated Shepherd. "What do you mean?"

"Simon, mum's the word, remember?" said Atkinson.

Shepherd narrowed his eyes, pretending that he didn't understand what was going on. "What's wrong?"

"Joe is just being over-cautious," said Hewson.

"You've lost me," said Shepherd, playing the innocent. He sipped his Lav. Palmer came over to join them, holding a bottle of lager.

"Joe, mate, John is one of us," said Hewson.

"He's a fucking journalist." Atkinson gestured at Shepherd. "No offence."

Shepherd faked a drunken grin. "None taken." He sipped his beer. "I was just asking. No sweat if you don't want to tell me. I'm easy either way." He grinned again. "I'm so bloody drunk I won't remember anything tomorrow anyway."

They all laughed. Atkinson was unsteady on his feet and he sloshed beer onto his trainers and cursed.

"What's going on?" asked Palmer.

"John was wondering what Gary's getting so busy about," said Atkinson.

"I was wondering that myself," said Palmer.

"Gary wants to buy some kit from Branko," said Hewson.

"Kit? What sort of kit?" asked Shepherd.

Hewson looked around as if he feared being overheard. "He wants to give the muzzies a taste of their own medicine."

"Are you serious?" said Shepherd, faking surprise.

"He's got a thing about it," said Hewson. "Says we've done enough talking, that we have to meet fire with fire. He says that we've let them walk all over us for years and that won't change unless someone stands up to them."

"By killing muzzies?"

"Simon . . ." said Palmer, but Hewson waved him away.

"That's nothing to what they've done," said Atkinson. "Bombs on our Tubes and buses, machete attacks on Parliament, cutting the heads off our soldiers. They think they can get away with it. Gary reckons if we hit them hard enough they'll back off. He says they're cowards at heart." More beer splashed onto his feet and he cursed again.

"He's probably right," said Shepherd. He drank more Lav and tried to act a lot drunker than he was. He looked over at the table. Branko was nodding and Dexter was patting him on the back. Moorhouse clinked his glass against Branko's. It looked like a deal had been done.

"This is your first time here?" asked Shepherd, turning his back on Dexter's table.

The three men nodded.

"How did you guys hear about it?"

Hewson nodded over at Dexter's table. "It was Gary's idea."

"But he hasn't been here before?"

"He found it on the internet," said Atkinson.

"It's been a blast," said Shepherd. "I'll be coming back." He sipped his beer as he ran through what he'd been told. It seemed a very haphazard way of buying an RPG, but then Dexter's options were obviously limited.

It wasn't as if you could order them on eBay. "What about you?"

"Maybe," said Atkinson.

Shepherd sipped his beer again. "So Gary is obviously pretty unhappy with Muslims. What's the story there?"

"He just doesn't like what they're doing to our country," said Atkinson. "None of us do."

"But it seems more personal with him."

Atkinson nodded. "Yeah. He met Lee Rigby. I mean they weren't friends, but Gary knew him. It was after some Army thing in London, Rigby was in a pub and Gary was there with his brother. This was a year or two before Rigby was murdered but when it happened . . ." Atkinson shrugged. "It affected him, big time. The way those two Nigerian bastards ran him over and hacked off his head. I mean, who the fuck does that?"

"Muslims," said Palmer. "That's who."

"If that had happened in America, the cops would have turned up and blown them away, no questions asked. But what do our cops do? They treat the killers with kid gloves and now they're in a nice cell with their own TVs and halal food. Gary's right, they don't give a fuck because they're not scared of us."

"Us being who, white people?" said Shepherd.

Palmer waved his glass under Shepherd's nose. "John, mate, last time I looked I was black."

"It's not about race, John," said Atkinson. "Those bastards who killed Lee Rigby were black, and he was white, there's no getting away from that. But they killed him because he was Christian and they were Muslims.

This isn't a race war we're in, it's a religious war. And if we don't start to fight back, we'll lose. And losing to these people means our lives will be over. They see us as being less than the shit on their shoes. That's the exact phrase they use. Shit on their shoes."

"So what are you? Some sort of group?"

"The British Crusaders," said Hewson. "We've got a hundred or so members but we're linked up with a lot of similar groups."

"Like UKIP?"

Atkinson laughed contemptuously. "No, mate, UKIP is about politics, about Europe and all that shit. We're about keeping our country what it has been for hundreds of years — a Christian country with Christian values. Mate, the muzzies throw gays off roofs and stone women for adultery. And they want to start doing that in England."

Hewson nodded and sipped his beer.

"And the Crusaders, your group, what is it planning to do, exactly?"

"It's about balance," said Atkinson.

"Balance?" repeated Shepherd. "I don't follow you."

"It's simple enough," said Atkinson. "At the moment there's no real Christian equivalent of the Muslim fundamentalists. What do they do? They burn poppies, they abuse our soldiers, they force halal food down the throats of our schoolkids, they insist on special treatment for pretty much everything. And what do we do? Nothing. We just let them get their own way and the more they get the more they want. So the Crusaders are going to give them a taste of their own medicine. We're going to stand up for the British. British British. And if enough of us stand up to them then they'll back down. That's how you deal with bullies. You stand up to them and you give them a slap and if you slap them hard enough they stop being a bully and start to behave themselves."

Shepherd nodded. "And how do you slap them, exactly?" He faked a frown. "Gary wants to attack mosques, is that it? With the sort of weapons we've been using here? Fuck me."

Atkinson opened his mouth to answer but Palmer waved his glass again and shook his head. "Joe . . ." he said.

Atkinson smiled and nodded. "Yeah, you're right," he said. "Better you ask Gary, John. Get it from the horse's mouth, as they say."

"There it is," said Katra, pointing at a three-storey flat-roofed building set back from the main road. Liam pulled up in the car park next to the concrete and brick structure. There were a couple of pickup trucks and half a dozen saloons parked to the left.

"Maybe I should go in on my own," said Liam.

"No, you'll need me there," said Katra. "Besides, I want to talk to Mia."

Liam wanted to argue but he realised that she was right. He spoke no Slovenian and didn't even know what Mia looked like. In all the years that Katra had been the Shepherd family's au pair, her family had never visited. Each year she would fly to Slovenia at least twice but they had never flown over to see her. His father had gone with her, but Liam had only ever seen photographs of the Novak family.

He parked the Clio next to a plumber's van and climbed out. There was a cold wind blowing from the woods behind the house and he shivered. Katra got out and rubbed her hands together. She smiled at him and turned up the collar of her sheepskin jacket. He could see the nervousness in her eyes so he went over and gave her a hug. "It'll be fine," he said. He patted his pocket. "I've got three thousand euros, I'm sure that'll be enough to get the ball rolling."

They walked to the front door. Liam knocked. There was no response and so he knocked again. This time the door was opened by a big man in a black suit. His head was shaved, he had a nose that had been broken and had healed badly, and he had cauliflower ears. He looked Liam up and down and opened the door wider, but stopped when he saw Katra. He barked at her in Slovenian. Katra smiled ingratiatingly and answered him. The heavy shook his head and started to close the door. Liam stuck his foot in the gap and shoved the door with his shoulder. The heavy pushed back but Liam grunted and gave it a hard shove. The heavy moved back and Liam slipped inside. "I just want to talk!" said Liam.

The heavy shouted something at him. Liam put his hands up. "I'm English, I don't understand," he said.

A second heavy appeared. This one had a crew cut and a diamond stud in one ear and was wearing a shiny black leather jacket. "Who are you?" he asked. "What do you want?"

Katra slipped through the door and began talking to them in Slovenian. Liam looked around. The ground floor was one large room with a pool table and sofas and tables and chairs, and at the far end was a bar where a barman in a tight black T-shirt was staring menacingly in their direction. A young girl in a black negligee was sitting next to a middle-aged man on a sofa and holding a bottle of beer to his lips while he used both his hands on her ample breasts. Another two scantily-dressed girls were playing pool with two middle-aged customers.

The heavy with the diamond stud in his ear pointed outside and shouted at her, clearly telling her to go. She answered back and Liam stepped forward, protesting. "Don't you touch her!" he shouted.

The guy with cauliflower ears punched Liam in the chest, just below the solar plexus, and the breath exploded from his lungs and he staggered back. Katra screamed and rushed over to Liam putting her arms around him as she shouted defiantly at the two heavies.

Diamond Stud slammed the door shut and grabbed Liam, pulling him from Katra's grasp and shoving him against the wall.

"Katra!"

They all turned to look at the girl who had shouted. It was Katra's sister, at the top of a flight of stairs to the left of the bar. Liam had seen pictures of her but never dressed the way she was, in a parody of a school uniform with her hair in pigtails. Mia was wearing high heels and she held onto the banister as she hurried down. Katra rushed over to her and they met at the foot of the stairs and hugged.

Liam tried to go over to them but Cauliflower Ears shoved him in the chest and pointed a warning finger at his face. "I just want to pay back the money that Mia owes," said Liam.

"Money?" the heavy repeated.

Liam reached into his pocket and took out the envelope of euros. The heavy took it from him, ran his thumb along the wad of banknotes, then grinned and put them into the inside pocket of his jacket.

"Hey, that's for Mr Žagar," said Liam, trying to grab the money back.

The heavy back-handed Liam across the face. Liam raised his hands to form fists but his eyes were watering from the blow and before he could focus the heavy had punched him twice in the stomach and Liam fell onto his knees, gasping for breath.

Diamond Stud laughed and kicked Liam in the chest, knocking him on his back.

Katra screamed and ran over to them. She grabbed the heavy's arm but he shook her off as if she were a child, then slapped her, hard. Katra's mouth opened in shock and she stared at the man in horror as if unable to believe that he had hit her.

Liam tried to get up but the heavy with cauliflower ears kicked him in the side.

Mia shouted at the men but Diamond Stud pointed at her and shouted back and she crumpled to the floor, crying.

Cauliflower Ears grabbed Katra by the arm and frog-marched her to the stairs. Liam started to protest but the other heavy produced a pistol from inside his jacket and jammed it up against his neck. He pulled Liam to his feet and walked him across the floor to the stairs, where Cauliflower Ears was already halfway up with Katra.

The barman shouted something over to Diamond Stud who shouted back as he left. He was holding the collar of Liam's jacket with his left hand and had the gun jammed against Liam's neck as they went up the stairs. Katra was crying now and tears were stinging Liam's eyes, partly as a result of being hit but also because he had never felt so powerless or humiliated. The girls and customers were watching, grinning or laughing. No one seemed to care in the least that they had been assaulted or that one of the men was brandishing a weapon.

Cauliflower Ears reached the top of the stairs. He was laughing at Katra's distress and said something to his colleague. The man laughed and there was a nasty edge to the sound and Liam's stomach lurched. Whatever they were talking about doing, it wasn't going to be pleasant, that was for sure. His mind raced, trying to think of something, anything, that he could say or do to get them out of their predicament, but he drew a complete blank. He was totally in their power. And so was Katra.

The flight back to London left Belgrade airport at ten minutes past ten. The coach had picked them up at the hotel at seven. Shepherd had been up at six for a breakfast of ham, cheese, bread and coffee with the McAdams, who were both bright-eyed and bushy-tailed. Atkinson, Palmer and Moorhouse had put in an appearance at a quarter to seven but had sat in the corner, nursing hangovers and drinking black coffee.

Dexter had appeared at five minutes to seven, looking very much the worse for wear, and when he saw that Hewson and Scott were still missing he went back to reception and called their rooms. They appeared with their bags just as Branko arrived. He did a quick headcount and then ushered them onto the waiting coach. Hewson and Scott clearly hadn't showered or shaved and had dark patches under their eyes. They sat at the back of the bus, Hewson to the left and Scott to the right. The McAdams sat at the front.

Shepherd chose the same seat as the last time and was surprised when Dexter came down the aisle and plonked himself down in the aisle seat. "Lightweights," he said, jerking his thumb at the two men at the back of the coach.

"It was one hell of a night," said Shepherd.

"You can handle your drink, all right. You look as fresh as a daisy."

Shepherd smiled. "My head's raging," he said. "I just hide it well."

Branko climbed in and pulled the door shut. The driver started up the engine and drove away from the hotel.

"So where do you live?" asked Dexter. "You still in Leeds?"

It was a friendly-enough question and Shepherd didn't think he was being probed. "London, now," he answered. "Hampstead. I never go back to Leeds. Not after what happened."

"We should have a night out when we get back," said Dexter. "I'm south of the river. Beckenham. But we could meet in Mayfair or something."

"Sure," said Shepherd.

"You could meet some of the guys."

"Guys?" said Shepherd, pretending not to understand.

Dexter moved his face close to Shepherd's. "The Crusaders," he said.

"I'm not sure I'm a political animal," said Shepherd. It was always better to play hard to get, during the early phase anyway.

"You hate what's happening to our country. And like you said, you've seen what happens, up close and personal. What they did to your sister, that was shit. It's time for you to make a stand, John. And you should meet a few other guys who feel the same."

"And do what, Gary? Go on a march and have eggs thrown at me? Fuck that."

"We don't march. Look, I can't say too much at the moment but we do have something planned and you're a natural."

"A natural at what?"

Dexter chuckled. "You can handle a gun. And the RPG."

"Scared the shit out of me when I pulled the trigger," said Shepherd. "It was a rush."

"You were bang on target."

"Beginner's luck."

Dexter punched him lightly on the shoulder. "You're one of us, Johnny boy," he said. "You need to get your arse off the fence and stand up for what you believe in."

"Yeah, maybe," said Shepherd.

"There's no maybe about it," said Dexter. "If we don't stand up and fight for our country, we'll lose it."

"You really believe that?"

Dexter opened his mouth to say something but then had second thoughts. "I tell you what, why don't you come along to one of our meetings, you can meet some of the guys. Are you on Facebook?"

"Sure. And Twitter."

"I'm not a fan of Twitter but I use Facebook a lot and the Crusaders have a page that has several hundred followers."

"I'm easy to find on Facebook. Send me a friend request."

"Will do. And can you like and follow the Crusaders page?"

Shepherd nodded. "I can do that."

Dexter grinned. "Damn sure you can. And you won't regret it."

Shepherd switched on his phone as soon as the plane touched down and he got a signal as it taxied up to its gate. He had received a text message. He assumed it was Katra but it was Pritchard, saying that he was in

274

the office and that he wanted Shepherd to report to him.

Shepherd went through the automatic passport gates with Dexter and his team, and they all shook hands in the arrivals area. "I'll drop you a line about meeting up with the rest of the guys," promised Dexter, patting Shepherd on the shoulder.

Dexter and his group headed off to the car park while Shepherd went to the black cab rank. He took a taxi to Thames House but had it drop him on the Embankment a short distance away. The nature of the work that went on in the building had long since ceased to be a secret, and being dropped outside almost always bought a cheery comment about spies or James Bond or Miss Moneypenny, even though the world's most famous secret agent actually worked for MI6 and would be based at the SIS Building across the river at Vauxhall Cross.

Shepherd walked to the front entrance. He showed his Home Office ID and passed through the metal detector. He waited while his holdall was checked by a uniformed security guard, and took the lift up to Pritchard's floor. His secretary wasn't at her desk and the director's door was open. Shepherd knocked lightly.

"Yes, come, come," said Pritchard. Even though it was a Sunday he was wearing a suit and tie, though he had taken off the jacket and slung it over the back of his chair. "Sit down," he said, still looking at his screen.

Shepherd dropped his holdall on the floor and sat down. Pritchard finished whatever he was doing and looked at him expectantly. "How did it go?"

"Extremely well," said Shepherd. "They were definitely there looking for kit. Grenades and RPGs. They practised with both while we were over there. The top guy there was called Branko, with three other Serbs, and I'm pretty sure they were all former Scorpions. Two of them, including Branko, had scorpion tattoos."

"The fact that your little jolly was in Sid should have been a clue," said Pritchard. "Once the Yugoslav Wars were over, a lot of the Scorpions moved to Sid. It became a bit of an enclave."

"I didn't know that."

"I was over in that part of the world during the nineties," said Pritchard.

"Me too," said Shepherd.

"Really? Where?"

"Sarajevo. 1995."

"During the siege? Those were bad times."

"Tell me about it."

"So you'd have been with the SAS back then?"

Shepherd nodded. "We were tasked with taking out a sniper. Got him eventually." Shepherd frowned. "If you don't mind me asking, what were you doing there?"

Pritchard smiled. "Sadly, that is still classified."

"You were there for MI5?"

"I admire your persistence, Daniel, but my lips are sealed."

Shepherd realised that Pritchard was in no mood to be questioned. "Anyway, I managed to get a look at Dexter's mobile," said Shepherd. "He'd been with a couple of guys from Combat 18, there were some selfies with them in London. Neil Burnside and Lee Barnett. And there were text messages from Burnside talking about Gunfire Tours. There were also several text messages from German numbers that were in English but a bit cryptic, which suggests that Dexter has been looking for weapons out there."

"That's certainly what we've been told," said Pritchard. "Dexter and two of his friends were out in Dortmund earlier this year meeting with representatives of a neo-Nazi group called Die Rechte, which translates as 'The Right', obviously. Die Rechte is careful to stay on the right side of the law — no pun intended — but their predecessor group, National Resistance Dortmund, was banned in 2012. The BfV has most of Die Rechte's leaders under active surveillance, and they passed on the intel to us."

Shepherd nodded. The BfV was the Bundesamt für Verfassungsschutz, the Federal Office for the Protection of the Constitution. It was the German equivalent of MI5. Because of the country's history, the government kept a close eye on rightwing groups and moved quickly to stamp on them the moment they broke the law.

"You say Dexter had photographs with these Combat 18 people?" asked Pritchard.

"Just selfies, taken in London," Shepherd replied.

Pritchard nodded. "Combat 18 has pretty much dropped below the radar these days, and their website has been down since 2014. But the individuals involved with Combat 18 are still very much involved with right-wing groups elsewhere. We've been looking at the internet footprint of the man you apprehended at the mosque attack, Tony Hooper. He's a regular visitor to a couple of US sites that are affiliated with Combat 18. And it turns out that Hooper's dad was a card-carrying member during the nineties. Hooper senior went on to become involved with National Action for a while but he's slowed down since he discovered he had prostate cancer."

"Any evidence that Hooper junior had been in touch with Dexter? I did mention the Acton attack to him and he was pretty disparaging, but I was wondering if he was faking it."

"There's no direct link so far," said Pritchard. "But these racists tend to move in the same circles so I'd be surprised if there wasn't a connection."

"Branko had no problem supplying us with RPG-7 rockets," said Shepherd. "He took our orders in the evening and they arrived before lunch the next day, so they can't be stored too far away from the quarry where we fired them."

"The former Yugoslavia is still awash with RPGs," said Pritchard. "A lot make their way to the Middle East, though the Chinese are more than happy to sell new ones to anyone with the cash. So what sort of rockets did they have?"

"Most of the group were firing practice fragmentation grenades," said Shepherd. "I was the only one who got the real thing — a bog standard PG-7V. Nothing special. A tank would shrug them off."

"Yeah, but they'd play havoc with a crowded mosque," said Pritchard. "If he can get one it's reasonable to assume he could come up with more. You said there were grenades, too?"

Shepherd nodded. "M75s."

"Kashikaras," said Pritchard. "Obviously, made in Yugoslavia. Though they manufacture them in Macedonia these days. How much was he charging for them?"

"A hundred euros."

The director smiled. "Greedy bugger. You know when the Yugoslav Wars were over the Serbs sold a massive shipment of them to a dealer in Sweden at three euros a pop. One of them turned up in Manchester in 2012, remember? A criminal by the name of Dale Cregan. Killed two cops and a couple of other people. And another two were used in a drug war in Antwerp in 2018."

"Yeah, well Branko clearly has a stock of them."

"And the cost of the RPG rockets?"

"Two hundred and fifty euros."

Pritchard chuckled. "PG-7Vs were changing hands for fifty dollars a time in Somalia at the height of the war there. But even at Branko's prices, they're still affordable."

"Yeah, I think Branko was definitely overcharging. He'd probably do a deal if he wanted the cash."

Pritchard nodded. "So, you have confirmation that Gary Dexter intends to purchase RPGs and grenades with a view to attacking mosques in the UK?"

"That's obviously what he's planning," said Shepherd. "He was deep in conversation with Branko, who was running the show. Branko hates Muslims, no question of that. Two of Dexter's men, Simon Hewson and Joe

Atkinson, told me that Dexter was talking to Branko about acquiring RPGs."

"Do they think you're one of them?"

"An Islamophobe? Sure. I didn't push it too hard but enough for them to think I could be recruited."

"And the fact that you're a journalist didn't worry them?"

"Dexter had Googled me and seen the sort of stuff Whitehill has had published. We're good."

"The Serbs running the tours, Branko et al — there are three men on the website, were there any others out there?"

"There was a guy called Neno. And two other guys were delivering equipment and food."

"Do you have pictures?"

"Some. And some video."

"Send me what you have. And check the IRMCT database, see if you can come up with any matches."

Shepherd nodded. The International Residual Mechanism for Criminal Tribunals was set up in 2010 partly to continue with work that hadn't been completed by the International Criminal Tribunal for the former Yugoslavia. The ICTY had been formed to prosecute those responsible for genocide and war crimes but prosecutions had tailed off and the IRMCT was now concerned mainly with paperwork. But there was a file of men still wanted, though they were no longer being actively searched for.

For the first time, Pritchard smiled. "It looks as if we're making progress," he said. "Well done. You made the right call when you suggested going to Serbia."

"Thank you," said Shepherd. "On that point, can I make a suggestion?"

"Go ahead," said the director, steepling his fingers under his chin. Shepherd wondered if he had practised the move in front of a mirror.

"Using Harry Dexter definitely paid off," said Shepherd. "If we hadn't given him the bugged phone we would never have found out about the shooting trip. But I don't see we'll be getting anything else from him. His father clearly isn't involved and the uncle only visits on a Sunday. So I'm suggesting that we stop using him as a source."

"You're still uncomfortable with using a minor, obviously."

"If he was an adult I'd still be recommending that we focus on my undercover investigation but I'm not going to deny that I'm not happy using children."

Pritchard nodded slowly. "I hear what you're saying." He took off his spectacles and began polishing them with a dark blue handkerchief. More displacement behaviour. "And I'm tempted to agree with you." He smiled and put his glasses back on. "You should continue in your role and we'll stop using Harry. Do you think you'll need anything in the way of resources?"

"I don't think so. Gary Dexter has offered to take me to a Crusader meeting and obviously as his guest I should have full access. I'm assuming he'll tell me more about what he has planned. Once we know how he plans to get the RPGs into the country we can intercept the consignment. Assuming that Branko can actually deliver."

Pritchard frowned. "What do you mean?"

"Dexter seems to be pinning his hopes on Branko supplying him with what he needs, but I don't know for sure if Branko agreed to that. It's one thing to supply RPGs to thrill-seekers in a Serbian quarry, quite another to ship them into the UK for a terrorist attack."

"Branko hates Muslims, you said."

"No question. But he managed to avoid prosecution for his activities with the Scorpions, I'm not sure he'd want to put himself at risk for someone he doesn't know."

"Good point," said the director. "I suppose we have to wait and see how it plays out."

"Sure, but if Branko doesn't come through, I could become more proactive."

"In what way, exactly?"

"I was thinking of me putting the Crusaders in touch with a genuine arms dealer. There's plenty on the Continent."

"How would that work with the cover you have?"

"I'd have to give it some thought," said Shepherd. "But if we could take out a dodgy arms dealer at the same time as Dexter, we'd be killing two birds with one stone."

"True," said the director. "But let's cross that bridge if and when we come to it. Let's assume that Branko will be the supplier. We need to let the RPGs into the country and pick up as many people as we can. Keep me informed, obviously."

"I should use the Hampstead flat that goes with the Whitehill legend. Once I'm up and running I'll liaise with Amar Singh regarding recording equipment."

"Do you have any idea of the time frame?"

Shepherd shrugged. "I got the feeling that Dexter wants to move quickly."

"That's good, the faster he moves the less likely he is to realise he's being set up." He looked over at his computer screen. Now familiar with the director's body language, Shepherd took that as his cue to leave. He stood up, grabbed his holdall and headed for the door.

The curtains were drawn and the lights were on. Liam couldn't see his watch, so he had no idea what time it was or how long they had been in the room when the door opened and Cauliflower Ears appeared. With him was a big man in a dark overcoat, chewing on a cigar. He had thick bushy eyebrows that almost met over a flat nose and a receding hairline that only half covered a liver-spotted scalp.

Liam and Katra had been tied to wooden chairs in the middle of the room with duct tape, and strips of tape had been plastered across their mouths. Diamond Stud had roughly searched them, taken their phones, and then left them alone. Twice during the night Cauliflower Ears had come in and checked their bonds. The second time he had stood behind Katra and molested her, slipping his hands inside her shirt and laughing as she had struggled. Liam had struggled with his bonds but the man had just carried on. He'd stopped eventually and left. There had been tears in Katra's eyes and if Liam had had a gun he'd have shot the man dead without a second thought.

The man with the cigar said something to Cauliflower Ears and he went over to Katra and ripped the duct tape away from her mouth.

"You know who I am?" the man with the cigar asked her.

She nodded fearfully. "You are Mr Žagar." She looked down at the floor.

"Don't look away. Look me in the eye."

Katra did as she was told.

"I remember you," said Žagar. "But you have been away for a long time now."

She nodded. "In England."

Žagar took a long pull on his cigar and then blew a cloud of bluish smoke towards her. He gestured at Liam with his cigar. "And who is this?"

"The son of my boyfriend. He came to help me."

Žagar laughed harshly. "And how is that working out for you?" He looked over at Cauliflower Ears and said something and the heavy started laughing.

"We just wanted to pay my sister's debt," said Katra.

"Ah, yes. The lovely Mia. She is a very popular girl."

Žagar took his cigar out and stabbed it in Liam's direction. Cauliflower Ears ripped the duct tape away from Liam's mouth. Liam licked his lips and cleared his throat. "Look, I've got money," said Liam. "I've brought cash and we can use my credit cards. Mia borrowed what, five thousand euros from you? I can

pay you six, so you get your money back and a profit."
He forced a smile. "That's what all this is about, right?
Making a profit?"

"Six thousand euros, that's what you're offering
me?" asked Žagar. He flicked ash onto the floor.
"That's a fucking insult."

"It's her debt," said Liam. "I'm here to repay it."

Žagar shook his head. "It isn't about her debt any
more. Now it's about her value to me. A girl like Mia,
she can earn five hundred euros a day. Maybe a
thousand. That's three hundred thousand euros over
the next year. Maybe more. Why would I give up an
asset like that for six thousand euros? Like you said, I
am a businessman. Why would I throw away a profit?"

Liam swallowed nervously. "How much would you
want?" he asked quietly.

Žagar grinned and stared up at the ceiling as he
pretended to consider the question. He took a drag on
his cigar, then lowered his head and blew smoke at
Liam. "Five hundred thousand euros," he said. "Half a
million. That is fair."

"How is that fair?" shouted Liam. "That's a hundred
times what she borrowed."

Žagar shrugged. "That is the price."

"Well I don't have it." He looked over at Katra. She
was close to tears. "Okay, I'll go back to the UK and
see what we can do about raising the money."

Žagar's eyes hardened. "I don't think so," he said.

"What do you mean? I don't have anywhere near
that much money. I'll have to go back to England and
see what I can do."

"You and your girlfriend will stay here until I get my money."

"She's not my girlfriend."

"Girlfriend, whore, slut, I don't care who the fuck she is to you. All I care about is getting my money and if you don't get it for me I'll cut you up into pieces to feed my pigs and your whore can work off the debt here."

"No!" said Liam. "That's not going to happen."

Žagar chuckled as he walked across the room to Liam. He stood in front of him, grinning as he took a long pull on his cigar. Then he took it and pressed the burning end into Liam's forehead. Liam yelped and Žagar pressed harder. He laughed as Liam screamed in pain, then took a step back. He sucked on the cigar to redden the end again, then he walked over to Katra, who was frantically struggling with her bonds.

"No!" shouted Liam. "Don't hurt her. Please."

Žagar turned to look at him. "If I do not get my money within forty-eight hours, she will be put to work here," said Žagar. "She can start by giving my man here a blow job. I'm sure a pretty mouth like hers will give a lot of pleasure. Though if we pull all her teeth out, I'm told that the pleasure is intensified."

"We don't have that sort of money," hissed Liam.

"You live in England, a rich country," said Žagar. "I'm sure you will know someone there who can help."

Liam nodded. "My dad," he said. "He'll help."

Žagar grinned savagely. "For both your sakes, you had better be right."

286

Shepherd went down to the second-floor hot-desk room. It was empty and he chose a terminal by the window. He dropped his bag on the floor, connected his phone and uploaded the photographs and videos that he had taken in Sid, then emailed a link to Pritchard.

He accessed the IRMCT database and clicked through the several dozen photographs of men still wanted for war crimes. None of them had been at the quarry. He logged onto John Whitehill's Facebook page. It had been well maintained by the footies, with recent posts related to the various articles that had been published under his name. He uploaded several of the photographs that he'd taken in Sid, being careful not to include any of Dexter and his friends, and mentioned that he was planning an article on adventure holidays. He did a search for Gary Dexter and sent him a friend request, then did the same for Roger Moorhouse, Charlie Palmer, Joe Atkinson, Simon Hewson and Matthew Scott.

He tapped in "British Crusaders" and found their page, and clicked the button to like it. As he was scrolling down it, his phone buzzed, telling him he had received a message. He disconnected it from the computer. It was from Liam's phone. He opened the message and frowned. It was all in capital letters. "WE HAVE YOUR SON AND YOUR GIRLFRIEND. WE WANT 500,000 EUROS. IF YOU CONTACT THE POLICE THEY WILL DIE. CALL THIS NUMBER WHEN YOU HAVE THE MONEY."

287

The number in the message was a mobile and the country code was Slovenia. Shepherd squinted at the phone. Was Liam playing some sort of sick joke, payback for him not being there at the weekend? He called Liam's number but it went straight through to voicemail. He ended the call and tried again. Still voicemail. He tried Katra but the same thing happened.

He sat back in his chair and ran a hand through his hair. It wasn't the sort of prank that Liam would play. So what the hell was going on? And why the Slovenian phone number? That was where Katra was from, but she hadn't been there for almost a year. His home in Hereford was a three-hour drive away, minimum. He called the mobile number of Major Allan Gannon, his former commanding officer. The Major answered almost immediately. "Spider, are you in town?" he asked.

"I'm afraid not, Boss," said Shepherd. "I need a favour. You still have my house key, right?"

"Sure."

"Can you pop around and see if Liam and Katra are there? I'm having trouble getting in contact with them."

"Is there a problem?"

"I know it sounds crazy, Boss, but I've been sent a text message saying they've been kidnapped. Liam was supposed to be at the house this weekend. Now his phone is off and so is Katra's and I've got this weird text message."

"I'll go straight round," said the Major.

"Thanks, Boss."

Shepherd ended the call. His heart was pounding and he took several long, slow breaths to calm himself down. He stared at the screen for several seconds as he considered his options. He entered Liam and Katra's numbers into the system and requested details of the location of the phones and any calls made. He flagged the request as "PRIORITY", though that was pretty much what everyone who made an application did. The phone companies were inundated with enquiries from the police and the intelligence services and there was a backlog of several days even for the urgent requests. The Security Service and MI6 tended to go straight to the head of the queue, but even so, it ultimately came down to some overworked and underpaid office worker accessing the phone company's records. In a perfect world MI5 would have access to the databases of all the phone companies but the world was far from perfect.

Flight records were a different matter. MI5 had direct access to the databases of all EU airlines. EasyJet, Adria Airways and Wizz Air all offered direct flights from London to Slovenia. Katra usually travelled with EasyJet when she visited family so he checked their flight records first. He found them on a Saturday midday flight from Stansted Airport, two seats in the middle of the plane. They had booked onto a return flight on Sunday afternoon but they hadn't been on board.

Shepherd sat back in his chair and rubbed the back of his neck. What the hell were they playing at? Why had they flown to Slovenia without telling him? He remembered that Katra had wanted to talk to him about something but he had been too busy to listen. Did she have some family problem? Why hadn't she told him? And how did that end up with her and Liam being kidnapped? His heart was racing again and he forced himself to breathe slowly and evenly.

He logged off the terminal and went downstairs with his holdall. He called for an Uber and it arrived within five minutes but the wait felt like hours. The seconds seemed to crawl by as he paced up and down the pavement.

Shepherd was still about ten minutes away from the Hampstead flat when his phone buzzed. It was the Major, calling on FaceTime. Shepherd accepted the call. "I'm inside," said the Major. His face filled the screen, showing his twice-broken nose and the deep cleft in his chin. "No sign of anyone." He held the phone up and showed Shepherd the kitchen.

"Was there a red Nissan Juke outside?"

"No. No car at all." The Major pointed his phone at the sink. "The washing up has been done and there are no signs of a struggle. The place is spotless."

"Yeah, I've checked flight details and they were on a flight to Ljubljana yesterday."

The screen showed the Major's face again, and Shepherd could see the concern in his eyes. "What's going on, Spider? You said kidnapped?"

"So far I've just got a text, Boss. I've been given a number to call in Slovenia but I wanted to check I wasn't being conned. Anyway, thanks, I'll take it from here."

"Hang on a minute," said the Major. "You're not planning on doing this on your own, are you?"

"I don't know what I'm doing yet, to be honest."

290

"Well as soon as you do know, just tell me what you need," said the Major.

"Thanks, Boss, I appreciate that."

"I mean it, Spider. Anything you want or need, you've got it."

Shepherd thanked the Major again and ended the call. He had tried to sound relaxed but he was far from calm. His heart was pounding and his mouth had gone so dry that he could barely swallow. He realised the driver was watching him in the mirror and he forced a smile and settled back in his seat. The Major's offer had come from the heart, he knew that, but the problem was that he had no idea what he needed. What he wanted was to get Katra and Liam home, but so far he had no clue how he was going to achieve that objective. He stared out of the window with unseeing eyes, wracking his brains for a solution.

The Uber dropped Shepherd on Hampstead High Street and he walked around the corner to the apartment block. It was built during the sixties to fill the gap left when two mews houses were destroyed during a Second World War bombing raid. The John Whitehill flat was on the second floor. He used his key to let himself in and tapped in the burglar alarm code. There was a small sitting room overlooking the street, a bedroom with just enough room for a double bed and a wardrobe, a cramped bathroom and a pokey kitchen. Shepherd dropped his holdall on the sofa and looked around the flat. It had been cleaned and there were recent copies of The Economist and National

Geographic on the coffee table. A shopper would make sure all the utility bills were paid and pop in once a week to collect the mail He went into the kitchen and checked the fridge, smiling when he saw the fresh milk and cans of soda water and a couple of Marks and Spencer ready meals for one.

He paced around the room, trying to quell the rising sense of panic that was threatening to overwhelm him. Panic wouldn't get him anywhere. He needed a game-plan, he needed a strategy, because without one he would never see Katra or Liam again. He dropped down onto the sofa and took out his phone.

Shepherd had a few numbers stored in his phone — even with his faultless memory it was usually quicker to call through the address book than tapping out the number. But considering she had left MI5 under a cloud, Charlotte Button's number was best left to his memory. He called and it went straight through to voicemail. He left a brief message and five minutes later she called him back. "It was a pleasant surprise to hear your voice but from your tone I'm assuming it wasn't a social call," she said.

"I'm sorry, Charlie, I've got a problem."

"Work or personal?"

"Personal," he said.

"Just tell me what you need," she said.

"Remember when we were on that container ship business, you said you used a negotiator who did a really good job."

"Chris Thatcher, yes, he was working for the shipping company. He was very professional. So much

292

so that when he retired we signed him up as a consultant. He's come in very useful."

"Would you mind if I picked his brains?"

"Of course not. I'll send you his numbers. Dan, is there anything else you need?"

"Just Thatcher's numbers will be fine."

"I know you like to play your cards close to your chest but I'm here for you if you need me."

"I appreciate that, I really do. But there isn't anything you can do. If that changes, I'll call you straight away."

"Make sure you do that," she said. "And give it a couple of minutes before you call Chris, I'll pave the way for you."

She ended the call. He stood up and began pacing again. He decided to make himself a cup of coffee and he was just about to add milk when his phone beeped. It was a text message with a mobile number and a landline. Shepherd called the mobile. Thatcher answered and said that he had already spoken to Button. "Charlotte said I'm to offer you every assistance, and that I'm to tell you that her company will bear any costs," he said.

"That's good of her," said Shepherd. "I don't want to go into this on the phone, whereabouts are you?"

"Islington," said Thatcher.

"I'm not far away," said Shepherd. "Where's a good place to meet?"

"There's a pub around the corner from me," said Thatcher. "The Angel, on Islington High Street."

"I'll see you there in an hour," said Shepherd.

He showered then checked the wardrobe. There were clean clothes, everything from socks and underwear to jeans and shirts and even a couple of suits. Shepherd chose a Ted Baker shirt and Diesel jeans.

He ordered an Uber on his John Whitehill account and went downstairs two minutes before it arrived. It took less than half an hour to get to Islington High Street. Shepherd walked into the pub and looked around. There was only one guy of retirement age sitting on his own, and Shepherd nodded at him. The man nodded back and gave him a small wave. He was wearing a dark suit that looked made-to-measure, with a starched white shirt and gold cufflinks. He stood up. He was tall and thin with a close-cropped grey beard and wire-framed spectacles. "Dan?" he said, offering a well-manicured hand.

"Chris, thanks for this." They shook hands. Thatcher was drinking a cappuccino and Shepherd went over to the bar and bought himself a regular coffee. When he got back to the table, Thatcher had taken out a small notebook and a gold pen. Shepherd didn't bother with small talk; it was clear that Thatcher was a professional. He explained what had happened and the text message he had received. He took out his phone and showed the message to Thatcher. He copied it down into his notepad. "You've had no proof of life?" asked Thatcher. "No photographs or voice message?"

"Just that one text message from Liam's phone," said Shepherd. "I've called his number and it's now off. I'm guessing that they have destroyed it and that the Slovenian number they are using is a throwaway."

294

"Have you called the Slovenian number?"

"Not yet. I want to get all my ducks in a row first."

Thatcher nodded. "Your son's name is Liam, right? So Liam Shepherd?"

Shepherd nodded.

"And your girlfriend?"

"Katra Novak. She has family in Slovenia. A mother. A brother. Two sisters. But she only visits twice a year. I wouldn't say they were close."

"What can you tell me about Liam?"

"He's twenty-one. He's finished his officer training at Sandhurst and is now learning to fly helicopters. If all goes to plan he'll be getting his wings next year. He was on leave and was coming to see us in Hereford at the weekend. I got tied up with work and their phones were off. When I got back I went to the house. There were no signs of a struggle and the two of them flew to Slovenia on Saturday, though I have no idea why."

Thatcher made notes as Shepherd spoke. "So what do you want me to do?" he asked as Shepherd finished speaking.

"I don't want to talk to them myself. I'm too close, my emotions will be running riot. I need a professional to handle the negotiations."

"That's the smart thing to do," nodded Thatcher.

"Plus I intend to go over to Slovenia and I need someone here to handle things." He smiled. "That someone to be you, obviously. If you are okay with that?"

"I'm on this for the duration," said Thatcher.

"Thank you," said Shepherd. "I plan to go to Slovenia tonight or tomorrow. Are you okay to do this from home?"

"Sure," said Thatcher. "I have recording equipment there, it wouldn't be the first time. How about I take you there now and we'll get started."

They downed their coffees and Thatcher led Shepherd around the corner to a small terraced house with a white door and a knocker in the shape of a lion's head. He unlocked the door and went in first, then held the door open for Shepherd. "First on the right," said Thatcher.

Shepherd walked into the room. It was a sitting room that was obviously used as a study, with a desk and filled bookcase by the window, and a scuffed leather sofa and two winged leather armchairs around a coffee table. There were two watercolours on the wall either side of a large cast-iron fireplace, and above it a gilt-framed mirror.

The room had an old-fashioned feel to it but there were two state-of-the-art Mac screens on the desk and a MacBook laptop. There were two phones, one of which was part of a fax machine. "Pull over a chair," said Thatcher as he sat down at the desk and opened one of the drawers.

Shepherd moved one of the armchairs closer to the desk. "I'm going to use my landline," said Thatcher. "Mobiles are all very well but they do go down from time to time." He took out a digital recorder from the drawer and plugged it into an adaptor on the floor. There was a wire running from the base of his phone and he plugged it into his recorder, then he took a pair of Sony headphones from the same drawer. He plugged the headphones into the recorder and gave them to Shepherd. Shepherd put them on.

"Good to go?" asked Thatcher.

Shepherd nodded, though he didn't feel good at all. There was a constant feeling of dread gripping his heart, squeezing it so hard that he could barely breathe. He forced a smile. "Ready when you are," he said, though his mouth was so dry that he had trouble speaking.

Thatcher opened his notepad and tapped the Slovenian number into his phone. Shepherd heard it ringing through his headphones. It rang for almost thirty seconds and Thatcher was about to cut off the call when it was answered. There was no voice at the other end, but they could hear heavy breathing. "My name is Chris Thatcher," said Thatcher, speaking slowly and carefully. "I am speaking on behalf of Dan Shepherd. Who am I talking to?"

There was no reply, but they could definitely hear breathing.

Thatcher repeated what he had said, word for word.

"I will only talk to the boy's father," said a voice. It was a man, not young, and with an Eastern European accent. Shepherd's ear wasn't sensitive enough to differentiate between the likes of Slovenia, Croatia, Bosnia and Serbia.

"Mr Shepherd isn't available at the moment," said Thatcher. "But he has given me the authority to speak on his behalf. We want to do what is necessary to bring Liam and Katra back to the UK."

"Where is he?" the man grunted.

"He is talking to his bank," said Thatcher.

"So he will pay?"

Thatcher caught Shepherd's eye. Shepherd nodded. He had caught the eagerness in the man's voice. He definitely wanted the money. Shepherd had been worried that there might have been another motivation for the kidnapping, but it was starting to look as if it was genuinely about the money.

"He wants his son and girlfriend back home," said Thatcher. "And we need you to help us make that happen."

"All you have to do is pay what I am asking," said the man.

"Who am I talking to?" asked Thatcher.

"You don't need to know my name."

"I think I do. In case I call and somebody else answers. My name is Chris. What can I call you?"

There was silence for a few seconds, then the man cleared his throat. "You can call me David."

Thatcher wrote the name down in his book. "Good, David, that's good. Now we know each other. I'm Chris and you're David. Now the next thing we are going to need is proof of life. You understand what I mean by that, David? Proof of life. We need to know that Liam and Katra are alive and well."

"They have not been hurt," said David.

"I'm sure that's the case, but you will understand that we need proof. That's why it is called 'proof of life'. The best way to establish proof of life is to put them on

298

the phone so that I can speak to them. Once I have spoken to them we can move forward."

"That is not possible."

"Why not, David? Why can't I speak to them?"

"They are not here."

Thatcher made a note in his notebook. "Well, can you send me a picture of them with a newspaper to show the date?"

"That will take time."

"We will need that, David. We need proof of life."

"We need to talk about the money."

"David, we cannot talk about the money until we have had proof of life. You must understand that. If we do not know for sure that Liam and Katra are alive, we cannot move on."

"It will take time."

"We will wait, David. How long do you think it will take?"

"A few hours."

"Then I will call you back in three hours, David. Will that be okay?"

"Four hours better," said the man.

"Four hours it is, David. I will call you back in four hours. Good-bye."

Thatcher replaced the receiver and sat back. Shepherd took off his headphones.

"That went all right, I think," said Thatcher.

Shepherd nodded. "We can assume his name isn't really David."

"It is a common name in that part of the world, but yes, the hesitation gave it away, didn't it? Did you note that he said 'all you have to do is pay what I am asking', which suggests that he is in charge. He did use 'we' as well but I think that was referring to him and me. When it was about the money it was 'I', so from my perspective he is the one calling the shots."

"And he isn't with Katra and Liam. He is saying it will take three to four hours to get proof of life which means that he is what, an hour or so away?"

Thatcher nodded. "That's how I read it. I think I'll call him back in about ninety minutes. If he's with them then I might be able to persuade him to let them talk to me." He put down his pen. "It's good news that it is about the money and we're not into any religious territory. It's looking like a purely financial transaction and they are always easier to deal with. I suspect that David is an established criminal. How old would you have put him at? Forty? Fifty?"

"In that area, yes."

"And I got the impression that he hasn't done this too many times. I don't think that kidnapping is how he usually earns his living. I could be wrong, of course."

"No, I understand what you're saying. He seemed quite willing to let you take the lead."

"So that suggests that this wasn't planned. Something happened to create a situation that David is now taking advantage of. And again that is good news. Whatever it was that happened, David just wants to be paid off. What about the money? How much can you get?"

"If I sell some shares, possibly a hundred thousand. I can probably borrow another hundred, maybe two hundred."

"The text message said five hundred, so two or three hundred might put you in the right ballpark."

Shepherd leaned forward. "That's going to be a fall-back position, Chris," he said. "I don't know this David, I don't know if we can trust him or not, so I'm going to head over to Slovenia and see if I can track him down there. The total population is a little over two million and there's only a quarter of a million people in Ljubljana. If I can talk to the right people . . ." He left the sentence unfinished.

Thatcher nodded. "I'm sure you know what you're doing," he said.

Shepherd grimaced. "I wish I was that sure," he said.

Shepherd had no way of accessing MI5's database at home so he took an Uber from Islington to Thames House. He went up to the second floor and logged on to a terminal. There was still no response to a request for information on Liam and Katra's phones. The phone companies were supposed to respond day and night to urgent enquiries but it was Sunday night so he hadn't expected an immediate reply.

He used his smartphone to check for flights to Slovenia. There were still plenty of seats available throughout the day but he wanted to wait for confirmation that Liam and Katra were definitely there.

He wasn't sure what arrangements MI5 had with Slovenia regarding phone traces. Slovenia was in the European Union so he assumed that there were protocols in place. He entered David's Slovenian mobile number, requesting location, calls and messaging, and flagged it "PRIORITY".

He stood up and stared out the window, considering his options. The problem was that just then he didn't have any. All he could do was wait.

Chris Thatcher sipped his coffee, looked at his watch for the tenth time, then pressed the redial button. David answered within seconds but said nothing. "David?" said Thatcher. "It's Chris."

"We said four hours."

"Yes, I know, but it occurred to me that as far as proof of life goes, it might be easier if you just put Katra or Liam on the phone. It would only take a minute and I only need to talk to one of them."

"That is not what we agreed," said David tersely.

"I appreciate that, David, I'm just trying to simplify things. If you would rather take a photograph with a newspaper and send it to me, that works, I simply thought it might make it easier for you just to let me talk to Liam or Katra and that way I would have proof of life."

"That isn't what we agreed," David repeated, but there was less conviction in his voice.

"David, I just wanted to simplify things, that's all. If it's impossible for me to talk to Liam or Katra then of course I will wait for you to send me the proof of life. It's up to you."

Thatcher took another sip of his coffee as he waited for David to come to a decision. There was no point in saying anything else.

302

"Okay," said David after several seconds. "Wait."

"No problem," said Thatcher. He checked that the recorder was working.

There was nothing for almost a minute then a woman's voice came on. "Hello?"

"Hello," said Thatcher. "My name is Chris Thatcher. Who am I talking to?"

"Katra," said the woman. "Katra Novak."

"Hello Katra, I am calling on behalf of Dan Shepherd."

"Dan? Is he okay?" Her voice was shaking, she was clearly afraid.

"He's fine and he's going to get you back, so you're not to worry."

"Tell him I'm sorry." She sniffed.

"Are you okay, Katra? Have you been hurt?"

"No, I'm okay."

"And is Liam with you?"

"Yes, yes, he is."

"And is he okay, Katra?"

"They hit him but he's okay now."

There was a yelp and then David was back on the line. "So you have proof of life? You are satisfied?"

"Yes, David. I am. Thank you."

"So now you will pay the money?"

"Mr Shepherd will talk to the bank tomorrow," said Thatcher. "The banks are shut now, obviously. But you have to understand he is not a rich man. He is a civil servant."

"He owns his own house, right?" said David. "Everyone in England owns their own house. He can borrow from his bank."

"Yes, but that will take time. And then he will have to get the money to Slovenia."

"No," said David. "You will hand the money over in London."

"To whom?" asked Thatcher.

"I will tell you who to give the money to once it is ready. You have twelve hours."

"David, I'm sorry but that is not enough time."

"If you do not pay half a million euros in twelve hours, they will die."

"But if they die you will get nothing," said Thatcher patiently. "If they die, nobody wins. Mr Shepherd loses his family, you lose your money. But if we work together to come to a satisfactory arrangement, then Mr Shepherd gets his family back and you get your money. Isn't that worth waiting a few hours for?"

"Twenty-four hours, then," said David tersely. "You have twenty-four hours to get the money."

"How about this, David. I will call you in the morning and I will update you then."

"Twenty-four hours or they will die," said David, then he ended the call.

Thatcher took off his glasses and smiled. That had gone better than he had expected.

Shepherd had just arrived back at the Hampstead flat when his phone rang. It was Chris Thatcher. "I've had proof of life," said the negotiator. "I've spoken to Katra and she says that she and Liam are okay."

"How did you manage that?" asked Shepherd.

"I gave David enough time to get to them and I called him. I explained that a phone call would work better than a photograph and he agreed."

"That's brilliant, thank you."

"So David wants five hundred thousand euros. I said you'd have to talk to the bank so that gives us some time. We can then go back with a counter offer."

"I can't thank you enough, Chris."

"Not a problem," said Thatcher. "If anything happens overnight I'll call you, otherwise we start again in the morning."

Shepherd ended the call and began pacing around the small room. David had gone to see Katra and Liam and had used his mobile phone. If the Slovenian phone company came through with a location map of where the mobile had been, there was a good chance he could find where Katra and Liam were being held. In the UK, the GPS function allowed for mobiles to be tracked within a few feet, but he didn't know if the same technology was available in Slovenia. He'd find out one way or another soon enough. All he could do now was wait, and waiting wasn't something he was especially good at.

Shepherd arrived at Chris Thatcher's house at nine o'clock the next morning. Thatcher was already wearing a suit, this time a dark blue pinstripe, with a starched pale blue shirt with a white collar and a dark blue tie. He took Shepherd through to a country cottage-style kitchen where he had prepared a large cafetière of strong coffee and laid out four croissants.

Shepherd didn't feel like eating but he gratefully accepted a mug of coffee and followed Thatcher along the corridor to the sitting room.

The armchair was where Shepherd had left it the previous evening, next to the desk. Thatcher sat down. "David will want to know where his money is. I'll tell him that you are talking to the bank but I will make sure he realises that he has to lower his expectations."

"We also need to know where he plans to do the exchange," said Shepherd. "I want to fly over this afternoon."

Thatcher nodded. "Let's do it," he said, picking up his good pen and flicking open his notebook.

Shepherd picked up the headphones and put them on.

Thatcher dialled the number. It started to ring and Shepherd felt the tension build in his stomach. The phone continued to ring but there was no answer and eventually the call went through to voicemail. Thatcher hung up and saw the look of concern on Shepherd's face. "He's making us sweat," said the negotiator. "He's just trying to assert his dominance. Don't worry."

Shepherd smiled thinly and nodded. Thatcher had a lot of experience at this, he knew what he was doing. But that didn't make him feel any less apprehensive.

Thatcher phoned again. The call went through to voicemail. Thatcher shook his head and smiled. This time he left a short message, identifying himself and saying that they needed to talk. Then he ended the call and began to eat his croissant.

"Now what?" asked Shepherd.

"If I was wanting to play games, I'd wait for him to call us back," he said. "He wants the money, so at some point we have to talk. But there's no point in trying to upset him." He took another bite of his croissant, washed it down with coffee, and called again. This time David answered. "Is that Chris?" he asked.

"Yes, David. This is Chris. Nobody else will be calling you on this number. I am your point of contact. How are you this morning?" He sounded amiable, as if it was a chat between friends.

David was considerably less friendly. "Do you have the money?"

"Mr Shepherd is talking to the bank now," said Thatcher. "The banks have only just opened and because of the size of the withdrawal he will have to speak with a manager. It is Monday morning so I don't know how quickly that will happen."

"I gave you twenty-four hours," snapped David. "If I do not have the money by then, the hostages will be killed."

"David, we obviously don't want anything to happen to Katra and Liam. That's why we are cooperating with you. And I understand your desire to bring this matter to a conclusion quickly, but you have to understand that these things take time. Mr Shepherd is not a wealthy man which means he will have to borrow the money. That takes time."

"Do you want me to cut off the woman's ear?" asked David. "Or the young man's finger? Would that speed things up?"

Shepherd's stomach lurched and he looked anxiously at Thatcher.

"David, how will hurting Liam and Katra help you in any way? You want your money and we are doing what we can to get that to you. Please, just bear with us. As soon as we have the money we will tell you."

"Twenty-four hours," said David.

"As quickly as we can, David. But there is something else we need to discuss. Where will we do the handover? The exchange? Where do we give you the money? Because it is difficult to move large amounts of cash out of the United Kingdom. There are laws to prevent money laundering."

"You are to hand the money over in London," said David. "I told you that already."

Shepherd leaned forward, frowning. "Does that mean that Katra and Liam are in London?" he mouthed. Thatcher made a patting motion in the air and Shepherd leaned back and folded his arms. There was no point in trying to second guess the negotiator.

"We can certainly give you the money in London if that is what you want," said Thatcher. "But what about Liam and Katra? How do we get them back?"

"We will release them in Slovenia once you have paid the money."

"David, that isn't how things are done and I am sure you know that. The exchange has to happen at one place. We check that Katra and Liam are alive and well and we hand over the money."

"You can check they are okay. Then you can hand over the money. The hostages do not have to be in the same place as the money."

"David, if that is what you want to happen, we will do it that way," he said. "But it will take us time to arrange to have someone in Slovenia. Where exactly will you be releasing Liam and Katra?"

"I will tell you that when you have the money ready."

"But will it be in Ljubljana? We have to make arrangements."

"I will tell you once you have the money ready. And my deadline of twenty-four hours still stands."

"Twenty-four hours from now?" said Thatcher.

"From when we spoke yesterday," said David. "Twelve hours from now."

"David, you have to help us, you have to give . . ."

"No!" said David. "You need to stop talking and start listening. I am in charge, I have the hostages, all you have to do is give me my money. And if you don't pay me today, I will kill the hostages."

The call ended.

Thatcher sighed, put down his pen and removed his glasses. "He's just talking, he doesn't mean it," he said.

Shepherd took off his headphones and put them on the desk. "He sounded angry."

"He was faking it," said Thatcher. "Did you hear how he kept saying 'me' and 'my' all the time? It's his money. He's not a middleman or a hired hand. This is his money and he knows that he won't be getting it if anything happens to Liam or Katra."

"I hope you're right," said Shepherd. He picked up his coffee mug and took a sip. "And what about paying him in London? That sounds like a set-up."

"No, it does happen," said Thatcher. "When the Somalian pirates first started seizing ships in the Gulf of Aden we used to have to drop the money onto the ships. They'd take the money and leave. But after a while their demands got so big that air drops became too unwieldy so we started delivering cash onshore, usually in and around Mogadishu. But by the end a lot of the Somalian warlords had moved their families to the UK and we were paying ransoms in London. Sometimes by bank transfer, I kid you not."

"That's madness," said Shepherd.

"It's business," said Thatcher. "And you should be grateful that it is about the money. If it was Islamic fundamentalists holding Liam and Katra, it would be a whole different dynamic and one that we would have a lot less control over. You can negotiate with businessmen; religious terrorists are a whole different ball game." He put his glasses back on. "He's not serious about that deadline, trust me. He wants to put us under pressure and he's doing that by threatening us. If he really wanted to hurt them he would have done it already. And the fact that he wants the money paid in London is also a good thing. It gives you two areas of enquiry."

"I suppose so," said Shepherd. He had a sick feeling in the pit of his stomach but he knew that Thatcher was a professional and had brought dozens of kidnappings to a successful conclusion.

Shepherd's mobile phone rang. It was the office. Pritchard's secretary. "Sorry, I have to take this," said Shepherd, getting to his feet.

Thatcher waved away his apology and Shepherd accepted the call. "Mr Pritchard would like you to be his guest at White's for lunch," said the secretary.

"I'm really sorry, I'm in the middle of something," said Shepherd. "Can you tell him I'll get back to him ASAP?"

"This wasn't a request, Mr Shepherd," said the secretary. "He will see you at twelve-thirty prompt. I assume you have the address."

Before Shepherd could reply, the phone went dead.

The taxi dropped Shepherd outside 37–38 St James's Street. It was a three-storey building of grey Portland stone with a slate roof. There were black railings either side of stone steps that led between two large ornate lamps to a black door. Shepherd went up the stairs feeling like a naughty schoolboy who had been summoned to see the headmaster. He knocked on the door and it was opened immediately by a liveried doorman. "Can I help you, sir?" he said, suggesting that perhaps Shepherd was at the wrong building.

"I'm here to see Mr Pritchard," said Shepherd.

"Ah yes, Mr Pritchard has gone through to the dining room already, sir. Follow me, if you would."

The doorman closed the door and strode across the hallway, taking Shepherd through a set of double doors to a wood-panelled dining room with a dozen circular tables, most of them set for two.

Pritchard was sitting at a corner table, away from the window and with his back to the wall. Shepherd wondered if it was tradecraft or luck of the draw, but it was the table he would have chosen if given the chance. Though, given the chance, he wouldn't have chosen the chair with its back to the door, but that was the one that Pritchard waved him to.

There was an open bottle of wine on the table, and a bottle of water. Pritchard nodded at Shepherd. "Your guest, sir," said the doorman.

"Thank you, Duncan," said Pritchard. Shepherd had no way of knowing if it was the man's first name or his family name.

As the doorman walked back across the room, an elderly waiter in a black suit took his place and handed Shepherd a leather-bound menu. "I'm going to have the potted shrimps to start, and then the partridge," said Pritchard. "I've ordered a bottle of the house white, it's very drinkable." He waved a languid hand at the bottle in a stainless steel bucket.

Shepherd gave the menu back to the waiter, unopened. "I'll have the same," he said. Food was the last thing on his mind. He couldn't remember the last time he'd eaten.

"Was that mirroring?" asked Pritchard as the waiter walked away. "Eating what I eat so that I'll feel closer to you?"

Shepherd smiled. "I just couldn't be bothered trying to work out what I wanted. And I've had partridge before and liked it."

312

"The kitchen here does marvellous things with game," said Pritchard. He picked up the wine bottle and poured some into Shepherd's glass.

"I bet," said Shepherd. He looked around the room. He could almost smell the history. Or maybe it was mildew. He wrinkled his nose.

"I can see that you're not a fan of clubs," said Pritchard.

"Not especially," said Shepherd. "I've been to the Special Forces Club a few times, but I'm not a member."

"Behind Harrods?" said Pritchard. "I've never been. I'm told they use trays to have toboggan races down the stairs."

"I've heard that, too."

"The thing about places like White's is that you're surrounded by insiders. I hesitate to use the word friends because there has been many a feud within these walls, but everyone knows everyone else. There are no strangers. Anyone who isn't known, who isn't trusted, isn't allowed in."

"Kim Philby was a member, wasn't he?" said Shepherd. "He met Maclean here, right?"

Pritchard smiled thinly. "I do like your sense of humour, Daniel," he said. "Yes, indeed, two of the most notorious British traitors did grace these premises. As did Oswald Mosley, back in the day. But those days are long gone. And my premise still stands, that whatever is said within these walls is as secure as if it were said in Thames House."

"But we're not meeting in Thames House, are we?"

"Indeed we are not, Daniel. Because the conversation we are going to have has no place there."

"Do you think we can cut to the chase?" said Shepherd, folding his arms. "If I'm to be sacked, a letter or an email or even a text would have done the job."

Pritchard seemed genuinely surprised by what Shepherd had said. He sat back in his chair and scratched his chin. "Why would you think that we would let you go?"

Shepherd shrugged. "Maybe my face doesn't fit any more."

"And that would be reason to terminate your employment? A man of your experience and talents? I think it far more likely that I would be shown the door than you, Daniel. You have talents and skills that MI5 needs. I'm an administrator. Any half-decent civil servant could do what I do."

"I doubt that," said Shepherd.

The waiter returned with their potted shrimps and small triangles of brown bread with the crusts cut off. It reminded Shepherd of the way Sue had always taken the crusts off for Liam when he was a toddler.

Pritchard tasted his potted shrimps and nodded. "Excellent."

He looked at Shepherd expectantly. Shepherd had no appetite but he picked up his fork and popped a prawn into his mouth and chewed. It had no taste and he had difficulty swallowing.

"I know we are in a business where dishonesty is a currency, but I'm going to need complete honesty from you, Daniel," said Pritchard.

314

Shepherd looked up from his potted shrimps, frowning.

"The reason I asked you here isn't just because of confidentiality, it's because the conversation we are having is very much off the record. No one other than my secretary knows that we are having lunch, and as far as I know I am the only member of Five who is a member here so there's no danger of anyone walking in on us. It's just you and me." He took a sip of white wine and gently replaced the glass on the crisp white linen tablecloth. "We both know that one never starts an interrogation without knowing the answers to the questions one is asking. So take a moment or two to gather your thoughts, then tell me about the shit you've found yourself in." He smiled and smeared butter over a triangle of bread and bit into it.

Shepherd picked up his wine glass and took a sip, his eyes never leaving the director's. He didn't need or want the alcohol, he just wanted time to think. There was no point in lying, he knew that. Lies always came back to haunt you. But when it came to telling the truth, there were degrees of honesty and it was a spectrum, all the way from saying nothing to leaving nothing unsaid. And he knew exactly what Pritchard was talking about. This wasn't about the job or the cases he was on, this was personal, which is why they were in White's and not in Pritchard's office in Thames House.

He put down his glass. "My son and my girlfriend have been kidnapped in Slovenia," he said. "I still don't know for sure what's happened, but they've been

315

kidnapped and whoever has them is asking for a ransom payment."

"How much?"

"I got a text message demanding half a million euros."

Pritchard grimaced. "Do you have the money?"

"I'm hoping to get it negotiated down to a level that I can afford."

"Your girlfriend is Slovenian?"

"Yes, but she's been here for fifteen years or so. I took her on as an au pair after my wife died and . . ." He shrugged, not sure what else he should say.

"When did this happen?"

"My wife dying?"

"I know about Sue passing away," said Pritchard. "I mean the kidnapping."

"While I was in Serbia."

"They didn't tell you they were going to Slovenia?"

Shepherd shook his head. "If they had, I could have driven over to see them. It's only a five-hour drive."

"Tell me everything," said Pritchard. He picked up his fork and speared another prawn.

There wasn't much to tell, but Shepherd ran through it. The text message from Liam's phone, the call to Slovenia, and the ransom demand.

"How are you supposed to deliver the money?" asked Pritchard.

"That's still to be decided. But they have said the money is to be paid in London."

"Do you think they want you to hand over the money personally?"

"I don't know. We've not reached that stage yet."

"You see why I'm asking?" said Pritchard. "Is it you they want or is it the money? Because if it's you it becomes a whole different ball game."

"I don't think they chose Katra and Liam because of me. I don't get the feeling they know who I am or what I do."

"Just wrong time, wrong place?"

"I think so."

"You have to be sure, Daniel. You've worked in that part of the world. Did you make enemies? Because they have long memories out there."

"I was a faceless SAS trooper when I was in Sarajevo taking out the sniper," said Shepherd. "I've been back since but not as Daniel Shepherd. And I don't remember crossing anyone."

"And with your memory, you would remember, wouldn't you?"

Shepherd nodded.

"What are your plans?"

"I've put in a request for location and usage details of Liam and Katra's phones. And I'm trying to get the Slovenians to do the same with the mobile we called in Slovenia." He stopped as a small smile flitted across Pritchard's face. "You know that, of course."

Pritchard shrugged carelessly. "You were accessing phone records for family members," he said. "And then you went on to look at flight records. We might well be the Security Service, but the Data Protection Act still applies. And the fact that I was in the office meant my attention was drawn to it right away. My first thought was that maybe they had run off together."

Shepherd laughed. "Katra has been like a mum to Liam."

"I didn't know that, obviously. Of course when I took a closer look at her phone records it became clear she had problems in Slovenia. And then I saw the message that had been sent on Liam's phone. It didn't take a Sherlock Holmes to work out what was going on."

"You've got the phone records?"

"Of course," said Pritchard. "I can tell you that Liam's phone was in Ljubljana when that message was sent but it's off the grid now. The Slovenians have assured me that they will have the location and phone records of the Slovenian mobile by the end of the day. You've called the number, I assume?"

"Not me personally. I've reached out to a hostage negotiator. He's made contact already and will talk to them from here while I go out there."

"What's his name?"

"Chris Thatcher. He was involved in a Somalian pirate thing a few years ago and he's freelance now."

Shepherd watched Pritchard carefully, wondering if he knew that Shepherd had been in touch with Charlie Button. And if he did know, how much of a problem would that be? While it had been several years since Button had left MI5, she was still *persona non grata* at Thames House. "I've heard the name," said Pritchard. He was studying Shepherd with a slight smile on his face and Shepherd waited for the second foot to drop. Pritchard's smile widened and Shepherd was sure that the director was able to look into his mind and see his inner thoughts, but it could well have been his subconscious playing tricks so he concentrated on meeting the man's gaze. Years of working undercover had taught him the importance of keeping the subconscious's misgivings under control. "So, this Thatcher has made contact with the hostage-taker?" said Pritchard eventually.

"Last night, and again this morning," said Shepherd. "The man he's speaking to is using the name David. We're not sure of his accent, but he's certainly from that part of the world."

"And you have proof of life?"

Shepherd nodded. "Thatcher spoke to Katra last night and she has confirmed that she and Liam are okay. Under the circumstances."

"Good to know," said Pritchard.

"The negotiator spoke to Katra on the guy's mobile. The first time we made contact, David said he was some distance away from where they were being held. He called him again later and he was with them and he persuaded David to put Katra on the phone."

"That was very stupid of him," said Pritchard. "Of David, I mean."

"We don't think he's a professional," said Shepherd. "Not a professional kidnapper, anyway. Obviously if we can utilise the GPS function of the phone he was using, we'll get the location of where Katra and Liam are being held."

"Fingers crossed," said Pritchard. "Now you said this David wants the ransom to be paid here in London?"

"Yes. In cash. Euros. Thatcher says it isn't unusual."

"It's actually an advantage, from our point of view," said Pritchard.

"Yes, it means they have people here which might be helpful in terms of identifying them. But it means I'll be paying the money without being able to see Katra and Liam," said Shepherd. "I'll be taking it on trust." He shrugged. "Trust probably isn't the right word."

"No, but it means the people here will have to be in communication with whoever has them hostage in Slovenia, and I can get GCHQ involved."

"You can do that?"

"I can. And I will."

"Thank you," said Shepherd. "I didn't expect that, I really didn't."

Pritchard took out his mobile phone. He tapped out a number and then spoke without introducing himself. "I have a mobile in Slovenia that I red-flagged with immediate effect," he said. "We think that it will be used to phone a London number, probably a mobile, can you prime GCHQ to be watching for that? Ideally we'd like a recording but at the very least a location." He looked over at Shepherd. "I'll need the number. I don't have your trick memory."

Shepherd told him the digits. Pritchard repeated them into the phone, listened and nodded. "Good, okay then, I'll leave it with you." He put his phone away, then smiled sympathetically at Shepherd. "You must be going through hell."

Shepherd grimaced. "I'm running on autopilot at the moment, trying not to think of the implications."

"Well you can rest assured that I will help," said Pritchard. "I'll do whatever I can."

"Thank you for the offer, really, but other than checking the phones I'm not sure that there's anything you can do. There's no point in contacting the authorities in Slovenia," said Shepherd. "If the kidnappers even think I've done that, they'll kill Katra and Liam."

Pritchard nodded. "Going through official channels was the last thing on my mind," he said. He waved at Shepherd's plate. "Eat," he said. "There's no point in doing anything on an empty stomach, in my experience."

"I don't really have an appetite, to be honest."

"I thought soldiers always ate on the basis that they never knew where their next meal was coming from?"

Shepherd smiled. "True enough," he said.

"And I'm not sure if we'll get the chance to eat when we get to Ljubljana."

Shepherd looked up from his plate. "I'm sorry, what?"

Pritchard smiled. "We're booked onto a 5.05p.m. flight from Heathrow that gets into Ljubljana at 10p.m. with a forty-five minute stop in Amsterdam." The director smiled at Shepherd's confusion. "Come now, Daniel, don't look so surprised. As I said, a good interrogator never starts an interrogation without knowing the answers to all his questions."

Shepherd didn't get a chance to talk to Pritchard about what was going on until they were sitting in the bar of the Grand Hotel in Ljubljana, with coffees in front of them. The car that took them to Heathrow had an office driver, and as he would obviously have been positively vetted he wouldn't be a security risk, but the questions Shepherd needed answering were best asked in private. The airport was busy, the plane to Amsterdam was packed, and they only had enough time at Schiphol Airport to walk between gates and board the plane to Ljubljana. The second plane was also packed, and Shepherd and Pritchard said barely a dozen words to each other during the flight. They had taken a taxi to the hotel, a large art nouveau building a few steps away from the central Prešeren Square, checked in and then went straight to the bar. Shepherd waited until the blonde bartender had walked away before turning to Pritchard. "I don't understand what's happening," said Shepherd, keeping his voice low. There were a dozen or so people in the hotel bar, mainly men in cheap suits and a redhead in a low-cut dress who may or may not have been a hooker on the make.

"We're here to rescue your girlfriend and son," said Pritchard. "That seems pretty straightforward to me."

"But why are you here? This is my problem, not yours."

"You're one of our most valued officers, Daniel. You're family. Why wouldn't we help?"

"But you personally? Don't get me wrong, I'm grateful, I just don't understand."

"One, I don't want it widely known what's happening. Two, I have form in this part of the world. Three, who else is going to help? The British Embassy

322

isn't in a position to do anything, it's out of the Met's jurisdiction, the NCA can't operate overseas and that leaves what. MI6? They'd see it as a personal matter. Which leaves your friends in the SAS who I am sure would do whatever you asked of them, but they don't have the sort of access to intel that you'll need to find Liam and Katra."

Shepherd nodded and stared at his coffee. He still didn't fully understand why his boss had flown to Slovenia with him. It seemed so out of character. "You say you have form here?" he said, still looking at his coffee. "And you told me you were in Sarajevo before. I don't get that. Why would MI5 be involved in Sarajevo?" He looked up and immediately Pritchard averted his eyes. Shepherd wasn't sure if that was because he was uncomfortable or because he was being evasive.

"What do you think, Daniel? That I'm a desk man, through and through? That I've never been in the field?" He forced a smile. "You know nothing about me."

"Only what I've heard on the grapevine," said Shepherd. "That's true."

"You've had enough legends to know that you can't rely on someone's CV," said Pritchard. He sipped his coffee. Displacement behaviour. But Shepherd could tell that Pritchard wasn't refusing to talk, he was just gathering his thoughts. "Obviously anything I tell you stays between us," Pritchard said eventually.

"Of course."

"My CV says career MI5. But that's not the truth. I was with MI6 for three years prior to that. I was recruited at university, back when things were done that way. A few chats with my tutor, a trip down to London for lunch, then the tests and the vetting. A year after I joined I was in the former Yugoslavia. I was good at languages. I still am. But it's not something I boast about. It gives me a huge advantage when people don't realise I can understand them."

"I've never been good at languages," said Shepherd. "My trick memory is a great thing to have, but it doesn't work with languages."

Pritchard nodded. "I'm the opposite. I find it hard to retain facts and figures though I am good at remembering faces, but I really seem to soak up vocabulary. Horses for courses. Anyway, it took me six weeks to get reasonably fluent in Serbo-Croatian and I was already fluent in German, Italian and Hungarian. I was gathering intelligence in Sarajevo but my main task was to get people in and out. This was just before the siege. We knew what the Serbs wanted to do but we weren't sure of the timing. The siege proper started on May 2, 1992. But throughout the spring the Serb forces were starting to encircle the city. In the year after the siege started they built the tunnel under the airport to get people in and out, but that wasn't an option in 1992. We had to take people overland and it got progressively more difficult. People never want to believe that the worst is going to happen. A lot of people thought it would blow over. Then by the time they realised it was really happening, it was almost too late."

He sipped his coffee. "About two days before the blockade started, I was taking a couple of diplomats and embassy office staff out. All men, most of the women had left weeks earlier. At the last moment I was asked to take a doctor and his wife out with us. He was a Bosnian Muslim, lovely man, he'd worked at the local hospital and his wife was a nurse there. They had a couple of kids but they'd sent the kids to live with her parents. But when it became obvious that the siege wasn't going to be a temporary thing they decided to call it a day. So we're in the vehicle and right away the more senior of the diplomats started kicking off, wanting to know who they were and what they were doing in a British Embassy vehicle. I explained that they were medical personnel being evacuated and that shut him up but he obviously wasn't happy. I kid you not, Daniel, this idiot had insisted that we take his golf clubs." Pritchard shook his head in disgust. "Anyway, we drove out of the city, using a route I'd travelled a dozen or so times before. We got flagged down by a group of soldiers. Nothing to worry about, they weren't really after civilians at that point. Or so I thought. I recognised one of the soldiers, I'd seen him a couple of times before. His name was Andrej. He knew me as Colin. I started to explain that I was evacuating diplomats but this big bruiser of an officer came over and began shouting the odds. He had two men with him. Tough bastards. I don't think they were regular Bosnian Serb Army, but they weren't Scorpions.

Somewhere in between. Anyway, the officer insisted we all get out of the vehicle. Fine. We did as we were told. Immediately he saw the doctor's wife in a hijab and he started pointing at her and wanted to know who she was."

Pritchard took another sip of his coffee. "I explained, and he told her to move away from the group. Her husband started to stand up for her and the officer smacked him with the butt of his rifle. He went down, his jaw broken. His wife screamed and the officer pointed his gun at her. He wasn't threatening her, his finger was on the trigger and he had murder in his eyes. She was screaming like a banshee and was clawing at his face and I could see that he was going to shoot her so I stepped in and punched him. I knocked him down, probably broke his nose. One of the other soldiers brought his gun up and I knocked his weapon to the side. The other soldier was swinging his gun around so I grabbed the sidearm of the man in front of me. I yanked it out of its holster. The other soldier was about to shoot, no warning, no nothing, so I pulled the trigger. I was lucky, there was one in the chamber and I hit him in the face. As he went down the officer was still on the ground and he was holding his rifle. He shot but he missed and I shot and I didn't miss. At this point I had no idea what I was doing, I was running on adrenaline. The soldier whose sidearm I'd taken was screaming at me and his finger was on the trigger of his rifle so I fired, two shots in the neck. I swung the gun around and there was only Andrej left and he was standing there with his mouth open, he couldn't believe what just happened and the next thing I knew I was pointing my gun at his face and squeezing the trigger. It was like time stood still, you know?"

Shepherd nodded. He knew. Often in combat everything appeared to slow down, a result of the brain going into overdrive because of the adrenaline and hormones coursing through the system. It sometimes felt as if the brain, or at least the conscious part, had stepped outside of the body and was watching and processing everything that was going on around it.

"So I was about to pull the trigger and kill a man who, while he wasn't a friend, was at least someone who had helped me in the past, and he had this look of total surprise on his face as he tried to work out what was happening. His gun was pointing at the ground, his finger wasn't even on the trigger, and yet I was going to kill him." Pritchard shook his head. "That image will stay with me until the day I die."

Shepherd understood exactly what Pritchard meant. Shepherd's own near-flawless memory meant that he could recall pretty much anything he had ever said or done, or heard, or seen. But some memories were burned more indelibly than others, and they usually involved the taking of life. His memories of combat were more technical, like recalling a video game, a series of images that ended with death and destruction, but those images tended not to come with emotion. He remembered what had happened, but not how he felt. But there were other times, usually when he'd killed up close and personal, when recalling what had happened brought with it the emotions he'd felt at the time, and more often than not they were the ones that woke him up in the middle of the night in a cold sweat with his pulse racing.

Pritchard held up his hand, his thumb and first finger almost touching. "I was this close to ending his life. A man who'd never done me any harm. The opposite, in fact. He'd helped me. My finger was tightening on the trigger and he wasn't moving, he was just staring at me, and then it was as if I woke up. Bang. Back in the moment. I lowered my gun and I remembered apologising to him. I just kept saying 'I'm sorry, I'm sorry' over and over again. Eventually I stopped and he put his hand on my shoulder and said that I had to go. The diplomats were already back in the vehicle. I asked Andrej what was going to happen to him and he said he'd come up with something and that we should leave. I helped get the doctor into the vehicle and we drove off. I remember looking back and seeing him scratching his head as he looked at the bodies on the ground. The diplomat was on my back all the way, he wouldn't let up, accusing me of putting his life at risk. He made an official complaint and demanded that I be sacked. I was summoned back to London and my boss read me the riot act. The thing is, I was sure I'd done the right thing. I still am. Luckily my boss agreed with me, but there was no getting away from the fact that I'd killed three Serbian soldiers. MI6 was going to have to let me go, but my boss pulled some strings and found me a slot in MI5. So far as the diplomat was concerned I'd been sacked, and it was made clear to me that I'd never be active overseas. So I was locked away in data analysis and I was actually very good at it. My language skills helped, of course, but I was good at spotting trends and anomalies and I had quite a few successes. I never got the credit, and I've always avoided any publicity anyway because what happened in Bosnia all those years ago could still come back to bite me." He shrugged. "To be honest, career-wise it was a good move. If I'd stayed as an MI6 officer I'd probably be burnt out by now, you know yourself what the job does to your nerves."

Shepherd sipped his coffee as his mind processed everything he'd been told. Pritchard was right, it was never a good idea to judge someone by their CV, especially when that CV had been put together by MI5. He had always assumed that the director was a career civil servant who had spent all his time behind a desk, where a papercut was the most damaging injury he faced, but now he realised that Pritchard had been prepared to put his life on the line to protect civilians he didn't even know. So was that why he was now in Slovenia? To relive his glory days?

His unspoken question was answered when Pritchard looked over at the entrance to the bar and smiled. "Speak of the devil," he said. "Here's the man himself."

Shepherd turned to look at the entrance to the bar. Pritchard was already on his feet. One of the men from Gunfire Tours, the one called Neno, was walking across the bar towards them, beaming from ear to ear. He was wearing a dark brown leather jacket, black jeans and gleaming white trainers. His eyes scanned Shepherd but

329

then returned to Pritchard and it was clearly him that the smile was aimed at. Pritchard met him halfway and the two men hugged, hard. They broke apart and Pritchard said something in Serbo-Croat and Neno laughed and the two men hugged again.

Shepherd watched in confusion. So Neno was Andrej, the soldier that Pritchard had almost killed in Bosnia. How had Pritchard tracked him down after all this time? The answer to the question hit him almost immediately. The previous night Shepherd had emailed Pritchard a link to the videos and photographs he'd taken in Sid. Neno hadn't been in any of the photographs on the tour company's website, but he was in the pictures that Shepherd had uploaded. So Pritchard must have seen Neno and recognised him as Andrej. But why were they now meeting in Ljubljana? Shepherd's mind whirled as he tried to process what he was seeing.

The two men had one final hug and then Pritchard brought Andrej over. "John, you obviously know Andrej," he said.

"Yes, but I know him as Neno," said Shepherd. He stood up and offered his hand.

Andrej shook Shepherd's hand. "Neno has been my nickname for many years," he said. "It's a small world, you knowing Colin."

"Isn't it?" said Shepherd. So Pritchard was sticking with Colin and Shepherd was continuing with his John Whitehill legend? It would have been nice to have been forewarned but Shepherd had the impression that Pritchard was enjoying keeping him on his toes.

Pritchard waved over a waitress and asked Andrej what he wanted to drink. He asked for a black coffee and pulled over a chair. "So you and Colin work together?" asked Andrej.

Shepherd nodded, unsure of what to say. He had no way of knowing how much Pritchard had told Andrej. He looked across at Pritchard. Pritchard was smiling, and he held his look for a couple of seconds before speaking. "I've explained to Andrej that he needs to steer clear of Gary Dexter and his team, that they are planning a terrorist attack in London. He's going to make sure that Branko doesn't sell them any weaponry."

"Okay," said Shepherd.

"He won't tell Branko that you were there following Dexter, he'll simply say that he has heard that Dexter has been approaching similar weapons training groups with a view to purchasing grenades and rockets and that the word on the street is that Dexter is under investigation by Europol."

"Once I tell him that, he'll have nothing to do with Dexter," said Andrej.

"Okay," said Shepherd again.

The waitress returned with Andrej's drink and Pritchard waited until she had walked away before continuing. "Andrej will also talk to Dexter. He'll tell him that Gunfire Tours won't be able to sell them weaponry, but he will give them the name and number of someone in the UK who can. And that someone will obviously be provided by us."

"Sounds like a plan," said Shepherd.

"I also asked Andrej if he'll help us with our current problem, and he has agreed," said Shepherd.

"Forgive me for asking, but when was all this agreed?" asked Shepherd.

Pritchard smiled. "Before you met me for lunch."

Shepherd nodded, impressed. "All this on the back of some video I took in Serbia and a few requests for phone records?"

Pritchard smiled thinly. "As I said before, I have a proven aptitude for data analysis."

Andrej leaned towards Shepherd. "Colin tells me that your girlfriend and son have been kidnapped?"

Shepherd nodded. "It happened yesterday. They were here, while I was with you in Sid."

"And they want a ransom paid?"

Shepherd nodded again. "Half a million euros."

Andrej blew softly between his teeth. "That's a lot of money."

Pritchard's phone rang. He looked at the screen and then hurried out to the corridor to take the call.

"You're okay to help?" asked Shepherd.

"Did Colin tell you how we met?"

"Sure."

"So you know he's a good man. So if a friend of his needs help, of course I'll do what I can. And tipping me off about Dexter helps me and helps Branko."

"Would you have sold the weapons to Dexter?"

"Branko said he would, but he couldn't deliver them to the UK, which is what Dexter wanted. Branko said Dexter could buy them here and then it was up to

332

Dexter to get them to the UK." He shrugged. "They were going around in circles."

"Why did Dexter say he wants grenades and rockets?"

"The story he told Branko was that he hates Muslims. Branko is the same."

"And you?"

"You have to understand our history," said Andrej. "The Ottomans moved into Bosnia and the Muslims took over. It was not a good place to be a Christian. Back then, only Muslims could buy or inherit land. If you wanted to own your own home, you had to convert. The Jews have a saying about what happened to them under the Nazis. 'Never again'. We have the same saying. We will never allow the Muslims to have power over us again. That was why Branko could be persuaded to sell weapons to Dexter and his group. But as soon as he knows that Dexter is under investigation, he'll have nothing to do with them."

Pritchard put his phone away. "David's phone was here in Ljubljana when you made your first call last night," he said. "Near the city centre, not far from where we are now, as it happens. The phone then moved east and when Thatcher made the second call, the phone was on the outskirts of the town of Novo Mesto, which is pretty much midway between here and Zagreb, linked by the A2 motorway. The phone's back in Ljubljana as we speak."

"So we go and get David now?" said Shepherd.

"I think not," said Pritchard. "I think our first priority is rescuing Katra and Liam. Besides, all we know about David is his name and the fact he has the phone. Say we turn up at his location and there are a couple of dozen heavies there? We won't know who's who. But there'll be no confusion when we find Liam and Katra." "Assuming that they haven't been moved," said Shepherd. "But yes, I hear what you're saying. If we go after David and something goes wrong, one phone call and they're dead. What about hitting the two locations at the same time?"

"We don't have the manpower," said Pritchard.

"What do we have?" asked Shepherd.

"You're looking at it," said Pritchard. "I was happy to take Andrej into my confidence because of our history, but that's as far as it goes. So it's the three of us."

They finished their coffees and left the hotel. Andrej had left his car in the street outside. It was a ten-year-old BMW that looked as if it had been recently resprayed dark blue. He took them around to the boot and opened it. Inside was a selection of weapons including three Glocks, a sawn-off shotgun, an AK-47 and three sets of night vision goggles. There were also several machetes and a baseball bat. Shepherd laughed and patted Andrej on the back. "I can't fault your kit, mate," he said.

The building was on the outskirts of Novo Mesto. There was a parking area to the left with a dozen vehicles lined up. Security lights illuminated the car park and the front of the building. It stood in a couple of acres of land and the nearest neighbour was a farmhouse about a hundred yards away.

Andrej parked a short distance away in a layby that gave them a view of the front of the building through a line of trees. There was a small pair of binoculars in the glove compartment and Andrej used them to check out the building, then he gave them to Pritchard. As he put the glasses to his eyes, the front door opened and two young men came out and headed over to a black pickup truck with landscaping equipment in the back. They climbed in and drove off. As they pulled onto the main road they passed another vehicle driving towards the house. It was a new-model Mercedes. The driver was wearing a suit and tie and he locked the car and went to the front door. It opened as he approached and he stepped inside. The door closed behind him.

The windows were all barred with decorative ironwork but Pritchard could see that the blinds were drawn. "It's a brothel," he said, lowering the binoculars.

Andrej nodded. "That sounds right."

"So David is what, a pimp?" asked Shepherd. "And he's keeping Liam and Katra in his brothel? What the hell's going on?"

"We don't know for sure that it's his place," said Pritchard. "But I'm guessing a brothel is as good a place as any to hide hostages. These places tend to pay off the local cops so they won't be getting any unexpected visits."

"So we're going in?" asked Andrej.

"Are you okay with that?" asked Pritchard. "I know you don't have a dog in this fight."

"I don't have anything else to do," said Andrej.

Pritchard twisted around in his seat to look at Shepherd. "I think we go in with concealed guns, get the lay of the land and play it by ear."

Shepherd nodded. "Sounds like a plan."

Pritchard grinned. "More of a premise than a plan, to be honest," he said. "The problem is, we don't know if they search the clientele. If they start to pat us down we'll have to go full tilt straight away."

"Either way we're going to have to pull out guns at some point. They're not just going to hand them over."

Andrej got out of the car, went around to the boot and opened it. He returned a couple of minutes later with the three Glocks. "I've got holsters, but I think tucked into the belt will work better," he said as he got back into the car. He handed a gun to Pritchard and another to Shepherd.

Shepherd knew that Andrej was right. Shoulder holsters were comfortable and reliable but they had a tendency to show themselves and a simple pat down would reveal the gun. If the weapon was hidden in the small of the back, a loose jacket would hide it and it would take a concerted search to reveal it. The downside was that drawing the weapon was an effort. Swings and roundabouts.

The Glock was a 17, possibly the same one that Shepherd had used in the quarry. He ejected the magazine. It was full, with seventeen rounds. He slotted the magazine back and pulled back the slide to slot one into the chamber. The Glock's safety trigger meant there was no way the gun could be fired accidentally

336

and having one in the chamber could save a vital second or two.

He tucked the gun into his belt. Pritchard and Andrej did the same.

"Good to go?" asked Pritchard.

Shepherd nodded.

Andrej drove the BMW along the main road and turned into the parking area of the house. As he stopped and switched off the engine the front door opened and a white-haired man appeared, his back stooped with age. The man waved goodbye to someone inside and then walked unsteadily over towards a rusting Škoda. A girl appeared in the doorway wearing stockings, suspenders and a babydoll nightie that left little to the imagination. She blew kisses at the old man as he opened the car door with a shaking hand.

"Clearly a big tipper," said Shepherd and Pritchard laughed.

The front door closed again as the three men climbed out of the BMW. The Škoda drove off.

"Best you let us do the talking," Andrej said to Shepherd. "They tend not to let foreigners into these places. If anyone says anything to you, just say 'Da' and pretend you're a bit drunk. Okay?"

"Da," said Shepherd.

They walked up to the building. Shepherd didn't see anything in the way of CCTV but he kept his head down anyway. Andrej knocked on the door. It was opened almost immediately by a heavily built man with a crew cut and a diamond stud in his left ear. He looked Andrej up and down, then scrutinised Shepherd and Pritchard. Andrej said something and the man grunted and held the door open. He was wearing a shiny black leather jacket with a belt that was swinging loose. Shepherd caught a glimpse of the butt of a gun in a holster under the man's left armpit.

Andrej said something to the heavy and the man laughed. He patted Shepherd on the shoulder and said something in Serbo-Croat. "*Da*," said Shepherd.

The heavy continued to laugh as Andrej took Shepherd and Pritchard over to a sofa by the window. Shepherd sat down in the middle. "What just happened?" he whispered to Pritchard.

"Andrej said you wanted a discount because you have a very small dick," he said. "The bouncer asked you if you really did have a small dick and you said yes." He grinned at Shepherd. "It was funny."

The ground floor was open plan, one large room with a small bar fronted by a line of wooden stools. There was a door at the side of the bar and next to the door was a wide staircase leading upstairs. To the left was a blue-topped pool table where a lanky man with greasy hair tied back in a ponytail was watching a plump blonde girl in a silver minidress try to balance on stupidly high stiletto heels to make her shot.

There was a second bouncer standing by the bar with his arms folded across a barrel-sized chest. He had cauliflower ears that suggested a former career as a wrestler or mixed martial artist, or maybe he had just been unlucky and had an abusive father.

The barman was as large and intimidating as the bouncers, though he was more casually dressed,

338

wearing a tight black T-shirt that showed off his bulging forearms and a gold medallion around his neck. The barman said something to the heavy and he nodded, opening the door at the side of the bar and disappearing inside.

There were three other customers in the bar: a guy in his fifties wearing overalls, standing at the bar, and two younger men sitting on a sofa, each with a girl straddling him. The girls both had waist-length hair, one blonde and one brunette.

A waitress in hot pants and a bright orange halter top walked over and Andrej ordered three beers. He asked the waitress a question that took at least two minutes to answer, and then she walked over to the bar, her hips swinging from side to side. As she reached it, the heavy came back through the door holding a bottle of spirits in each hand.

Andrej leaned towards Pritchard and Shepherd and lowered his voice. "Customers can sit here as long as they keep buying drinks. If you want to sit with a girl, you have to buy her a bottle of champagne." He grinned. "A hundred euros a bottle, if we're on expenses. If you want to take a girl upstairs, that's two hundred euros, paid in advance. Two shots."

"Two shots?" repeated Pritchard.

"You get to come twice," said Andrej.

"Good to know," said Pritchard, dryly. He looked around. "Do you think there's a basement?" He nodded at the door by the bar. "There maybe? Katra and Liam could be there. And there's two floors of bedrooms upstairs, right?"

"We need to get upstairs to take a look around," said Shepherd. "I don't see a toilet here, maybe that's upstairs."

The waitress returned with their beers and put them down on the table in front of them. Pritchard paid her in cash. He spoke to her in Serbo-Croat and she pointed at the stairs. "You're right," said Pritchard, once she'd left. "The loos are upstairs on the left."

"So one of us goes up and looks around?" said Shepherd. "Can't be me, obviously. '*Da*' isn't going to get me very far if I walk in on a couple in flagrante delicto."

Andrej frowned, not getting the reference, so Pritchard translated for him and he laughed.

Shepherd stiffened as he saw a young girl coming down the stairs. She looked as if she was drunk and she kept one hand on the banister as she carefully took one step at a time, tottering on heels that were clearly too high for her. At first glance he thought she had made a bad job of applying her make-up but then he realised she had purplish bruises on her face. Somebody had hit her. Her hair was bunched into pigtails and she was wearing a cropped white top with a mini necktie and a short blue skirt. It was only as she reached the bottom of the stairs that he recognised her; she looked totally different from the last time he had seen her.

"Guys, we might have a problem here," said Shepherd, keeping his voice low. "That's Katra's sister. Mia."

"Does she know you?" asked Pritchard.

"We've met a couple of times," said Shepherd.

Mia went to the bar where the barman poured her a shot of slivovitz which she downed in one. She asked for another and the barman shook his head but then the heavy waved that he was to give her another so he poured it and again she drank it down in one gulp.

A man appeared at the top of the stairs, buttoning his flies. He was huge, close to seven feet tall, with a shaved head and a square chin, and thick eyebrows that met over a bulbous nose. He staggered drunkenly down the stairs and over to the front door. The heavy with the diamond stud in his ear already had the door open for him and he pretty much fell across the threshold and lurched towards the car park. The heavy closed the door, took out his smartphone and studied the screen.

Mia leaned against the bar and surveyed the room. Her eyes settled on the three of them and she jutted up her chin and blinked as if she was trying to focus. Shepherd looked away, desperately avoiding eye contact. There was no way she would have expected to have seen him in a Slovenian brothel so with any luck she wouldn't recognise him, especially in her drunken state. It was every undercover agent's worst nightmare, to come across someone who knew who they really were.

She tottered towards them. Shepherd stared at the floor. Her high heels came into view. "Dan?" he heard. "Is that you?" She was slurring her words and swaying unsteadily. She had met Dan twice before when he had visited the family with Katra.

Shepherd looked up and tried to throw her a warning look, but she was too drunk to pick up any subtext. "It is you!" she said.

She rushed over, pushed Pritchard to the side and sat down next to him, grabbing his arm with both hands. "You have to help me," she said. "They won't let me go." Unlike her sister she had a very heavy Slovenian accent, but he understood every word.

"Don't worry," said Shepherd. "What about Katra and Liam. Are they here?"

Mia shook her head. "They took them today. I don't know where. Please, you have to help me."

"Okay, okay," said Shepherd. "Just stay calm." He looked around the room. Her voice had carried and the barman was looking over at them, frowning. The heavy with the diamond stud in his ear had put away his phone and looked in their direction.

"Liam and Katra, are they okay?" asked Pritchard.

Mia nodded, then looked at Pritchard, clearly wondering who he was. "He's a friend," said Shepherd. "His name is Colin. And this is Andrej."

She flashed Andrej a tight smile, then tightened her grip on Shepherd's arm. "Please, take me out of here."

"We will," said Shepherd. "Who has got Liam and Katra? Who took them?"

"The man who owns this house," she said. "He is a Serb. Zivco Žagar. He's a gangster."

The heavy walked over from the door, glared down at Shepherd and said something in Serbo-Croat. "Da," said Shepherd, waving him away.

The man growled again and this time Pritchard answered.

Shepherd didn't understand what they were saying but guessed it was because Mia was sitting with them

342

and they hadn't bought her a drink. The heavy tried to speak to Shepherd again. Shepherd shrugged. Again Pritchard did the talking but that just seemed to annoy the heavy even more. He pointed at Shepherd and started shouting. Mia shouted back.

Andrej stood up and backed to the side, his arms loose. He was clearing his line of sight, Shepherd realised; getting himself into a position where he could fire his gun without hitting Shepherd or Pritchard. Andrej began to talk to the heavy, presumably asking him to calm down. His words had no effect.

The other heavy walked across the room to stand by his colleague. They both stood with their feet apart, arms folded and heads tilted back.

Andrej fell silent and he stared at the two heavies.

Pritchard started talking again. He stood up as he spoke, the action appearing casual but Shepherd could see that he was preparing himself to pull out his gun. Shepherd looked at Mia and gestured with his chin for her to get off the sofa. She didn't get the message and gripped his right arm even tighter. That was going to be a problem because he was going to need it when the shooting started, and it looked like that was going to be sooner rather than later. Liam and Katra were probably already in Ljubljana. The heavies would be on the phone the moment Shepherd, Pritchard and Andrej left the building and as soon as Žagar found out they were heading his way there was every chance he would just cut his losses and kill his hostages. The only way they could reach Žagar was to incapacitate everyone in the brothel, or at the very least make them incapable of reaching out to him. Mia interrupted Pritchard and started shouting at the two heavies. The one with the diamond stud pointed at her. "*Zatvori usta kučka!*" he hissed, which presumably meant "shut up" because she did, staring down at the floor.

Pritchard had stopped moving. Like Andrej, he had cleared his line of sight. The two heavies didn't seem to realise the danger they were in. They were just thugs who relied on their physical bulk to intimidate, they had no military training or understanding of tactics.

A third heavy appeared at the top of the stairs. He was shaven-headed and had a pair of sunglasses on top of his head and a thick gold chain around his neck. From the way he shouted down at his two colleagues it seemed he was their boss. He came down the stairs two at a time, his game face on. These were bog-standard alpha males, used to getting their own way with a show of force. They had a shock coming.

Shepherd put his face close to Mia's and held her look. "Stay down," he said.

"What?"

Sunglasses reached inside his jacket. So did Diamond Stud.

"Just don't get up," he said to Mia. He stood up, grabbed her and threw her over the back of the sofa. As he turned he pulled the Glock from the waistband of his jeans.

The heavy with sunglasses already had his gun out. So did Andrej, but the heavy was staring at Shepherd and didn't see him. He was still staring at Shepherd when the two bullets ripped into his chest. Blood

344

blossomed on his white shirt and a look of confusion flashed across his face before his eyes went blank and he collapsed to the floor.

The heavy with the diamond stud had his gun out and he aimed at Shepherd's chest and pulled the trigger but nothing happened. He didn't have a round in the chamber. Shepherd did and when he pulled the trigger his Glock kicked in his hands and the man staggered back as blood spurted down the front of his chest. Shepherd raised his gun and his second shot hit the man in the centre of his face. Blood and brain matter splattered out of the back of his skull and he went down.

The heavy with cauliflower ears was carrying his gun in the small of his back but he was having trouble reaching it and he was still struggling when Pritchard shot him in the face.

The barman ducked down behind his bar. He didn't seem the type to be hiding, so Shepherd kept his attention focused on the man and sure enough he reappeared holding a pump-action shotgun. As he pumped in a cartridge and swung the gun around, Shepherd fired twice. Both rounds hit the barman just below his neck and he fell backwards against a display of bottles that crashed around him as he slumped to the floor.

The room was suddenly deathly quiet and Shepherd's eyes were stinging from the cordite in the air. The customers who had been on the sofa with the girls had jumped over the back and were cowering behind it. The man with the ponytail who had been playing pool was standing with his cue in both hands as if he was preparing to use it as a weapon but he hurriedly dropped it when Shepherd glared at him and it clattered to the floor.

"Andrej, check upstairs," said Pritchard. "Bring everyone down." He went over to the door and bolted it, then flicked off the outside lights. He looked over at Shepherd. "That back room by the bar, see what's in there," he said. Shepherd hurried over to the bar. Pritchard raised his gun in the air and spoke loudly in Serbo-Croat. The girls and customers moved towards the bar, holding their hands in the air.

Mia appeared from behind the sofa and stood where she was, shaking with fear.

Shepherd pulled open the door. It was a storeroom, about ten feet wide, lined with shelves full of bottles and cans. There was no window and no other door.

"We can put them in here," said Shepherd.

Pritchard nodded and barked instructions at his captives. They began to strip off their clothing. As each person disrobed enough to prove they weren't carrying a weapon or a phone, Shepherd ushered them into the storeroom. No one argued or protested; they realised that the alternative was to join the dead heavies on the floor.

Andrej appeared at the top of the stairs. There were three middle-aged men with towels wrapped around their waists and four girls in various stages of undress. Andrej herded them downstairs. There was no need to search them and they were pushed into the storeroom.

346

Pritchard spoke to them harshly, waved his gun, and then closed the door.

Mia was watching them anxiously. "What do we do with her?" asked Pritchard.

"We can't leave her here," said Shepherd. "She can stay at our hotel."

Pritchard thought about it, then nodded. "You're right. Okay, so we have to go to Žagar's place. That's presumably where we'll find Liam and Katra." He gestured at the storeroom door. "The question is, what do we do with them?"

"They're not the bad guys," said Andrej. "Just working girls and customers."

"Except the girls are being held against their will," said Shepherd. "This isn't their fight." He waved Mia over. She threaded her way between the bodies on the floor, tottering on her high heels. "Mia, you don't want to work here, right?"

She shook her head tearfully.

"So why are you here?"

"I owed Žagar money. He said I had to work here to pay off my debt."

"And the other girls? They owe money to Žagar?"

Mia nodded. "Most of them."

Shepherd looked at Andrej. "See what I mean? These girls are being raped on a daily basis."

Andrej nodded but didn't say anything.

"No one's suggesting we hurt them, but we can't let them go, not until we've resolved the situation in Ljubljana," said Pritchard. "If they tell the police or Žagar then we'll never get to Liam and Katra. I don't see any way of locking this door and even if we do there's no guarantee that they won't break out. Someone has to stay. It can't be Mia, obviously. You need to get to your family. So that leaves me and Andrej."

"I'll stay," said Andrej.

"Are you sure?" asked Pritchard.

"It's fine. I'll turn off the lights and you can call me when you're done."

"What about transport?" said Shepherd. "We've only got the one vehicle."

"You can take my car. When we are done, I'll take one of the cars outside and dump it in Ljubljana."

"That works for me," said Pritchard. He patted Andrej on the shoulder. "Thanks for this."

Andrej grinned. "I had nothing planned for tonight."

Pritchard put his gun back into his holster and went over to Diamond Stud. He picked up the dead man's gun. "It'll muddy the waters if we use these guns," he said.

Shepherd followed his example and picked up the gun that Cauliflower Ears had been carrying. It was a Glock 19. Shepherd ejected the magazine and checked it. It was full. He slid the magazine back in and pulled back the slide to slot a round into the breech. "Mia, do you have any things you need to take with you?" asked Shepherd.

"Upstairs," she said.

"Go and grab what you need," said Shepherd.

Mia took off her high heels and ran upstairs.

"You should call the negotiator and get him to make a call to the Slovenian number again," said Pritchard. "He can say anything, we just need to confirm the location."

Shepherd nodded and walked over to the door. He took out his phone and called Chris Thatcher. He answered and Shepherd asked him to make a call to David. "Tell him we have the money ready and we want to confirm a handover location," said Shepherd.

"Is that true?" asked Thatcher.

"No, but by the time he realises I don't have the money, it'll be over one way or another."

"Usually I'd spend more time getting the price down," said Thatcher.

"I appreciate that," said Shepherd. "But this is more about getting his location. Just keep him on the line as long as you can."

"I will do," said Thatcher. "How's it going out there?"

Shepherd looked down at the dead heavies sprawled across the floor like broken toys. "So far so good," he said.

Pritchard was a careful driver, his eyes in constant motion, flicking to the rear-view mirror and the side mirrors. Shepherd had put the Glock that Andrej had given him in the glove compartment and the gun he had taken from the dead heavy was tucked into his belt. The beams of the BMW cut through the night. There were now streetlights on the road and they could see the beams of oncoming traffic long before they reached them.

Mia was sitting in the back, her legs drawn up against her stomach, but she seemed happier now that the brothel was several miles behind them. "What happened, Mia?" asked Shepherd, twisting around in his seat. "Why were you working there? You said you owed Žagar money?"

"Our farm had bad luck," she said. "Our cows got sick and then we lost our sugar beet crop and our mother couldn't pay the bank what we owed them."

"Why didn't you tell Katra?"

"We did. She said she'd talk to you. I don't think she realised what a big problem it was. Anyway our mother needed money to pay the bank and someone said if I went to Žagar he'd lend me money and he did. Five thousand euros, which was enough to pay the bank for two months. Then we had a fire and we lost a barn and a load of equipment and it turned out our mother hadn't paid the insurance. So I went back to Žagar and he was so nice, he lent me another three thousand euros. I was supposed to pay him a thousand euros a week for twelve weeks but then I lost my job and . . ." She shrugged. "We had so much bad luck."

"And then what happened?" asked Shepherd.

"Two weeks ago I couldn't get the money to pay him. I went to see him and he said if I couldn't pay, I could repay the debt by working. That sounded like a great idea because I didn't have a job so he said I could work in a restaurant." She sniffed and wiped her nose with the back of her hand. "I knew as soon as I walked

350

in that it wasn't a restaurant. I tried to leave but they wouldn't let me. The barman, he grabbed me and took me upstairs and raped me. Then the other men there came into the room, one by one." She shuddered. "They all raped me. They said that they owned me, that I was their property, and that if I tried to escape or refused to do what I was told, they'd kill me and they'd kill my family. That first night I had four customers. The busiest night I had seven." She shuddered again.

"I'm sorry," said Shepherd. He didn't know what else to say. There were no words that were going to make her feel better.

"After a week I managed to call my mother. A customer was in the shower and his phone didn't have a password so I called her and told her what had happened. She said she would call the police and I told her the police wouldn't help. The cops come to the house, I've seen them. They come to have sex. They know what's going on, they just don't care."

"They'll be paying off the police," said Pritchard. "Par for the course with places like that."

"I just wanted to let my mother know I was okay." She forced a smile. "Well, not okay, but I was still alive. If I worked long enough then I'd pay back what I owed and I could go home."

Shepherd shook his head. "No, Mia, that's not how it works. They were never going to let you go home."

She sniffed and nodded. "I know. There are girls who have been there for two years. They said no matter how many men they went with, Žagar always said they were still in debt."

351

"So your mother called Katra?"

"I don't know. All I know is that on Saturday, Katra and Liam arrived at the house. They locked them in an upstairs room so I couldn't talk to them. Then this afternoon the men came back and took them." She put a hand up to her face. "I called out to Katra when they brought her downstairs and Anton slapped me." She rubbed a bruise on her cheek.

"Anton? Which one was Anton?"

"The barman," said Mia.

Shepherd smiled tightly. Anton wouldn't be slapping or raping anyone else. He'd had no regrets about shooting the barman but now he was actually pleased that he'd put two rounds in the man's neck.

"Do you have any idea where they were taking Katra and Liam?" asked Pritchard.

Mia shook her head.

"What about when you went to see Žagar? Where did you go?"

"He has a big house in Ljubljana. Everybody knows it."

"Can you show us the house?" asked Pritchard.

Mia nodded.

Shepherd's phone rang and he answered it. It was Chris Thatcher. "I've spoken to David," said Thatcher. "He has agreed on three hundred thousand euros and he wants it paid at nine o'clock tomorrow morning. Charing Cross station. Do you want the details?"

"Sure."

"The money is to be in a backpack. No tracking devices, no tricks, whoever picks up the money will check. The person delivering the money should wear a blue baseball cap and carry a banana."

"A banana?"

"I know," said Thatcher. "I don't know what movie he's been watching. But yes, a banana. I suppose it's one way of making sure the wrong person isn't approached. The handover is to be under the clock on the concourse. The money is to be handed over and the man who collects it will walk away. Once it has been confirmed that the money is okay, Liam and Katra will be released in Ljubljana. Close to a police station."

"Okay Chris. Thank you. Can you monitor the phones for a few hours more, then I think we should have this resolved."

"I will do. Good luck."

"Thanks," said Shepherd. He ended the call and looked across at Pritchard. "Žagar is expecting the ransom at nine o'clock tomorrow morning."

"Well he's got a big surprise coming, hasn't he?" Pritchard's phone beeped. He took it out and held it against the steering wheel, slowing the car as he read the message, then he passed the phone to Shepherd. "Europol have just got back to me about Žagar."

Shepherd studied the phone. There was a head and shoulders photograph of a hard-faced man with receding hair, a flat nose and a thick brow staring at the camera as if he wanted to tear the photographer limb from limb. There was a brief summary of the man's criminal record — human trafficking, extortion, drugs, murder — though most of the allegations remained unproven in a court of law. He'd served two short prison sentences in the mid-eighties, both times for violent assaults. Since then he'd been charged with offences several times but the cases had never gone to court. Witnesses — including police officers — had a habit of disappearing. Zivco Žagar was clearly a nasty piece of work.

Žagar's house was modern, the sort of mansion that would be found in a gated community in Florida. There were two-storey columns either side of a double door, large windows and a triple-doored garage to the side. It stood on several acres of landscaped gardens. In Florida it would probably have been painted white or a subtle shade of beige but someone had decided that this one should be a vivid lilac colour. There was a black Bentley and a Mercedes SUV parked in front of the garage. The gardens were surrounded by an ugly concrete block wall topped by coils of military razor wire. There was a tall wrought iron gate through which they could see two heavy-set men in camouflage pattern jackets standing in the drive carrying shotguns. Pritchard drove by without slowing so all Shepherd got was a glimpse of the building.

"Crime obviously pays in this part of the world," said Shepherd.

Pritchard pulled over at the side of the road about a half a mile away from Žagar's house. "The guards look serious," he said. "And carrying guns like that in the open means he has the cops on the payroll."

"The wall looks daunting, so I guess we have to go in through the gate," said Shepherd.

"The wire looks vicious but we can cut it," said Pritchard. "And we can use the night vision goggles and come in through the back."

"We don't know how many guards there are in the grounds," said Shepherd. "Maybe a diversion at the front and we go in at the back." He nodded to himself. "It might work. But with just the two of us it's going to be tight." He twisted around in his seat to look at Mia. She was hugging her knees to her chest, clearly upset at being so close to Žagar's house. "Did you go inside, Mia?" She nodded fearfully and Shepherd flashed her an encouraging smile. "How do you get in? You just went to the gates?"

She nodded. "He will see anyone who needs help."

"Especially pretty young girls, I bet," said Pritchard.

"He is a sort of local godfather," said Shepherd. "Is your Serbo-Croat good enough to pass yourself off as a local?"

"He speaks perfectly," said Mia. "But Žagar knows everybody. He will know he is a stranger."

"I could get around that," said Pritchard. "You're right, I could talk my way in, but what then?"

Shepherd turned around to look at Mia again. "They just let you in? You told them you wanted to talk to Žagar and they opened the gate?"

She nodded.

"And you walked up the drive yourself?"

"One of the guards took me. He knocked on the door and there was another guard inside."

"With a shotgun?"

She shook her head. "He had a gun in a thing under his arm."

"How many guards did you see inside the house?"

Mia's brow creased into a frown as she tried to remember. "Three," she said. "Or four." Her frown deepened and then she nodded again. "Four. The one who opened the door and then three more."

Pritchard's phone beeped and he checked it. He studied his screen for almost a minute before looking up at Shepherd. "The phone isn't there, it's in a building about three miles away," he said. He twisted around in his seat and showed the phone to Mia. It was showing a Google Maps satellite image of a couple of blocks of the town. "Do you know where this is?"

Her frown deepened as she stared at the screen. "I'm not sure. I don't think so."

Pritchard took the phone back and switched to a street view. He showed her the screen again and she immediately recognised the building. "It's a nightclub," she said. "The Hangar Club, Žagar owns it."

Pritchard turned back to look at Shepherd. "That's probably where Katra and Liam are."

"Have you been inside, Mia?" asked Shepherd. She shook her head.

Pritchard put the BMW in gear and drove off. It took less than ten minutes to reach the Grand Hotel. Pritchard parked the car and they walked in together. They went up in the lift to Shepherd's room and he unlocked the door. Mia went in first and sat down on the bed. "I'm so tired," she said.

"You should shower and then sleep," said Shepherd.

"What are you going to do?" she asked.

"We're going to get Liam and Katra."

"I can help," she said and he smiled at her enthusiasm.

"No, we'll handle it," he said. He looked at Pritchard, who was helping himself to a bottle of water from the mini-bar. "Got any clubbing gear?" he asked.

Pritchard held up his Glock. "Just this," he said.

Pritchard parked the BMW in a side street around the corner from The Hangar Club. He and Shepherd got out of the car and checked each other out. They were both carrying their guns tucked into the back of their jeans and were wearing their shirts loose under their jackets. Pritchard did a full three-sixty, holding his arms out. There were no signs that he was carrying a concealed weapon. Shepherd did the same.

"What's the plan?" asked Shepherd as they walked towards the nightclub. It was a two-storey windowless flat-roofed building, the ground floor painted black, the top floor grey, with a huge logo of an aeroplane propeller in the middle. Stainless steel riveted plates spelled out the name of the club above a black awning under which there were two big men in dark coats with the hard faces and cold eyes favoured by bouncers around the world.

"I don't see that we've any choice other than to play it by ear," said Pritchard. "The phone is in there somewhere, and that means Žagar is there and with any luck that's where he's keeping Liam and Katra."

357

There was a line of four brass poles linked by a red rope but there was no queue of people waiting to go in and the bouncers just nodded as Pritchard and Shepherd walked by. Pritchard greeted them in Serbo-Croat and one of them grunted. It was still early for a nightclub so Shepherd figured they were letting anyone in.

Inside there was a reception area with red carpets and black walls and lots of UV lights. To their right was a hatch to a cloakroom where a blonde girl wearing a black beret was tapping something into her smartphone. Next to the cloakroom was a flight of stairs leading to the upper floor, blocked off with a thick red rope from which hung a sign saying "STAFF ONLY". To the left was another hatch and above it a notice saying there was a twenty-euro entrance charge. They could hear the thump of techno music coming through double doors. Pritchard paid a young bearded hipster type and they went through the double doors into the club proper.

It was a huge room with a bar at one end and a DJ booth set against a wall where a blonde girl in a leather dress and large padded headphones was nodding to the track while a brunette with full sleeve tattoos flicked through a box of LPs. There were a few dozen clubbers dancing, all about half Shepherd's age, but there were plenty of middle-aged men clustered around the bar or standing or sitting at high circular tables around the dance floor.

Shepherd followed Pritchard over to the bar. Pritchard bought two beers and handed a bottle to

Shepherd. "*Na zdravje*," he said and clinked his bottle against Shepherd's.

There was an area of sofas in a corner of the club, and they went over and chose one that gave them a full view of what was going on. Above the bar was a VIP area, reached by a wide flight of stairs that was guarded by two more bouncers, wearing tight-black T-shirts with the name of the club on the front.

"I think the offices are reached by the stairs in the reception area," said Pritchard. "The VIP area doesn't seem to lead anywhere."

Shepherd nodded. That had been his thought, too. He sipped his beer as he looked around. Two bouncers outside. Two guarding the VIP area. Another three wandering around looking to nip trouble in the bud. Big men who could clearly handle themselves if things got physical, but they weren't carrying guns.

Getting upstairs would be easy enough, but what then? The bouncers weren't armed but there was every chance that any heavies upstairs were. On the plus side, nobody in the nightclub would hear any shots over the thumping music.

Pritchard sipped his beer. "Ready when you are," he said.

"You're okay with this?" Shepherd asked.

"Daniel, I wouldn't be here if I wasn't."

Shepherd smiled thinly. "Thank you."

"No need to thank me," said Pritchard.

Shepherd put down his beer. "Let's do it," he said.

They walked towards the exit. Shepherd pushed through the double doors. Two men in leather jackets were on the other side and Shepherd and Pritchard held the doors open for them. The two men were followed by two young women with dyed blonde hair and too much make-up, wearing minidresses and knee-length boots. The girls followed the men into the nightclub and then Shepherd and Pritchard let the doors swing shut.

Shepherd stepped over the rope blocking the stairway and headed up. Pritchard followed him.

Shepherd reached behind him and pulled out the Glock he had taken from Cauliflower Ears.

The stairs turned sharply to the right. Shepherd peered around. There were another twelve stairs up to a small landing. At the top of the stairs was a door with another "STAFF ONLY" sign on it. There was no CCTV. Shepherd reckoned that Žagar didn't want a record of the comings and goings.

Shepherd kept the gun low as he walked up the stairs. Pritchard followed, his pistol at the ready.

They reached the top of the stairs and stood either side of the door. During his years in the SAS, Shepherd had practised entering a hostile room thousands of times, but that didn't make it any easier. Usually he would have an idea of what lay behind the door — he'd have seen a floor plan or had the layout described to him, and more often than not he'd have intel on the nature of the enemy that he would be facing. On this occasion all he knew was that Zivco Žagar was probably there with an unknown number of men carrying an unknown number of weapons.

He could feel the dull throb of the nightclub's sound system coming up through the floor as he reached out to hold the door handle. He looked at Pritchard and nodded. Pritchard nodded back. Shepherd was surprised at how calm Pritchard was under pressure. He had misjudged the man completely. Pritchard flashed him a tight smile as if he'd read his mind. Shepherd turned the handle. The door opened inwards.

There was a single room with a huge oak desk at the far end, behind which Žagar was sitting in a high-backed chair. On the wall behind him was a painting in a gilt frame that appeared to show Žagar in a nobleman's uniform riding a black horse and brandishing a sabre.

Žagar was smoking a cigar and he took it out of his mouth as he stared at Shepherd and Pritchard, more out of surprise than fear, despite the guns they were holding.

There were two sofas — one to the left, one to the right — with a large wooden coffee table, which appeared to have been carved from a single tree trunk, between them. Each sofa was occupied by a big man dressed in black, one totally bald, the other with grey hair tied back in a short ponytail. Both men had left their guns on the table and they reached for them until Pritchard barked at them to stay where they were. Both men raised their hands in the air. Pritchard spoke to them brusquely and they both put their hands behind their necks and interlinked their fingers. Pritchard stepped forward, picked up the two pistols, and stood back.

There were no windows, the walls were painted a dark purple and even with three fluorescent lights the room still had a gloomy, claustrophobic feel to it.

Žagar flicked ash from his cigar into a large brass ashtray that stood on his desk next to a bottle of brandy and a chunky tumbler and growled at Pritchard in Serbo-Croat.

"English would be better," said Pritchard. "My friend here isn't familiar with your language, and I'm a little rusty."

"Who the fuck are you?" snapped Žagar.

"Where are you keeping them?" asked Shepherd. "Liam and Katra?"

Žagar narrowed his eyes. "You are the negotiator?" His frown deepened. "No, you are the boy's father." He grinned. "They are not here. Now fuck off and get me my money."

"Where are they?" asked Shepherd. "Your house?"

Žagar shrugged. "You pay me what I am owed and you will get your family back." He took a long slow drag on his cigar and then blew smoke towards them.

"How much did Mia borrow from you?"

Žagar shrugged again. "That doesn't matter. You know the price for your family. You pay it or you'll never see them again."

"You don't think I'll kill you?"

"If you kill me, you'll never see your family again." He took another pull on his cigar.

Shepherd walked over to the sofa and pointed the gun at the heavy with the pony tail. The heavy flinched and turned his head away. Shepherd bent over, grabbed

362

a cushion with his left hand and then pressed it against the barrel of his Glock as he aimed at the man's knee and pulled the trigger. The cushion muffled a lot of the explosion. The man grunted in pain and grabbed his injured leg. Shepherd looked over at Žagar. "The next one goes into his head, the one after that will be in your stomach."

The bald heavy stood up but Pritchard shouted at him in Serbo-Croat and he sat down again.

"Okay, okay, you've proved that you're serious," said Žagar. "What do you want?" He picked up his tumbler and took a long drink of brandy. His hand wasn't shaking, Shepherd noticed. Žagar wasn't a man who frightened easily.

"I told you what I want. I want my family."

Žagar waved his glass around the room. "As you can see, they are not here."

"Where are they? In that shitty lilac castle of yours?"

Žagar took another drink from his glass. He studied Shepherd as he swallowed, like a fox weighing up a chicken.

"What do you think?" Pritchard asked Shepherd.

"The house is a fortress," said Shepherd. "High walls and razor wire and armed guards. We could go over the wall with night vision goggles but I'm thinking that going in through the front gates would be so much easier."

"That's exactly what I was thinking," said Pritchard. He looked over at Žagar and spoke to him in Serbo-Croat.

Žagar sneered at him. "You will die," he said. He spat on the floor. "Better you just kill yourselves now because if I get my hands on you you'll spend a long time dying."

"Sticks and stones," said Shepherd, but it was clear from the way Žagar frowned that he didn't understand the reference. Shepherd pointed the Glock at Žagar's face. "Listen to me and listen well. The only way you are going to get out of this alive is if you get us into your house and we get out with Katra and Liam."

Žagar glared at him with undisguised hatred.

Shepherd took off his jacket, then removed his underarm holster and tossed it behind Žagar's desk. He draped his jacket over his Glock, making sure that Žagar could see that his finger was on the trigger.

"We're going to walk out of here like we are the best of friends," he said. "We're going to walk to our car and you're going to sit in the front seat next to my friend here, and I'll be sitting behind you. One mistake and I will shoot you and I will do it with a smile on my face."

Žagar stood up and wriggled his shoulders like a boxer preparing to fight. "You don't scare me," he growled.

"I don't care if you're scared or not," said Shepherd. "All I care about is that you do as you're told."

Pritchard spoke to Žagar in Serbo-Croat. Žagar grunted. "I was telling him that I'll be listening to what he says to the staff downstairs and that one wrong word means we'll start shooting."

"Dead right," said Shepherd.

364

"I will need my coat," said Žagar. He nodded at a cashmere overcoat on a hanger on the back of the door. "It is cold outside."

Shepherd grabbed the coat and checked that the pockets were empty before handing it to Žagar.

The guy who Shepherd had shot was now white in the face, still clutching his injured leg. "You'll be okay," said Shepherd. "Take off your belt and apply a tourniquet above the knee. Not too tight."

The man did as he was told. Žagar put on his overcoat and buttoned it up. Shepherd kept his gun trained on Žagar's chest. "Sit down," he said. "We're not ready to go yet."

Žagar went back behind his desk and dropped down into his executive chair. Shepherd went over and checked the makeshift tourniquet on the injured man's leg. Much of the bleeding had stopped. "You'll live," said Shepherd.

"Fuck you," snarled the man.

Shepherd pointed his Glock at the man's face. "Now lie on the sofa, face down." He gestured at the other heavy. "You too."

Pritchard repeated the instructions in Serbo-Croat and they obeyed, but were clearly fearful that they were about to be killed.

Shepherd grabbed the telephone on Žagar's desk and ripped the wire out of the wall, then pulled the wire out of the phone. He went over to the bald heavy and used the wire to bind his wrists and ankles. The heavy was wearing a tie and Shepherd took it off and fashioned a gag.

He looked around the room. There was an electric heater against the wall and he ripped the wires from that and used it to bind the injured man, ignoring the man's moans and yelps. The man wasn't wearing a tie so Shepherd pulled off his shoes and socks and tied the socks together to gag him.

Once he had bound and gagged the two heavies, he waved his gun at Žagar. "Time to go," he said.

As Žagar walked around his desk, Pritchard moved with him, keeping his gun aimed at his chest.

Pritchard opened the door and went out, putting his gun back into its holster before beckoning the gangster to follow him. As Žagar walked out. Shepherd followed a step behind him, keeping his gun levelled at the man's waist. They walked down the stairs and stepped carefully over the rope. The man taking the entrance fee looked over and his eyes widened when he saw Žagar. Žagar immediately said something in Serbo-Croat and the man smiled. Shepherd looked over at Pritchard who nodded. All good.

Žagar spoke to the woman in the cloakroom, and from the way she hurriedly put her phone away, Shepherd figured he had told her off. They walked to the exit. Shepherd tensed. If there was going to be a problem it would be when Žagar was with the bouncers. That would be when he would feel the least threatened. His finger tightened on the trigger. The bouncers hadn't appeared to be armed but they were big men and wouldn't hesitate to get physical. They walked outside. The bouncers were talking to two long-haired blondes in miniskirts and knee-length

366

suede boots. They turned to see who was coming out and were clearly surprised to see Žagar. Žagar patted one of them on the back and said something that made them laugh.

Pritchard said something and the bouncers nodded. Shepherd kept the concealed gun trained on Žagar. If it all went wrong he'd put one bullet in Žagar, take care of the bouncers, and then shoot Žagar again. That was his fall-back position, but it wasn't necessary. Žagar and Pritchard started walking to where the BMW was parked and Shepherd followed them. Only when they turned the corner did Shepherd relax. So far, so good.

As the BMW approached the wrought iron gates, Pritchard spoke to Žagar in a quiet monotone. Shepherd listened. He knew nothing of the language but he could guess what Pritchard was saying. Something along the lines of "keep smiling and tell them that your car has got a problem and your two nice friends have offered to drive you home and don't say anything that will tip them off that something is wrong because if you do you'll get a bullet in the back of your head."

Žagar nodded sullenly. "*Da*," he said, which Shepherd did understand.

Pritchard brought the BMW to a halt in front of the gates and pressed the button to open the passenger window. Shepherd had his Glock down close to the floor, his finger gently touching the trigger. If it went wrong and Žagar did call out for help then he'd shoot Žagar then the two guards and Pritchard would stamp on the accelerator and hopefully smash through the gates, but that was very much plan B.

One of the guards approached the gate, cradling his shotgun. Žagar waved and spoke to him. Pritchard smiled at the man and nodded. Shepherd did the same.

The guard opened the gates. Pritchard closed the window and drove through. He reached the house and parked next to the Bentley. "Nice car," he said.

"Imported," growled Žagar.

"Obviously," said Pritchard. "How much would a car like that cost in Slovenia?"

"I don't know," said Žagar.

"You don't know?"

"I have a car importing business. I acquired it through the company."

Pritchard nodded. "Must be nice not to worry about the price of things," he said. "Right, so this is what is going to happen. We will get out of the car. We walk into the house together. My friend here will have his finger on the trigger at all times and if we even suspect that you are trying something, he will shoot you dead and then we will shoot everyone in the house. Then we will take Liam and Katra but you and everyone who works for you will be dead. Are we clear?"

"Yes," said Žagar. "I am not fucking stupid, despite what you seem to think."

"Once we have Liam and Katra we will leave and you are free to do whatever you want to do."

Žagar nodded and Pritchard smiled brightly. "Right, let's get started." He opened the door and got out. Shepherd also got out, keeping his jacket draped over

368

his Glock. He kept the barrel pointing at Žagar as the gangster slowly got out of the front passenger seat.

They walked together towards the front door, Shepherd slightly behind Žagar, the gun pointing at the man's left kidney.

The front door opened as they approached. A heavy with a shaved head wearing an Adidas tracksuit looked at the three of them, frowning. Žagar spoke to him and the man relaxed and opened the door wide.

They walked through into a large marble hallway. There was a massive modern chandelier hanging over their heads and a life-size model of a growling lion at the base of a curved marble staircase. There were four doors leading off the hallway, one of which led to a kitchen full of stainless steel appliances. A middle-aged woman came out, wringing her hands. At first Shepherd thought it might be Žagar's wife but it was clear from her obsequious tone and his brusque reply that she was a member of staff.

Žagar gestured at the staircase with his chin. "*Uz stepenice*," he growled.

Pritchard nodded. They went up the stairs together, Žagar and Pritchard leading the way.

The woman went back into the kitchen and the heavy in the tracksuit disappeared into one of the ground floor rooms.

They reached the upper landing. Hallways led off left and right. To the right a man was standing facing them, his hands clasped over his groin. His head was shaved and he had a rope-like scar across his neck that looked more like a war injury than the result of a bar brawl.

Žagar spoke to the man and the man turned and opened the door he was standing in front of.

Žagar went in first. As Pritchard reached the heavy, he pulled out his Glock and jammed it against the man's throat. He hissed at him in Serbo-Croat as he reached inside his jacket and pulled a pistol from the man's holster. He tucked the gun into his waistband and pushed the man into the room. Shepherd followed them, taking his jacket away to reveal his Glock.

Katra was lying on the bed, her wrists and ankles bound with duct tape. There was a strip of duct tape across her mouth. Her eyes widened when she saw Shepherd and she tried to speak but the gag muffled any sound.

Liam was tied to a chair with duct tape and he had also been gagged. He grunted and strained at his bonds.

Shepherd closed the door. "Against the wall," he said, gesturing at Žagar with his gun. Žagar did as he was told. The heavy followed suit as Pritchard motioned with his gun. The two men stood facing the wall as Shepherd hurried over to the bed. He put down the gun and carefully pulled the duct tape away from Katra's face. "Dan," she gasped. "I'm so sorry."

"Shush," he said. "It's going to be fine." He looked around for something to cut the duct tape but there was nothing obvious. He took his key ring from his pockets and used a key to hack away at the tape binding her wrists. After half a dozen slashes the tape parted. She threw her arms around his neck and kissed him tearfully. "Steady," he said, untangling himself

370

from her arms. "Let me get all the stuff off you and I can untie Liam."

He removed the tape from around her ankles, then went over to Liam. He gently pried the tape away from his son's mouth. "What took you so long?" Liam joked, but Shepherd could tell how scared he was.

"Traffic was terrible," he said. "Are you okay?"

Liam nodded. "I'll be better when I'm out of here," he said.

Shepherd pointed at the burn on Liam's forehead. "What happened?"

"Nothing, I'm fine," said Liam. "Can we just get the hell out of here?"

Shepherd used the key to hack through the tape binding his wrists to the chair, then freed his legs as Liam massaged the circulation back into his wrists.

When he had finished untying Liam, he went back over to Katra who was now sitting on the bed. "Are you okay?" he asked, sitting next to her. "Did they hurt you?"

"Not really," she said. "I mean, yes, but not . . . you know . . ."

She began to sob and Shepherd put his arm around her. "Where are your shoes?" he asked.

"I don't know," she sobbed. "I'm sorry."

Shepherd stood up and looked around. He spotted her trainers by the bathroom door and he went over and got them for her. "We're going home now," he said.

"Dan, I'm sorry, but Mia is in trouble."

"Mia's back at the hotel," said Shepherd. "We'll go and see her."

Liam went over to the window and looked out through the blinds. "Let's get ready to go," Shepherd said.

"I'm so sorry," said Katra, starting to cry again. "This is all my fault."

"No, it isn't, and don't say that," said Shepherd. "Sometimes bad people do bad things."

"I thought if I came over here I could sort it out. I asked Liam to help."

"No, I offered to help," said Liam.

"Guys, all that matters is that we get out of here, okay? Katra, put your shoes on. Liam, are you good to go?"

"Can I have a gun?"

Shepherd shook his head. "We're not shooting our way out," he said. "We're going to go downstairs and get into our car and drive away. No one is going to try to stop us."

"What about him?" asked Liam, nodding at Žagar.

Katra sat on the edge of the bed and started putting on her trainers.

"What do you think?" Shepherd asked Pritchard. "What do we do with him?"

Pritchard looked over his shoulder. "He's not going to let . . ." Žagar pushed himself away from the wall and pulled the gun from Pritchard's belt. He fumbled with the handle and as Pritchard turned, Žagar slammed the barrel against the side of his head.

Pritchard staggered back, stunned.

Žagar was surprisingly quick for a man of his size. He took two steps over to the bed and grabbed Katra,

372

putting his left arm around her neck and dragging her to her feet as he pressed the barrel of the gun against the side of her head.

Liam moved towards Katra. "Liam, no!" shouted Shepherd. "Stay back!"

Liam took a couple of steps back.

Shepherd used both his hands to aim his Glock at Žagar's face but Žagar kept moving, keeping Katra between him and Shepherd.

Žagar glared at Shepherd. "You're not going anywhere," he said. "You think you can come here and threaten me? In my own house?"

Shepherd moved to the side but Žagar kept Katra in the way. Katra stared at Shepherd in horror.

"Let the girl go, Žagar. We can all walk out of here."

"You're lying," said Žagar. "You're going to kill me."

"Not if you let the girl go," said Shepherd.

Žagar pulled Katra back, keeping the gun against her head, until he was standing in the doorway to the bathroom. "You go," said Žagar. "You leave now or I will put a bullet in this bitch's head."

"Dad, shoot him!" shouted Liam. "Shoot him before he hurts Katra!"

Pritchard had his gun pointing at Žagar, but now he was in the doorway he could only be approached face on and Katra was in the way.

"We just want to go home," said Shepherd. He had a clear shot and his finger tightened on his trigger but then the moment passed and Katra was in his sight line again.

"Dan . . ." she gasped, but then Žagar tightened his grip on her throat. She only had one trainer on, Shepherd realised; the other was by the bed.

"You walk away and send me my money," said Žagar. "Then I will let the woman go."

Shepherd shook his head. He dropped his aim and had a clear shot of Žagar's hip but he needed to be sure that his first shot was fatal.

"If you hurt her I will kill you, I swear!" shouted Liam, his hands bunched into fists.

"Liam, let me handle this," said Shepherd, keeping his eyes fixed on Žagar, looking for the shot that would save Katra's life.

Katra began clawing at the arm around her throat. It looked as if she was getting close to passing out and Žagar was having trouble keeping her upright. Her eyes widened in panic and she opened her mouth but no sound came out.

"Žagar!" shouted Shepherd. "Let her go!"

Žagar grinned. He aimed the gun at the ceiling and pulled the trigger. The bullet thwacked into the ceiling and flecks of plaster sprinkled down like a light snow fall.

They heard shouts from downstairs. Shepherd looked over at Pritchard. They had only seconds before Žagar's men would be outside the door. Pritchard grimaced. "I'm out of ideas," he said.

Shepherd looked back at Žagar. "This doesn't have to go this way," he said. "Just let us go. No one else needs to get hurt."

374

"Fuck you!" shouted Žagar. "This is my home! My fucking home! Who the fuck do you think you are?"

Shepherd took a step back. He pointed his gun up at the ceiling but kept his finger on the trigger. "I just want my family back. That's all I want. Nobody else needs to die."

There were rapid footsteps on the stairs and muffled shouts.

Žagar grinned in triumph. "Fuck you!" he said, and pulled the trigger. The side of Katra's head exploded and blood splattered across the bed.

Liam screamed in horror.

Shepherd's mouth opened and he blinked, unable to process what he had just seen. Time seemed to stop. He could see the blood spraying from Katra's head; he could see the look of disbelief in her eyes; the snarl on Žagar's face; the gun, ready to fire again; Pritchard turning to look at Žagar; the heavy preparing to rush Pritchard.

Time picked up speed again and Katra fell to the side like a marionette whose strings had been cut. She fell onto the bed but immediately rolled off and sprawled across the floor, smearing blood across the bedding.

Liam rushed towards Žagar, his arms outstretched, fingers curled into talons. Žagar was roaring now and turning the gun towards Liam.

Shepherd fired twice and both shots hit Žagar in the head. Shepherd felt no satisfaction as the man fell to the floor, his face a bloody mess. He felt nothing at all.

The heavy was grabbing for Pritchard's gun. Shepherd turned and fired, shooting him in the chest.

There were more shouts outside. Shepherd gestured for Pritchard to move to the side and he fired through the door three times. There was a grunt and the sound of a body falling to the floor.

"Liam, get down," shouted Shepherd. Liam did as he was told, kneeling behind the bed.

Pritchard was down in a crouch, his gun in both hands. "Door," said Shepherd, moving to the side. They had to move quickly; if it became a siege situation it would end badly.

Pritchard shuffled forward, still bent low, and used his left hand to turn the door handle. He pulled the door open and stepped back. As the door swung open, Shepherd saw the man in the tracksuit lying on the floor. He was still alive and holding a pistol. Shepherd shot him in the head and then ducked out. The stairs were to his right so he kept low and swung the Glock in that direction, letting off two quick shots to keep any attackers on the back foot. He stepped over the body of the man he'd shot and saw there were two men in the hallway, one with a shotgun, one with a pistol. Shepherd shot the guy with the shotgun first, two quick shots to the chest, then moved to the left and fired as the guy with the handgun pulled his trigger. Both guns fired at the same time. The heavy's shot went high and whizzed by Shepherd's left ear, embedding itself in the wall. Shepherd's shot hit the man in the throat and blood gushed down his shirt front. The gun was still pointing in Shepherd's direction so Shepherd fired

376

again and put a bullet into his heart. The man fell to the floor.

Shepherd had fired fourteen shots. There had been fifteen in the clip. There were more shouts from downstairs and Shepherd rushed down the hallway. There was no going back now.

He picked up the dropped shotgun and tucked the Glock into his belt. The shotgun was a Mossberg 500, five cartridges in the magazine and one in the chamber. It was a nice weapon and appeared brand new. The ambidextrous safety was already in the off position. Shepherd couldn't tell what type of cartridges it contained but no matter what they were they would be good for shock and awe. He reached the top of the stairs and looked down. There were three men heading up, brandishing pistols. He pointed the shotgun at the man in the middle and pulled the trigger. The shotgun kicked in his hand and the blast knocked the man backwards, reducing his face to a mangled mess. From the damage Shepherd guessed the weapon was loaded with magnum shells. He ejected the spent cartridge, pumped in a second round and shot the man on the left, then ducked down to reload. Two shots smacked into the wall behind him, then he stood up and fired in a smooth, fluid motion. The shot caught the man square in the chest and he fell over the banister and hit the marble floor with the sound of a wet towel slapping against a wall.

The heavy who had taken the second shot was sitting with his back to the wall, blood pouring down his chest. He was still holding his gun and he raised it with a shaking hand but then the life faded from his eyes and the gun clattered on the marble stairs.

"Dad, look out!" shouted Liam.

A man appeared from the kitchen wearing a long black coat and flat cap, holding an Uzi. Shepherd started to pump in a new shell but he knew he was going to be too slow and was bracing himself for a hail of bullets when there were two rapid shots from behind him and the man with the Uzi staggered back. Shepherd took a quick look over his shoulder. Liam was at the top of the landing, holding a Glock with both hands. Pritchard was standing behind him. As Shepherd watched, Liam fired a third time.

The man with the Uzi fell onto his back, his lifeless eyes staring up at the ceiling.

Shepherd stepped over the two bodies on the stairs and went down to the front door. There were at least two guards outside, probably more, and they would have been certain to have heard the shots.

He hurried over to the guy with the Uzi. Liam had hit him in the chest with all three shots and blood was soaking into the man's shirt. Shepherd pulled the coat off him and put it on. There was hardly any blood on it and it was a reasonable fit.

Pritchard came down the stairs. "Good idea," he said as Shepherd put on the man's cap, he laid the shotgun against the wall and picked up the Uzi. It wasn't a genuine Uzi, he realised, but a Croatian clone, probably manufactured during the Yugoslav Wars. At just over eight pounds it was heavier than the original and the markings on the selector switch were different — the clone had R for full automatic fire, P for single shot, and Z for safe. The gun was set to full automatic and Shepherd clicked it to single shot. He ejected the magazine. It was full. Thirty-two 9 mm rounds. It had a folding metal stock, locked in place.

Liam was still standing at the top of the stairs. "Nice shooting," said Shepherd. "But stay where you are for the moment."

"Okay, Dad," said Liam.

Shepherd buttoned up the coat and went over to the front door. He kept his head down as he opened it. Pritchard moved to the side, covering the door with his Glock. Shepherd pulled open the door and looked out. The two guards who had been at the gate were striding along the drive, cradling their shotguns. Shepherd kept his head down and the Uzi at his side. He waved with his free hand, then stepped back into the hallway and pushed the door so that it was just ajar. He nodded at Pritchard. They both kept their guns trained on the door.

Five seconds later they heard muffled voices and the door swung open. Shepherd stepped to the side. As soon as the two men came into view he fired, two shots into the man on the left, two in the one on the right. The door continued to open as the two men slumped to the floor. Shepherd sprang forward and stepped over the bodies, sweeping the area with the Uzi, finger on the trigger. The driveway was clear. He looked to the left. Clear. He looked to the right, just as a man emerged from behind the garage. He was holding a pistol but didn't have time to raise it before Shepherd put two shots in his chest. Shepherd ran to the garage. The man was still alive so Shepherd shot him in the head and then ducked around the garage. Two more heavies were running towards the house, one with a handgun, the other cradling a shotgun. They stopped when they saw Shepherd. The heavy with the pistol raised his hand in salute and shouted something in Serbo-Croat.

"*Da!*" Shepherd shouted back, then he swung up his gun and put two shots in the man's chest. The guy with the shotgun stood fixed to the spot, still trying to process what he was seeing. Shepherd shot him twice, then jogged around the back of the house, looking for any other guards. There didn't seem to be any. It took him a full thirty seconds to jog all the way around the house and back to the front door. He took another look down the driveway, then went inside. An ashen-faced Liam had joined Pritchard in the hall. "All clear outside," said Shepherd. He put the Uzi on the floor and took off the coat and hat.

"I'll drop you and Liam back at the hotel then I'll go and collect Andrej," said Pritchard. "I'll take the guns back and put them in the hands of the dead heavies in the brothel. It'll muddy the waters."

"What about Katra?" asked Liam. "We can't just leave her here."

"We have to, Liam," said Shepherd, tossing the hat and coat onto the floor by the body of the man who had been wearing them. "The police will be here later, they'll take her body away."

"You can't leave her with strangers, Dad."

380

Shepherd put his hand on Liam's shoulder. "She's dead, nothing's going to change that," he said.

"Dad!" There were tears in Liam's eyes.

"I know, I know. I know exactly what you mean."

"You don't leave your people behind, Dad. Isn't that what the SAS says?"

"This is different," said Shepherd. "Slovenia is her home."

"Her home is with us. How can you say that?"

"This is where her family is. The police will handle everything, her family can identify her, then there'll be a funeral and we can come to that."

Liam shook his head. "They can't have the funeral here. She belongs with us."

"This is where her family is, Liam," said Shepherd. He heard the tremor in his voice and he took a deep breath. "She came back here to help them. This is where she needs to stay now." He smiled sadly. "I understand. I do. But even if we put her in the car and drive her away from here, what do we do? We can hardly take her body back to the UK, can we? She's dead, Liam. We have to let her go." He reached out and took the Glock from Liam's shaking hands.

"It's like you don't care," said Liam, bitterly.

The words hit Shepherd like a punch in the stomach. "I care," he said, earnestly. "Believe me, I care. I loved Katra. I still love her. But there comes a point when you have to let go and that's the point we've reached. We can come back for the funeral. We can take as long as we need to mourn her. But her body has to stay here."

"He's right, Liam," said Pritchard. "What's done is done. Now we have to move forward."

Liam looked as if he wanted to argue, but then he nodded. "Okay." He looked up at the stairs. "I want to say goodbye to her."

Shepherd shook his head. "You're better remembering her as she was," he said. "Don't let what's upstairs be the memory you keep with you. Remember her laughing, smiling, remember her cooking for us, sitting on the sofa watching *Britain's Got Talent* and laughing until she cried. Remember the holiday we had last year in Florida. Remember all the good things."

Liam kept looking up the stairs, then he nodded as he realised that Shepherd was right. "Okay," he said.

Pritchard nodded. "Let's go," he said.

Pritchard dropped Shepherd and Liam outside the Grand Hotel and then headed back to Novo Mesto. Shepherd took Liam up to his room. His heart was pounding all the way up in the lift at the thought of what he was going to have to say to Mia. She was sitting on the bed when he let them into the room and she smiled when she saw Liam but then her smile turned to confusion when she realised that Katra wasn't with them. Shepherd sat down next to her and took her hands in his and she burst into tears before he even started to speak. She kept her head down and sobbed quietly while Shepherd told her what had happened in Žagar's house. When he'd finished she lay down and turned on her side. Shepherd patted her shoulder, not knowing what to say to comfort her.

He stood up and went over to Liam, who had sat down in an armchair by the window. "Are you okay?" asked Shepherd.

"Not really," said Liam. He rubbed his face with his hands. "Why did Žagar kill Katra?"

"I don't know," said Shepherd. "It might have been an accident. He was angry, he fired up at the ceiling, maybe the second shot was a mistake. Maybe he wanted to hurt me. I don't know."

"It made no sense," said Liam. "He didn't gain anything by killing her. He could have just let us go and everyone would have been okay. He would be alive now and so would Katra. Why are people so fucking stupid sometimes?"

"They just are," said Shepherd. "He was an evil shit, you know that. You saw how he treated the girls in that place, and he thought nothing of threatening to kill you and Katra."

"But by killing Katra he killed himself. You wouldn't have killed him if he'd let her go, would you?"

Shepherd didn't answer. It was a difficult question. After everything that had happened, he couldn't see how he could have let Žagar live. The gangster would have wanted revenge. More than that, he would have needed it. If he hadn't struck back then he'd have appeared weak and in Žagar's line of work weakness usually ended in death. Shepherd didn't see that Žagar would have had any choice other than to come after him with everything he had, and he wouldn't have stopped until Shepherd was dead. So the answer to Liam's question was yes, he was never going to let

Žagar go, no matter how it had played out. Had Žagar known that? Was that why he had pulled the trigger?

"Dad?" asked Liam.

Shepherd forced a smile. "There's no point in going over it," he said. "What happened, happened. We can't change that." Images flashed through his mind. Katra's eyes, filled with tears. The hand clamped around her throat. The gun. The shot. The blood spraying across the bed. He shuddered.

"I'd have let him go," said Liam. "I'd let a hundred guys like him go just so I could keep Katra with us."

"I understand," said Shepherd. He gripped his son's shoulder. "What you did on the stairs. That was good shooting."

Liam shrugged. "I'm a soldier, Dad. I fly helicopters but I've been trained to use guns."

"World of a difference between targets and people," said Shepherd. "You put three rounds in a man's chest."

"He was going to shoot you. I wasn't about to let that happen."

Shepherd nodded. "You saved my life."

"Which is why I won't give it a moment's thought, if that's what you're worried about. I don't feel the least bit guilty and I'm sure I never will. And if I could have killed Žagar, I'd have done that happily."

"Okay."

"What happens now?" asked Liam.

"We wait for my friend to get back."

"Who is he?"

"Someone I work with."

"He doesn't look like a cop."

Shepherd nodded. He had never told Liam that he worked for MI5. There had been no need. And the work he did for the Security Service was similar to what he'd done for the police and the Serious Organised Crime Agency. "Looks can be deceptive," he said. "Do you want to shower? I've got clean underwear and a shirt if you want them."

Liam smiled wearily. "Yes to the shower and the shirt, but I'll pass on the underwear." He hugged Shepherd, hard, then headed to the bathroom.

Pritchard returned after two hours. Shepherd let him into the room and Pritchard looked worried when he saw Mia curled up on the bed. He gestured for Shepherd to follow him next door and the two men went through to Pritchard's room. "We need to get back to London before the shit hits the fan here," said Pritchard.

Shepherd nodded. He had already reached the same conclusion. "I don't really want to fly out of Slovenia, even if we are using legends," said Pritchard. "Croatia would be better. There's a 6.25a.m. Lufthansa flight leaving Zagreb that will get us in to London City Airport at 9.30 with a change in Frankfurt. I've booked seats for you, me and your boy."

"What about Mia and her family?"

"I've spoken to Andrej and he'll arrange for protection for them. I'm pretty sure the debt will die with Žagar. But if anyone does try to give the Novaks any grief, Andrej will be there."

Shepherd sighed. He knew Pritchard was right. He wasn't happy at leaving the country so soon after Katra had been killed. But if the authorities realised that he was in the country, it would raise all sorts of awkward questions, none of which he would be able to answer without condemning himself to a world of trouble. He had to be back in the UK when the Slovenian cops started their investigation.

He looked at Liam. "Have you got your passport?"

Liam patted his back pocket. "Sure."

"How do we get to Zagreb?" Shepherd asked Pritchard.

"Andrej will send us a car. He'll wait until our plane is in the air before he tips off the cops about the brothel."

"And when the police realise that we took Mia from the brothel, what then?"

"She tells them nothing. She says she was in shock, that she doesn't know why she was taken, that she was dropped in the city and found her own way home." He shrugged. "I know it's weak, and they'll realise straight away that Katra and Mia were sisters, but they'll still see them both as innocent bystanders in all this."

"The girls and the customers in the brothel will have our description."

"Witnesses are always unreliable, you know that. I doubt that the clients will be saying anything and the girls, most of them owe Žagar no favours." He looked at his watch. "We need to get going, we have to check in before five."

They reached Zagreb an hour before their flight was due to leave. As they waited to pass through security, Shepherd took out his personal phone and switched it on. There were several missed messages and a dozen messages on voicemail, including two from Liam and three from Katra. Shepherd's face tightened. He wanted to listen to Katra's messages but knew that he wasn't ready, not yet. He went through to the John Whitehill Facebook account. Dexter and his friends had all accepted his friend requests. And there were three messages from Dexter, inviting him to a British Crusader meeting that night at a pub in Croydon. He held the phone out so that Pritchard could read it. The director nodded. "Perfect," he said.

The Lufthansa flight touched down at London City Airport bang on time and within half an hour of the plane landing, Pritchard and Shepherd were in a black cab heading west. Liam had taken his own taxi to the flat Shepherd was using in Lambeth. Shepherd had given him his key. Until the Dexter investigation was done and dusted, Shepherd needed to base himself at the John Whitehill Hampstead flat.

"We can talk over breakfast," said Pritchard.

"Sure," said Shepherd, though food was the last thing on his mind. He couldn't stop thinking about what had happened, how Katra had died and how he had been powerless to help. There were so many "what ifs", so many things he could have done differently. He should have shot Žagar the moment the gangster had grabbed Katra. He should have tied the man's hands or knocked him out as soon as they had found Katra. He had given Žagar too much time. Instead of talking, Shepherd should have just put a bullet in his head. He couldn't stop thinking about what had happened and his perfect recall made the memories all the more painful. He could remember everything in minute detail and there was nothing he could do to block out the images.

The cab pulled up in front of a neat semi-detached house. Shepherd frowned; he had been so busy with his own thoughts that he had lost track of where they were. Pritchard paid the driver and they climbed out. There was a paved driveway leading up to a single garage and a front door with leaded windows. Pritchard unlocked the front door and Shepherd followed him inside.

There were two rooms leading off to the left, a sitting room with a floral print sofa and framed watercolours on the wall, and a dining room with an oval table that would seat six and an oak sideboard on which stood a collection of animal figurines. The house had a feminine feel, and the kitchen was no different — it was bright yellow with country-style cabinets, a shelf of cookery books and pots of herbs growing in small terracotta pots along the windowsill.

Pritchard took off his jacket and hung it over the back of one of the chairs around a circular pine kitchen table then took a frying pan from an overhead cupboard. It was twice the size of the frying pan that Shepherd had at home, and divided into five compartments. He put it on the stove and took bacon,

388

sausages, mushrooms and a box of eggs from the double-doored fridge.

"Daniel, can you make the coffee?" asked Pritchard, gesturing with a spatula at a Nespresso machine.

Pritchard put bacon in the largest of the compartments, cracked eggs into another two, then added the sausages and mushrooms.

Shepherd made two mugs of coffee while Pritchard deftly fried the food. He saw Shepherd watching him and he smiled. "You're wondering if I'm married, or gay, or all of the above."

"No, I'm not," said Shepherd, though that was a pretty accurate assessment of what had been going through his mind.

"It's what you do. You have to assess people so you know how to deal with them. If you didn't, you wouldn't last long undercover."

"You're not a case, though."

"So tell me you weren't wondering about my marital status."

"It's a nice house. But you seem to be here alone."

Pritchard nodded. "My wife died, about five years ago. No kids. Partly by choice, partly because we ran out of time." He smiled wearily. "I would have been a shit father, anyway. Probably in my genes."

"I'm sorry," said Shepherd.

"For what? My wife, my shit father, my genes?"

"Your wife, mainly."

Pritchard started putting the food onto plates. "She had breast cancer," he said. "She had chemo and surgery and she was lucky, for a few years she was clear, and then it came back and when it came back . . ." He shrugged. "She wasn't so lucky."

"Sorry."

"Nothing to be sorry about," said Pritchard. "Five years is a long time. And it's not as if there were any 'what ifs'. There was nothing anyone could have done any differently. She got cancer and she died."

"I know what you mean about 'what ifs' all right," said Shepherd. "I'm going to spend the rest of my life wondering if we should have handled Žagar differently."

Pritchard put the frying pan down. "I blame myself. He grabbed the gun from me."

"I should have killed him as soon as we were in his house," said Shepherd. "There was no way he was coming out of the situation alive, I should have done it straight away." He forced a smile. "Should've, could've, would've. What happened, happened. There's no going back. That's what I told Liam."

"He seems to be taking it well." Pritchard finished putting the food on the plates and put the frying pan into the sink. He carried the plates over to the table and both men sat down. Shepherd added Heinz ketchup to his plate, Pritchard went with HP sauce.

Shepherd stared down at his plate. He had absolutely no appetite. "I haven't really had the chance to talk to him," said Shepherd. "But I will."

"The question is, where do we go from here?" said Pritchard. "I have a contact in Europol who will keep an eye on the Slovenian police. The only police who'll be overly concerned will be those on Žagar's payroll

390

and I'm not sure they'll want anyone looking too closely at his death in case it turns the spotlight on their involvement. Same with the men who died, none of them were innocent civilians. They'll probably put it down to inter-gang rivalry."

"But what about Katra?" asked Shepherd. He cut into his egg. Pritchard had cooked it perfectly. "They're going to wonder what she was doing in Žagar's house."

"She's local, remember? There's no reason for the cops to think that she was anything other than a local girl who got caught up in a gang war. If they do dig then yes, they might discover that she was living in the UK. Worst possible scenario they start looking at when and how she arrived in Slovenia and find that she flew in with your boy. Hopefully they won't spot that he flew out of Zagreb the day after she died."

"And if they do?"

"We'll cross that bridge when we come to it. But what I can do is get his name removed from the EasyJet manifest so it looks like Katra flew out there alone." Pritchard sipped his coffee. "I know you're still worried about her family, but Andrej will make sure they're okay. And again, I'm pretty sure it will end with Žagar's death. Another gang will move in, natural selection will out."

Shepherd popped a slice of sausage into his mouth and nodded. Everything the man said rang true.

"This might sound a tad callous, and I apologise for that, but we need to discuss what we do about Gary Dexter," said Pritchard. "I would prefer to strike while the iron is hot, obviously."

391

Shepherd chewed and swallowed. He couldn't taste anything. "I understand."

"But if you need time, I think we could probably move ahead without you."

Shepherd shook his head. "No. I'm in."

"Are you sure? After what you've been through . . ."

"After what I've been through, I need to keep working," said Shepherd. "I need to keep myself occupied."

"Okay, good," said Pritchard. "I'll get Andrej to talk to Gary Dexter. He can put him in touch with our dealer."

"I can suggest someone for that," said Shepherd.

"Jimmy Sharpe?"

"He's played an arms dealer before. And he's got access to the sort of weaponry we need."

"I was already thinking about him as a possibility," said Pritchard. "Do you think you could get yourself involved?"

"I don't see why not," said Shepherd. "Dexter said I should get in touch with him. I'll do that today and arrange a meeting. Maybe we can time it so that Dexter gets the call from Andrej while I'm there."

"Where does Dexter plan to get the money from?"

"I'm not sure. Why, do you think I should suggest funding?"

Pritchard shook his head emphatically. "Absolutely not," he said. "We've got to be careful we don't cross the line into entrapment. It's bad enough that we come up with the arms dealer, if we use our cash then a good lawyer will get him off. He needs to use his own cash."

392

"I'll get in touch with him as soon as I'm done with your breakfast."

Pritchard grinned. "It's good?"

Shepherd nodded. "Damn good." He smiled enthusiastically but the truth was he was eating because his body needed fuel, no other reason.

Shepherd drove to Croydon but parked well away from the pub and went a circuitous route to check that he wasn't being tailed. The pub was full and it took Shepherd several minutes to find Dexter and Moorhouse. They were standing close to the toilets, drinking lager. They both shook hands with Shepherd and eagerly accepted his offer of a drink. It took him almost ten minutes to get served. The clientele was predominantly white and male and under forty, with a dozen or so skinheads gathered together at one end of the bar. The only two women Shepherd saw, other than bar staff, had dyed blonde hair and St George's crosses tattooed on their arms.

He bought lagers for Dexter and Moorhouse and a pint of shandy for himself, then threaded his way back to them. They were just finishing their drinks when he reached them and they put their empty glasses on a nearby table and took the fresh ones from him.

"This is a good turnout," said Shepherd.

"We've got a lot of support in Croydon," said Dexter. "We're among friends."

"What's the story?" asked Shepherd. "Are you giving a speech?"

"I'll do the introductions," said Dexter. "Then we've got three speakers. Two of them are with Combat 18, I've known them for donkey's. And we've got a guy from Sweden who's going to talk about the problems they're having with the muzzies. Then I'll do an appeal for funds and we'll pass a bucket around."

"Sounds good," said Shepherd.

The meeting started at nine on the dot. Dexter had stood on a chair and shouted to get everyone's attention. Most of the drinkers had filed upstairs to a large room. There was a small stage at one end with a couple of microphone stands. On the wall behind the stage were several anti-Islam banners and St George and Union Jack flags.

More than eighty people crowded into the room. The skinheads all gathered at the back. Several were clearly drunk, laughing and pushing each other, though they stopped when Dexter got onto the stage and appealed for quiet. He started with a tirade of how he saw Muslim immigrants destroying the country he loved, and pretty much repeated the comments he'd made in Sid, about it being time for the English to make a stand. His remarks were greeted with cheers and applause, and having worked up the crowd he introduced the speakers from Combat 18. They turned out to be the men that Dexter had taken selfies with — Neil Burnside and Lee Barnett. The two men had a microphone each and did a racist double act that had the audience cheering and waving their fists in the air. Much of their anger was directed at Muslims, and the two men threw out all sorts of statistics about Muslims in prison, Muslims claiming benefits, and Muslim terrorist plots. Shepherd knew that most of the figures they quoted were exaggerated or just plain wrong, but the audience either didn't know or didn't care. At one point, Barnett praised the attack on the mosque in Acton, and he had details of the explosives used that hadn't been released by the police. Shepherd made a mental note to talk to the cops in charge of the investigation. If Barnett hadn't been actively involved in the attack, he was clearly in contact with someone who had been.

The final speaker was introduced as a father whose daughter had been killed by a Muslim grooming gang in Stockholm, but Shepherd hadn't heard of the case and the more the man ranted and shouted, the more Shepherd doubted that he was telling the truth. He certainly had a Swedish accent but Shepherd figured that a bereaved father would be showing more grief and less hatred. The man declared that white people were no longer safe in Sweden and that the English should do everything they could to make sure their country didn't go the same way. The audience clapped and cheered but Shepherd was fairly sure they were being played. Not that they cared. They clearly weren't there for a thoughtful discussion on the pros and cons of Islam, all they wanted was to have their bigoted prejudices confirmed. Shepherd had no choice other than to join in with the applause, though much of what the man said made him sick to the stomach.

When the Swede finally ended his tirade, Moorhouse went around with a blue plastic bucket to collect donations.

Dexter took to the stage and thanked everyone for coming, telling them that if the British Crusaders were indeed to lead the fight, they needed funds. By the time Moorhouse had finished his collection there were several hundred pounds in the bucket.

Moorhouse went over to the stage where he bundled the notes and put them in a jiffy bag, and what coins there were went into a plastic bag. As the audience headed back downstairs, Dexter came over to Shepherd. His pupils were dilated and his face was bathed in sweat. "What do you think?" he asked.

"Awesome," said Shepherd.

"We could fill much bigger venues but if we do that the lefties start protesting and the cops come and shut us down."

Moorhouse nodded in agreement. "We could fill the fucking O2," he said.

Shepherd wanted to ask what happened to the money, but instead he repeated some of the things that the Swede had said and threw in a few Islamophobic remarks that had Dexter and Moorhouse nodding in agreement.

Moorhouse finished dealing with the cash and suggested they go downstairs for a drink. Shepherd bought a round, then said he needed to pee and headed for the toilet. The toilet was unoccupied and he took out his phone and sent a text message to Pritchard: "GO". He washed his hands and went back to the bar. A couple of minutes later Dexter's phone rang. He looked at the screen and grinned. "It's Neno," he said. "I'll take it outside."

"I'll come with you," said Moorhouse.

Shepherd stayed where he was as the two men left the pub. He would have loved to have gone with them, but he couldn't afford to appear too keen. He sipped his drink and kept an eye on the door, constantly scanning faces to make sure that there was nobody in the pub that he'd crossed paths with before.

They came back after about five minutes. Dexter was pumped up and his cheeks had reddened. "We're on," he said.

"On what?" asked Shepherd.

"Neno has found us a dealer here in the UK. Some guy called Viktor. Sounded foreign. I spoke to him just now and Viktor says he can get whatever we want and that it's already in the country, no need for shipping. He was a bit cagey on the phone but he says we can meet him tomorrow, at The Dorchester," said Dexter.

"Park Lane," said Shepherd. "I've done a few interviews there over the years."

"It's posh, right?"

"You won't get in with shorts or trainers, but it's fairly relaxed," said Shepherd.

"He's talking about afternoon tea."

Shepherd laughed. "Now that is posh."

"You'll come with us, yeah? You, me and Rog."

"You're sure?"

"Yeah, you know your way around. You're a good judge of character, John. I trust your judgement. And the more the merrier."

Shepherd raised his glass. "Then I'll be there."

The blonde woman who greeted them at the entrance to The Promenade, the foyer at the heart of The Dorchester hotel, was model-pretty and dressed as if she expected to be featured on the cover of Vogue magazine. Dexter gave her the name that Sharpe was using and she led them through the opulent room, where ornate modern chandeliers were hanging from the ceiling and the walls were lined with silk drapes. Well-dressed customers sat on elegant sofas and plush armchairs as liveried waiters delivered plates of finger sandwiches and trays of delicate cakes. A pianist on a grand piano was effortlessly filling the room with soft music. Many of the diners were taking photographs on their phones, of themselves and their food, and nobody paid the men any attention as they were led to their destination. Sharpe was sitting on an overstuffed sofa next to his NCA colleague, a good-looking bearded guy in his thirties who Shepherd knew was called Vito Serafino. Shepherd had never met the man and Serafino didn't know who or what Shepherd was, but Sharpe had told him that Serafino was one of NCA's top undercover agents. He had posed as an arms dealer on several occasions, in the UK and overseas on loan to Interpol.

Dexter looked at Sharpe and Serafino, obviously wondering who was who. Serafino took the lead, standing up and offering his hand. He was wearing an immaculate black Boss suit, a crisp shirt and a blue tie, and had a chunky gold Rolex on his wrist. "I am Viktor," he said.

398

"Viktor, mate, good to meet you," said Dexter, shaking Serafino's hand enthusiastically. "Neno says good things about you."

"Not too much, I hope, we like to keep our activities low profile," said Serafino. "The fewer people who talk about us the better."

"Yeah, he wasn't mouthing off, just said that you can get us what we need."

"I'm sure we can," said Serafino. He gestured at Sharpe. "This is my colleague, Barry."

Sharpe took it in turns to shake hands with Dexter, Moorhouse and Shepherd, then they sat down. They had two sofas and three armchairs arranged around two square tables. The pianist began to play "Happy Birthday" and a waitress carried a small chocolate cake with a single burning candle over to a table where a whitehaired old lady in a Chanel dress and pearls sat with a man in a dark suit who was probably her grandson. The man clapped as the old lady blew out the candle, her eyes flashing with the excitement of a little girl. People at the neighbouring tables applauded quietly as the candle went out, and the pianist went back to playing show tunes.

"Why The Dorchester?" asked Dexter, looking around. "Why couldn't we meet in a pub?"

Sharpe waved his arm around the lavish surroundings. "Plenty of room between the tables, so we can't be overheard," he said. "In the unlikely event that the cops are taking an interest in us they'll stick out a mile, but the real reason is that I just love their egg and truffle sandwiches." He grinned. "And if you baulk at picking up the bill, we'll know that you're short of cash and that you're wasting our time."

"We've got the cash," said Dexter.

"Glad to hear it," said Sharpe. "Let's have some bubbly as well then, shall we?" He waved over at a waiter and ordered champagne to go with their afternoon tea.

Two large plates of finger sandwiches arrived immediately after their champagne had been poured. There were Sharpe's favourite egg and truffle, along with cheese and cucumber, prawn salad, pastrami with mustard and coronation chicken. Sharpe tucked in immediately. Dexter was more cautious, opening up each sandwich and sniffing it before taking a bite.

They waited until the waiter had walked away before discussing the matter in hand. Serafino did the talking. "Grenades are pretty standard, and we can get you a type that's similar to what you saw in Serbia," he said. "But Neno said you wanted RPG-7s and we don't have any of those in the UK. We can get them, and we can have them shipped over, but it'll take time and there'll be an extra cost."

"We definitely want them," said Dexter.

"Not a problem, we can get them, but I'm in a position to offer you something else. Swedish-made AT4s, single-use anti-tank high-explosive missiles made by Saab, the car people. Far more effective than the RPG-7 and with red dot targeting. You just put the red dot on the target and pull the trigger."

"How much?" asked Dexter.

"One and a half thousand pounds," said Serafino.

"Each?" said Dexter.

"Of course," said Serafino.

"That's a bit steep," said Dexter. "The RPGs in Serbia were only a couple of hundred euros."

"That's because all you were buying was the rocket," said Serafino. "With the RPG, the launchers are reused. The AT4 is a single-use anti-tank weapon. You fire it and then throw away the launcher. It's much more efficient. You've fired an RPG-7 and, as you know, it's very hit and miss. Literally. The AT4 is much more reliable. It's very accurate up to three hundred metres and you can easily hit a large target up to half a kilometre away. Plus, there's a big difference in price between here and the Continent. I didn't get the impression from Neno that money was going to be an issue. I hope my time isn't being wasted here."

Dexter put up a hand to placate him. "I was only asking," he said. "Your price is your price, I get that. Now how many can you get?" asked Dexter.

"How many do you want?"

Dexter looked across at Moorhouse. "What do you think, Rog? Four?"

Moorhouse nodded. "We've got the funds."

Dexter looked back at Serafino. "Okay, we'll take four."

"And what about grenades?" asked Sharpe.

"How much are they?" asked Dexter.

"Ninety quid each," said Sharpe. "But you can have a dozen for a grand."

"We'll take a dozen," said Dexter. "Fuck it, two dozen. How soon can you get them?"

Sharpe looked at Serafino. "Tomorrow okay?"

"Tomorrow works," said Serafino.

"Where can we pick them up?" asked Dexter.

"We like to do any transactions far away from prying eyes," said Sharpe. "We've got a farm we use, just outside London. I'll text you the address first thing tomorrow morning. Just make sure you've got the cash."

"We'll have it," said Dexter.

"Excellent," said Sharpe. A waiter brought over a plate of scones with dishes of jam and clotted cream. Sharpe rubbed his hands together. "Lovely," he said.

The meeting lasted an hour and a half, and Sharpe was still tucking into The Dorchester's famed fancy cakes when Dexter, Shepherd and Moorhouse left. Dexter had paid the bill in cash though Shepherd noticed that Sharpe had pocketed the receipt. They gathered together outside the hotel. "What do you think?" Dexter asked Shepherd. "You're a journalist, you've got a feel for people."

"They seem to know what they're doing," said Shepherd. "And it's easy enough, you don't pay until you've seen the merchandise."

Dexter nodded. "That's what I thought," he said. He patted Moorhouse on the shoulder. "So you can get the money this afternoon?"

"Sure," said Moorhouse.

"I think I'll bring Charlie tomorrow as well," said Dexter. "Get him to check the gear before we buy."

"Sounds like a plan," said Shepherd.

"Are you up for it, John?" asked Dexter.

"Hell yeah," said Shepherd.

Dexter grinned. "Good man. Now let's find a pub and grab some beers. Those bloody sandwiches have given me a thirst."

Shepherd was up before eight the following morning. He was drinking a mug of coffee as he watched Sky News when his phone rang. It was Gary Dexter. "We're off," he said. "You're in Hampstead, right? We'll pick you up in about an hour."

As soon as Dexter ended the call, Shepherd phoned Pritchard and brought him up to speed.

"Good job," said Pritchard.

"Best not to go counting chickens," said Shepherd.

"Your pal Sharpe is a pro, I'm sure it'll go like clockwork," said Pritchard. "Call me when it's over."

"Will do."

"How are you getting on?"

"I'm okay."

"If you need time off, take as much as you need," said Pritchard.

"To be honest, I prefer to be working," said Shepherd. "Stops me dwelling on what happened."

"The Slovenian police have identified Katra and informed the family, so you'll be contacted soon. They haven't looked at flight records yet so it looks as if they're treating it as a local crime. As we thought, they're not shedding any tears over the death of Žagar or any of his minions. If anything, champagne corks were popping."

"Good to know," said Shepherd sourly.

"I'm sorry, I didn't mean to be flippant. I just wanted to point out that so far you and your boy are below the radar."

"Okay," said Shepherd. "Thanks."

"How's Liam bearing up?"

"Same as me, throwing himself into his work. His CO wasn't happy about him being late back to base, but it's all good now."

"I am so sorry about what happened. For your loss."

"Thank you."

"There are never any words, are there?" said Pritchard.

Shepherd smiled ruefully. No, there weren't. There were no magic words that would make it any better. Katra was dead and that was the end of it. Nothing anyone could say would make it any easier. "I'll phone you once Dexter and his team are in custody," he said, and ended the call.

He finished his coffee and picked up a dark blue blazer that was hanging over the back of an armchair. He had a Glock 43 in a holster in the small of his back. He wasn't expecting trouble but that didn't mean he wasn't going to be prepared for the worst. The Glock 43 was the perfect gun to be carried covertly. It weighed just over twenty ounces fully loaded and the barrel was just over three inches long. The magazine held six 9 mm rounds and one in the chamber made seven. Shepherd put on the blazer and examined himself in the mirrored wardrobe in his bedroom. There was no way the gun could be spotted. He stared at his reflection. It felt strange to be working instead of grieving, but just then that was what he wanted. He didn't want to sit and think about what had happened to Katra and keeping busy meant that the grief stayed in the back of his mind until he felt he was ready to deal with it. He felt a wave of sadness wash over him and his stomach lurched, so he forced himself to concentrate on the matter in hand. He wasn't Dan Shepherd, grieving for the woman he loved, he was John Whitehill, journalist, and potential right-wing terrorist.

He paced up and down, constantly looking at his watch. Eventually his phone buzzed to let him know he had received a message. It was from Dexter: "OUTSIDE IN 5 MINS".

Shepherd took a last look at his reflection, then let himself out of the flat and went downstairs.

Dexter arrived in his Mercedes. Roger Moorhouse was sitting in the front passenger seat. He and Dexter were casually dressed in pullovers and jeans. Charlie Palmer was in the back seat wearing a combat jacket with sunglasses perched on top of his head. Shepherd got in next to him. "All right, John?" asked Dexter.

"All good," said Shepherd. He looked at the GPS. According to the screen, the farm where they were due to meet Sharpe and Serafino was just over half an hour away.

The blue Transit van drove slowly down the track towards the farm. Jimmy Sharpe watched from his vantage point in the barn where he had parked his

Jaguar, well away from the main farmhouse. The farm was up for auction and had been empty for the past two months, following the death of the owner and his wife in a pile-up on the M25.

There were six SFOs with him in the barn, standing next to their two grey BMW SUVs. There was a yellow circle the size of a beermat in the windshield of both vehicles indicating that they carried firearms. The officers had Glocks in holsters on their hips. There was no indication that Dexter and his pals would be carrying guns so the police wouldn't be bothering with their carbines. They would remain locked in the gun safe, between the rear two seats. "Right, that's Vito arriving with the weapons," said Sharpe. The plan was for the police to stay out of sight until the transaction had been completed. There were four regular cops with a Mercedes Sprinter van parked in another barn that would be used to transport the prisoners to the nearest police station for processing.

Sharpe's phone rang and he took it out of his jacket pocket. It was Julie Bacon calling. He walked away from the SFOs and took the call. "Jimmy, they've sent Harry a text asking him to do a run today."

"Bugger," said Sharpe. "I'm going to be tied up all morning. Can you deal with it?"

"It's already in hand," said Bacon. "I've arranged surveillance there and back and I'll be in the safe house waiting for him. I'm not expecting any problems."

"Good girl," said Sharpe.

"That's sexist, Jimmy."

"Good person," said Sharpe. He chuckled and ended the call. He went over to the SFOs and looked at his watch. "The targets should be here within half an hour. We'll show them the goods, then there's a chance they'll want a demonstration, in which case we'll give them one. Once they've said enough for the tape and they've produced the money, you guys can move in. The signal again is me saying 'good to go'. Just in case the radio packs in, the fall-back signal will be me rubbing the back of my neck with my left hand." He showed them the action and the SFO who would be monitoring the radio transmission nodded. Sharpe and Serafino were wired up and Shepherd would be recording on his phone. An NCA photographer was in the attic of the farmhouse and would be videoing everything.

Sharpe took a head and shoulders shot of Dan Shepherd from his jacket pocket and showed it around. "Just so you know, this guy is one of ours and he will be carrying a handgun. He's not to be arrested, he'll stay with me."

The cops studied the picture and nodded. Sharpe put it away. "Right, let's get to it."

Harry Dexter got off the train from Reading at Paddington and took the escalator down to the Bakerloo Line, followed by NCA surveillance officer Andrew Mosley in his businessman garb. As they went down the escalator, Mosley sent a text message — "HAVE EYEBALL" — to Julie Bacon who was running the surveillance operation from the safe house in Reading.

Mosley followed Harry to Waterloo and took a seat at the opposite end of the platform. Harry played on his iPhone until the teenager arrived with the grey North Face backpack. As usual, the teenager sat down two seats along from Harry and put the backpack down between them. When the next train arrived, the teenager got on and Harry headed for the northbound Bakerloo Line platform. Harry took the Tube back to Paddington where he boarded the next train back to Reading. He was followed on the train by NCA surveillance officer Oliver Tomkinson.

Harry played with his iPhone all the way to Reading. When the train arrived he walked to the safe house. He paid no attention to Tomkinson, who was walking ahead of him. Following a target by walking ahead of them was an excellent way of keeping close but it was of little use in counter surveillance and Tomkinson completely missed the tough-looking man in a dark overcoat who was following Harry on the other side of the road.

Harry reached the safe house and rang the bell. Julie Bacon let him into the house, and he helped himself to a Coke from the fridge as she opened the backpack and took samples of the drugs inside.

"Where's Jimmy?" asked Harry.

"He's busy today," said Bacon. She finished taking a sample of cannabis, rewrapped the block and put it back into the backpack. "There you go," she said.

Harry drank the rest of his Coke and took the backpack from her. "When are we going to be done with this?" he asked.

"Soon," said Bacon.

"You always say that," groaned Harry.

"It's true, Harry," she said. "We're almost done."

"Do you think I'll get some sort of reward?" he asked.

Bacon tilted her head to one side. "Reward? Why?"

"For what I'm doing. Helping to catch the bad guys."

"Harry, your reward is that you don't face criminal charges for your drug dealing and you go back to living a normal life," said Bacon. "Frankly, you should be thanking your lucky stars."

"The thing is, when this is over, I stand to lose money," said Harry. "When you bust them, I won't have a job any more."

Bacon looked at him in disbelief. "Harry, you're a drugs mule. You've been breaking the law. You're lucky you're not going to prison."

"I'm just saying . . ."

She held up her hand. "I know what you're saying. Now get that backpack to where it needs to be and then get off home."

Harry sighed and shook his head as he walked towards the front door. "I never get no respect," he said.

She put a hand on his shoulder and turned him around. "Harry, I have the utmost respect for what you're doing, seriously. And we are truly grateful for the way you've helped us. I promise you we are nearly done. It's only because the Albanians took over from Dancer and Swifty that it's gone on as long as it has. I want this to be over as much as you do, okay?"

Harry nodded. "Okay."

She ruffled his hair. "You're a good lad," she said.

He laughed and shook her off. "Don't mess up my hair," he said. She reached for him and gave him a hug and ushered him out of the door.

Harry walked away from the house and down the pavement. Oliver Tomkinson was a hundred yards ahead of him, on the other side of the road. Neither of them saw the man in the overcoat, following some distance behind, a mobile phone clamped to his ear.

When Harry reached the house where he was to deliver the drugs, Tomkinson sent a text to Julie Bacon. As he was bent over his smartphone, the man in the overcoat walked by, talking on his. There was a white windowless Mercedes van parked down the road. The man walked up to it, pulled open the driver's door and climbed in.

Harry walked around to the back of the house. He took off his backpack and was about to knock when the door opened wide. He stepped back in surprise. It was Stuart Bradley, wearing a black Adidas tracksuit and gleaming white trainers. Bradley smiled showing yellowing teeth and blinked at Harry through the thick lenses of his glasses. "How's it going, Harry?"

Harry had never liked Bradley, there was something not right about his smile or the look in his eyes. Harry

410

always felt as if Bradley was picturing him naked and the way the man licked his thin lips made Harry's skin crawl. He held out the backpack but Bradley didn't take it. Instead he waved for Harry to enter the kitchen.

"What's wrong?" asked Harry hesitantly.

Bradley's smile widened. "Nothing's wrong, lad. Just get your arse in here."

Harry stepped across the threshold and Bradley slammed the door behind him. Harry turned to look at the door. When he turned back, two big men in suits walked out of the hallway. They were the men who had been at the house in Kilburn, the ones who had told him to show them Bradley's house. Harry's heart pounded. The men stared at him with cold eyes. One of them bared his teeth like a dog that was about to bite. "Who's been a naughty boy, then?" growled the man.

Bradley ripped the backpack from Harry's hands and disappeared into the hallway. The two men stepped menacingly towards Harry and he backed away, holding up his hands in a vain attempt to protect himself.

"Here they come," said Sharpe. He was standing with Serafino at the rear of the Transit van. In the distance, Dexter's white Mercedes was heading down the track from the main road. Sharpe had been following the car's progress on his phone, courtesy of the MI5 tracking device. Serafino was wearing a dark blue Ted Baker suit with a floral shirt and gleaming black Bally shoes. Sharpe was also suited and booted and wearing a dark raincoat to better conceal the transmitting device that was taped to his chest. The microphone was in one of the buttons of his suit.

They had parked the van in the yard of the farm, in front of the single-storey farmhouse. To the left was a vehicle storage area, in which were parked a couple of mud-splattered tractors, and a large storage shed, the door chained and padlocked. The barns and a large white silo were about a hundred yards away and facing the farmhouse was a field that had been ploughed but didn't appear to have been planted with anything.

The Mercedes drove into the yard, its tyres crunching on the gravel. Dexter parked and the four men got out. Sharpe and Serafino walked towards them. They all shook hands. "You've got everything?" Dexter asked Serafino.

"Of course. Do you have the money?"

Dexter gestured at the boot of the Mercedes. "Counted it twice to be sure," he said. He walked over to the rear of the Transit. Serafino went with him and opened the rear doors. The men crowded around, trying to get a look at the boxes inside.

"Guys, come on," said Sharpe. "Let the dog see the rabbit."

The men backed off while Serafino opened one of four metal trunks. Inside, nestled in foam packaging, was a grey rocket launcher. "Check it out, Charlie," said Dexter, moving to the side.

Palmer peered into the trunk and nodded. "Yeah, that's an AT4."

412

Dexter patted Serafino on the shoulder. "You don't mind opening up the other three, do you? I'd hate to get home and find out that I'd paid for an empty box."

Serafino laughed. He opened up the three other trunks. Each contained a pristine launcher.

Dexter nodded. "Excellent," he said. "And what about the grenades?"

Serafino opened up a square metal trunk. Inside were two dozen olive green spheres the size of a small orange, each with a matt black handle. They were wrapped in bubble wrap. Serafino took one out and unwrapped it.

Dexter frowned. "What sort of grenade is it?" he asked.

Serafino grinned. "It's the sort that goes bang when you pull the pin," he said. "What sort of grenade were you expecting?"

"The ones we saw before had square dimples over them. They were more oval shaped."

Serafino laughed. "A grenade is a grenade," he said. "These are L109A1 high-explosive fragmentation grenades, as used by the British Army since 2001. It's the standard NATO anti-personnel grenade, it weighs 465 grams and has a fuse delay of between three and four seconds. And if you need proof, it has 'GREN HAND' written on the side."

He held the grenade out. It did indeed have "GREN HAND" stencilled on the side in yellow capital letters.

Dexter gestured at Palmer. "What do you think, Charlie?"

Palmer took the grenade and looked at it. "Yeah, it's the real thing," he said, weighing it in the palm of his hand.

Dexter took it from him. "And it's what, lethal up to thirty feet?" asked Dexter. "Same as the Serbian ones?"

"Thereabouts," said Serafino.

"I want to try it," said Dexter.

"You pay for it, you can do what you want with it," said Sharpe. "But we don't give away free samples."

"Where?"

Sharpe gestured at the neighbouring field. "Knock yourself out. Just make sure you're well away from us."

Dexter looked at the grenade in his hand as if he was having second thoughts, then he shrugged and strode over to the field. He walked fifty feet or so away from the vehicles, then stopped. "Gary, mate, remember the shrapnel!" Shepherd shouted at him. "Drop to the ground after you've thrown it, just in case."

"Fuck that, I'm going to throw it and run," Dexter shouted back.

Shepherd didn't bother arguing. Assuming Dexter could throw it fifty feet or so, dropping would be the safest option, but if he ran and didn't trip he'd be okay. "Suit yourself," he said.

Dexter pulled out the pin, drew back his arm and threw it as hard as he could. As soon as he released the grip on the grenade the handle flew off. Dexter was already running before the handle hit the ground. Shepherd began counting off the seconds. Two, three, four. The grenade exploded with a dull thump, kicking up a plume of soil. There was a greyish white cloud

414

about twelve feet across that was quickly dispersed by the wind blowing across the field.

Dexter whooped as he ran over to Moorhouse who clapped him on the back. Dexter was still holding the pin and he showed it to Moorhouse. "A souvenir," he said.

"You're a mad bastard, Gary," said Moorhouse. The two men walked over to the van, laughing.

"Satisfied?" asked Serafino, stroking his neatly trimmed beard.

"Hell, yeah," said Dexter.

"What about the money?" asked Sharpe.

"Don't worry, Jock, we've got the cash," said Dexter. He nodded at Moorhouse, who went over to the Mercedes and opened the boot. He took out a large padded envelope and brought it over to Dexter. Dexter gestured at Serafino who held out his hand. Moorhouse gave the envelope to Serafino, who opened it and peered inside. There were bundles of fifty-pound notes. Serafino put the envelope on the floor of the van and took out one of the bundles. He flicked through it, then removed one of the banknotes and held it up to the sky. He nodded. "All good."

"Of course it's all good," sneered Dexter. "What, you think we'd bring dodgy notes?"

"Always best to check," said Serafino.

"Can you guys help us put the gear in the Merc?" asked Dexter.

"Good to go," said Sharpe.

Dexter looked confused. "What?" he said. "What do you mean?"

His question was answered by the roar of engines as two grey BMW SUVs came screeching out of one of the barns. They were Metropolitan Police ARVs, each with three specialist firearms officers on board.

"What the fuck!" shouted Dexter.

"Just stay where you are, lads," said Sharpe. "It's over."

"Like fuck it's over," said Dexter. He reached into the van and pulled out a grenade from the box.

The two ARVs came to a halt and the SFOs piled out, aiming their Glocks at their targets. Shepherd continued to play his role and raised his hands in the air. Moorhouse stood rooted to the spot, too shocked to move. Palmer slowly raised his hands. Dexter ripped the bubble wrap from the grenade.

A grey-haired sergeant aimed his gun at Dexter. "Put the grenade on the ground and step away from it!" he shouted.

Dexter held the grenade in the air. "I'll throw it!" he shouted.

"Gary, mate, don't be stupid," said Shepherd.

"It's the only way," said Dexter. He pulled out the pin.

"You'll kill us all," said Shepherd.

"Not if they let us go," said Dexter. He waved the grenade above his head with his right hand and the pin with his left. "This'll kill everyone within twenty feet," he said to the armed cops. "So you need to get back into your cars and fuck the fuck off."

"We're not going anywhere," said the sergeant. "Just stop being a bloody fool and put the pin back in."

416

"Fuck you," said Dexter and he threw the pin at the sergeant. It bounced off the sergeant's Kevlar vest and fell onto the concrete. Dexter held the grenade up again. "You shoot me and I let go and it goes off and we're all dead."

"Gary, please, come on," said Shepherd. "You don't want to do this."

"I've no fucking choice, John."

"You've been caught buying weapons," said Shepherd. "Big fucking deal. A few years inside. But if you throw that and kill somebody, that's you behind bars for life."

Dexter took a step towards the armed police, and they all took a step back, though they kept their Glocks trained on Dexter's chest.

"Gary, don't do anything stupid," said Shepherd.

"John, mate, just go. They won't stop you. Not while I've got this." He looked at Moorhouse. "Leg it, Rog. You too, Charlie."

"Leg it where, Gary?" said Moorhouse. "John's right. They've got us, we're fucked, but blowing up cops is only going to make it worse."

"The police are part of the problem, don't you see that? If they treated the Muslims the way they treat us, our country wouldn't be in the state it is. They treat the muzzies with kid fucking gloves."

"Gary, the cops aren't the problem," said Shepherd.

"They fucking are!" shouted Dexter. "They have a duty to protect us, the citizens, but they don't and we have bombs on our buses and our trains and they burn poppies and they mow citizens down with their cars and the police do fuck all about it. They know who the jihadists are, they know their names and where they live, but they're too scared to do a damn thing about it. Fuck them!" He drew back his arm and threw the grenade at the armed cops.

The police officers stood transfixed as the grenade flew through the air. It wasn't until it landed on the ground that they began to run. Sharpe didn't move, he had a look of astonishment on his face. Serafino also stood transfixed. The grenade bounced once on the concrete and then slid to a halt. Shepherd knew that there was no way they would be able to outrun the deadly shrapnel. Dexter, Palmer and Moorhouse were also running. There was a chance that they might survive, but it was a slim one.

Shepherd had started counting the moment that Dexter had released his grip on the grenade. One thousand. Two thousand as the grenade hit the ground. Sharpe still hadn't moved, he was staring at it in disbelief. Shepherd reacted instinctively, throwing himself over the grenade, covering it with his chest. Three thousand. Shepherd closed his eyes. He knew he'd feel nothing, the blast would turn his body into vapour, pretty much. He thought of Katra, and the look of horror on her face as she had died. Shepherd wasn't a great believer in heaven or hell but part of him was sure that he'd be with her again. Four thousand. Shepherd gritted his teeth as he waited for the end. Five thousand.

"You soppy bastard," said Sharpe.

Shepherd opened his eyes. Six thousand. Was it a dud?

"You didn't really think they were all live, did you?" said Sharpe. "Give me some credit."

Shepherd rolled off the grenade and sat up. "Wouldn't be the first time you'd screwed up," he said, trying not to show just how relieved he was.

"But good to know you'd throw yourself on a grenade for your old pal." He offered his hand and Shepherd grabbed it. Sharpe hauled him to his feet. The armed cops realised what was happening and gave chase after Dexter, Palmer and Moorhouse, who were making slow progress across the ploughed field. "You okay?" Sharpe asked Shepherd as they watched the police round up the three men.

"I'm okay," said Shepherd, brushing dirt off his blazer with his hands.

"You sure?"

Shepherd considered the question for several seconds, then he nodded. "I'm sure."

"That was a bloody crazy thing to do, you know that."

Shepherd shrugged. "I knew it wasn't live," he lied.

"You can't kid a kidder," said Sharpe. He put his arm around Shepherd and hugged him. "Anyway, it's the thought that counts."

"Don't get all emotional on me, Razor. Please."

Serafino was staring at them in astonishment. Sharpe grinned. "Dan here's one of us," he explained. "Used to be a cop but he's secret squirrel now."

"You might have told me," said Serafino. He put out his hand and Shepherd shook it.

"I figured it was one less thing for you to worry about," said Sharpe.

As the police handcuffed Dexter, Palmer and Moorhouse and marched them back to their vehicles, Sharpe's phone rang and he answered it. He frowned as he listened, swore under his breath, said "yes" a few times and then ended the call. "We've got a problem with Harry," he said.

"What sort of problem?" asked Shepherd.

"A fucking huge one," said Sharpe. "He was asked to do a pickup and delivery. Julie organised the surveillance and was at the safe house to take samples. The team followed him to Warwick and Bradley's house and were monitoring him on the iPhone you'd given him. Bradley said they wanted him to go inside and when he did it was obvious that two of Kriezis's men were there. They've bundled him into a van and are taking him back to London as we speak."

"I thought we were done with using Harry undercover?"

"Julie says Teflon wanted to keep Harry and the other county lines up and running for a while longer."

"Bloody hell, Razor. If anything happens to that kid . . ."

"It's not the end of the world, Harry still has his phone on him so we can track them."

"What about ARVs?"

"Julie didn't have armed support, it was a regular delivery."

420

"What about now?"

"Teflon is organising ARVs in London but he told Julie he wants to adopt a wait-and-see posture."

"He what?"

"His exact words, apparently."

"Harry's been taken hostage, Razor. If we wait and see he could end up dead." He took out his phone and looked at the App linked to Harry's iPhone. He smiled with relief when he saw that it was working. Harry was on the M4, heading east.

The police officers from the Mercedes van ran over to the SFOs and took the fugitives into custody.

Sharpe went over to the sergeant, whose Glock was now back in its holster. "We've got a situation with one of our assets," Sharpe said to him. "Can you offer us assistance?" He gestured at Shepherd. "This is Dan, he's with us."

The sergeant shook his head. "No can do, we've been told to attend a scene in Stoke Newington," he said. "Guy threatening to kill his wife. Sorry."

"No problem," said Shepherd. He gritted his teeth and considered his options. Yes, Ron McKee was running the investigation into Frenk Kriezis but Harry Dexter had been an MI5 asset so Shepherd was at least partly responsible for what happened to him. He looked at Sharpe and could see from the look on his friend's face that he knew what Shepherd was going to say.

"Your call," said Sharpe.

"McKee won't be happy."

Sharpe chuckled softly. "I'm just a consultant. Worst he can do to me is not sign off on my expenses."

"Let's go," Shepherd said, patting him on the back.

Sharpe took him over to the other barn where he had parked his red Jaguar.

"You're using your own car on an undercover job?" asked Shepherd. "That's a bit risky isn't it?"

"I'm using NCA plates, and it means I get to claim mileage," said Sharpe.

They climbed in. Sharpe's phone rang and he looked at the screen. "Speak of the devil," he said. "It's McKee." He put the phone on hands-free as he drove out of the barn. He brought the chief inspector up to speed as he drove along the rutted track that led to the main road. McKee listened and as soon as Sharpe had finished he confirmed that he had already put in a request for armed support. "Liaise through me," said McKee. "Keep me appraised of the boy's location."

"Will do, Sir," said Sharpe and he ended the call. He looked across at Shepherd. "Well that's a turn up for the books," he said. "I was sure he was going to be pissed off at me and tell me to get back to Peel House. Instead it's all hands to the pumps."

"Maybe you misjudged him, Razor. It happens." Shepherd looked at his phone. Harry was still on the M4, heading to London.

Kriezis turned around in his seat and jabbed his cigar at Harry. "Stop your fucking snivelling," he said.

"I want to go home," said Harry in the rear of the van, wiping his eyes with his sleeve. He was boxed in by Shkodra and Prifti.

"We'll have a talk and if you tell me what I want to know, you can go home."

Kriezis took a pull on his cigar and blew smoke towards the windshield. He had no intention of letting Harry go home — the interrogation was only going to end one way.

Dushku slowed the van and indicated to leave the main road.

They were in Chingford and ahead of them was the industrial estate where they had dealt with Christy "Vicious" Miller and his crew. Dushku pulled up in front of the unit and Kriezis used his remote control to open up the red metal door at the delivery area. Dushku drove through and came to a halt in the middle of the building. He switched off the engine and sat holding the steering wheel with both hands.

"Is something troubling you?" Kriezis asked him, in Albanian.

"He's a kid," said Dushku, staring straight ahead.

"If I'm wrong, he can go home."

"But you don't think you're wrong, do you?"

Kriezis shook his head. "No. And neither do you. The kid's fucked us over and if we don't get rid of him, we're in the shit. And he's not a kid. Look at our lives when we were his age. Were we kids?"

"Our lives were different," said Dushku. He shrugged. "Don't get me wrong. I'll do what needs to be done. I was just saying, I don't like killing kids or women."

Sharpe pounded on his horn in frustration. The middle-aged woman in the grey Volvo ahead of them was driving at just below the speed limit, with a mobile phone clamped to her ear. "The problem with the Jag is that I don't have blues and twos," he said. He pulled out to overtake but there was a large cement truck heading their way, so he braked and dropped behind the Volvo again.

Shepherd studied his phone. The red dot that marked the progress of the van was no longer moving. "They've stopped," he said. "It's an industrial estate in Chingford."

Sharpe looked at his satnav. They were about five minutes away. The cement truck flashed by. "What do you want to do?" he asked, pushing down on the accelerator to overtake the Volvo. He glared at the woman as he went by but she was too engrossed in her phone conversation to notice.

"Razor, they're not taking him there to play hide and seek. You know what they're going to do."

"You want to go in?"

"I don't want to go in, no, but I don't see we've any choice."

Sharpe smiled thinly. "We?"

"We can't wait for the armed cops, not if his life is on the line."

Sharpe nodded as he drove. "I hear you," he said.

Shepherd reached behind his back and pulled the Glock from its holster. Six shots in the clip and one in the chamber. The Glock 43 was a great weapon to carry covertly, but at that moment Shepherd would have preferred a few more rounds in the magazine.

Shkodra opened the side door of the van and climbed out. He turned and grabbed Harry. "Out you come," he growled. Harry stumbled out of the van. Shkodra kept a tight grip on the teenager's collar. Prifti followed and they stood either side of the boy, dwarfing him with their bulk.

Kriezis and Dushku got out of the front of the van and slammed the door shut, the sounds echoing around the empty unit. Dushku went over to flick the switch that turned on the unit's overhead fluorescent lights as Kriezis used the remote control to lower the metal door.

Kriezis walked slowly over to Harry. He stared at the boy, then blew smoke into his face. Harry turned away and started coughing. Kriezis flicked ash from his cigar. "Where did you go today, Harry?" he asked.

Harry swallowed nervously. "Waterloo," he said. "Same as I always do."

"And then where did you go?"

Harry swallowed again. "Reading," he said.

"And when you got to Reading? Where did you go?"

Tears were running down Harry's face.

"You need to tell me, Harry," said Kriezis. "I do not like being lied to." He took another long pull on his cigar.

"I took the bag to Reading," said Harry. "I took it to the house. You know that. You were there. The house I always go to."

Kriezis slapped Harry across the face, hard. "Do not lie to me, you little shit!" he shouted.

"I did, that's what I did, I delivered the drugs the same way as I always do." He glared defiantly up at Kriezis, his eyes brimming with tears.

Kriezis lowered his head so that his face was level with Harry's. "I know exactly where you went and what you did," he said. "Yes, you delivered the drugs, but before you did that you went to another house, didn't you? The house with the green door." Kriezis grinned when he saw the look of confusion flash across the boy's face. "Yes, Harry. I know everything. But I need to hear it from your own mouth."

Harry sniffed and wiped his wet cheeks with the back of his hands. "I'm sorry," he said.

"You don't have to tell me you're sorry," said Kriezis. "You just need to tell me the truth. Who did you meet in the house?"

"The police," said Harry, his voice a hoarse whisper.

"And the police checked the drugs?"

Harry nodded. "Yes."

"And you do that every time? Before you deliver the drugs, you visit the house with the green door?"

"Yes," said Harry. "I'm really sorry. I won't do it again, I promise."

"I know," said Kriezis.

426

"They followed him," said Shepherd, staring at his phone in horror. "How did that happen, Razor?" They could hear most of what was being said, but Harry's phone must have been in his jacket or pocket because the sound was muffled.

They had parked at the entrance to the industrial estate. The unit where the Albanians had taken Harry was directly ahead of the Jaguar. It was a single-storey building with an entrance on the left-hand side and a delivery area with a large metal shutter to the right. There was a line of parking spaces next to the entrance but they were all unoccupied which meant that the Albanians had driven their van inside.

"I don't know," said Sharpe. "We were winding down the investigation, someone must have taken their eye off the ball."

"We need to get in there, now," said Shepherd. "They're going to kill him."

"The ARVs are on their way."

"We don't have time." Shepherd gestured with his Glock at the metal loading-bay door. "There's only one way in."

Sharpe looked at the door, then back at Shepherd. "You are fucking joking."

"It's the only way, Razor."

"This motor's almost brand new."

"Harry's in danger."

"I'm still paying for it."

"You'll be reimbursed."

"I fucking love this car." He looked back at the door. "Fuck."

Shepherd checked his seatbelt.

"Fuck," said Sharpe again. He turned the car towards the door and accelerated, hard. The engine roared and the Jaguar leapt forward.

Sharpe kept accelerating, both hands gripping the steering wheel so tightly that his knuckles were white.

Shepherd reached out with his left hand and opened the door. The Jaguar was a sturdy car but it would buckle when it hit the door and Shepherd didn't want to risk being trapped inside the vehicle when it crashed.

The speedometer was a fraction off forty miles an hour when the Jaguar hit the door. The car weighed close to one and a half tons and its momentum ripped it through the door with the scream of tortured metal.

The shattered door clattered on the roof of the Jaguar as Sharpe slammed on the brakes.

Shepherd looked to his left. Time seemed to have slowed and he saw Kriezis staring at them, open mouthed. His three heavies were standing with their backs to the car and had yet to react. Harry was standing between them.

The Jaguar screeched to a halt. Shepherd kicked the door open and brought his gun to bear on the four men. "Hands up, now!" he shouted. He moved away from the Jaguar. "Stay where you are, Razor," said Shepherd. Sharpe wasn't armed and Shepherd didn't want his friend getting caught in the crossfire.

Kriezis threw away his cigar and grabbed Harry while the three heavies turned to look at Shepherd.

"Hands in the air, now!" shouted Shepherd, and he fired a warning shot up into the roof. "Harry, get over here!"

Harry struggled but Kriezis had a tight grip on his collar. "Help me!" Harry shouted.

Kriezis held Harry with his left hand while his right reached inside his coat.

Marko Dushku and Jetmir Shkodra had turned and began moving towards him, seemingly oblivious to the gun he was holding. "Stay where you are!" he shouted.

"Fuck you!" shouted Dushku.

The third heavy, Gëzim Prifti, moved to the right.

Shepherd gritted his teeth. The Albanians clearly had no intention of backing down. They were all reaching inside their coats. Shepherd didn't want to shoot until they were actually holding their weapons. In a war zone the rules were different, but London wasn't a war zone, despite what was published in the more strident tabloids, and if he were to kill unarmed men he'd be letting himself in for a whole world of trouble.

Kriezis pulled a revolver from his coat and waved it over Harry's head. "Drop your weapon or I'll shoot the kid," he shouted.

Harry was staring fearfully at Shepherd. A damp patch spread around the crotch of his trousers. He'd wet himself.

Shepherd stared at Kriezis but his mind flashed back to Slovenia. The fear in Katra's eyes, the hatred pouring out of Zivco Žagar, the finger tightening on the trigger. Shepherd gritted his teeth. There was no way he was going to let Harry die.

"Drop your fucking gun or the kid is . . ."

Shepherd fired twice and both shots ripped through the man's face, splattering blood and brain and fragments of skull across the wall behind him. For a second Kriezis remained upright and then he collapsed and his gun clattered onto the concrete floor.

Shepherd was already moving, dropping down and turning to the left. There were two men there so they were the major threat: Dushku and Shkodra. Dushku's hand was emerging from his jacket. He was holding something but it wasn't a gun. Shkodra's hands were at his sides, he was staring in horror at the body on the floor.

Shepherd heard rustling to his right. He stepped back and turned, still keeping low to make himself as small a target as possible.

Prifti had a gun in his hand but his arm was shaking and when he saw Shepherd turn he panicked and the shot went low, hitting the ground close to Shepherd's left foot and ricocheting off behind him.

Shepherd was holding his Glock with both hands and fired twice, a textbook double tap to Prifti's chest. Prifti staggered back and fell to the floor. Shepherd had fired five shots which meant he only had two left.

He turned again and Dushku was moving towards him, a cut-throat razor in his right hand. Shepherd brought his gun to bear on Dushku's throat and the heavy stopped, clearly realising that there was no way he could reach Shepherd before the trigger was pulled. Shkodra was putting his hands in the air. "Don't shoot," he said.

430

Harry staggered over to Sharpe and Sharpe put his arms around the boy. Harry buried his face in Sharpe's chest and sobbed.

Shepherd kept his gun trained on Dushku's throat. The two men locked eyes. Dushku was still trying to work out if he could get to Shepherd, but then the fight went out of him and he folded the razor. He started to put it back in his jacket pocket but Shepherd shook his head. "On the floor," he said.

"No," snarled Dushku. "It was my father's razor."

Shepherd lowered the Glock and shot the man in the leg. Dushku screamed in pain and threw the razor down. "Get down on the floor," said Shepherd. "Both of you."

The two men did as they were told, dropping to their knees and then lowering themselves down. Shepherd fished out his phone with his left hand and called 999.

The police car stopped about a hundred yards down the road from the Dexter house. Shepherd and Sharpe were in the back, sitting either side of Harry. "Give us a minute, please," Shepherd said to the driver, a young constable with a rash of acne across the back of his neck. Sharpe's Jaguar had been pretty much written off when it had crashed into the industrial unit, a fact that Sharpe had mentioned at least three times during the drive to Reading.

Sharpe and Shepherd climbed out and stood on the pavement. Harry joined them.

Shepherd patted the teenager on the shoulder. "Harry, are you okay?" Even though the teenager nodded Shepherd wasn't convinced. Harry was avoiding eye contact and had a worried look on his face.

Shepherd looked across at Sharpe, wondering how he felt about the state the boy was in. Sharpe shrugged.

"Harry, if you want, I could go with you and explain to your mum and dad what's happened," said Shepherd.

Harry shook his head fiercely. "No way," he said.

"I think you'd be surprised," said Shepherd. "You're their son, they'll understand."

"I said no!" hissed Harry. He looked over at Sharpe. "You said they'd never know. That's what you said."

"And what I said, stands," said Sharpe.

"Whatever you want to do, we'll abide by your decision," said Shepherd. "I'm just saying that you've been through a lot today and you might feel better if you confided in your mum and dad. If my son did something wrong I would still support him, no matter what."

Harry sniffed and rubbed his nose with the back of his hand. "You think I did something wrong?"

"No. That's not what I meant. You were helping the police and if you tell your mum and dad that, they'll be there for you."

"You don't know my dad."

"No, but I am a dad myself. And trust me, dads love their kids, no matter what. Mums probably even more."

Harry shook his head. "I don't want them to know."

"That's fine," said Shepherd. "It's totally your call. But if you do change your mind, remember what I said.

They'll support you. And if you ever want to talk to me, you can call me. Any time, day or night."

Harry forced a smile. "Thank you," he said. He opened the car door and got out. He waved at Sharpe, shouldered his bag, and walked towards his house.

"He'll be okay," said Sharpe as they watched him walk away. "He's a tough kid."

"I hope so," said Shepherd. "But he's still got the phone so I'll be able to keep an eye on him."

"An ear, you mean," said Sharpe with a grin.

"That, too," said Shepherd. Harry turned into the driveway. He turned to look at their car, gave them a small wave, and disappeared from sight.

"You'll be his guardian angel, is that it?" asked Sharpe.

"Exactly."

"For how long?"

"For as long as he needs me," said Shepherd.

Shepherd parked his BMW X5 in front of the garage and let himself into the house. He had to stop himself calling out Katra's name. He flashed back to the last time he'd arrived home and his stomach churned at the memory of her rushing towards him and leaping into his arms. He closed the front door and walked down the hallway to the kitchen. He dropped his holdall by the table and took a bottle of soda water from the fridge and a handful of ice cubes from the freezer. He dropped the cubes into a glass and added half the soda water, then went through to the living room. He picked up a bottle of Jameson whiskey from the drinks cabinet and sat down on the sofa. He added a slug of whiskey to his glass and sipped it, then took out his phone. He took another long pull on his whiskey and accessed his voicemail. He sat back, put the phone on speaker, and pressed the button to listen to the first of Katra's messages.

Other titles published by Ulverscroft:

TALL ORDER

Stephen Leather

He is one of the world's most ruthless terrorists, codenamed Saladin. He plans and executes devastating attacks and then, ghost-like, he disappears. Ten years ago he blew a plane out of the sky above New York — and now he's struck again, killing dozens in London. But one of the latest victims is the goddaughter of the acting head of MI5, who knows exactly who she wants on the case: Spider Shepherd. Dean Martin, a psychologically damaged former Navy SEAL, was the only person in the world who can identify Saladin. But Martin was killed ten years ago — wasn't he? Shepherd must find Martin and take him back to the killing fields on the Afghanistan-Pakistan border. Revenge on the world's most wanted terrorist is long overdue, and Shepherd is determined to deliver it . . .

LIGHT TOUCH

Stephen Leather

Working undercover is all about trust — getting the target to trust you and then betraying them in order to bring them to justice. But what do you do when you believe an undercover cop has crossed the line and aligned herself with the international drugs smuggler she was supposed to be targeting? When Lisa Wilson stops passing on intelligence about her target, MI5 sends in Dan "Spider" Shepherd to check that she's on the straight and narrow. Now two lives are on the line — and Shepherd discovers that the real danger is closer to home than he realised. As Spider finds his loyalties being tested to the limit, an SAS killer is on a revenge mission in London, and only Spider can stop him . . .

DARK FORCES

Stephen Leather

A violent South London gang will be destroyed if Dan "Spider" Shepherd can gather enough evidence against them while posing as a ruthless hitman. What he doesn't know is that his work as an undercover agent for MI5 is about to intersect with the biggest terrorist operation ever carried out on British soil. Only weeks before, Shepherd witnessed a highly skilled IS sniper escape from a targeted missile strike in Syria. But never in his wildest dreams did he expect to next come across the shooter in a grimy East London flat. Spider's going to have to proceed with extreme caution if he is to prevent the death of hundreds of people — but at the same time, when the crucial moment comes, he will have to act decisively. The clock is ticking . . .

BLACK OPS

Stephen Leather

When MI5 Agent Spider is asked to assume the identity of the contract killer hired to take out President Vladimir Putin, he knows he'll become a wanted man. And things are about to get more complicated: Spider is told that his MI5 controller and close friend Charlotte Button has been running an off-the-books assassination operation, taking vengeance on the men who killed her husband. Spider owes his life to Button — but this discovery will stretch his loyalty to the limit. Because he is told to betray her. Worse, he's asked to cooperate with his nemesis at MI6, Jeremy Willoughby Brown, in taking Charlie down. And he will have to cross the assassin Lex Harper, currently on the trail of two Irish terrorists, who may be able to lead him to his ex-boss . . .